# One Wish

## MARIA DUFFY

HACHETTE
BOOKS
IRELAND

First published in 2014 by Hachette Books Ireland

A CIP catalogue record for this title is available from the British Library.

ISBN 978 1444 743 692

Typeset in Adobe Garamond Pro by Bookends Publishing Services, Ireland.
.Printed and bound by Clays Ltd, St Ives plc

Hachette Books Ireland policy is to use papers that are natural, renewable and
recyclable products and made from wood grown in sustainable forests. The logging
and manufacturing processes are expected to conform to the environmental
regulations of the country of origin.

Hachette Books Ireland
8 Castlecourt Centre, Castleknock, Dublin 15, Ireland

A division of Hachette UK Ltd.
338 Euston Road, London NW1 3BH

www.hachette.ie

For Una. Always in our hearts.

# January 2013

Deano sat in the corner and watched as a guy in a scruffy overcoat pushed his way to the top of the queue. Nobody seemed willing to challenge him. His eyes were scary in a glazed over sort of way, and everyone seemed reluctant to even look at him. Red Ron, as he was known, had apparently been coming here for years and had well and truly marked his territory. He took his bowl of coddle and sat in his usual spot by the window. Even when the place was packed to the brim, Red Ron's seat was always left untouched. It would be a brave man or woman who'd dare to sit in *that* seat.

Deano turned his attention to his own coddle. He wiped up the rest of it with a piece of bread which he stuffed in his mouth. He'd always hated coddle. Scummy water, he used to say to his mother when she served it up. Scummy water with raw rashers and sausages – how could anyone want to eat that? But here things were different. Here you took what you could get and were grateful for it.

He'd come here first only a couple weeks ago but hadn't been interested in making friends. He wasn't like them. He couldn't associate with people like that. All he needed was something in his stomach to tide him over for the night. His was just a temporary situation – a little glitch that would sort itself out soon. There was no point in getting to know people when he'd be moving on and, let's face it, *his* world wasn't part of theirs.

Wiping the crumbs from his trousers, he took his jacket from the back of his seat and stood up. He'd always prided himself on his appearance. His philosophy was that if you looked smart and

1

respectable, people would treat you with respect. Even under the present circumstances, Deano managed to wash most days and kept his black hair neat and tidy. He hauled his rucksack onto his back and nodded his thanks to Liz behind the counter before heading out into the cool November air.

It was like déjà vu as he walked along the Liffey towards O'Connell Street. He remembered watching that movie, *Groundhog Day*, and thinking how head-wrecking it must feel to wake up and repeat the same day again and again. But that was exactly how he felt. Time was just blurring and he was even losing track of what day of the week it was. This wasn't his life. He wasn't a drug addict or an alcoholic. He wasn't a gambler and he wasn't lazy. But one thing Deano was, although he hated to admit it, was homeless.

# Chapter 1

**Seven months later**

Bloody spots! Becky Greene had always prided herself on her lovely dewy skin but her face seemed to be screaming objection at turning thirty by popping out unsightly red lumps. She sighed as she painstakingly applied another layer of Mac concealer to the affected areas. At least she was able to tease her wavy blonde hair to hide the ones at the side of her face. She took a black kohl pencil and lined her green eyes more thickly than usual in the hope of drawing all the attention to that part of her face. 'It will have to do,' she sighed to herself as she smacked her plump lips together to spread her trademark pink lip gloss.

Half past eight. At least she was finished her preening before the toilets were overrun by a gaggle of women fighting for a place at the mirror. She hated making small talk and tried to be at the office before anyone else so that she could avoid their inane gossip. She didn't dislike any of her co-workers; she was simply indifferent to them and kept out of their way as much as possible. She knew they considered her stuck-up, but she really didn't care.

Everything Becky did, she did well, and her job as an assistant manager in the bank was no exception. She was in charge of commercial foreign transfers and had her own desk at the very back of the open-plan office where, thankfully, she was mostly left to her own devices. When she'd been transferred to the city-centre branch three years earlier, everyone had been very welcoming. She'd come from a smaller branch on the south side of the city and her new workmates

3

had been keen to include her in their after-work social activities. She'd politely declined every invitation and now the offers were few and far between. She wasn't there to make friends – it was a means to an end. A job that would keep her brain active, her wallet full and keep her safe in the knowledge that she'd never, ever end up like her mother.

She washed her hands just as the door swung open and two girls arrived in, talking nine to the dozen.

'Hi, Becky,' they practically sang in unison.

'Morning,' said Becky, as the girls tottered over to a mirror on their too-high heels. Although Becky was fond of her heels, she could never understand why these young girls wore shoes like that to do a job that involved being on their feet all day. Both girls were new, having started on the same day the previous month, and Becky had immediately pegged them as gossipers.

'I love your eye make-up,' the one called 'Lynda with a y' said, although Becky could see she was clearly eyeing up the unsightly spots on her face.

'Ooh, yes,' the other joined in. 'It makes you look sooo young.'

Becky gritted her teeth. 'Thanks. We old folk have to do all we can to keep up with you youngsters. Right, better get back to it.'

She took a final glance in the mirror before plucking some blonde hairs from her navy suit jacket and heading out the door. She wasn't at all surprised to hear the words 'sarky bitch' being uttered as she walked back into the main office. It was water off a duck's back.

She stopped at the front desk where two of the staff were sorting through the post. 'Anything for me?' she asked, leafing through the unopened envelopes.

One of them, a guy who seemed about twelve and looked to Becky as though he was making his confirmation in the oversized suit, looked at her fearfully. 'We've only started going through them, Becky. I'll drop yours down to you as soon as they're sorted.'

Becky looked at her watched and tutted. 'Make sure you do. And you know when it's *your* week to do the post, you need to be in early and have it sorted before anyone looks for it.'

'Yes … I … it was just … sorry.'

Becky shook her head disapprovingly and headed down to her desk. The place was beginning to come alive with chitter-chatter as the staff arrived but Becky was happy to feel invisible. She powered up her computer and began sorting through the mound of paperwork in her in-tray. It was then she noticed the date: 26 August. There was a time when that date had meant something to her. Not any more.

'Morning, Becks. Look at you all bright-eyed and bushy-tailed. How on earth do you manage to look so fabulous this early in the morning? I've barely brushed my hair!'

Becky smiled at Kate, a small, fiery redhead and Becky's only ally in the place. 'Well, the difference is that I *need* all this slap whereas you're just naturally beautiful.'

'Ah, go away with you.' Kate blushed, lighting up the freckles on her pale face. 'But what's the story with Carl on the post desk? I saw you having words with him and he looked like a scared schoolkid.'

'I'm just sick of the young ones slacking off, that's all. They think they can make their own rules but I'm not having it.'

'Ah, Becky, you have to ease up. You don't always have to be on people's backs.'

Becky sighed. 'I know – I just can't seem to help it. But luckily I have you to keep me in line. How are you, anyway?'

'Grand, not a bother.' Kate shifted some of Becky's paperwork and perched on the edge of the desk. 'Do you fancy lunch today? I'm just in the mood for a big stodgy burger. Me and Garreth went down to Spillane's last night and had a bellyful.'

'I could never do that on a Sunday night, knowing I'd have to face a whole week in work after.'

Kate's eyes twinkled. 'Well, Sunday has become one of our BBB nights and I wouldn't miss it for the world.'

'Do I even want to know?'

'Well, let's just say it's something that you should try sometime.'

Becky was intrigued. 'Go on, what is it? Is it something to do with *Big Brother*?'

'Nope.' Kate was giggling like crazy.

'Well, don't have me guessing or we'll be here all day.' Becky was anxious to get back to work. The thought of lunch and a chat with Kate sounded great, but she had a mountain of stuff to get through first.

Kate lowered her voice. 'Beer, burger and bonk! And I can't recommend it enough. Now I'd better fly and help Trisha take out the cash or there'll be wigs on the green.'

Becky laughed as she watched her friend input the combination on the door of the large safe and disappear inside. Being English, she found a lot of the Irish expressions hard to understand and Kate was always full of them. She made a note to google 'wigs on the green' later.

Becky loved Kate's company. Despite her vow to keep her distance from everyone, she'd warmed to her from the very beginning. She was different from the others. She wasn't giggly and gossipy and part of any clique – she was mature, intelligent and self-assured, despite her mere twenty-three years. She said things as they were, and Becky liked that. When Becky had refused to go for drinks with the staff on her first Friday in the job, Kate had come over to her and asked why the hell she wouldn't go. Becky had balked at first and thought Kate was rude but the more she got to know her, the more she'd liked her outspoken ways. She liked the fact that Kate wasn't into the touchy-feely stuff and didn't pry too much into her personal life. They'd formed an unlikely friendship.

Her eyes were drawn to the date on the computer again. She'd tried to blot out certain dates over the past few years but some were more difficult to forget. Today was her mother's birthday. She'd be sixty-two years old. She briefly let her thoughts wander to the house she'd once called home in London. She doubted there'd be any celebrations there today. She gave herself a mental shake – she wasn't going to let herself think about it for one more minute. The morning would fly by with so much to do and then she could relax over a lovely, gossipy lunch with Kate.

❀

'So, go on. Tell me what's up with you.' Kate launched into her double cheeseburger with gusto, squirting tomato sauce all over the table.

'God, Kate. How on earth do you manage to stay so slim when you eat so much? If I looked at that burger, I'd put pounds onto my hips.'

'I'm lucky with my metabolism, I suppose. Although sometimes I think I should be more careful what I eat. I'm fed up not getting anywhere with this modelling and maybe if I was skinnier, I'd do better.'

'Are you joking me? You're a size eight and absolutely gorgeous.'

'Thanks, Becks. But I'm also way older than most successful models out there so if I'm going to get anywhere, everything needs to be perfect. And anyway, stop changing the subject. I was asking what's up with *you*.'

Becky raised her eyebrows as she sipped her coffee. 'What do you mean?'

'I know there's something wrong, Becky. You haven't been yourself lately.'

'In what way?'

Kate licked the sauce that was running down her arm. 'Well, for starters, you're paler than usual and a hell of a lot grumpier!'

'Oh, thanks for that. Kick a girl while she's down.'

'But that's just it, Becky. Why are you down? What's going on?'

Becky sighed. 'It was just a figure of speech. But I probably do need a bit of a pick-me-up, if I'm honest. I think I'm just overworked and not getting enough sleep.'

'Maybe. When was the last time you've had a check-up with the doctor? You don't look after yourself enough. Why don't you make an appointment? I can even come with you, if you like.'

'Honestly, Kate. I know you're only looking out for me but there's nothing to be worried about. And anyway, you know you become a snivelling mess at the mere thought of going into a doctor's surgery.'

Kate nodded. 'Well, that's true. Remember the time Garreth made me go with him so he could get the lump on his balls checked out? Oh, God, the mortification!'

'How could I forget?' Becky giggled. 'You spent the whole morning trying to think of an excuse not to go with him.'

'But I went in the end, didn't I? Even if I did end up fainting as soon as the doc began to examine poor Garreth's private parts!'

'Haha! God, I would have loved to have seen that.'

'What? Garreth's private bits?'

The two girls burst into fits of giggles and Becky's heart lifted. Kate was a tonic and exactly what she needed. 'Well, you certainly don't need to worry about coming to any doctor with me. A few early nights and I'll be as right as rain.'

'I would come with you, you know,' said Kate, her face becoming serious. 'I know I can be a bit flippant at times and I like a good laugh, but you can talk to me about anything. You know you can rely on me, right?'

Becky smiled at the younger girl. 'I know I can, Kate. And you're the first person I'd come to if I had a problem, but I can promise you everything is absolutely fine.'

Kate exhaled. 'That's a relief. Maybe a few nights away would be the perfect tonic for you. Why don't we head down to Galway or something – just the two of us?'

'I'd love to but I can't. You know I can't.'

'But there has to be a way, Becks. You're still a young woman – you should be out there having fun.'

Becky's face darkened. 'But I *am* having fun, Kate. Maybe it's not your idea of fun, but it's my life and I wouldn't have it any other way.'

Kate knocked back the last of her Coke and looked at Becky. 'I know and I'm sorry. I didn't mean anything by it but I'd just love to see you getting out and about a bit more.'

'I don't do too badly, considering,' Becky said, picking at the croutons in her salad. 'I was barely home all weekend.'

'Yes, but that's a different sort of going out. I'm not talking about walks in the park and trips to the shops – I'm talking about proper let-your-hair-down nights out. I couldn't believe you didn't even celebrate your thirtieth last month.'

'We have different lives, Kate. And as far as I'm concerned, I *did* celebrate. Alice cooked a delicious meal at my house and we had a lovely evening.'

'You see!' Kate looked triumphant. 'That's just what I'm talking about. Borrrrring!'

'Reel your head in, Kate, will you? I'm sick and tired of you nagging me.'

'I'm sorry,' said Kate, looking sheepish. 'It's just that I—'

'God, have you seen the time? We're going to be dead late. Let's go.' Becky jumped up suddenly and grabbed her jacket from the back of the chair. She was glad of an opportunity to change the subject. The two of them didn't argue much but when they did, the seven-year age gap was more evident. Although Kate was mature for her age, she didn't understand responsibility. And why would she? She was young and free and could do what she wanted with her life and she seemed to think that Becky should want to be like that too.

But Becky hadn't been lying when she said she was having fun. She loved her life. It may not have been the life she thought she'd have. It may be far removed from how she thought things would turn out, but she was happy. It was the life she'd chosen and she wouldn't change it for the world.

# Chapter 2

'How are you, Mr Grimshaw?' said Becky, waving to her next-door neighbour as she arrived home. 'Is the leg any better?'

'Ah, it's not too bad at all, Becky, love. Another few days and I should have the dressing off.'

'That's great news.' She opened her silver-painted gate and walked up to the front door. She loved her little two-bedroomed terraced house in Cabra. It wouldn't win any prizes for looks, with its ugly red-stone cladding and varnished front door, but it was quaint in its own way. It was the neighbourhood that appealed to her more than anything. It was a small cul-de-sac of fifteen houses, most of which were occupied by elderly people who'd lived there all their lives. Everyone looked out for each other but they didn't intrude. Becky felt safe there. Safe and happy.

She'd been delighted to move from the drab bedsit she'd lived in before. As soon as her transfer had been confirmed, she'd trawled the internet to see what was for sale within walking distance of her new job. She'd fallen in love with the little house as soon as she'd seen it and the sale had gone through quickly. She'd been glad about that because her situation had meant that she needed to be settled as soon as possible.

'Only me,' she said, as she pushed open the front door. She kicked off her shoes in the hall and hung her jacket on the banister. 'Something smells delicious. Have you two been baking again?'

'Mummy, Mummy, we're in here. Come and see what we're doing – it's so cool.'

Becky followed the little voice into the kitchen and had to stifle a giggle at what she saw. 'Oh, sorry, I think I'm in the wrong place. I was looking for my house but I see this is a beauty salon.'

'Silly Mummy,' giggled Lilly, Becky's four-year-old daughter. 'It's me – see?' She took the two pieces of cucumber from her eyes to convince her mother that it was, indeed, her. 'Alice got new face stuff that's going to make her ten years younger so we were just trying it out.'

Alice had removed the cucumber from her eyes and looked sheepish. 'Sorry, Becky. I didn't expect you home early. I'll get all this cleaned up now.'

'You're fine. It was quiet this afternoon so I managed to slip out. I'm glad you two have been having a good time.' Becky plonked herself down on a kitchen chair and looked in amusement at the two brown faces in front of her.

'And, no, we haven't been baking,' Alice said, wiping the thick brown substance first from Lilly's face and then her own. 'It's this chocolate face mask I bought in town last week. The girl told me that cocoa contains loads of antioxidants that protect your skin from damage and it even has brilliant anti-ageing properties.'

Becky laughed at that. 'Alice! How much have you spent already this year on anti-ageing stuff? I wish you wouldn't believe everything they tell you. Honestly, they could package seaweed in a jar, tell you it's good for wrinkles and you'd buy it!'

'How did you know, Mummy?' Lilly jumped up onto Becky's lap and snuggled into her.

'How did I know what?'

'Come on now, Lilly,' said Alice, turning a deep pink. 'Let's go and get a bath ready for you.'

Lilly shook her head, her straight blonde hair flying from side to side. 'Not yet, I want to tell Mummy about the seaweed.'

'You didn't,' said Becky, looking at Alice.

'I, em …'

Lilly continued. 'Alice brought seaweed last week. She said not to

11

tell you because you'd think she was mad. We just had to wet it and leave it on our faces for twenty minutes and our skin was all smooth and shiny after.'

'Gosh, Lilly. If you keep up these treatments, you'll be two years old in no time.' Becky's eyes twinkled.

'Silly Mummy! It doesn't make *me* younger – only Alice. She says she's never, ever going to be fifty. Even if she lives to be a hundred!'

Alice wagged her finger at Lilly. 'Don't you be giving my secrets away, Missy. Or else everyone will want to be trying them out.'

'Well, your secrets are safe with me,' Becky said, pulling herself up out of the chair with Lilly still attached. 'You get on off home, Alice, and I'll see you in the morning.'

'Are you sure? I can stay and throw together some dinner for you if you like.'

'Thanks, but I think we might order a pizza and have a movie night. What do you think, Lilly?'

'Hooray, hooray, can we, can we?' The little girl's eyes almost popped out of her head at the prospect, and Becky's heart filled with love.

'Yes, but it's a bath for you first and then into your pjs.'

Alice cleared the last of the mess from the kitchen table and washed her hands in the sink. 'She's been a great girl today, Becky, and tried two new things – a kiwi and some turnip.'

'Good girl.' Becky beamed at her daughter. 'And did you like them?'

'The kiwi was fun. It felt kind of furry and tasted like grapes. But the turnip was nasty. It made me want to throw up.'

Becky laughed at that. She wasn't a fan of turnip herself. 'Well, at least you tried.'

'Right, I'm off.' Alice came over and took Lilly from her mother's arms to get a cuddle before she left. 'You be good for Mummy and I'll see you in the morning, okay?'

''Kay, Alice. I love you.'

'I love you too, sweetheart. See you tomorrow.'

After a quick call to order a pizza, Becky carried Lilly upstairs to the bathroom and began to run a bath. She smiled when she thought of the scene she'd come home to. Alice was forever trying to make herself look younger. Although Becky couldn't understand why – at forty-seven, she was a fine-looking woman. The short black hair that framed her face had yet to turn grey and she barely had a wrinkle on her pale skin. Her body was in good nick too, although she claimed her size-eight frame was more to do with genetics than exercise or diet.

Despite her eccentricities, Alice was the most wonderful nanny she could ever have wished for, and not a day went by when she didn't thank God for finding her. She'd been working for another family, minding twins, when the mother had decided suddenly she couldn't cope with work and wanted to be at home with her babies. It had left her without employment so she'd taken a part-time job in a local playschool. One of Becky's new neighbours had a child in the playschool and had told Becky all about the wonderful Alice. That had been nearly three years ago and both Becky and Lilly loved her dearly.

'Why is Alice not a mummy?' Lilly searched her mother's face as she splashed in the bath.

'I've told you this before, sweetheart. Alice was never lucky enough to have her own children, but she loves you just like you were her daughter.'

'But she could have her own children and still love me, couldn't she?'

Becky sighed. How do you explain the devastation of infertility to a four-year-old? 'Well, she could, but she wants to save all her love for you.'

'But I wouldn't mind if she had some children. Or you could have some more, Mummy. I could be their big sister and play with them and mind them and everything.'

'You'd make a great big sister, darling. Maybe some day.'

'And could we get a daddy too? I think maybe we need one to get more babies.'

13

Becky didn't know whether to laugh or cry, but Lilly continued. 'Rachel in *Friends* got a baby and Ross was the daddy but Phoebe had *three* at the same time and there wasn't *even* a daddy. It's a bit confusing.'

'Since when did you watch *Friends*?' Becky couldn't contain her surprise.

'It comes on sometimes after my programmes. Why don't I have a daddy?'

Jesus! 'Because sometimes that's just the way it is, sweetie. And I can do the job of a Mummy *and* Daddy. See these muscles?'

Lilly giggled as Becky flexed her muscles and made a silly face. 'So can we get a baby?'

'Quick, I think I hear the pizza man outside. Let's get you out of that bath and into your pjs. You can pick the movie while I'm getting out the plates.' Thankfully the conversation was averted for the moment. Becky loved that her daughter was chatty and inquisitive but sometimes she just didn't have the answers to her questions. That wasn't the first time she'd asked about her daddy and Becky was never sure what to say. She suddenly felt exhausted. Pizza in front of a movie seemed like the best idea she'd ever had and she was looking forward to relaxing for the next couple of hours.

❋

'Night, sweetheart. I love you. See you in the morning.'

'Night, Mummy.' The words were barely a whisper before Lilly's eyes closed. Becky sat for a moment, drinking in her face. The little girl never failed to take her breath away. She watched as her little mouth relaxed open and her head dropped to the side. Her long, straight blonde hair was fanned out on the pillow and she looked like an angel. Becky kissed her lightly on the tip of her button nose before tip-toeing downstairs.

Becky was exhausted and knew she should really just go to bed herself but Kate's words were playing on her mind. She really had become very settled since Lilly was born. Yes, she had responsibilities and couldn't just go out at the drop of a hat, but Kate was right. She was still young and should be making a better effort to get out and about. She so badly wanted to be a good mother to her little girl that she sometimes forgot that life was passing her by.

She headed into the kitchen and filled the kettle with water. Maybe a coffee and a *Coronation Street* catch-up before bed would help her relax and have a good sleep. Kate made fun of her for watching *Corrie* – said it was for old fogies – but Becky found it fascinating to get such an intimate look into the lives of others, regardless of the fact that it wasn't real.

She poured her coffee and headed into the sitting room where she curled her legs up underneath herself on the brown leather sofa. As she flicked on the telly, she looked around the stark room and made a vow to jazz it up a bit as soon as she got a chance. She'd always intended to inject a bit of colour into the clinical-looking room, but she just hadn't got around to it yet. She'd bought the house for a song, but the décor had been so old-fashioned and fussy that she'd just painted every room cream and had oak laminate floors fitted throughout. The only thing that added a bit of homeliness to the room was the gorgeous portrait of a two-year-old Lilly hanging over the fireplace.

Just as she was about to press play to start watching *Corrie*, the shrill tone of the phone ringing almost caused her to spill her coffee.

'Shit!' Although she was tempted to ignore it, she didn't want it to wake up Lilly. Leaving her coffee on the floor, she ran to grab the phone from the hall table.

'Hello.'

'Hiya, Becky. It's Kate.'

'Oh, hi, Kate. What's up?' She was almost sorry she'd answered it now.

'I just thought I'd give you a buzz to see how you are and to … well … I'm sorry for saying what I did today. You know what I'm like. Me and my big mouth.'

Becky relaxed and took the phone into the sitting room. 'Don't worry about it. I know you mean well and, to be honest, I probably *should* try and get out a bit more.'

'Exactly, Becks. I know I probably said it the wrong way earlier, but I just think it would be good for you.'

'I know,' conceded Becky. 'And Alice is always offering to babysit so Lilly wouldn't be a problem.'

'That's brilliant. Why don't we make plans for this weekend? It can be your proper, grown-up birthday celebration. See if Alice will stay late on Friday and we could even go straight from work.'

'Definitely not straight from work, Kate.' Becky was adamant. 'I'll need to go home and see Lilly first. I feel guilty enough as it is, being out at work all day every day.'

'Well, see what you can do. Let me know which night suits and we can plan something. We might even find you someone to have a BBB night with!'

Becky laughed at that. 'Do I look like a BBB sort of girl?'

'Ah, come on, Becks. From what you've told me about Lilly's father, I'd say you're *exactly* that sort of girl!'

Becky stiffened and didn't answer.

'Becky … are you there? I was only joking, you know. I didn't mean anything by it. I just think you've gone long enough without … you know … I think you could do with a bit of … oh, God, help me out here!'

'I could do with a bit of what?'

'Do I have to spell it out, Becky? From what you've told me, it's been years since you've had a man in your bed. You could do with a good seeing to.'

'Jesus, Kate!'

'Look, I'm sorry that I don't say things in a proper way, but I'm just saying it as I see it. I really don't mean to offend you.'

'I know you don't, Kate. Look, I'd better go and check on Lilly.

She was a bit unsettled tonight. We can chat tomorrow about the weekend, okay?'

'Okay,' said Kate, sheepishly. 'And sorry again. I just can't seem to help saying the wrong thing.'

'Don't worry about it. Chat to you tomorrow.'

Becky threw the phone on the sofa beside her and fought the urge to scream. Damn Kate. She was too bloody honest for her own good. She always said stuff that nobody else would dream of saying – the thing about it, though, was that she was often right.

The reminder about Lilly's father had unsettled Becky. She'd always felt she'd done the right thing in not pursuing him. What man would want to hear that he'd got a woman pregnant from a one-night stand? She'd had a shock when she'd realised she was pregnant but, in true Becky style, she'd focused and decided what she needed to do. She was a strong, independent woman and she was going to raise her child alone. It hadn't been easy and there'd been times when she felt she'd taken on too much but she'd got through it – was still getting through it.

But what had Kate meant when she said she was exactly 'that sort of a girl'? Flirty? Flighty? Irresponsible? Is that what people thought of her? She'd worked very hard to develop a thick skin over the years and she really didn't care what others thought but what she *did* care about was Lilly. She'd hate to think that any decisions she'd made in the past weren't in her daughter's best interests. Everything Becky did, she did for Lilly, and her only wish in life was that Lilly would grow up happy, healthy and secure.

She suddenly felt exhausted. She drained the last of her coffee from the mug and switched the telly off. *Corrie* would have to wait for another night. Dropping her mug into the sink in the kitchen, she switched off all the lights, set the alarm and headed upstairs. Lilly was snoring softly, the covers tangled around her legs and one arm hanging off the bed. Becky's heart melted at the sight of her. She tucked her in and kissed her gently on the cheek. Yes, she'd done the right thing. She was a good mother and Lilly was a very happy, well-adjusted child.

She hopped into bed herself and barely had her duvet pulled up over her before she began to drift off to sleep. But it wasn't a restful sleep. Something had unsettled her. She couldn't be sure what it was, but she had a horrible feeling of foreboding. Becky liked to pretend she was unbreakable but, underneath, she was really still the same vulnerable child who had hugged her knees to herself as she sat on the landing listening to what was going on downstairs.

# Chapter 3

'You don't think this is too much, do you? I mean, I know we're just going to a pub but it's ages since I've been out in town and I want to make an effort.' Becky could tell by Kate's face that she'd gone over the top.

'Well, em, you look really nice but—'

'Right,' sighed Becky, turning to head back up the stairs. 'I'll go and get changed. I wouldn't want to—'

'No!' Kate lunged off the sofa and startled Becky by grabbing a hold of her, almost sending her flying. 'You look gorgeous. Now please, can we just go?'

'Relax, Kate. It's not even nine yet. Just let me run to the loo and we'll be off.'

She ignored Kate's eye-roll and flew back upstairs, where she locked herself in the little bathroom. Maybe she *had* gone over the top with her outfit but she didn't go out at night very often and had wanted to give her new Calvin Klein dress an outing. She'd picked up the little black number the previous weekend in TK Maxx when she and Lilly were having a girlie shopping day. It was tight-fitting and quite a few inches above the knee but she knew she had great legs and wasn't afraid to show them off along with her size-twelve curves. She'd teamed it with a gorgeous pair of Kurt Geiger lipstick-pink heels which brought her five foot seven height up to nearly six foot.

She rooted in her make-up bag and found her bronzer. She'd do a quick touch-up job before heading back down. She was glad now that she'd let Kate talk her into going out. She wasn't going to go mad –

just a few drinks and then home – but she'd promised Kate that next time she might let her drag her to a club after. Thankfully, Alice had offered to babysit so at least she knew her daughter would be in safe hands.

Giving her hair another blitz of hairspray, she was finally happy with how she looked. She was going to keep her outfit on. Kate was gorgeous and looked amazing in just a pair of jeans and t-shirt but Becky felt she needed a bit more than that to look good. She liked her glamour and the main thing was she felt good in it. She could hear giggles coming from Lilly's room so she couldn't resist one last peep in before she left.

'What are you two whispering about?' she asked, wagging a finger at her daughter and Alice, who were lying on the bed side by side. 'I hope you're not planning a party or anything while I'm out.'

'Becky! How could you suggest such a thing? I'm deeply offended.' Alice winked at Lilly, who tried to look serious but couldn't hide the giggles.

'Well, you be good for Alice, Lilly, and I'll be back in a few hours. Night night.' She kissed her daughter on the lips and hugged her tightly. 'And thanks for this, Alice. I owe you one.'

'You owe me nothing. Sure isn't it me who's the lucky one, having this little one for company. Now go on out and enjoy your night.'

'Jesus, I thought you'd gone for a nap or something,' moaned Kate, as Becky appeared back in the sitting room. 'Come on, will you. It will be closing time before we get there at this rate.'

'Bloody hell, Kate. I'm here now so let's go.' She ushered her friend out the front door and the two girls headed down towards the main road where they planned to get a taxi into the city centre.

Half an hour later, they were pushing open the door of the buzzing pub, glad to get in out of the nippy night air. The Duke was a small and popular pub just off Grafton Street – and Becky had always loved it. She'd gone there a few times with the girls from her last branch but hadn't been inside the place since she'd moved. She shivered slightly as she looked around and memories of the past came flooding back. It seemed like a lifetime ago.

'You go and find us a table and I'll get the drinks in,' Becky said, aware of stares from both men and women. 'A pint of Bulmers?'

Kate nodded. 'Lovely. Look, I'll grab us those two stools over there. There's a shelf we can put our drinks on.'

Becky gave the barmen the order and let her eyes wander around the room as she waited. Something inside her had come alive as soon as she'd stepped inside the pub. Her life had changed completely when she'd had Lilly and although she wouldn't change it for the world, there were certain things she'd started to miss about her life pre-motherhood.

'There you go.' She was jolted out of her reverie when the barman placed the drinks in front of her. She paid for them and headed over to where Kate was busy with her phone.

'Kate Murray! I'm going to hide that phone on you one of these days. Who are you texting?'

Kate looked sheepish and slipped the phone back into her bag. 'I was tweeting, actually.'

'Even worse! I honestly don't get what's so great about Twitter. You're chatting to a whole load of people you don't even know. I'd understand if you had no friends and were looking for company, but you've got loads of real-life ones.'

'I'm determined to get you tweeting one day. I bet you'd become addicted just like the rest of us.' Kate's eyes twinkled as she took a big glug of her pint.

'Never!' Becky laughed. 'I have no interest and never will.'

'And what about men?' Kate looked at her warily.

'What *about* men?'

'As I said the other night, maybe you should think about meeting someone. I know you keep saying that men are off the menu, but surely you must think about it.'

'Kate, I haven't got the time for a man. There just isn't room in my life right now. Maybe when Lilly is all grown up and off in college or something.'

'Jesus, Becky. You'll be ancient by then.'

'Oh, thanks for that.'

'But you must have … you know' – Kate moved in closer and lowered her voice – '… *urges*.'

'Nothing I can't sort out myself.'

'And nobody can do it like we do ourselves, but don't you want more? Wouldn't you sometimes like a bit of male company – even to have someone on hand for a booty call now and then.'

'Kate! You're sex mad. There's more to relationships, you know.'

'I know. But the sex is the best bit.'

Becky laughed at that. 'Well, as I said, it's not something I'm too bothered about at the moment.'

She took a sip of her wine and tried not to meet Kate's eye. She wasn't being entirely truthful, but she didn't want to get into a heavy conversation about it. She could barely admit it to herself, let alone anyone else, but a part of her would love to be in a relationship. She hadn't been with a man since the night Lilly was conceived and, until recently, she hadn't felt as though she was missing out. But the truth was, she *was* lonely. Lately, she'd been thinking a lot about her situation and imagining what it would be like to be with someone. She'd been letting her thoughts drag her down and wasn't sleeping well as a result. But she wasn't ready to share how she was feeling with anyone yet. She wasn't the sort to wear her heart on her sleeve and she liked to appear unbreakable, when she was anything but.

'Becky, are you okay?'

'Sorry, I was miles away.'

'I knew it! I've got you thinking about getting it on with some sexy hunk, haven't I?'

'Well …'

'Becky Greene. Spill the beans. Are you keeping something from me?'

'I wouldn't dare. I was just thinking about Len Sherwood and how he keeps asking me out when he comes in to the bank.' It was the first thing that had come into her head.

'Ah, the lovely Len. Now he wouldn't be my idea of a sexy hunk – too clean-cut. But maybe it's about time you put him out of his misery and went out on a date with him. He seems like a really decent guy.'

'Hmmm. It's become a game with him, I think. We're like Tom and Jerry. It just wouldn't be the same if Tom caught Jerry, now would it?'

'Haha! You're mad. But I still think he's worth taking a chance on.'

Becky smiled to herself. 'It's nice this, isn't it? The two of us out on the town. We should do it more often.'

'That's exactly what I've been saying. There's no reason why having a child should stop you from having a life of your own. It's about time you … What is it, Becks? You've gone white as a ghost.'

Becky's mouth dried up and she suddenly felt she couldn't breathe. Her hand went to her chest and she looked to the ceiling in an attempt to gulp in as much air as she could. But her breaths were short and sharp and her chest was tightening.

'Jesus Christ. What's wrong?' Kate jumped from her seat and went to put her arm around her friend.

'I … I'm fine,' said Becky, barely whispering the words. Her breath had begun to even out again. 'I'm okay, honestly.'

'You frightened the life out of me. I thought you were having a heart attack. Are you sure you're not? We should probably just go. What are you looking at?'

Becky was staring over at the bar, where two men in suits were deep in conversation.

'Who are they?' Kate asked, sitting back onto her stool. 'Do you know them?'

'I thought I knew one of them but it was a false alarm.' She stopped staring at the men and turned her attention back to Kate. 'I'm sorry for giving you a fright. I think it was a panic attack. I've had a few of them over the past year but they're nothing to worry about.'

'Oh, God, poor you. I never knew.'

'It's no big deal. They come and go usually within a minute or two.'

'But why did you panic when you thought you knew that guy?'

'Because there are people from my past I'd rather not see again.'

'Oh, well, now you *have* to tell me more.'

Becky could see Kate wasn't going to let it go. 'I thought he was Lilly's father.'

Kate gasped. 'Really? And is it definitely not him?'

'Definitely not, thank God.'

'And would it have been such a bad thing if it *was* him?'

'Yes!' Becky slammed her drink down on the table. 'I don't need him coming into our lives and complicating things. We're fine just as we are.'

'But aren't you even a little bit curious about him? I know you told me it was a one-night stand and you haven't seen him since, but aren't you ever tempted to look him up?'

'Absolutely not.' Becky shook her head vehemently. 'He's nothing to us.'

'Was he nice? I mean, did you get to talk to him much before … you know …'

Becky sighed. 'There wasn't much talking, if I'm honest. Dennis was a—'

'Dennis? Was that his name? That's the first time I heard you say it.'

Becky nodded. 'He was pretty well known in the area for his womanising. He ran an estate agency close to where I worked and, by all accounts, he was loaded. I'd often see him out and about flashing his cash. In fact, I used to see him in here sometimes. That was probably on my mind when I thought I saw him.'

'That makes sense,' Kate said, sipping her drink and listening intently. 'You should have said and we could have gone somewhere else.'

'I hadn't even thought about it until I walked in the door. But it's not as if I'd been here on a date with him or anything. In fact, I'd never even spoken to him until the night that ... you know ...'

'And how come you didn't tell him about the pregnancy? I mean, surely you thought about it.'

'Of course I did. I thought about nothing else for months but, in the end, it just didn't feel right. We'd only chatted briefly in a crowded club before he brought me back to his flat. He seemed like a nice enough guy but I was just another of his conquests, I suspect.'

'But, still, it's a pretty big decision to make not to involve him at all.'

'Kate, I've been through enough in my life to know that we can only truly rely on ourselves. I thought about it long and hard but, in the end, I decided it was going to be just me and my baby. To involve someone else someone I didn't even know – would have been way too complicated.'

'God, you really are brave. Do you think you'll ever tell Lilly about him?'

'I'll definitely tell Lilly when she's older. I'll give her any information I have and she can make her own decisions. But I have a long time to go before I have to think about all that.'

Kate drained her drink and stood up. 'Right, let's have another. I think we could do with it after the shock you've just had. Same again?'

Becky nodded, glad not to have to explain herself any further. Her conversations with Kate were usually more gossipy than deep and meaningful. That's probably why she'd never spoken to her about Dennis before. She had told Alice the whole story – but Alice was different. She was maternal and understanding and, despite her mad obsession with everything anti-ageing, she was always full of good, sound advice. Becky often said she was her Irish Mammy to which Alice would always say, 'Sister, I'm your Irish sister!'

'Here we go,' said Kate, returning with the drinks. 'That barman is a bit of all right, isn't he?'

Becky laughed. 'Now, now. You're taken, remember? What would poor Garreth think if he heard you talking like that?'

'I can look at the menu, can't I? Where's the harm in that?' She took a gulp of her drink. 'So what do you say to a club after this? Can I tempt you?'

'Not this time. Although I wouldn't say no to a Big Mac.'

'You really know how to party, don't you?' giggled Kate. 'But now that I've got you in the mood, I'm definitely taking you clubbing next time. And maybe you'll have even got it on with Luscious Len by then.'

'I wouldn't bank on it. Now drink up, I'm starving.' Becky took a big slug of her wine and winced as the liquid burned the back of her throat. Her head was spinning, but it wasn't from the alcohol. She was trying hard to get Dennis Prendergast out of her head. She hadn't thought much about him in years and now between Lilly asking questions and her eyes playing tricks on her, thoughts of him were filling her head. She and Lilly were doing just fine and Becky didn't need memories of the past coming back to haunt her.

❄

Kate kicked her shoes off and snuggled into Garreth on the sofa. It hadn't exactly been a wild night – if she was honest, it was actually pretty boring. Except for Becky's story about Lilly's father. That had definitely been the highlight of the evening. She loved Becky and really wanted to see her happy, but sometimes she didn't help herself. She was a good-looking woman with a good job but she was letting life pass her by. Any man would be lucky to have her but Becky was still being all prissy, saying she needed to give Lilly her full attention. What she actually needed was a good shag to make her realise what she was missing!

The mere thought of sex, mixed with the headiness of the pints she'd had, made her hot with desire. She glanced at Garreth, who was engrossed in football on the telly, and slowly slipped her hand down the waist of his jeans.

'Kate Murray! I should send you off with your friends more often if this is what I get when you come home.'

'There's more where that came from. Let's go upstairs and I'll show you what I've got.'

Garreth didn't have to be asked twice and they both raced upstairs, discarding clothing along the way. Kate had an insatiable appetite for sex, although she'd been a bit of a late starter. But when she'd brought herself to orgasm that first time, she'd realised what she'd been missing, and sex became a huge part of her life. She'd gone through a huge number of men before she'd met Garreth – not because she craved different men but because they just couldn't keep up with her and were frightened away.

She'd landed on her feet the day she'd met Garreth, a year earlier. It had become clear very early on that they both wanted the same things from life – money, fun and a lot of sex. But all their aspirations weren't shallow ones. Garreth was a singer-songwriter trying to make it big in the music business. He spent most of his time gigging in pubs and clubs and dreaming of one day making it big. Kate understood his drive because she had her own eyes on a modelling career. She'd had some small successes in her late teens but she'd recently signed with a new agency who assured her that there was still time to make it big in the industry. The job in the bank gave her the money to invest in herself and she was hoping one day it would pay off.

Her mind turned to Garreth and his naked, supple body bearing down on hers. He was an amazing lover – he always sensed whether she wanted it fast and passionate or soft and gentle. They knew each other intimately and nothing was off limits. But what made their relationship different to all the ones she'd had before was the fact that she loved him. She had no doubts that he was the man for her and, despite her sexual appetite, she didn't want to be with anyone else.

'That was amazing, love,' said Garreth, rolling onto his back, the duvet a tangle around their feet. 'You're just so beautiful.'

'You're not so bad yourself. But I could definitely do with losing these love handles.' Kate pulled at the almost non-existent fat on her waist.

'Don't be ridiculous. You're absolutely perfect. I really love you, you know.'

She knew. Her mind wandered to the bullies in school who'd made her life hell. How many of them were as happy as she was now? None, she hoped. Her six years in secondary school had been a nightmare because of those girls. They'd taunted her about everything, from her ginger hair to her lack of boobs. And when they'd approached their Leaving Certificate years and most of them were sexually active, they'd called her frigid. Just because she wasn't ready. Bitches. If they could only see her now.

She moved in closer to Garreth and spooned him. She felt protected and loved. It was like living in a bubble that nobody could touch, and she just hoped against hope that it would never, ever burst.

# Chapter 4

'I'm delighted you had a good night out,' said Alice, zipping up her jacket at the front door. 'And sure Lilly's an angel – I'd mind her every night of the week.'

'Thanks, Alice. You're so good. What would I do without you?'

'Well, you'll never have to find out. Now get yourself up to bed. If I know that little girl, she'll have you up at the crack of dawn.'

Becky rolled her eyes. 'Seven on the button! She's never late. And to think I used to love my sleep.'

'She's worth it though, isn't she? Night, love. I'll see you bright and early on Monday morning.'

Alice kept the smile plastered on her face as she drove off, waving to Becky until she was out of sight. She'd barely turned the corner when the tears came. Big, fat tears falling right down her neck and soaking her top. She parked the car at the side of the road and banged her fists on the steering wheel. It wasn't fair. It just wasn't fair.

Why was it that somebody like her, who had so much love to give, wasn't blessed with a child of her own? She'd always imagined a life surrounded by children but she'd never thought that none of them would be hers. She'd been nanny to numerous families over the years and had loved every minute of it, but none of the children had been as special as Lilly. Lilly was as close as she'd ever come to having a child of her own. There was a mutual love there – a closeness like she'd never experienced before. Maybe it was down to the fact that there was no father on the scene and Alice was, in a way, playing the part of a second parent.

She pulled a tissue out of her pocket and wiped the tears from her face and neck. Her sobs had subsided and she was left feeling empty and alone. When she'd been married, her family and friends had known about her desire to have children, which, in the end, had only added extra pressure on an already pressurised relationship. She'd only been twenty-five when she'd got married and they'd started to try for kids after a year or so. Thirteen years and numerous disappointments later, he'd left her for a woman with a ready-made family. She could hardly blame him. He'd wanted to be a dad just as much as she'd wanted to be a mother.

She started the car again and drove the short mile back to her own empty house. After she'd let herself in and turned on some lights, she filled the kettle with water and plonked down on a kitchen chair. She could feel the lump in her throat beginning to form again – big juicy sobs threatening to rise to the surface. She didn't usually get maudlin and she didn't like it one bit. She managed most of the time to put her infertility out of her mind. What was the point in dwelling on something you couldn't change?

Right, she wasn't going to spend the night crying and feeling sorry for herself. It was only just after midnight so it wasn't too late. She pulled her mobile out of her handbag and dialled a number.

'Frank, it's me. Any chance you'd come over?'

❋

'Are you feeling better now, love?'

'*Much* better,' said Alice, pulling the duvet up around her and cuddling into Frank's warm body. 'You always manage to cheer me up.' The one good thing about being infertile was that they never had to use protection. Alice wasn't stupid, of course. When she'd met Frank two years earlier and they'd decided to take the relationship to the next level, she'd suggested they both get tested for STDs. She knew it sounded very clinical but it was also the sensible thing to do. They'd been together since, in a monogamous relationship, and the sex was amazing.

'So do you want to tell me what happened? Why were you in such a state?'

Alice sighed. 'I honestly don't know what came over me. I had such a lovely time with Lilly tonight and just seeing her asleep in her bed ... it was just ... it was just ...'

Frank pulled her into his arms and kissed the top of her head. 'I know, I know, love. Life is just shit sometimes. You'd have made such a wonderful mother.'

'Don't get me wrong. I'm happy. You know I am. But the pain inside me just never goes away.'

Frank stroked her hair and didn't say any more. That's what she loved about him. He always instinctively knew the right things to say but he also knew when no words were required. When her husband had walked out eight years ago, Alice had vowed she'd never let another man into her life. She was done. She was going to die an old spinster. But when Frank had come along to pave her patio, they'd hit it off immediately. They'd been seeing each other ever since but despite his numerous hints, she was still hesitant about letting him move in – though she knew in her heart that it was just a matter of time before he did.

'You know my Louise adores you, don't you?' Frank was talking about his own daughter who was gone off to travel the world. Louise was twenty-five, a product of a teenage romance, and although Frank hadn't stayed with the mother, he'd been fully involved in his daughter's upbringing. 'She's always asking for you – thinks you're the best thing that's ever happened to me.'

'Thanks, but it's hardly the same, is it? She looks on me more as a friend than a mother – maybe if we'd met when she was younger things would have been different, but not at this stage.'

'But there are always options, Alice. We could think about fostering at some point. I mean, if we were living together, maybe we could apply to foster a child.'

'Oooh, I see what you did there,' Alice said, smiling at him. 'We'll add that to the list of reasons why you should move in!'

'It never even crossed my mind.' But his eyes were twinkling mischievously.

'And anyway,' continued Alice, 'I'm forty-seven and probably too old. I'm sure they'd want young, fit mothers for foster children, not withered old bats like me.'

Frank suddenly pulled away the duvet and stared at Alice's naked body. 'Now I'm no expert, but it looks to me as if there isn't one damn thing that's withered on that body of yours. And, come to think of it, there's nothing withering here either!'

'Come here so,' laughed Alice. 'We may as well test the fitness levels too while we're at it.'

Alice felt more content than she'd been in years. Frank wasn't exactly a looker. From behind, he had the look of George Clooney, a striking figure with his tanned neck and black-flecked, silver hair. But that's where the similarities ended. The skin on his face was rough from the years working outside as a builder and his long nose served as a slide for his small glasses. But he was kindness personified. He was a good man with a big heart and Alice loved the very bones of him. As their passion built again, she thanked God for giving her such a gift. The pain of not having a child would never go away but the love of a good man would definitely make her life easier.

❖

Glad to be in bed after her night out, Becky lit the French Linen Water candle on her locker and lay back in bed to inhale the fresh scent. The candle had been a present from a customer and she'd taken to lighting it every night for a few minutes before settling down to sleep. It relaxed her and she was convinced it made her sleep more soundly.

Despite her panic attack in the pub, she'd really enjoyed the night. Kate was fun to be around and always made her laugh. She was glad now that she'd agreed to go out and made a vow to do it more often in the future.

She thought about the man she'd seen in the bar earlier. The Dennis Prendergast lookalike. It was a name she hadn't heard of in a long time and one she thought she'd never hear of again. She'd managed to blot him right out of her mind when she'd come to the decision not to tell him about her pregnancy so it was no wonder she'd had a fright when she thought she saw him.

Dennis Prendergast. Dennis Prendergast. Dennis Prendergast! She couldn't get him out of her head now. She blew out the candle and turned onto her side, pulling the duvet up around her neck. She didn't want to think about him. But that was easier said than done.

Maybe what she needed was to have a fling to help her forget about him. Was that what happened after she'd made love with Dennis? Had he moved on to his next conquest and forgotten all about her? Of course he had – that's what he did. Jesus! There she was thinking about him again. What the bloody hell was wrong with her?

Dennis had been a gorgeous-looking man. He was half Spanish – at least that's what she'd heard. But you only had to look at his sallow skin and dark features to see there was something Mediterranean about him. That was obviously where Lilly had inherited her dark brown eyes because Becky's were a bright green. It was weird to think of her daughter having the eyes of a man she didn't even know and who didn't know of her existence. In the early days, Becky used to wonder about Dennis' family. Did Lilly have grandparents she didn't know about or aunts and uncles? But when life had settled down and she'd become used to being a single mother, she'd cleared her head of all such thoughts.

She sat up a little in the bed to punch her pillow into a better shape. She'd been promising herself a new bed and pillows for months now but had just never got around to it. She thought of Kate and the friendship they'd formed. Kate and Alice had become her best friends but it was funny how they both took a different role in her life.

Becky had tried very hard to keep her two friends at a distance in the beginning, but she'd soon given up. She'd clicked with them both very soon after meeting them and the friendships had developed from there. In a way, they were like her family.

Her own family were the reason she'd left London in the first place, back in 2006. She didn't talk about them much because it was too painful to even think about. There'd been some contact initially but it had fizzled out and Becky had come to terms with the fact that she was better off without them. It wasn't that she didn't think about them – because she did – but it was better this way.

A thud came from the other bedroom and she sat up straight.

'Mummy, Mummy, Mummy!'

Becky jumped up and dashed into the room where Lilly was sitting on the floor, rubbing her eyes, still half-asleep. She swept the little girl up into her arms. 'What happened to you, sweetheart? Did you fall out of the bed?'

'I think so,' she whispered, almost falling back asleep in Becky's arms. 'I'm a silly moo.'

'You *are* a silly moo,' said Becky, tucking her back in. 'But you're *my* silly moo and I love you soooo much!'

'Love you, Mummy.' She was back asleep again in seconds and Becky sat for a moment and stared at her angelic face. She felt like the luckiest woman in the world. If she could only freeze time and stay in this moment forever. But she could sense things were changing. And change didn't always have to be bad, did it? Sometimes change was for the better. But only sometimes.

❦

Deano looked at his reflection in the mirror and, just like he did every time, balked at what he saw. Who was that man looking back at him? Who was the bearded guy with the unruly hair and dead eyes? It was nobody he knew. Not any more.

It was ten months since Deano had first found himself on the streets. They'd been the longest and hardest months of his life, but it was probably no less than he deserved. What he'd initially seen as a temporary situation had become his life. It was hard to believe he'd once driven fast cars, eaten in fine restaurants and lived the high life. But he only had himself to blame.

And blame himself he did. 'Did you hear about Alan McCabe?' said his mate, Simon, one day. And that was the moment when his life changed forever. Deano had thought he'd be able to pick himself right back up after his business failed, but, after the revelations about Alan, he'd started on a downward spiral. Taking to the streets had never been a consideration at first but with money rapidly running out, no support network and a head full of guilt, it hadn't left him with many choices.

He finished trimming his beard and threw some cold water over his face. In the early days of his homelessness, he'd tried to keep himself as well groomed as possible, but some days now he couldn't even muster up the energy to brush his teeth. They were the days when he felt like ending it all. They were the days when he couldn't find the sun and the black clouds hung over him like a cloak of darkness. When he'd woken up numb with the cold earlier that morning, his mood had been really low. Like so many other days, he'd felt physically sick at the thought of facing the day. But somehow he'd managed to lift himself. He wasn't feeling any joy, but at least he wasn't contemplating throwing himself off a bridge. His jeans and t-shirt were wrinkled but it was the best he could manage. It was important that he looked respectable today.

He nodded to the girls who were busy dishing up dinner at the day centre before he headed out into the sunshine. As he walked through the busy streets of the city centre, he allowed himself to imagine that he was just like any normal person. People were dashing around, busy getting on with their lives – and there he was, getting on with his. There was nothing about him to suggest he was homeless. Even the rucksack on his back with his sleeping bag and blanket could mean he was mistaken for a tourist. But from what he'd learned about people these past few months, most wouldn't care even if they knew.

When he sat in shop doorways at night time, people would mostly do what they could to avoid him. If they didn't walk across the street, they'd look the other way as though he was invisible. He hated that. It was an embarrassment that others considered him the bane of society. Few stopped to speak to him and even those that did, seemed afraid. He couldn't blame them really. In his previous life, he'd have done the same. He'd have thought that all those living on the streets were either out of their mind on drugs or mentally ill. He wouldn't have stopped for them either.

He arrived at his bus stop and rooted in his pocket for the change he'd collected the previous night. Tapping, they called it. Nobody in the homeless community called it begging. He didn't like to be tapping, but sometimes he left a little box beside him while he buried his head in his sleeping bag. Every now and then he'd hear the jingle of coins and another little bit of him would die inside.

He hadn't long to wait because his bus arrived within minutes and he threw the change in the slot and took a seat. Today he was visiting his mother like any normal person. He'd regale her with tales of business meetings and clients. He'd tell her about parties and girlfriends. He'd become lost in his stories and, just for a little while, they'd become the truth. Then, later, he'd find himself back in a shop doorway, huddled into his sleeping bag and wishing for an end to it all.

# Chapter 5

'I'm really happy you both came in with Lilly this morning.' Glenda, the middle-aged owner of Lilly's new playschool, beamed at Becky and Alice. 'We welcome diversity here and like to teach the children to embrace it.'

Becky was confused. 'Em, yes. We thought we should both come in on the first day. I'll be back in work tomorrow so Alice will be managing things from here on in.'

Glenda nodded approvingly. 'Wonderful. And you clearly both have defined roles so that's good for Lilly. Continuity is very important.'

'Mummy, mummy. Look at this shop with all the pretend food. I love playing shopkeepers and Ella said she'd play with me.'

'That's brilliant, sweetheart. I told you you'd love it here.' A huge weight lifted off Becky's shoulders when she saw Lilly was already settling in. She'd no doubt the little girl would thrive in playschool. She was clever and, thanks to Alice, she already knew her numbers and alphabet.

'Gorgeous little thing, isn't she?' said Glenda, beaming at Lilly. 'And just so we know, does she call you both "Mummy" or does she have ways of differentiating between you – like one "Mummy" and one "Mam"?'

Alice and Becky stared at her for a moment until Alice burst out laughing. 'You think we're a couple? Haha! That's hilarious. Besides the little fact that I'm old enough to be Lilly's grandmother!'

Glenda turned a deep crimson. 'Oh, God, I'm sorry! I didn't mean to make assumptions – I just thought … I just …'

'Don't worry about it,' laughed Becky. 'Alice is Lilly's nanny. I work full time and just got the day off today so I could come down and settle her in. She's the one who'll be bringing her here every day.'

'Well, why don't you two go off and get a coffee or something and I'll see you back here in an hour. I reckon Lilly has already fitted right in.' The three looked over to where Lilly was taking a crying boy by the hand and showing him a box of toy cars.

'That's our girl,' beamed Alice. 'Come on, Becky. Let's leave her for a bit. I don't think she'll even notice we're gone.'

Becky reluctantly agreed, a sob forming in her throat, but she managed to wait until she was outside to let it escape.

'Ah, come on now,' Alice said, hugging her friend. 'It'll be good for her. She's getting fed up with being stuck with me all day and this will get her ready for big school next year.'

Becky dabbed at her eyes with a tissue, careful not to smudge her mascara. 'I know you're right, Alice. It's just she's growing up so quickly and I feel I'm missing so much.'

Alice put her arm around Becky as they headed towards The Cake Corner. 'Becky, you're a fantastic mother. You've got to stop beating yourself up just because you go out to work.'

Thankfully, the little coffee shop was quiet enough so they ordered a pot of tea and two scones and took a seat in the corner.

'Is there something else bothering you, love?' Alice's soft tones brought tears to Becky's eyes.

'Jesus, what the bloody hell is wrong with me?' She dabbed the corner of her eyes. 'I've turned into a snivelling mess lately.'

A cheery young girl placed the tea and scones in front of them and when she left, Alice reached out for Becky's hand. 'You don't have to put on an act with me, Becky. I know you're not as hard as nails. I know you have a big, soft heart in there, despite what you try to portray.'

'What?' Becky's hand flew to her mouth in mock surprise. 'Are you saying that all my efforts to be a bitch these past few years has gone to waste? Does everyone think I'm actually a softie?'

'Well, I wouldn't go that far. From what Kate was telling me, I'm sure plenty of your work colleagues think you're a bitch!'

Becky laughed. 'Well, that's something to cling on to, I suppose.'

'But seriously,' said Alice, watching Becky carefully, 'I can sense there's something troubling you. Look, I know I'm not family and I know you don't like to talk much about personal stuff, but I hate to think of you bottling things up.'

'Alice, *you* are more like family to me than anyone else in my life has been. And it's true that I don't really talk much about personal stuff but you're the only one I'd talk to if I had a problem.'

'And have you? A problem, I mean.'

Becky sipped her tea and thought for a moment. 'To be honest, I don't really know. I always thought my life was sorted. I was happy, with a good job, a wonderful child and enough money to keep us comfortable.'

'But don't you still have those things? What's changed?'

'Nothing's changed in a physical sense, but I'm just feeling a bit unsettled. And then my night out with Kate got me thinking.'

Alice slapped her hand on the table a little too hard. 'Bloody Kate! Why am I not surprised? What has she said now?'

'Ah don't be so hard on her. She did say one or two things about me getting out more but I'd been thinking about it myself lately. Sometimes I feel like life is passing me by.'

'But your life is so full, Becky. You have your job and Lilly and your friends. It's not as though you're sitting at home depressed every night.'

'I know you're right but when Lilly is in bed and all I have is a glass of wine and *Coronation Street* for company, it can be a bit lonely. Maybe it's time that I got back out there and started meeting people again.'

'You mean like an actual *man*!'

Becky laughed at that. 'Well, yes, I suppose so. I'm not planning a mission to find one or anything, but I might not be so against the idea if something turns up.'

'Well, I think that's great,' Alice beamed. 'And you know I'm available for babysitting whenever you need me.'

'You're so good to us, Alice. I honestly don't know what we'd do without you.'

'Don't be silly. Sure don't I love that little girl as though she was my own? I'll be forever grateful to you for bringing me in and making me a part of your little family.'

'Ah, stop, Alice. You'll have me going again.' Becky took a large sip of her tea in an effort to stop the tears.

'But surely it's a *good* thing that you're going to get out and about a bit more. Is there something else?'

'It's just the whole situation with Lilly and her father. I'm wondering if I've done the right thing in keeping Lilly from him.'

She quickly filled Alice in on what had happened at the pub and Lilly's questions about her father. She told her about filling in the forms for playschool and hovering over the next-of-kin section. That had really brought it home to Becky that there was no father for Lilly, no grandparents or aunts and uncles – it was just the two of them. It had been quite confronting.

'Becky, love, you made the decision that was right for you at the time. And nobody can deny the brilliant job you've done with Lilly. She's a real credit to you. But it's never too late if you want to do something about it now.'

Alice's words startled Becky. She'd expected her to say that the father didn't need to be involved. That he had never been a part of Becky's life so he didn't need to be a part of Lilly's.

Alice continued. 'I mean, we can make decisions about things and just because we might change our minds later doesn't mean that the original decision was wrong. Do you get what I mean?'

'So are you saying that I should try and find Lilly's father now?' Becky was trying to take in what her friend was saying.

'I'm not saying that at all. All I'm saying is that there's no harm in re-evaluating the situation. You may still decide that you don't want anything to do with him but at least you'll have thought about it.'

Becky sighed. 'You're right. Even talking about it is helping. I've got to learn to open up more.'

'Well, have a think about things and we can talk about it again. And if you do decide to look him up, I'll be right there behind you.'

'Thanks, Alice. And don't go telling anyone I'm not as tough as I look, will you? I have a reputation to uphold.'

'Your secret is safe with me. And do you realise that it's been an hour since we left Lilly and you haven't even cried about her once? That makes you one tough lady.'

Becky jumped up from her chair, shrugging on her jacket and looking at her watch. 'I can't believe an hour is gone already. And I thought I'd be watching every minute ticking by.'

'Well, if nothing else, our chat got you through your daughter's first morning in playschool.'

'It was more than that,' said Becky, linking Alice as they headed back to collect Lilly. 'It was like a counselling session. I think you've missed your calling.'

'Ha! Counselling is just one of my sidelines. Working with children all these years has qualified me for a lot of things. I could be a nurse, a baker—'

'A candlestick maker! Well, I'm grateful you had your counselling hat on today.'

Lilly was busy doling out plastic meals to the other children and spotted them as soon as they walked in. 'Mummy, Alice, come and look at the dinner I made. You can have some too.'

'She's been a great girl,' said Glenda, beaming. 'I think we have a lovely little group here and Lilly is definitely going to be a wonderful addition.'

Becky's heart swelled with pride as she looked at her little girl. Alice had been right. Lilly was a great kid. She was clever, loving, kind and an absolute joy to be around. Despite her earlier reservations, Becky knew she'd done a great job with her. And she'd done it on her own. She was mad to consider rocking the boat now by adding a father to the mix. She felt relieved. She felt sure.

'Mummy, do you want sauce on your eggs?' Lilly beamed as she held out a plate of pretend food to her. Becky's heart did a flip. If she was so sure, why was it that when her daughter looked up at her, she saw Dennis Prendergast's eyes staring back?

# Chapter 6

'Kate, have you got a second?' Becky was sitting at her desk in work. There was a mound of paperwork to deal with, but she didn't feel much like working.

'Jesus!' puffed Kate, arriving at Becky's side looking flushed. 'Those bloody bags of coins weigh a ton. It's a wonder someone hasn't broken their back carrying them from the safe every morning. Don't you think we should have porters to do—'

'Listen, I don't want to keep you from your work. I was just wondering if you could call over some evening this week. I need your help with something.'

Kate looked put out that her concerns weren't being taken seriously. 'Yes, well, of course I can. But someone needs to do something about those bags. Honestly, it's an accident waiting to happen.'

'I have a meeting with Andrew later and I'll bring it up.' Andrew was the branch manager and the most indecisive man Becky had ever met. He seemed to spend all his time shuffling papers about and it was almost impossible to get him to deal with anything. But it seemed to appease Kate for the moment.

'Okay, good. And what was it you wanted me to help with?'

'Oh, just some computer stuff.' Becky tried to be nonchalant. 'Nothing too important but you know what I'm like when it comes to technical stuff.'

'Ooh, are you finally going to join this century then? I knew you'd eventually give in. I'll have you Tweeting and Facebooking in no time.'

'Well, that's *never* going to happen. But I may call on your Facebook expertise to help me with something.'

Kate pushed some of Becky's paperwork aside to sit on the edge of the desk. 'Now that sounds intriguing. Come on, don't leave me in suspense.'

'I'll explain when you come over.' Becky changed the subject quickly. 'Look, it's almost ten so you'd better get set up before customers arrive in.'

'Shit! I didn't think it was so late. Right, I'll catch you at lunchtime and you can fill me in then.'

Becky sighed as she tried to focus on a document in front of her. At this rate, she'd never get all her transfers done before her eleven o'clock cut-off.

She'd just have to put everything out of her mind and focus on the job. It was so unlike her to be distracted. She always prided herself on her diligence and her ability to leave her personal life at home while she was working, but now the seed of Dennis Prendergast had been sown in her mind, she hadn't been able to shake it. Part of her wanted to wipe his name from her memory but the other part felt that maybe now the time was right to try and make contact with him again. She'd no idea what would happen if and when she found him. She was just taking the first steps and she'd see after that. It was a huge step to take and something told her that her life was about to change forever.

❂

'So why didn't you tell *me* you needed help with computer stuff?' Alice looked a little miffed when Becky told her Kate was coming over.

Becky laughed. 'Why do you think? You're not exactly a whizzkid when it comes to technology, are you? In fact, I'm probably even slightly ahead of you – and that's saying something.'

'So what's with the sudden interest in the world of computers, then?'

'It's not computers I'm interested in at all. It's just what they can tell me.'

'Go on,' said Alice, slipping her coat on and heading out into the hall.

'Well, I was going to tell you but I was waiting to see what I could find out first.' Becky looked into the kitchen, where Lilly was sitting at the table, drawing. She lowered her voice. 'I've decided to take your advice and look up Lilly's father.'

Alice gasped. 'Seriously? So you're going to tell him about Lilly? When did you decide this?'

'I've been thinking about it since our chat last week. And I haven't decided anything yet – other than I'm going to see if he's still around. If I do find him, I'll have to have a think about what my next step, if any, will be.'

Alice clasped her hands together. 'Oh, but it's still very exciting. So Kate's going to help you find him on the computer?'

'Well, yes. I tried googling him myself but I couldn't find anything and that's just about as far as my knowledge of computers goes. I searched the business he ran and nothing came up, so I'm guessing it's not there any more. A couple of options for his name came up for Facebook but when I clicked on them, I couldn't see any information. That's why I need someone who's up to speed on that sort of stuff.'

Alice had been about to head out the door but hesitated. 'But do you think Kate is the right person to help you? Yes, she's probably a whizz with the computer but you know what she's like. If you find him, she'll have a date arranged before you have a chance to think.'

'I do have a brain of my own, you know,' said Becky, put out that Alice would think she'd be so easily led. 'This is only an initial search. I just want to find out a little bit more about him before I decide what I'm going to do.'

'Hmmm. Well, just be careful, okay? I know it would be easy to get swept away in a moment – especially with a young, enthusiastic girl like Kate egging you on and she might encourage you to—'

'Well, why don't you stay and give us a hand, then?'

'Are you sure? I wouldn't like to intrude.' Alice already had her coat off and was heading back into the kitchen. 'I mean, I wasn't having a go at Kate or anything. You know I only have your best interests at heart.'

'I know you do, Alice. Now why don't you stick the kettle on and I'll go for a quick shower. We can have a chat ourselves before Kate comes over.'

Becky smiled to herself as she stepped into the warm shower. Alice was so transparent. She'd clearly wanted to stay and had been waiting for an invitation. She lathered some Clarins foaming cleanser onto her face and allowed the water to wash over it. Although she was nervous about the prospect of finding out about Dennis, there was also a huge bubble of excitement inside her. Her life was good but it wasn't exactly full of thrills. The thought of adding a new dimension to it was very appealing. Of course she was going to have to think carefully every step of the way. Lilly was her priority and she couldn't lose focus of that.

Ten minutes later, she was dressed and heading downstairs when the doorbell rang. She pulled open the door to see Kate standing there, hopping from foot to foot and blowing on her hands.

'Jesus, anyone would think it's December rather than September,' she said, stepping inside and rubbing her hands together. 'It's absolutely freezing out there.'

Becky smiled at her friend. 'Come on into the kitchen. It's much warmer in there. Did Garreth give you a lift over?'

'Yes, he's so good to me … oh, hi, Alice. I didn't realise you'd still be here.'

'Hiya, Kate. Yes, Becky asked me to stay to give a hand. Lilly and I were just doing our nails, weren't we, Lillypop?'

Lilly giggled and waved her sparkling pink nails in the air to show them off. 'I'm not Lillypop, silly. I'm just Lilly!'

'Okay, okay. Sorry about that, Lillypop.' Alice stuck out her tongue and the little girl was off in fits of giggles again.

Kate took off her jacket and hung it on the back of a chair. 'Ah, you're going to mind Lilly while we do our computer stuff.'

'No. Lilly will be going to bed in five minutes. I'll be giving you two a hand.'

'Oh, right.' Kate looked put out but turned her attention to Becky, who was loading cups into the dishwasher. 'Are you excited about the prospect of finding him?'

'Finding who?' Lilly's head popped up and her eyes were inquisitive. 'Who are you going to find, Mummy?'

Becky was stunned for a moment but Alice piped in. 'Mummy has to find someone in work to be her assistant because she's so busy. It's all boring bank stuff really.'

Lilly lost interest immediately and continued blowing on her nails.

Kate looked sheepish and mouthed sorry to Becky. Becky knew Kate hadn't meant any harm but also knew she would have to warn her about the dangers of talking too openly in front of Lilly. Alice knew those sorts of things instinctively, but Kate was completely at sea when it came to children.

'I think it's time for your bed, Missy,' said Becky, anxious to get started on the search. 'You run on upstairs and brush your teeth and I'll be up when I clear away this stuff.'

Becky began to gather up the nail polishes. 'I'll do that, Becky,' Alice said. 'You go on up with her and get her settled. Night, night, sweetheart.'

'Why are your fingers purple?' asked Kate, staring at Alice's hands as she cupped them around Lilly's face for a kiss.

Alice blushed. 'Oh, it's probably just paint from earlier today. Lilly and I were doing art.'

'It's from the blueberries, Alice, 'member?' Lilly looked from Kate to her mother. 'Did you know that if you eat a punnet of blueberries every day, your skin will be all smooth and lovely?'

Becky had to stifle a giggle. 'I didn't know that, sweetheart. Aren't you a clever girl?'

'Alice told me. And she brought some beetroot for our lunch today because it's full of anti-sausages or something and makes you young.'

Even Alice, despite her mortification, couldn't help laughing at Lilly's information. 'Antioxidants, sweetie. And what did I tell you about keeping my secrets?'

'Sorry, Alice. But Kate and Mummy might want to try them too.'

'Okay, let's get you to bed,' said Becky, lifting her up and hugging her closely. 'You two might grab the laptop from the counter over there and get it set up on the kitchen table – and make some coffee. I'll be down as soon as I've read this little one a story or two.'

'Right,' they said in unison and Becky sighed. If those two were going to be at each other's throats all evening, she'd scream. The last thing she needed was friction. Besides Lilly, they were the two people who meant most to her in the world and they were going to damn well get along whether they liked it or not.

⁂

'I might have known we'd hit a dead end,' said Becky, stretching her hands above her head and yawning. 'I suppose it would have been too easy to just read all about him from the comfort of my little kitchen.'

Alice patted her hand. 'I wouldn't give up yet, love. There are a lot of other ways you can trace him.'

'Yes, you could go to where he lived and just confront him.' Kate looked excited at the prospect. 'In fact, we could even come along for a bit of moral support.'

'Well, I didn't quite mean that,' said Alice, glaring at Kate. 'I meant a bit of gentle digging – not full-on confrontation.'

Becky looked thoughtful. 'Kate might have a point actually. I don't mean to confront him straight away, but it mightn't be a bad idea to go to where his business used to be. He lived in the flat over it but if the business is gone, I'm guessing he's gone from there too.'

'You see?' Kate gave Alice a triumphant look. 'I knew it was a good idea. When should we go? What about tomorrow? God, this is exciting.'

'Don't be ridiculous, Kate,' said Alice, shaking her head. 'We can't all go off on a wild-goose chase. It's not a game – it's Becky's life.'

'Oh, for God's sake, Alice. Get off your high horse. Becky said it was a good idea, didn't she?'

'But she didn't say that we should all—'

'Right, I think we'd better call it a night.' Becky was sick of the two of them bickering and she needed time to think.

Alice was the first to push her chair back and stand up. 'Of course. You must be exhausted, Becky. You need to sleep on it and we can talk again tomorrow.'

'Yes,' said Kate, quickly. 'Let's have lunch tomorrow and we can have a good chat.'

Becky ushered them both out of the kitchen towards the front door. 'You've both been great. Thanks for all your help. I'll have a think about what I want to do next and I'll talk to you *both* about it.'

She waved them off and breathed a sigh of relief. At least Alice had offered to drop Kate to the taxi rank. Hopefully they wouldn't kill each other in the car.

She set the alarm and switched off the lights downstairs. Walking up the stairs to bed, she felt weary. Her head was so full of stuff, she was afraid it might explode. Her friends were great and she really appreciated their help but sometimes – just sometimes – she wished she had a family to talk to. Her thoughts wandered to London and she wondered where they all were – what they were doing. It wasn't as painful as it had once been to think about them, but it still hurt.

She'd often heard it said that nothing was as powerful as a mother's love and it made her desperately sad that she didn't have that. But it made her all the more determined to make sure her daughter had it in abundance. She tip-toed into Lilly's room and stood watching her for a moment before placing a feather kiss on her forehead.

'I love you, sweetheart. And whatever happens, you'll always have me. You'll always have your mother's love.'

# Chapter 7

Deano sat in the bus shelter and buried his chin in his scarf. The days were getting colder and it looked like there was going to be a steady downpour. He'd woken up that morning to the icy rain biting into his face and had been forced to abandon his sodden bed. As luck would have it, it had been a lucrative night and his tapping cup was half full. It meant he'd been able to buy a steaming hot cup of tea and breakfast bagel and, more importantly, an hour in the comfort and warmth of a fast-food restaurant.

The wind was blowing the rain into the shelter and Deano moved further into the corner as he tried to stay dry. He stared over at the house across the road and wondered what was going on inside. Were they sitting down enjoying a nice calm breakfast or were they rushing around like crazy to get ready for the day ahead? The latter, he assumed. Because every day must be crazy and hectic in that house.

He remembered the day the house went on the market. 'A wonderful buy', the blurb had said. 'Close to the bus and just one stop away from The Pavilions Shopping Centre … A gorgeous, detached cottage with a vast and spacious interior.' There was no doubt it was all true. And its price tag of six hundred and fifty thousand euro had even seemed fair, considering the country had been in the height of a property boom. He reckoned it couldn't be worth more than three fifty now. Three hundred grand of equity down the drain. It didn't bear thinking about.

He checked the time on his battered old watch. Twenty to nine. Ten more minutes and the door would swing open, with Isabella shouting at the kids to hurry up. It never failed to amaze him how she managed to run things like clockwork when it was clear that she had so much to juggle.

Deano had come here first a few months ago – partly out of curiosity and partly to punish himself. He wanted to see the family for himself. He was inexplicably drawn to them and had become fascinated with their lives. They didn't know he came, of course. To them, he was invisible. He was nobody. But they consumed his thoughts. How could they not?

The bus shelter had become packed with commuters and he was glad when a bus arrived to pick them all up. He watched somewhat bemused as they seemed incapable of forming an orderly queue but instead gathered six or eight abreast waiting for the driver to open the doors. Most wore business suits. Deano found it hard to believe that he had been one of them once. It seemed like a lifetime ago. It *was* a lifetime ago.

Ten to nine. He glanced across the road again and just as he'd expected, the door opened and Isabella came out. She was carrying the little girl but the twin boys made a beeline for the front door of the car. Even from where he was, he could hear their shrill voices.

'It's my turn. You were in the front going to Granny's on Sunday.'

'But you were in it twice yesterday.'

'Yeah, only for like five minutes. Granny lives hours away.'

Deano strained to hear what Isabella said to the boys but a motorbike going past drowned out the sound. Whatever it was, it had left them in no doubt that she wasn't taking any nonsense from them. Both skulked into the back seat beside their sister and Isabella went back into the house. She emerged a few seconds later with her arms full of school bags and her face showing the strain of the morning.

She was only in her thirties but the furrows on her brow and tired lines around her eyes suggested she was older. She seemed to be ageing rapidly, but it was no wonder. Deano had come to that spot enough times over the last year to know her routine pretty well. Sometimes, he wished he had a car to follow her and see exactly how her day panned out, but that would probably be taking things a step too far.

She reversed the car out onto the main road and was gone in seconds. Deano sighed and closed his eyes. Why did he do it to himself? He always felt like shit afterwards, but he still kept coming back for more. He often wondered if anyone noticed him there in that same spot. Were people taking note of his face in case it turned up on *CrimeCall* some day? Did he look like a stalker – or somebody about to commit a crime? He'd laugh if it wasn't so tragic.

The rain had stopped so he threw his rucksack over his shoulder and headed down the road. He didn't feel like getting on a bus yet. He wanted to walk to clear his head. There were times when he'd almost spoken to Isabella. He'd even crossed the road one day as she was getting into the car, but fear had let him down at the last minute. What would he say to her? What *could* he say?

He quickened his steps as the rain began to pelt down again. A few minutes and he'd be inside the warm shopping centre. Since he'd woken up that morning, his chest had felt tight and he seemed to have the beginnings of a raspy cough. He was lucky really that he didn't get sick too often and he'd managed to stay healthy enough during his time on the streets. The sickest he'd been was one morning when he'd been suffering the effects of alcohol poisoning. It was back in the early days when some guy he'd met in the soup kitchen had told him that the only way to stay warm at night was either to down a full bottle of whiskey or get into the heroin game and become oblivious to it. There was no way Deano was going down the slippery slope of drugs, so he'd gone for the whiskey option. Never again. It had taken him three days to empty the contents of his stomach and it was an experience he wouldn't like to repeat.

He'd stayed clean since that day and he'd clung on to the hope that if he kept a clear head, he'd be able to figure a way out of the awful situation he was in. But it was almost nine months later and he was still trying to figure it out. He felt sure that if he could only keep the dark days at bay, he'd be able to think straight. But depression was a real factor when you lived on the streets.

He sometimes went to a social club which was run by one of the homeless charities. He'd hated the idea of it at first – he didn't want or need charity. He deserved nothing. But he soon began to realise how valuable the club was. It was somewhere to go. Somewhere to meet others. Somewhere he didn't feel so alone.

He'd even listened to one of the charity workers in there, who explained to him about what payments he was entitled to. He registered himself as homeless but when faced with endless paperwork to claim a payment, he'd fallen at the final hurdle. The combination of his pride and his growing depression had caused him to rip the forms up and storm out of the very building that could have been his key to a better life.

The truth was that he didn't want to join the many homeless people who collected money from the state each month. What he really wanted was to find himself a job. If he could get himself back into the workforce, he could rent a little flat and become self-sufficient. But he'd never again go back to the sort of life or job he had before. The more time he spent on the streets, the more he felt distanced from his previous life. The person he'd been before was the very sort of person he detested now, and he realised that the things he'd had in his life had just been superficial. He'd thought he'd had loads of friends but where were they now? Nobody had stood by him when he'd begun to hit hard times. Nobody had wanted to know.

At first when things had gone belly up, he'd felt secure in the knowledge that he had plenty of friends who'd support him through it all. 'Come and sleep on my sofa for a bit,' one of them had said. And another: 'There'll always be room at my place until you get yourself sorted.'

But the cold, stark reality was that people were all talk. A few nights on a mate's sofa and his wife was screaming blue murder that her house was being taken over. He'd managed a few weeks between various friends' places, but his pride had kept him moving on for fear people would brand him a loser. It had dawned on him soon enough that he only had himself to rely on.

A waft of warm air hit his face as he walked through the automatic doors of the shopping centre. He'd treat himself to a doughnut and a sit down before heading back into town. It was weird but he didn't like to be away from the city centre for too long. It was his home now. A fit of coughing overcame him and he was forced to lean against a wall for support. Bloody rain. He wasn't looking forward to another night of it.

He paid for a doughnut and a tea in McDonald's, making sure he had enough change for his bus fare, and gladly took the weight off his feet. Isabella's face popped into his head again and he wondered if he would ever see her smiling. Was her life just drudgery now? Did she feel a bit like him in that every day was the same? He closed his eyes and swallowed a mouthful of hot tea but he felt the guilt stick in his throat and threaten to suffocate him. Would it ever go away? Would he ever be rid of the guilt he felt when he looked into Isabella's sad eyes?

# Chapter 8

Becky laughed as she listened to Dermot and Dave's banter on 98fm. She was driving over to the south side on a mission, and was glad of the distraction of the comedy duo. She knew that if she thought too much about what she was doing, she'd just turn right around and go back home.

She'd left work early, claiming she had a dentist appointment, but it wasn't true. She'd been thinking about what she should do about Dennis, and then it had come to her.

She'd decided not to say anything to the girls. It was still early so Alice wouldn't be expecting her home and Kate probably hadn't even realised she was gone. This was something she needed to do by herself and, besides, she didn't think she could handle the two girls bickering and disagreeing about everything.

She turned off at the Donnybrook Road and headed down towards her old life. She hadn't been back at all since she'd moved and it felt strange to see the familiar street names and landmarks. She parked on a little side street and allowed herself to sit quietly for a moment. Right, she wasn't going to over-think things. She rooted in her bag and pulled out her pink lip gloss. If she was going to be asking questions of people, she may as well make sure she looked good. She straightened her navy pencil skirt as she stepped out of the car and began walking.

She'd really had some fun times in this neighbourhood. It had been her first home when she'd come over from London in 2006, and she'd great memories of how welcoming the people had been and how she'd immediately felt that Ireland would be her home for a very long time. A waft of freshly baked bread filled her nostrils and she smiled as she realised Monica's Tearooms must still be in operation. She used to live off Monica's breakfasts, never having time to make one for herself, and had been a regular customer in the afternoon when she'd sometimes pop in for tea and one of Monica's famous scones.

A few minutes later, she stood outside the bank where she'd once worked. She wondered if many of the old gang still worked there. She hadn't kept in touch with any of them and they hadn't bothered with her. It was sad in a way, because she'd spent a lot of time with them. But that was how she'd wanted it. A clean start.

She continued walking as the autumn sun tried to break through the clouds. And then she was there. Dennis Prendergast had once run his little empire from this very shop. His estate agency had seen the boom but, by the looks of things, it had seen the Celtic Tiger crash through the floor too. There was no trace of what was once Prendergast Estates. In its place was Howie's Hardware – a drab-looking shop, a million miles from Dennis' sleek, contemporary offices.

It was now or never. She took a deep breath and pushed the door, setting off a jingle from a bell above. A grey-haired man of about seventy with a beige shop coat and glasses held together by some duct tape appeared from beneath the counter, reminding Becky of a scene from an old sketch show.

'What can I do for you, love?' The man burst into a fit of coughing.

'I'm, em, just looking at your floor mops.' She needed to buy some time.

'You won't get any better than those,' he said, waving his hand to indicate the wall of mops. 'All top-of-the-range stuff we have here – cheaper and better than you'll get in those big stores. And you get it all with a smile here.' He flashed his broken teeth and Becky winced at their yellowness.

'So have you been here long?'

'Oh, I'd say since about ten this morning. I usually don't open up too early because it takes me a while to straighten my back and—'

'No, I mean how long has your shop been here?' Becky could see this wouldn't be easy.

'Ah, I get you now. Coming up to a year now. Came out of retirement when I saw this little beauty up for sale, I did.' He leaned over the counter as though to share a secret and Becky moved closer to hear. 'Got it for dirt cheap. It was a repossession – came with the flat and all over it.'

So Dennis really *had* fallen on hard times if the bank had repossessed his business and home. It was no wonder, really. It would have been difficult for anyone in that line of business to keep their heads above water when the bottom fell out of Ireland's property market. Becky remembered people in the area speaking about Dennis Prendergast and how he was doing so well keeping his business alive through the bad times. It had obviously got him in the end.

'So are you having it, then?'

Becky was startled out of her reverie. 'Having what?'

'The mop. Are you taking the mop?'

'Yes, I'll take this one.' She grabbed for the first one to hand and rooted in her bag for her purse.

'Hang on,' said the old man and disappeared underneath the counter again. Becky watched the empty space where he'd been until he rose up a few seconds later with a toothy smile. She could smell the smoke a mile away. He was obviously having a sneaky cigarette. She couldn't help laughing to herself.

'So did you know the person who owned the place before you?' She was still rooting for her purse to play for time.

'No, didn't know him at all. Dennis Prendergast was his name. I know that because I regularly get post for him and have to give it back to the postman. He didn't leave any forwarding address, so what can I do?'

Becky's heart fell. Without a forwarding address, she didn't have much hope of tracing him. 'So you've no idea? You've no clue where he might have gone to?'

'Sorry, love, I can't help you there. But you did say you were going to buy the mop, didn't you? Business is pretty quiet at the moment so you know yourself. Every bit counts.'

'Of course.' She pulled out her purse and handed him a twenty euro note. There was no point in spending any more time there.

She was heading out the door feeling deflated when the old man's voice called after her. 'You could always try Jack Berry across in the chipper. Jack's been here for years so he might know something of Mr Prendergast.'

'Thanks. I might just do that.' Becky felt buoyed up again and headed across the road. There were eight or ten people in the queue for chips so she stood behind the last one.

'Can I help you there?'

'Eh, just a bag of chips, please.' She could hardly start asking questions in front of the other customers so she'd just have to bide her time. There was something really depressing about the silence of the shop. In fact, it struck her that the whole area was depressing. It wasn't the street she remembered. When she'd lived around there, it had been buzzing and full of life. But like so many places, the recession seemed to have taken its toll and the sparkle was gone.

'Salt and vinegar?'

She looked up and couldn't believe she was already at the top of the queue and even better, there was nobody behind her so she was free to ask questions. 'Yes, please. And do you mind if I ask you about the hardware shop across the road?'

She waited for an answer but since none was forthcoming, she continued. 'Did you know the guy who used to be there beforehand? The estate agent.'

'I've only been here myself since last month but Jack might know. Hang on.'

Becky's heart was beating like crazy, waiting for this Jack guy to come out and tell her what he knew. The harder it was becoming to get information, the more she wanted it. It was almost turning into a challenge.

'You're looking for Dennis Prendergast?' The guy Becky assumed was Jack appeared out at the counter, eyeing her up suspiciously.

'Yes, I used to know him. I was just wondering how he was doing.'

'Are you a debt collector or something?' Still those suspicious eyes.

'No! Not at all. As I said, I used to know him, that's all.'

'Well, it wouldn't have mattered even if you were. Dennis disappeared from here over a year ago and I haven't seen him since.'

'You knew him, then?'

'Only in passing. He often came in here for his lunch or he'd pop over for a late dinner. He lived above his shop, you know.'

Becky nodded, thinking about her one and only time to visit his flat above the shop.

Jack continued. 'Decent enough guy, but a bit flash. He used to throw the cash around like it grew on trees and he always had a different girl on his arm.'

Becky winced at that. It was just as she'd thought. Maybe she'd had a lucky escape. From what she was hearing, maybe it was a good thing she hadn't found Dennis. She wasn't sure what she'd been expecting, but just hearing about his womanising again was like a wake-up call.

'Well, thanks for that information.'

'No problem. Sorry I couldn't be of more help.'

'Oh, you've helped plenty,' said Becky, heading towards the door. 'In fact, you've done me a huge favour.'

'I can't imagine how but I'm glad. And are you forgetting something?' She turned to see him holding up a brown paper bag of chips.

'Sorry, I'm such a scatterbrain.'

She quickly paid and, glancing for one last time at what used to be Prendergast Estates, she headed back down the road. She hadn't got what she'd wanted from today, but it had been far from a wasted journey. It had made her realise that revisiting the past wasn't necessarily a good thing. She and Lilly were happy with how things were and she was scared to risk messing that up. She tucked the long pole of the mop underneath her arm as she walked back towards the car. She willed her tears not to come but as she stuffed her mouth with the vinegar-laden chips, she couldn't help it. Why did her life have to be so complicated?

❁

'I can't believe you went off looking for Dennis without telling us. I wish you hadn't gone on your own.'

Becky was sitting at the kitchen table with Alice and she'd just filled her in on the events of the afternoon. 'There was no need for anyone to come with me, Alice. All I was doing was asking a few questions.'

'But what if you'd come face to face with him? It could have brought back all sorts of memories. You might have been upset.'

Becky thought for a moment as she cupped her hands around the warm tea Alice had made. 'I really don't think I'd have been upset. And I wasn't planning on saying anything to him just yet. I only wanted to see where he was in his life and have a think about what to do.'

'But you mightn't have had a choice if he'd seen you. What would you have said if he'd recognised you?'

'He wouldn't. I told you, Alice, it was just one night. And even the guy in the chipper said he had a different woman on the go every night so I was just one of a long line.'

Alice started to say something, then hesitated.

'What?' said Becky.

'It's just I've often wondered about you getting pregnant. Did you not use protection?'

'That's why it came as such a surprise. We used a condom so it never occurred to me that I could get pregnant. How naïve was that?

They're only ninety-eight per cent safe, you know. That's a statistic I'll *never* forget again!'

'God, Becky. I hope you realise how lucky you are. Honestly, two bloody per cent and you manage to get yourself pregnant whereas I've spent almost half my life trying and got nowhere.'

Becky looked at Alice and to her dismay she saw tears running down her face. 'Oh, Alice,' she said, jumping up from her chair and going to comfort her friend. 'Sometimes I forget.'

'I'm fine, I'm fine,' Alice said, quickly wiping her tears with her sleeve. 'I'm just so hormonal these days. Every day that I go through this bloody menopause, I feel cheated and angry. I'm only forty-bloody-seven, for God's sake!'

Becky sat back down but reached across and took Alice's hand. 'I can't imagine how hard it is for you. And yes, I *do* realise how lucky I am. It didn't feel like it at the time but it was the best thing that ever happened to me.'

'Why are you crying, Alice?' The two women were startled as Lilly appeared in the kitchen.

'I thought you were watching telly,' said Becky, pulling her daughter onto her lap. 'You've got five more minutes and then it's bed for you, Missy.'

'But why is Alice crying?' She kept her eyes fixed on her beloved nanny.

Alice plastered a smile on her face. 'I'm not crying, silly. The tears are because I was laughing so hard at your mummy's joke.'

'Oh,' she said, hopping down from Becky's lap. 'Usually mummy's jokes are soooo bad.'

They both burst out laughing as Lilly skipped back in to the sitting room to watch telly.

'She's getting cuter by the day,' said Alice, shaking her head.

Becky nodded. 'She's growing up so fast. I need to enjoy every precious minute I have with her. And I can start by putting the name Dennis Prendergast firmly out of my head.'

'Do you really mean that, Becky?'

'Yes! I'm not going to turn my life upside down trying to play detective when I don't even know if it's what I want.'

'Okay, okay. I get it.' Alice stood up and put her cup into the sink. 'Right, I'm off. I'm doing a few weeks of going to bed really early to test the theory that sleep is good for the skin. Did you know that the term "beauty sleep" isn't just an old wives' tale? It's supposed to be really good for your skin.'

Becky rolled her eyes. 'Well, at least *that* remedy won't cost you anything. See you in the morning.' She closed the door and turned the key in the lock. Maybe she should take a leaf out of Alice's book. She could do with more early nights herself. She felt exhausted a lot of the time and her skin could do with a bit of tender loving care.

She began to load cups in the dishwasher as she let her mind wander back to the events of the day. Part of her felt relieved that she hadn't come face to face with Dennis. It would have been very confronting. But she was also a little sad. It had felt exciting to be on a mission – to be about to embark on something that could possibly have a huge effect on her life. Where was Dennis Prendergast now? What was he doing? Was he married with children of his own? Maybe Lilly had some half brothers or sisters. The thought made her shiver. Well, wherever he was, it was of no interest to her any more. Her one wish in life was that Lilly would grow up happy and fulfilled and right now, she didn't need a father for that.

# Chapter 9

Kate sat in the waiting room with about fifty other girls. She'd just had a casting for a major fashion show that was happening at Christmas and she felt sure she'd make the cut. They'd seemed impressed by her look and her dedication. They'd oohed and aahed as they took pictures and had made numerous comments about her 'amazing' red hair.

'God, the waiting is excruciating, isn't it?' said a skinny blonde girl sitting beside her. 'I don't think I'll ever get used to it.'

Kate glanced at her. She was about eighteen and more than six foot but was so thin that her bones protruded in her neck and arms. There were certain people in the fashion industry that considered that to be a positive thing, but Kate just thought it looked like she was starved half to death.

'Have you done many of these?' The girl was still talking.

'I've done loads,' said Kate, feeling smug. 'And you do get used to it after a while. Is this your first?'

'No, I've done a few but I'm still fairly new to it all. Angel is the name.' She held out a painfully skinny hand.

'I'm Kate Murray. And don't worry if you don't get called. It sometimes takes a while to get yourself noticed.'

'Oh I've got the job each time I did one of these.' Angel opened her green eyes wide. 'They usually say they like a new, fresh face.'

'I see.' Kate was mortified. She should learn to keep her mouth shut. Still, the three judges on the panel had been impressed with her so she was feeling very positive.

A murmur rippled through the room all of a sudden as one of the judges appeared at a doorway. It was time.

'Okay, if you hear your name called out, please stay back. Otherwise you can leave. You haven't been successful at this time but I thank you all for your participation.'

'I love this bit,' whispered Angel, full of excitement. Kate just felt like a bundle of nerves.

'So we have Donna Sherringham, Elaine Moorehouse …' The names meant nothing to Kate and with every name called, she felt her hopes dissipating. '… Angel Filan and finally Kate Murray.'

'We're both in!' squealed Angel. 'They called us both.' Kate was over the moon. It was only the shortlist but she mostly didn't even get called on to that, so it was a step forward.

As the girls who hadn't been called started to leave, the judge continued, 'So we're just looking for two girls today and we'll make our decision fairly quickly. If you can all just walk up and down the centre of the room until we tell you to stop.' The other two judges had come into the room and they were poised and ready to give their verdict.

Kate knew how to work the floor. She sashayed up and down, making great use of her long, wavy hair and throwing shapes with her hips. This was hers. She could taste it. She wanted it so badly. The Christmas fashion shows that this particular store put on were spectacular and everyone in the modelling world wanted a piece of the action.

'Okay, thank you, girls. We're just going to have a chat for a few moments and we'll announce the two names then.'

Angel found Kate and grabbed her hand, squeezing it tightly. 'I hope it's you and me, Kate. Wouldn't that be fabulous?'

'Yes, it would.' And she meant it – but she felt old when she looked at the other girl, who was so young and excitable. Kate was growing tired with the constant anticipation and then the inevitable rejection.

'Okay, girls. This is it. The two girls we're taking to the show with us this year are …'

Kate could barely breathe. This was it.

'… Orla Devine and Angel Filan. Remaining girls, give yourselves a clap. You came very close. Better luck next time.'

Kate was devastated. Angel had suddenly forgotten about her and was hugging the other successful girl. They were both around the same age and as skinny as each other. She couldn't even bring herself to congratulate them but grabbed her bag and coat and headed outside into the cool evening air.

Tears streamed down her face as she walked down the street. She caught a glimpse of herself in a shop window and felt disgusted. At twenty-three, she was a write-off. She was too old and too fat. In the modelling world, size eight just didn't seem good enough. Those girls must have been barely a four and both were way taller and younger than her. Well, she could do nothing about her age, but she was in control of her own body. There was no way she was going to change her hair either – but she could lose some weight.

She felt a little better as she quickened her step. What she needed to do now was get online and find out the quickest, easiest way to shed some weight. The next time she'd go to one of those castings, she'd be a new, skinnier version of herself and they'd be falling over themselves to give her a job. Angel may have trumped her in this one, but she'd better watch out, Kate Murray was going to be the name on everyone's lips very soon.

❁

The sounds of Deano's cough echoed in the air as he shuffled towards his accommodation for the night. He'd been trying to fend off a cold since he'd gone to watch Isabella earlier in the week but the incessant rain had ensured he was permanently drenched to the skin. The nights were the worst, when even the layers of blankets and his sleeping bag couldn't keep the dampness from creeping right into his bones.

He'd felt very unwell earlier and hadn't even been able to bring himself to get up. Usually he'd have his stuff packed up before the hustle and bustle of the morning but when he'd woken up, it had felt like somebody was standing on his chest. Every cough had hurt and every movement was painful.

He'd spent the day drifting in and out of sleep, aware of stares of passers-by, but he hadn't cared – he realised he was at an all-time low. The next time he'd opened his eyes, there was a woman standing over him, eyes full of concern, her head set at a compassionate tilt.

She was from one of the homeless charities. They'd got a phone call from a concerned member of the public to report a homeless man who didn't seem at all well. The woman who'd rung had passed him on her way to work and, although she hadn't wanted to approach him herself, she'd gone to the trouble of ringing to make sure someone would. When he'd heard this, a tiny light had gone on inside his head. Somebody cared. It had been a long time since he'd felt that. Maybe there was a bit of hope after all.

He stopped outside an old, red-brick building and took a card from his pocket. This was the place. The woman had told him to go there and he'd be given a bed for the night. He'd had a couple of nights in hostels in the early days of his homelessness but had decided it wasn't for him. Maybe it would be diffcrent here, he said to himself. He knew he needed to get out of the wet and cold for at least a night or two so he really didn't have a choice.

I le was shown to a room shared by a number of people. It was stark and grey with prison-like beds and a stench of desperation. But compared to the streets, it was pure luxury. They were going to have him see a doctor. He was going to be looked after and given medicine. He'd have a hot meal and maybe even a chance to wash.

He allowed himself to lie back on the bed and relax. It felt soft under his aching body and he immediately felt himself drift off to sleep. But his fever took over and his head filled with thoughts of a previous life. As he shifted restlessly, he dreamed of the exhilaration of landing a great business deal and the pleasure of a night of passion with a woman. He thought about delicious food in fine restaurants and nights of careless abandon getting drunk with friends. He might not want to go back to that life, but he did wish for one that was better than what he had now.

'Man, what are you doing in my bed?'

Deano woke with a jolt. 'I … I was told to go here. Is it yours? Sorry. I can move to this one.'

'You see, that one's me mate Terry's and the one beside it is Rasher's.'

'Is there any one I can take? I really don't mind where I go.' Deano forced himself into a sitting position, every bone in his body aching from the fever.

'I'll tell you what. You can stay put if you have any blow on you. Me and the lads are dyin' for a buzz.'

'Sorry but I don't use. I have nothing.'

'Well, fuck you!' Before Deano could respond, the guy had him by the scruff of the neck, a syringe threatening to break the skin. 'Now, do you want to rethink the blow situation?'

'I'm telling you, I don't have any. I swear, I don't even—'

'Ah, relax,' the guy cackled, sticking the syringe back into his pocket. 'I'm only messin' with you. I wouldn't do that to anyone.'

Deano breathed a sigh of relief but kept his guard up as the guy was still hovering over him, swaying from side to side.

'Any ciggies, then?'

'None of them either, I'm afraid. Look, I have a few euro here I got from tapping last night. You can have that if you want.' Anything to get rid of him.

'Ah, thanks. And sorry again for the needle thing. I never would have done nothin'. Catch you again if you're stickin' around.' He stuck the change in his pocket and swayed off out of the room.

Deano had no intentions of sticking around. He'd hang around to see a doctor if he could and get some medicine but, after that, he was out of there. The streets might be cold, damp and lonely, but they were safer than places like this. He'd never close his eyes if he stayed there – fearing what would happen to him in his sleep. Tonight, he'd shuffle on back to his spot in the doorway – his little piece of home.

# Chapter 10

Alice took a deep breath before ringing the doorbell. She'd done everything she could to cover up her two black eyes but she knew Becky would notice immediately. She could lie and say she'd had an accident but somehow she didn't think that would wash with Becky. She'd just have to tell the truth and listen to the lecture.

'Hi, Alice.' Becky swung open the door, a roller brush stuck in her hair and one shoe on. 'Thank God you're early because I'm running a bit— Jesus, what the hell happened to you?'

'You'd want to see the other guy,' said Alice, grinning as she stepped inside and closed the door.

'Seriously, are you okay? Come on in and sit down and you can tell me about it.'

'Honestly, I'm fine, Becky. You don't want to make yourself late. Go on and get ready and I'll tell you all about it later.' Alice had already taken her coat off and was starting to unload the dishwasher.

'You're not getting away with it that easily.' Becky closed the dishwasher and indicated for her to sit down, pulling her own chair up close to her. She took her hand gently. 'Did Frank do this to you? You know you don't have to stay—'

'Jesus, Becky. Are you insane? Of course he didn't. Why on earth would you think that?'

'I … I'm sorry. I just thought—'

'Hi, Alice.' Lilly bounded into the room dressed in her favourite floral leggings, her blonde hair up in two uneven ponytails. 'Oh, look at your eyes. So you did the Dracula thing. Yay!'

'I sure did, sweetheart. What do you think?'

'It's sooo cool,' said Lilly, coming to have a closer look.

Becky looked from one to the other. 'Dracula thing? Anyone care to explain?'

Alice laughed. 'I told you, Becks. I had a procedure done. That's why my eyes look black. It's called Dracula therapy and it's going to make me look younger.'

'I don't believe it.' Becky slumped back in her chair and ran her two hands through her hair. 'A bloody anti-ageing procedure! I should have known.'

'I thought you said you wouldn't judge, Becky.'

'I'm not judging – I just hate that you put yourself through stuff like this.'

'It's okay for you, with your perfect skin and complete lack of wrinkles. Wait until you get to my age and you'll be doing whatever you can to stall the tides of time.'

Becky sighed and nodded. 'Maybe.'

'And getting back to what you were saying before Lilly interrupted us,' said Alice. 'Why did you jump to the conclusion that Frank had hit me? It's a pretty big assumption.'

'Sorry. I must be watching too much telly. Now I'd better go and get myself organised for work or I'll be dead late. Would you mind doing a couple of pieces of toast for Lilly please?'

'No problem,' said Alice. 'That's what I'm here for.'

As Becky flew upstairs to get ready, Alice felt uneasy. She got the feeling Becky was hiding something. Imagine her thinking Frank would do a thing like that. Maybe she'd had experience of it herself. Alice shuddered at the thought. She should really try and find out more about Becky and the past that she never wanted to talk about.

She buttered two slices of toast and cut each into quarters. She headed into the sitting room where Lilly was curled up on the sofa watching cartoons. 'Here you go, sweetie. Don't get crumbs everywhere, now.'

'Thanks, Alice. Does it hurt much?' She stared at Alice's face and scrunched up her nose.

'Not a bit. It looks a lot worse than it feels and the blackness will be gone in a few days.'

Sometimes Alice wished she could just be happy with how she looked instead of always wanting to look younger or thinner. She'd never been like this in her thirties. It was really only in the past few years that she'd started trying out all the anti-ageing regimes, though she knew in her heart that it was just her way of controlling something in her life. She hated the fact that her fertility was completely out of her hands. The doctors had never found anything wrong, so she'd always lived in hope that she'd fall pregnant. But when her husband had left just before her fortieth birthday, her hopes had disappeared with him.

'I'm off, Alice. I'll see you later.' Becky's voice echoed in the kitchen and snapped her out of her reverie.

She finished unloading the dishwasher and peeped in on Lilly, who was still munching happily on her toast. Back in the kitchen, she made herself a cup of tea and sat down at the table. She was definitely going to have a proper chat with Becky later. They hadn't really had a chance to talk much since the whole Dennis thing had come to a halt last week and Alice had certain thoughts on that. And she wanted to try and get to the bottom of why Becky had jumped to certain conclusions about the black eyes. If there was something in her past preventing her from moving on with her life, Alice was going to do her best to get to the bottom of it.

❖

The morning was warm and humid so Becky decided to walk to work. Even though she was tight for time, sometimes it was just as quick to go on foot anyway. It would only take her half an hour if she walked briskly. When she crossed the traffic lights at Hanlon's Corner, she was on a long, straight road down to the quays.

She thought of Alice and her black eyes and could have kicked herself for jumping to conclusions. When she was growing up, black eyes had been a regular occurrence. Her dad had been a violent alcoholic and her mother had been on the receiving end of his fists many times. He'd never once hit her or her sister, but she'd often wished he would, just so that she could hit him back and show him how much she hated him. When he was sober, he was careful to keep his punches to her mother's stomach or back – anywhere that wouldn't cause visible injuries. But on drunker nights, he hadn't cared and her mother's face took the brunt of his anger. Becky had spent many nights sitting at the top of the stairs, listening to the arguments and wincing at every punch her father threw.

As she'd got older, she'd begged her mother to leave him. She'd wanted them to go and start a new life – somewhere they could feel safe and not be crippled with the fear of what was going to happen next. But her pleas had fallen on deaf ears until Becky had come to realise that her mother would never leave. She loved him too much, she'd said. She understood him like nobody else, she'd said. Becky had begun to hate her mother too by then and had vowed she'd make a better life for herself as soon as she could. She'd managed to put herself through college with the proceeds of a part-time job until she'd finally landed her dream job in a bank. By then, her mother was an alcoholic too and had retreated into herself. The beatings had decreased only because now they got drunk together. When Becky was twenty-two, a position had become available in a Dublin branch and she'd looked on it as her opportunity to get away from the chains that had dragged her down all her life and she'd jumped at the chance to get as far away as possible from her dysfunctional family.

A car horn startled her as she stepped out onto the road and she was surprised to realise she was almost in the city centre. She barely remembered the walk, she'd been so consumed by thoughts of the past.

She opened the door of the bank with her key and walked straight down towards the toilets. As she looked at herself in the mirror, Dennis Prendergast popped into her head. She wondered if she was being fair to Lilly. Had she ever been fair to her? She hated to admit it, but her decision not to tell Dennis she was pregnant had probably been a lot to do with her own upbringing. How different things would have been for her and her mother if her dad hadn't been around. They would have had a chance of a good life. She would have grown up in a proper family and had a sister to confide in.

Bringing Lilly up on her own was her way of proving that having no father was better than having a bad one. But since she'd started looking for Dennis, she realised that she couldn't lump all fathers into one box. For all she knew, Dennis could have turned out to be a great dad.

She looked at herself in the mirror. There were dark circles around her eyes and her skin looked dull. Maybe if Alice's Dracula therapy was a success, she should think of something like that for herself. But she dismissed the thought. What she needed was a good night's sleep and to have that, she needed peace of mind. And as far as she could see, the only way she'd get that was to know that she'd done the right thing by her daughter. After all, Lilly was the only thing that mattered at the end of the day.

Deano spat out a lump of phlegm as he tried to fix the cardboard in such a way that he was sheltered from the wind. It was his third day of taking the medicine and it was finally starting to loosen his cough. He'd barely had any sleep since he'd left the hostel on Friday so he was determined to make himself as comfortable as possible tonight. There was a time when comfortable had meant a soft mattress and feather pillows. Now it was an extra layer of cardboard on the concrete to stop the ice cold riding up through his bones.

'There you are, Deano. Settling in for the night?'

Deano spun around to see Lorcan from one of the homeless

charities holding out a steaming cup and a sandwich. 'Yep. Nothing much on telly so I might as well.'

'Can we not convince you to take a bed tonight, mate? It's going to be a cold one.'

'Thanks but no thanks. I've told you I'm not going into one of those places. I'll have the soup, though. That'll keep me warm.'

Lorcan handed over the cup. 'It's your call.'

'If I could just get this cardboard to stay in place, it'd be like a room at the Ritz.'

'Here, let me help.' He expertly manipulated the cardboard to form a wall around Deano's sleeping bag and stood back to survey his work. 'Not bad, if I say so myself.'

'Not bad at all. Thanks, Lorcan.'

'It's no problem. So how's the form anyway?'

Deano shook his head. 'Shite, if I'm honest. I don't know how much more of this I can take.'

'And no luck on the job front?'

'Nothing. Nothing's ever going to fucking change.'

'You don't know that, Deano. Listen, I've got to go, but I'll see you tomorrow night, right?'

Deano leaned against the railings but didn't say anything.

'Deano?'

'Yeah, see you then.'

Lorcan reached out and rubbed Deano's shoulder gently. 'Keep the faith, bro.' And then he hopped into his van and drove away.

Deano pulled his hat down over his ears and eyes and buried himself in his sleeping bag. The warmth of Lorcan's hand was still burning on his shoulder. Some day, he'd tell him that he and others in the charity were the reason he was still living. That little piece of human contact – that one touch – helped him forget about the desolation and guilt and focus on the fact that he was still here. And as his mother used to always say – where there's life, there's hope.

# Chapter 11

'So that was it, really,' Becky said, picking at her chips. 'The trail ran cold at that point so I just gave up and came home.' Becky had taken Kate over to the pub across the road for lunch and was filling her in on her search for Dennis.

'But how come you went off looking on your own, Becks? I would have gone with you if you'd just asked.'

'I know you would have. But don't be cross with me for not telling you. It was just something I felt I had to do on my own.'

'Hmmmm. I see.'

'You know, if I'd wanted someone to come with me, it would have been you.'

Kate sighed. 'I know. Don't worry about it.'

Becky eyed her friend suspiciously. Usually Kate would get way more animated than that. 'Are you okay, Kate? You don't seem yourself today.'

'Well, I'm sorry I'm not singing "If you're happy and you know it" or anything. Sometimes even *I* get a bit fed up with things.'

'But I told you the reason I—'

'God, Becky. Everything isn't about *you*. Sometimes there are other things in life other than The Becky Greene Story!'

Becky recoiled at the viciousness in her voice. 'What is it, Kate? This isn't like you.'

Kate sighed. 'I'm sorry. I'm just fed up with this modelling lark. I went for another job on Friday and felt sure I'd get it but they gave it to someone younger and skinnier. It just gets me down sometimes that I can't seem to catch a break.'

'Ah, I'm sorry. I'm sure your time will come. You have so much to offer. Someone is going to see that soon enough.'

'Right,' said Kate, pushing her barely-eaten salad away and sitting up straighter in her chair. 'Let's not talk about me. Tell me more about your search.'

'No, forget about me. What happened on Friday?'

'Honestly, Becky, there's really nothing to talk about and I'm sorry I snapped at you. Tell me your story. It'll be a distraction for me.'

Becky looked at Kate's face and felt guilty for always assuming she had no problems. 'Well, as I said to Alice, I was just trying to get a sense of what Dennis was up to these days. I thought by snooping around, I might find out more.'

'Hold on. Rewind there for a minute. You've told Alice already?' Kate pouted and played absently with the sachets of salt in front of her.

Becky laughed. That was more like the Kate she knew and loved. 'Don't be like a sulky child. I only told her because she was minding Lilly while I was gone and it just sort of all spilled out when I got home.'

This seemed to appease her. 'Okay, but what are we going to do about it now? The trail can't have gone completely cold. We just have to figure out what our next move is.'

'That's *exactly* what I hoped you'd say,' beamed Becky, glad to have Kate's enthusiasm again. 'I told Alice I wasn't going to bother looking any more but, to be honest, I can't get Dennis Prendergast out of my mind.'

'Ah, so as far as Alice is concerned, it's over?'

'Kate! It's not a competition between you two. If I continue to look for him, I'll tell Alice but for now, I'm asking *you* about it.'

Kate had the grace to look sheepish. 'I'm sorry. But I just think Alice over-thinks things. Sometimes, you have to just go with your gut and do what you feel is right.'

'Exactly!' Becky shoved her sandwich to one side and leaned on the table. 'I know Alice has my best interests at heart but what I feel I need right now is your determination and drive. I don't want to leave things as they are. I want to continue looking for Dennis and I think you're the very girl to help me.'

'You can count on me, Becky. Now, let's see … if he didn't leave a forwarding address, is there anyone you can think of who might know something of his whereabouts?'

Becky shook her head. 'Nobody. As I told you before, I didn't know him or any of his friends. I just knew him by reputation.'

'That's it!' Kate banged her fist down on the table, causing heads to turn in their direction.

Becky was startled. 'What's *it*? And can you lower your voice please? People are staring.'

'Sorry, but that's how we'll find him – his reputation.'

'I don't follow.'

'Listen, if Dennis was so well known around the area that he had a reputation, someone somewhere must know where he is. It's a no-brainer.'

'But other than knocking on doors, I don't see how we can find out more.'

Kate pulled her chair in closer to the table. 'Well, let's think logically. You worked in the bank close to his business, right?'

'Right.' Becky didn't know where she was going with this.

'Well, I'm guessing that he was often the hot gossip around the canteen. Am I right?'

'Yes! You could be on to something there. But I'm not in touch with any of the old gang. There was the odd phone call in the beginning after I transferred but it all just fizzled out.'

Kate's eyes twinkled. 'Well, maybe now is the time to renew some of those friendships.'

'Kate Murray. Are you suggesting I befriend someone solely for the purposes of acquiring information?'

'That's exactly what I'm suggesting. They were hardly good friends if they didn't bother keeping in touch so what would be the harm in ringing one of them for a catch-up and just casually ask some questions?'

Becky wasn't so sure. 'I just don't want to start up a friendship with those girls again, Kate. We had some fun together but we really weren't any more than mates who went out for a few drinks. They weren't true friends like you and Alice are.'

'I'm not asking you to host dinner parties for them. Come on, Kate. It could be our best chance of finding out more information about Dennis.'

'Hmmmm. Maybe. I'll have a think about it.'

'Come on. You know I'm right.'

Becky looked at the other girl's pleading eyes and laughed. 'I suppose you are. But just give me a day or two to think about it, okay? If I do decide to ring one of them, I'll have to make sure I can ask the appropriate questions without stirring their suspicion.'

'Easy peasy,' said Kate, sipping her coffee. 'All you need to do is ask about everyone you used to know – how people are doing, what they're up to, etcetera. If their branch is as gossipy as ours, they'll know every last detail about what's happened to Dennis Prendergast.'

'Gosh, you're a right little detective, aren't you? I think you've missed your calling.'

'Ha! Garreth says the same. I always figure out the endings to books before I've read them and it drives him mad when I guess who the killer is in every crime drama we watch.'

'Well, there might well be some killings if we don't get ourselves back. Did you see the time?'

Kate looked at her watch and jumped up, grabbing her coat and bag. 'Jesus, how can it already be ten past. Fergal will go mad. I can just hear him now saying: "Jaysus, Kate. I could eat the scabby leg off a donkey. What kept you?"' She mimicked Fergal's thick Cork accent as they flew out the door of the pub.

Becky roared laughing. 'You have him off to a tee. Poor Fergal. We'd better hurry. I wouldn't want him fading away on us.'

❁

'And it was lovely talking to you too, Laura. We must keep in touch.' Even as she heard those words coming out of her mouth, Becky knew she'd probably never talk to Laura again. She threw the phone down on the sofa beside her and took a sip from her glass of water. She wasn't quite sure what to do with the information she'd been given but she knew someone who would. She picked up the phone again and dialled.

'Hi, Kate. I hope it's not too late.'

'Ah, hiya, Becks. Not at all. Garreth is downstairs watching some boring house-building programme and I've just come up to bed to read. What's up?'

'I did it. I rang one of the girls I used to know and got talking to her.'

'Wow! That was quick. I thought you were going to take some time to think about it first.'

'I was, but I decided there's no time like the present. There was no harm in getting some information if I could – I wouldn't have to act on it straight away if I didn't want to.'

'And?'

Becky drew a breath. 'Well, I asked her about lots of people we knew and I just threw in Dennis Prendergast's name. I said I heard his business had closed and asked if she knew what had become of him.'

'And …?'

'One of the girls saw him a few times in a shop on the quays on her way home from work.'

'Brilliant. A sighting. And was she sure it was him?'

'Well, apparently this particular girl had had a *thing* with Dennis. He'd taken her phone number but hadn't rung and she'd been really upset about it at the time. So when she saw him in the shop, counting out his change for a quarter of pear drops, she'd come into work delighted to report on how the mighty had fallen.'

'And you said she saw him a few times?'

'Yes. Three or four, I think, and each time the same scenario – he'd buy a quarter of pear drops and slowly count out the change. He must either work or live around the area.' Becky took another sip of her water before tucking her legs up underneath her on the sofa. 'So what do you think I should do now?'

'Well,' said Kate, slowly, 'I think we should go to the shop in question and ask about him. What have we got to lose? If he's a regular customer, they'll probably know something about him and, who knows, we might even see him while we're in there.'

Becky remembered something else. 'That's another thing. Apparently his appearance has changed a lot. He used to be really clean-shaven and a slick dresser. This girl said that he had a beard and looked a bit dishevelled. She even thought he might have been drunk because of the way he was moving.'

'I love a man with a beard.' Kate sounded dreamy. 'I'm always telling Garreth he should grow one but he doesn't think it would suit his—'

'I'm more concerned about the dishevelled and drunk bit. I'd definitely need to find out more about him before I'd even consider bringing him into our lives. Maybe he's turned to drink if things aren't going well for him and, to be honest, if that was the case, I wouldn't want to know him at all.'

'Well, don't jump to any conclusions. Sleep on it and we can have a chat again in the morning. Maybe we could pop down to the shop at lunchtime and have a little snoop.'

Becky balked at that. 'I don't know if I'm ready for that, Kate. What if I actually saw him there? It would be a bit of a shock. I know I said before that I was happy at the thought of bumping into him but based on what I've heard since—'

'Look, I won't force you into it tomorrow but you should definitely have a think about it. I know what you're like. You haven't been able to get Dennis Prendergast out of your mind these past few weeks and I suspect you won't rest until you've found him.'

'You're right,' sighed Becky. 'I don't know what it is and why it's so important all of a sudden, but something keeps telling me to go after him.'

'Well, trust your gut, is what I say. Do what feels right and if finding him feels right, that's what you should do. And besides, if you get that out of your system, maybe you'll turn your attentions to poor Len.'

'Len Sherwood? What's he got to do with this?' Becky was confused.

'I saw him today staring at you while you were explaining something to him. He's completely besotted. If you weren't so caught up with this Dennis business, you might see that.'

'Ha! I see it all right, but I just choose not to acknowledge it. I have too much on my mind at the moment to go there.'

'Well, never say never. I still think you two could be great together.'

'Hmmm. I'm not so sure. But in relation to Dennis, I'll sleep on it. And thanks, Kate. You've been brilliant in all this.'

'It's no problem. And I haven't done anything really other than listen.'

'Sometimes that's the best way of all to help. Right, I'll let you get back to your book and we can talk again tomorrow.'

Becky got up to go and make herself a sandwich. She'd been trying to cut out the night-time snacks because she could feel the pounds piling on her hips, but she just couldn't resist a cheese toastie.

'Mummy, look at my picture.' Lilly appeared at the door of the kitchen, almost frightening the life out of Becky.

'Lilly, I thought you went to sleep ages ago. What are you doing up this late?' She lifted the little girl up into her arms and kissed the top of her head.

'I drawded this for you in school today and I wanted to show you.' She held out a page with a very colourful picture on it.

'That's beautiful, darling. You really are a clever girl. And who are all these?' Becky pointed to the matchstick people who seemed to be holding hands and were surrounded by flowers.

'That's me and you.'

'And who's that holding your other hand? Is it Alice?'

'No, silly. It's a boy. It's a daddy.'

Becky paled. 'Wha – what do you mean?'

'Not a *real* daddy,' said Lilly, oblivious to her mother's shock. 'It's just a pretend one. Teacher told us to draw our families and everyone else was drawing a mummy and a daddy, 'cept for Samantha. She has two mummies.'

Becky didn't know what to say so she just kissed her daughter on the nose and hugged her tightly. 'Right, Missy. That's a beautiful picture but I think we should get you back to bed. You'll need all your energy tomorrow if you're going to produce wonderful pictures like that again.'

Becky tucked Lilly into her bed and came back downstairs. That was the second time Lilly had mentioned a daddy recently. Becky was a firm believer in signs and they didn't come any clearer than that. If she'd had any reservations about finding Dennis Prendergast and telling him about Lilly, she didn't now. Lilly was entitled to know about her father and she was going to make sure it happened, no matter what can of worms she might open in the process.

# Chapter 12

Becky had never before been late for work but she knew she would be this morning. She'd decided to go to the shop where there'd been sightings of Dennis and see what she could find out. She'd been itching to look since she'd spoken to Laura last week but Lilly had come down with the flu and Becky had been trying to juggle looking after her daughter with the demands of her job and hadn't had a second to herself.

The shop was quiet, except for a couple of customers browsing the magazines. She could see a shop assistant watching them eagerly, as if challenging them to leave without buying one.

'Hello, can I help you?' Becky was startled by the voice of a second shop assistant behind her and almost crashed into the tins on the aisle where she'd been lurking.

'Hello, yes. I mean, no. I'm just browsing.' Shit. Who browses in a small convenience store?

He looked at her for a moment before his face exploded into a grin. 'Okay. You have a browse and let me know if I can help you with anything.'

There was nobody else in the shop now and Becky was conscious of both men watching her. What was she like? All she wanted to do was ask a question and instead she was playing for time and looking like a shoplifter. She picked up a packet of digestives and headed to the till.

'Just this?' Shopkeeper number one raised an eyebrow. They definitely thought she was a shoplifter. Shopkeeper number two had obviously warned him and they weren't buying the 'I'm just browsing' story.

'Yes. Well, actually, no. I wanted to ask you about someone. I'm trying to find a man.'

'Ah, I see.' Shopkeeper number two nodded approvingly.

Jesus! 'No, no, what I mean is I'm looking for someone.'

'Aren't we all?' Shopkeeper number one winked and Becky wanted the ground to swallow her up. They were two guys in their twenties and were obviously taking great pleasure in making her squirm.

She decided to ignore their taunts and just ask the question. 'I'm trying to find an old friend of mine. I couldn't get him at his old address and someone told me he comes in here frequently. He's a tall, dark guy with a beard – apparently buys a quarter of pear drops when he's in.'

'Can't say that rings a bell. Ever since we got those old-fashioned jars of sweets in, we can barely keep enough in stock. Every second customer buys a quarter of something or other. I think it's the old-style brown paper that—'

'Okay, thanks for your help anyway.'

'Sounds like it's important,' said Shopkeeper one. 'You're not a detective, are you? Is this guy wanted for something?'

'As I said, he's just an old friend.'

'And if we do happen to see someone of that description, who should we say is looking for him?'

'There's no need to say. But I'd really appreciate any information you could give me. I'll pop in again during the week and see if you've any news.'

'You do that, darling.' Shopkeeper two was leering at her now and she couldn't get out of there quickly enough.

She headed back up the quays towards O'Connell Bridge. It was ridiculous. Somebody somewhere must know where Dennis Prendergast is. People didn't just vanish into thin air. The shop had been her best lead but that had turned out to be a dead end. She wasn't much of a detective really. She'd have to get Kate on the case again.

She headed into the office and could see the raised eyebrows from staff already sitting at their desks. It was probably the first time they'd ever seen her arrive later than everyone else. Well, let them think what they want, Becky thought. If anyone dares say anything, I'll give them a piece of my mind. As far as she was concerned, she worked her socks off every single day in that place so if she wanted to be late, she'd damn well *be* late.

'Are you actually slacking off, Becky Greene? What time do you call this?' Kate had followed her into the toilets and was wagging a finger playfully at her.

'Get lost, Kate. I give this place enough of my time.'

'Calm down, will you? I was only joking. What's up with you?'

Becky threw her black Guess bag on the counter and turned to face her friend. 'Sorry, I'm just tired and frustrated. I went to that sweet shop this morning and nobody knew anything of Dennis.'

'Ah, Becks, that's a bummer. But don't be disheartened. I'm not letting you give up that easy. We'll think of something else.'

Becky tried to fight back the tears. It wasn't like her to get teary but the whole Dennis Prendergast thing had made her very emotional. It was like something was pushing her on. She *needed* to find him. She'd gone more than four years not giving him a second thought but now it was consuming her life. It was as though finding him was going to be important for her and Lilly's future.

'Are you okay, Becks? Don't cry. We'll work it out.' Kate put her arm around her and pulled her into a hug. Becky wasn't one for displays of affection but accepted Kate's embrace. For some reason, her sister popped into her head, making her cry even harder.

'God, what is it? Is this all about Dennis or is there something else?' Kate surveyed her face, trying to figure out what was going on.

'I was just thinking of my family. Sometimes I wish they were here to help me with stuff.'

Kate looked thoughtful. 'You don't talk much about them. I mean, you've said your parents are still alive but I've never wanted to pry too much.'

'They're still there in London all right but we don't talk any more. I have one sister too – Joanna – but we were never close.'

'A sister! I didn't know that.' Kate wiped the counter beside the sink with some toilet roll and sat up on it. 'For some reason, I always thought you were an only child.'

'I may as well have been. Joanna was ten years older and left home when I was only eight. She kept in touch initially but her visits and calls became further and further apart until they stopped altogether.'

'God, that's terrible. So your parents don't see either of their daughters?'

Becky began to shift uncomfortably, rooting in her bag while she decided what she was going to say. She looked Kate straight in the eye. 'They don't. And they don't deserve to.'

Kate seemed to realise that it was Becky's way of ending the conversation. She hopped down from the counter and checked her reflection in the mirror. 'Well, you have your own family to worry about now. And for what it's worth, I'm happy to be your stand-in sister.'

Becky had already begun to refresh her make-up, giving herself the mask of confidence that everyone knew her for. 'Thanks, Kate. And sorry for being such an eejit.'

'Haha! I love it when you say words like 'eejit' in your English accent. We're winning you over to our way of talking, bit by bit.'

Becky headed back towards her desk, her head awhirl with emotion. She'd witnessed a lot of stuff in her childhood years and it had made her tough. Tough as old boots Becky. That was her. What was happening to her?

She noticed Lynda, one of the new girls, leaning across her desk showing a colleague something apparently hilarious on her phone.

'Lynda Harrington!'

The girl almost jumped out of her skin.

'There's a time and a place for silly playground stuff and it certainly isn't here. If you don't have enough work to do, come down to my desk and I'll sort you out with plenty.'

Becky click-clacked back to her desk in her pointy black Kurt Geiger heels. She didn't turn her head when she heard the rumblings of discontent from some of the staff. They needed to know their place. She felt better now. Normality had been restored.

❋

Alice watched Lilly launch on her bowl of soup with gusto and felt a rush of pride. She wasn't a picky eater like so many children her age. Alice had made sure to introduce her to as many different foods as possible from a very early age and her perseverance was now paying off. She'd been off her food when she was sick but thankfully it had only taken the waft of Alice's home-made chicken pie to get her back on track again.

'How's the soup, sweetie? Do you like it?'

Lilly dipped a huge piece of bread roll into her bowl and sucked the soup off it. 'It's nice. But it's a bit greenish. Did you put spinach in it again for your wrinkles?'

Alice had to stifle a giggle. She probably shouldn't teach Lilly so much about her quest to look younger.

Lilly continued. 'I don't think you should bother putting the spinach in any more because it's not making your wrinkles go away.'

'Are you saying I'm an old, wrinkly nanny, then?' She reached under the table to tickle the little girl's knee. 'Like Nanny McPhee?'

'Eeewww!' Lilly scrunched up her nose. 'Not like her. She's kind of scary and has a funny tooth. You have nice teeth.'

'Well, thank God for small mercies,' laughed Alice, finishing off her own soup. 'So, did you have a good day in playschool today?'

'It was ace! Glenda read us two stories. One was about a little boy called Sean who had no mummy.'

Alice watched Lilly carefully. 'Come over here and sit on my lap and you can tell me all about it.'

Lilly didn't need to be asked twice and made herself comfortable on Alice's knee. 'The little boy kept being angry because he thought it wasn't fair that he didn't have a mummy. He was being naughty in school and when he got into trouble, he'd say it was because he had no mummy.'

'And what happened then?'

'Well, a new boy came to his class who was very sad. He told Sean that his mummy and daddy didn't really care about him and had sent him to live with his granny.'

'Oh, that's very sad. The poor little boy.'

'Well, you see,' said Lilly, intent on finishing the story, 'Sean began to realise that he was very lucky to have a daddy who loved him and cared for him.' She paused. 'I think Mummy is mad with me.'

Alice was thrown by Lilly's sudden change in conversation. 'What do you mean, sweetie?'

'I showed her the picture I drawded and I think it made her sad.'

'What picture? Do you want to show it to me?' Alice was intrigued.

Lilly ran upstairs and came down with the picture. Alice studied it for a moment. 'Is this you and your mummy?'

'Yes.' Lilly dropped her head.

'And who's this with you?'

'It's a daddy. Not mine. I haven't got one. This is just a pretend one.'

Alice chose her words carefully. 'And you think Mummy is angry because you drew that? I bet she's not. I bet she thinks you're the cleverest little girl in the world.'

'Do you think so?' Lilly's eyes lit up. 'Because I love my mummy and I don't care about not having a daddy.'

'Well, I think that as soon as Mummy comes home this evening, you should tell her you love her. I bet that will make her the happiest mummy in the world.'

Lilly raced upstairs to put her picture back in her room and Alice shook her head. Rearing children was certainly a minefield. You just never knew what you were going to hear next. It was funny how Lilly had started to think about a daddy at the same time as Becky was thinking about finding him. Those two were certainly in tune with each other. Alice envied their relationship. She had a great bond with Lilly but it would never be as close as a mother–daughter one.

She stood up and began rinsing the soup bowls before putting them into the dishwasher. She wouldn't allow her mind to go there. She'd had a few wobbles lately and Frank had been great, but it was about time she accepted the status quo. It just wasn't her role in life to have children. She had a very happy life now with a wonderful man and great friends. Lilly was as close as she'd ever get to having a child of her own and she was going to cherish that little girl for as long as Becky would allow her to be a part of their lives.

# Chapter 13

Becky felt a little unsettled when she found herself standing outside the shop again. She'd left work at five and instead of heading to her bus stop on O'Connell Street, she'd walked towards O'Connell Bridge and turned right down the quays.

She took her phone out of her bag and pretended to text, trying not to look conspicuous. She peeped inside and was relieved to see a young girl behind the counter. Not a sign of Tweedledum and Tweedledee. Maybe this girl would know more. With a renewed hope, she stepped inside and went to loiter in the biscuit aisle until there were no customers in the shop.

After what seemed like ages, listening to the ping of the cash register and watching people come and go, Becky decided she'd had enough. She'd come back again when the shop was less busy – unless Kate came up with a better idea. As she headed for the door, she bumped into a guy who was counting his change as he came in.

'Sorry about that,' he said, not even looking up at Becky.

Becky sniffed disapprovingly. She hated when people didn't look at her when they spoke. But something made her stop in her tracks. She wasn't sure what it was. She looked over to where he was holding a tube of toothpaste and counting out his money to the shop assistant. She could only see the back of his head but she felt her stomach do a flip.

'Just this,' he said, 'and a quarter of pear drops.'

*A quarter of pear drops!* Oh, God. It was him. She hadn't seen his face but that voice – low and husky, so distinctive. She could feel her chest tightening and she was glued to the spot. Her breathing became heavy and she felt as though the air was being squeezed out of her. She looked over at the counter again and saw the shop assistant was measuring out the sweets. She had to get out of there. Her legs felt like jelly but she managed to stumble outside where she gulped in big lungfuls of air. She couldn't believe it. Dennis Prendergast, right there inside that shop. She had to think quickly. She couldn't let him go now that she'd found him.

Before she had a chance to think any further, Dennis came out of the shop and stopped right beside her to put his purchases into his big rucksack. There was no doubt it was him but, God, he looked so different. When Becky had met him, his jet-black hair had been really short. Now it fell in wavy tufts around his face and was dotted with grey. It was weird looking at him with a beard too. Rugged. That's how Becky would describe him. He had the look of an Australian backpacker with his outdoorsy tan and crumpled clothes.

He suddenly hauled the rucksack onto his back and walked right past her as though she was invisible. But why would he give her a second glance? She was nothing to him. She knew she'd have to act quickly, so she followed him. She felt stupid to be stalking him like that but what other option did she have? She was hardly going to go right up to him and say something like *Excuse me, do you know you're the father of my child?*

He walked quickly despite the weight on his back and she was having trouble keeping up in her heels. She followed him across a road and around a few corners until he suddenly disappeared inside an old, run-down building. Becky stopped a few feet away and thought for a moment. She could hardly follow him in.

There were no signs on the building indicating what it was. Maybe it housed offices and he was going in to a meeting. Or maybe he worked there. If he'd lost his premises, maybe he was renting a cheaper office space, trying to build up his business again. She moved a little closer to see if she could get a look inside. Nothing. He'd vanished from sight and Becky felt strangely empty.

There was nothing more she could do. She took a note of the address and headed back in the direction of O'Connell Street where she'd get her bus home. She'd check out the place on Google Maps on the way and take it from there. At least she had a lead now. She quickened her step and her heart felt a little lighter. Bubbles of excitement rose up inside her and she couldn't wait to get home to investigate more.

❁

'I can't believe you actually saw him, Becky,' Alice said, staring wide-eyed as Becky relayed the story.

'I can barely believe it myself. I've been dying to get home to fill you in.'

Alice shook her head. 'And how did you feel? Were you not tempted to talk to him? I think I would have had to say something. Were you not afraid you wouldn't see him again?'

Becky laughed at her friend's enthusiasm. 'It felt really strange, actually – like I was stepping back in time. I got that bubble of excitement in my stomach, just like I did when I met him that first time.'

Alice looked at her carefully and dipped a gingernut into her tea. 'I think you need to be careful, Becky. Things have changed drastically for you since then. And by the sound of things, for him too. You've just got to be sure you know what you're getting yourself into.'

'It's something I need to do, Alice. I know that now.'

'Hmmmm.'

'And what does that mean? I hate it when you make that disapproving noise.'

'I don't disapprove – in fact I was the one encouraging you to look for him.'

'But ...?'

'I just don't want you to get caught up in a fairy tale. You feel the time is right to tell Dennis about Lilly and that's great, but don't be presuming a perfect happy ever after.'

Becky sipped her coffee. She was almost afraid to respond to that for fear it would end in an argument. She hated that Alice was so cynical. She'd had some tough times but she really shouldn't impose her negativity on others.

'I'm sorry if that's not what you wanted to hear, Becky. I'm just trying to be realistic.'

'Look, Alice, I appreciate your concern but I'm really not expecting anything from Dennis and I certainly don't think it's a fairy tale.'

Alice at least had the grace to look sheepish. 'Maybe I didn't word it right but what I meant was you should focus on the task in hand. Don't get caught up in the romance of it all and expect the three of you will end up playing happy families.'

'Are you nuts?' Becky was incensed. 'I have absolutely *no* romantic interest in Dennis Prendergast. Why on earth would you think that?'

'Well, you were saying that you got bubbles of excitement in your stomach, just like when you first met.'

'Oh, for God's sake, Alice, I didn't mean it the way you think I did. It was just seeing him brought me back to a moment in time. Didn't you ever get that feeling? A sight or a smell that brings back memories of happy times? It doesn't mean I want to take him to bed again.'

They both fell silent and sipped their drinks. They rarely argued about anything and Becky didn't like it when they did. She knew Alice would never hurt her purposefully – but she *did* feel hurt by her words. She wasn't a silly little sixteen-year-old, chasing a dream. She was just trying to do what was best for her daughter. The doorbell rang and startled them both.

'That'll be Kate,' said Becky, jumping up from her chair, glad of the distraction. 'I asked her over so we could all discuss the situation. You've both been great and I want to continue this with the two of you at my side.'

Alice nodded, teary-eyed. 'I'm sorry, Becky. I didn't mean to upset you. Of course we'll both be here for you.'

The doorbell went again and this time Becky rushed out to answer it. 'Sorry about that, Kate. We were just nattering. I'm delighted you could come over.'

'As if I'd miss out on the hot gossip. I'm intrigued to hear what the big news is.' Kate threw her denim jacket on the banister and followed Becky into the kitchen.

Alice and Kate nodded politely to each other and Becky took out another cup. 'Tea or coffee?'

'I'd murder a glass of white, if you had any.'

'Coming up,' said Becky, opening the fridge. 'I had a feeling you'd say that so I have one chilling.'

Kate laughed. 'I'm so predictable. So tell me what this is all about.'

Becky spent the next ten minutes filling her in on the events of the day. Alice remained quiet and Becky suspected she was feeling the emotion of the argument they'd had.

Kate clapped her hands together. 'That's brilliant, Becks. So where do you go from here? You really need to act quickly on this.'

'Well, I'm not sure I agree,' said Alice, speaking up for the first time since Kate had arrived. 'I think Becky needs to sit on the information for a bit. Give it time to sink in and then decide her next move.'

Kate shook her head vehemently. 'No, she needs to do something about it *now*. How do we know Dennis won't disappear again?'

Becky didn't want to upset Alice again but Kate was right. 'The truth is,' she interrupted them, 'I've made the decision to talk to him, so there's no point in hanging around. But the only thing is, I've checked Google Maps and there's no indication of what the building is.'

'We should go take a look.' Kate was already up off her seat. 'Let's go now. All three of us. Do you mind driving, Becks?'

'Em, there's just one little problem,' said Becky.

'Come on,' groaned Kate. 'Don't put obstacles in the way. The sooner we find out more information, the sooner you can act on it.'

'I think the obstacle Becky is talking about is the little four-year-old one up in bed!' Alice couldn't hide her smugness.

'God, sorry, Becks. I wasn't thinking. Alice, do you think you could—?'

'Kate!' Becky was mortified at Kate's cheek.

'No, it's okay, Becky.' Alice stood up and began to clear the table. 'You two go off and see what you can find out. I'm feeling tired anyway and I may as well watch telly here as in my own place.'

'Are you sure? I mean, you've been here with Lilly all day. I really can't ask you to—'

'Go! I'll be happy when you both come back and tell me what you've found out.'

Becky stood up and flung her arms around Alice. 'You're a gem, you know that? We won't be long, I promise.'

❀

Alice sat down heavily on the sofa and flicked on the telly. Her head was pounding and she felt rotten. She'd put it down to that detox tea she was drinking but if she was really honest with herself, it was probably just another symptom of the menopause. She was like a text book case – the insomnia, headaches, nausea. Come to think of it, she hadn't eaten much today either, other than a few biscuits and a slice of cake. She'd want to watch that or her skin would be breaking out in spots and blemishes.

She flicked around the channels but there was nothing on. Not that she could concentrate on anything anyway, with so much to think about. She knew finding Lilly's father was the right thing for Becky to do, but she was worried that it would cause all sorts of upset when things were out in the open. What if Dennis wanted to start seeing Lilly? What if Lilly didn't want to see him? It was a real can of worms and, though Alice hoped it would all work out, she had her doubts.

Laying her head back on the sofa, she could feel her eyes closing. She was exhausted. Part of her wanted to be home, tucked up in bed, but the other side of her hated to go home to an empty house. Why on earth did she insist on keeping Frank at arm's length? It seemed so stupid. She was just going to have to learn to trust again or she'd never be entirely happy.

She opened her eyes and rubbed them roughly. She needed to stop wallowing. Flicking around the channels again, she came across *Michael McIntyre's Comedy Roadshow*. He was hilarious. It was just what she needed. She turned the volume up and laughed at the mere sound of his voice. Within minutes she was feeling more positive. She needed to take her own advice. There she was trying to sort out Becky's life, telling her to confront things, when she herself was avoiding her own problems. She'd talk to Frank soon. It was time for her to let go of the past. Frank was her future and she was going to make sure she didn't let this one go.

❀

Deano took an extra sweater and jacket out of his rucksack. The skies were clear, which was a sure sign that it was going to be a bitterly cold night. That horrible dose he'd caught had lasted two weeks and he was hoping to avoid another one like it. He was glad at least to have had some time in the warmth of the social club. He'd taken up an art class and was surprised to find he actually enjoyed it. It was a couple of hours of escape from reality – from the thoughts of self-destruction and guilt that were constantly swallowing him up. He double-checked to make sure his area was clean and paint-free before heading towards the door.

'Night, Deano. Stay safe, man.'

'Night, John. Probably see you over the weekend.' Deano smiled at the other man. But the smile faded as soon as he walked outside. He liked John. He was a decent guy and good company. He'd lost everything in a fire some years back – his wife, his two children, his life. Deano felt desperately sorry for him, but John's story just added to his own feelings of guilt and desperation. John was where he was through no fault of his own. Deano was there because of his own bad decisions, selfishness and stupidity.

He headed up the quays towards O'Connell Bridge, where he'd cross over to his usual spot. His rucksack felt heavier than usual. His steps felt slower. He wished he could just rid himself of thoughts that were weighing him down. He thought about Isabella and wondered what she was doing at that moment. Was she making lunches for the children for school tomorrow? Was she crying herself to sleep? He tried to blink away his own tears as the cold wind cut into his face. He suddenly felt the need to see her again. It was more than two weeks since he'd last been to her house and he needed to feed his guilt again. It was no more than he deserved. Watching Isabella reminded him of the man he had been and the man he never wanted to be again. Much as he hated his life now, it was nothing to the hatred he felt for the life he'd once lived.

# Chapter 14

A social club for the homeless. That's what the guy in the bike shop across the road said the building was. It had completely thrown Becky. She hadn't expected to hear that. The Dennis Prendergast who'd had a certain reputation about town didn't seem the sort to get involved in charity. Although, apparently, they ran a lot of classes there so maybe he was on the payroll teaching business or something. That sounded more like it. That was as much as they'd found out the previous evening. The building had been locked up by the time they got there and, even though they'd peered through the big old wooden-framed windows, there'd been nothing to see except darkness.

Now, in broad daylight, Becky was back. She'd slipped out for an early lunch break while Kate was still busy at the counter. She was grateful for the girl's help but she didn't always want her holding her hand. It felt to Becky as though she was becoming weak. She'd always been this strong, independent woman but lately she'd been feeling a bit fragile, relying on her friends far too much. Ultimately, this was *her* problem so she was going to make sure to be the one to sort it out. She stared up at the weathered red-brick building and pushed open the door.

'Can I help you?' A young girl appeared from another door to Becky's left and took her by surprise.

'I, em, yes.'

The other girl smiled, waiting.

'I'm looking for someone. Dennis Prendergast. I think he might teach a class or something here.'

The young girl shook her head. 'I can't say that name is familiar. Are you sure you have the right place?'

'I'm sure. He's tall with dark hair and a beard. Sort of Spanish looking.' Becky held her breath, willing the girl to know him.

'Hmmm. Nope, doesn't ring a bell at all. Are you sure he teaches here?'

'I really don't know. But I know he comes in here and it's really important that I talk to him. Can you think of anyone matching that description at all?'

'Well, now that I think about it, it sounds a bit like Deano. But you said it's a Dennis you're looking for?'

'Yes, Dennis Prendergast. He was here last night, if that helps at all. Maybe you could see what was on?' Becky knew she was clutching at straws, but she wasn't ready to give up yet.

'Oh, well, in that case, maybe it *is* Deano you're looking for. He was here for the art class.'

Becky felt a spark of hope. 'Maybe Deano is his nickname. Do you know where I can find him?'

The girl eyed her up suspiciously. 'And you are?'

'I'm, em, Alice. Alice O'Malley.' Jesus, why had she said that? She'd suddenly felt panicked about giving her real name and Alice's was the first one that came into her head.

'Hold on a sec, Alice.' The girl disappeared back into the room, leaving Becky standing there, sweat running down her back. The closer she was getting to finding Dennis, the more nervous she was becoming.

She began to pace up and down the room, wondering if the girl was going to come back with an address. Or maybe she was gone to ring him to check if it was okay to give out his personal details. She checked her phone anxiously to see what time it was. She only had twenty minutes left and she hadn't even eaten yet. Not that she could have swallowed a bite at that moment. Her heart was beating right up into her throat.

Suddenly the door opened again and Becky looked around expectantly.

'You were looking for me? Alice, is it?'

Becky froze. There standing in front of her was Dennis Prendergast. She hadn't expected him to be there! God, her mouth was dry and she couldn't find any words.

'Martina said you asked for me by name. How do you know me?' He stood watching her suspiciously and all she wanted to do was run. What had she been thinking? What on earth was she going to say to him?

'Well, are we going to stand here looking at each other all day or are you going to tell me what you want?' He was clearly getting agitated.

'I … I'm sorry. It's just the girl … Martina … didn't say you were here. I thought she was just gone to get your details or something.'

He smiled faintly. 'Martina is like our mammy. You did well getting any information out of her at all.'

'Oh, I see,' said Becky, relaxing a little. 'It's just that I—'

'So I'll ask you again. What do you want?'

His face was dark and Becky felt a little bit frightened. He didn't look like the Dennis she remembered. 'I'm sorry. I was just … I wanted to talk to you …'

'Yes?' He leaned on a windowsill and stared at her. Lilly definitely had his eyes.

'The recession. You see, I'm writing about it. Yes, I'm writing about how the recession has changed people's lives.' Oh, Jesus. That had just come out.

'And what's that got to do with me? And you still haven't said how you know me.'

Oh, God. 'A friend – well, more a friend of a friend saw you come in here and recognised you. She knew I was looking for people to talk to for my articles and she said you had a business that went bad.'

'And who is this friend?'

'Well, em, I probably shouldn't disclose my source.' Oh, sweet Jesus! How ridiculous did that sound? *Disclose her source!*

'Well, you can tell your *source* that I'm not interested in speaking to anyone about my past. I don't need my mistakes printed in a paper for everyone to read. It's enough that they're engrained in my head. Goodbye, Alice.'

'Wait!' She suddenly felt panicked as he began to walk away. 'It won't be a negative piece. It can be upbeat as well as—'

'Ha!' He turned around to face her but his eyes were angry. 'How can a story like mine be upbeat? Now, why don't you go and chat to some yummy mummies or children in the playground. They'll give you upbeat if that's what you're after.'

'Do you know what? I'm sorry I thought you were worth talking to in the first place.' She turned and began to walk away. She knew she didn't have a right to be angry at him but she couldn't help it. There was no excuse for talking to her like that.

'Alice, wait…' He caught up with her and blocked her path. 'I'm sorry.'

She saw a glimmer of hope. 'Does that mean you'll talk to me?'

'About what exactly? The fall of the mighty estate agent?' There was an edge to his voice.

'Look, Dennis, I didn't come here to offend you or to make you think of things you'd rather forget. It's just that the recession has affected so many people. I thought it would be nice for the reader to be able to relate to someone like you. Someone real.' She held her breath. It seemed like ages until he spoke again.

'Okay. If it's something that might help others, I'll do it. Should we go and sit down somewhere?'

Becky's heart was beating like crazy and she felt another panic attack coming on. It was all happening too quickly. 'I … I can't talk to you now. I have to be somewhere. But maybe we could meet up later for a chat?'

'I suppose,' he said, his face turning dark again. 'When and where?'

'Let's say Monday at one o'clock. I noticed a little coffee shop at the end of the road – Martha's I think it's called. How about there?'

He nodded. 'It's a date.'

Becky blushed and she thought she saw his lip curl into a half-smile before he turned back towards the club. It was all very surreal. She felt excited as she walked back to work but, at the same time, she was nervous. This could be the start of a whole new chapter in her life but something told her it could get very, very complicated.

❀

She'd looked vaguely familiar. Dennis couldn't put his finger on it, but something about her made him think of the past. She was certainly pretty, with her blonde hair tumbling over her face and sticking to her soft pink lip gloss. And those green eyes. Women hadn't been on his radar since he'd walked away from his old life. Except for Isabella, but that was different.

He walked back into the room where a few of them had been playing cards and sat back down.

'Are we dealing you back in for this one?' said Red Ron, shuffling the cards. 'John got a poker while you were gone – fleeced us of matchsticks, he did.'

Dennis nodded and watched as the older man dealt out the cards. But his mind wasn't on the game. The pretty stranger had unsettled him. Alice, she'd said her name was. Alice O'Malley.

'Are you in or out?' John was getting impatient.

'I'm out.' Dennis threw his cards on the table. 'And I'm going to call it a day, lads. See you tomorrow.'

He grabbed his coat from the back of the chair and headed outside, dragging his rucksack behind him. Why the bloody hell did he feel so strange? Maybe it was just being in close proximity to such a beautiful woman. Her musky scent had filled his nostrils and made his head spin. He'd felt himself stir in places that had been dormant for quite a while.

He walked out onto the quays and shuffled along by the river, lost in thought. If he was honest with himself, it wasn't just her beauty that had unsettled him. She'd transported him back to a place in his past that was almost alien to him now. And she'd called him Dennis. It had been a while since he'd answered to that name. Everyone knew him as Deano and he was used to that now.

There was a cold wind blowing in from the Liffey and he pulled his coat tighter up around his neck as he approached O'Connell Bridge. So he was meeting this beauty for lunch on Monday. For just a moment, he felt a bubble of excitement. But it was short-lived as he began to realise what she must think. To her, he must seem repulsive. A guy who lives on the streets, eats in shelters and grabs a wash where he can get it.

As he reached the bridge and took a right, he had a sudden urge to see his mother. It wasn't important that she didn't understand. He always found it a great comfort just to be there with her, losing himself in his stories and escaping his life for an hour or two. He crossed over and headed towards the bus stop on Westmoreland Street. He could even tell her he had a date for Monday and it wouldn't be a lie. Well, not exactly.

He wondered what exactly Alice O'Malley was expecting from him. Did she want the harrowing tales of the darker side of life on the streets or a dumbed-down version? Or maybe, since she seemed to know a bit about his previous life, she was looking for an account of his life before and after. Well, he wasn't too sure about that. He had no doubt it would make an interesting tale but he didn't really want to be dragged into a detailed conversation about the life he'd had before. His focus was now on getting himself out of the slump he was in and he didn't need to be reminded of how he'd got there in the first place.

His bus came into sight and he rooted in his pocket for some change. The Dennis Prendergast of old wouldn't have been seen dead on a bus. It had been taxis all the way – unless of course he'd been driving one of his flash cars. He shook his head and shivered. He'd spent the whole year trying to forget his old life and he hated now that little snippets were popping into his head. Damn that Alice. She may have been beautiful, but Dennis feared that she was going to bring trouble with her. Well, he'd just have to wait until Monday to see.

# Chapter 15

'Get away!' Kate's mouth gaped open as Becky told her she'd come face to face with Dennis Prendergast. 'God, I can't believe you actually spoke to him. And how did you feel? Were you nervous? Shocked? It must have been mad weird.'

'It was strange all right.' Becky grinned at her friend's enthusiasm. They'd both managed to escape to the little kitchen for a ten-minute coffee break so that Becky could fill her in on what had happened at lunch. She still hadn't quite got her head around things herself yet.

Kate continued. 'You must be excited. Or are you terrified? Or both?'

'Both! It was silly to pretend I was writing something about the recession but it was the first thing that popped into my head.'

'It mightn't be such a bad thing though,' said Kate, gulping the last mouthful of her coffee. 'It'll give you an excuse to ask a load of questions; like how he got involved with the charity and what his role is there. It will be interesting to see what his real job is now though. He'll need to have a good income if he's going to provide for you and Lilly.'

'Kate!' Becky was appalled. 'He will *not* be providing anything for me and Lilly. That's *not* why I'm getting in touch. You know perfectly well that I'm self-sufficient. I don't need a man for anything!'

'Calm down, Becks. I wasn't really thinking when I said that. But even if you don't want him to contribute financially, you'll want to know he's a decent, law-abiding citizen with a good job and a clean slate.'

'I suppose. Although if he's doing charity work, he can't be all that bad.'

Kate raised her eyebrows. 'But in fairness, you really don't know anything about him. You may have known about him years ago, but where has he been and what has he been doing since he lost his business? He could have been in prison for all you know.'

Becky paled. 'Don't be ridiculous. Why would you even think that?'

'Well, the Dennis Prendergast you described to me from four years ago didn't seem like someone who'd give freely of their time to help others. Maybe the charity work is part of a sentence – community service or something.'

'Look, we don't even know what exactly he's doing at the homeless centre. For all we know, they could be paying him to give a class. I think I'd have heard if he committed some sort of crime.'

'Like you heard his business had folded? Like you heard he'd left the area?' Kate seemed determined to rattle Becky.

'Kate, why are you trying to put me off?'

'All I'm saying is that now you have the perfect opportunity to question him. Just don't play all your cards too soon. Wait until you get some information from him before you tell him who you are.'

'I suppose you're right.' Becky stood up and rinsed her mug in the sink. 'Let's just hope that the meeting goes well. It could be the start of Lilly getting to know her father and vice versa. I never thought it would happen, but somehow it just feels right now.'

Becky headed back to her desk. Just a couple of hours left before she could go home. She looked at the heap of paperwork in her 'to do' pile and sighed. How could she be expected to concentrate on that when there was so much happening in her personal life? But she needed to not lose sight of who she was. She was Becky Greene – independent woman and mother.

❋

'Alice?'

'Yes, love?'

'Who's Dennis?'

Alice was glad she and Lilly were lying back on the sofa enjoying face masks because she wouldn't have been able to hide her shock at the little one's question. She needed time to think.

'We're not supposed to talk while we have these on, Lilly. Remember I told you we have to lay here quiet for fifteen minutes until they go hard on our faces.'

''Kay.'

Thank God for that. Jesus, what was she going to say to the child? More importantly, what had Lilly heard? She touched her face and found the oatmeal mask still wet so she probably had five more minutes before they'd need to take them off. Fed up with spending a fortune on creams and potions in her quest to look younger, Alice had decided to give some tried and tested home remedies a go. This one was simply oatmeal mixed with honey and milk and according to a lady who called herself BYoung2 on one of the forums, it was going to give her soft, dewy skin like she hadn't seen since her thirties.

'Can we take them off now, Alice? My nose is itchy.'

Alice sighed. There was no putting it off any longer. 'Okay, sweetie. Take the cucumber off your eyes and we'll go and wash the mask off.'

Five minutes later they were back in the sitting room, faces squeaky clean and glowing with health.

'Did it work, Alice? Are you less than forty yet?'

'I don't know, Lilly. What do you think?'

'Hmmm,' said the little girl, shoving her face right up to Alice's. 'You might need a bit more work. Can we do the chocolate one again next time? Pleeeeeease?'

Alice laughed out loud. 'I reckon you're right. I think I need a *lot* more work. How about we give the masks a rest for a few days and we'll do the chocolate one in a week?'

'Yay! And Mummy too? Can she do a mask too?'

'If she wants to – but I'm not sure it's her thing, love.'

'But it would make her laugh. I think she's sad because she needs to talk to Dennis. Who's Dennis?'

Oh, Jesus! 'Who said she needs to talk to Dennis?'

'I heard you talking the other night. When Kate was here. Mummy said she needed to talk to Dennis. I think it must be *ferry* important.'

Alice hesitated. 'You know, I think it must have been when your mummy was talking about Dennis in work. He's always late and she needs to talk to him about it.' It was the best she had.

'Oh. Will he get in trouble?'

'I don't know, sweetie. Now let's not worry about him. Why don't we bake some buns and you can decorate them in pink for your mummy.'

'But Alice. Maybe Dennis doesn't mean to be—'

'I'm home! Where are my two favourite girls?'

Thank God. Becky's timing was perfect. Alice felt uncomfortable lying to Lilly but, under the circumstances, she didn't know what else to do.

'Mummmmyyyyy!' The little girl ran into her mother's arms and hugged her tight. 'We did masks again. Look. Look at Alice. Isn't she nearly under forty now? I told her she might need another little while though.'

Becky laughed and hugged her daughter. 'Well, I think Alice looks perfectly lovely as she is without wasting her money on promises in a bottle.'

'Thanks, Becky,' said Alice, turning red. 'But you can rest easy. These masks were completely home made. When I saw my credit card statement, it put years on me so it kind of defeated the purpose!'

'Ha! Didn't I say it would end in tears? But changing the subject, do you have time to stay around for a coffee? I have a bit of news I'm dying to tell you.'

'I do. And I want to tell you something myself.'

Becky put Lilly down and looked at Alice worriedly. 'Nothing bad, I hope?'

'No, not exactly.' She indicated to Lilly and Becky understood.

'Lilly, sweetie,' said Becky. 'Can you go upstairs and put your pjs on, please? Then you can watch some telly while I have a little chat with Alice.'

Lilly was out the door in a flash and Becky flopped down on the sofa. 'So what is it you have to tell me?'

'Don't panic but just before you came in, Lilly was asking about Dennis.'

'She *what?*'

'She overheard us talking about him the other day so she was asking who he was. But I fobbed her off, saying he was somebody at work you needed to talk to.'

'Jesus, thanks for that, Alice. The sooner this thing comes to a head the better. I hate all the sneaking around.'

'Ta-da!' Lilly stood in front of them again, all dressed for bed, her pink, floppy-eared bunny under her arm.

'Good girl,' said Becky, hugging her again. 'Now you can watch telly in here while Alice and I go into the kitchen for some tea.'

'So what's your news, then?' Having insisted that Becky sit down, Alice busied herself making tea.

Becky paused before answering and Alice turned to look at her. 'You won't believe it, Alice, but I met Dennis today.'

'What? You actually met him? Oh, my God. Tell me more.'

Over the next few minutes, Becky recounted the events of the day, with Alice hanging on her every word.

'And I'm happy to be meeting him,' Becky continued, 'but sometimes I wonder about the effect it might have on Lilly. I'm doing this for her, but what if it doesn't work out?'

'Becky, no matter what happens, she'll always have you. And it sounds to me like you're doing everything right. You're sussing him out before making any decisions so whatever you decide after that is going to be the right thing. They say a mother's instinct is the best one.'

Becky took a sip of her tea. 'Thanks, Alice. You really are like a big sister. I've been thinking lately how sad it is that I don't have any family I'm close to. Maybe if I did, I wouldn't feel the need to bring Lilly's father into our lives.'

'Is that what it is?' Alice put her cup down and stared at Becky. 'Is that the real reason you're after Dennis? Just so that Lilly can have another blood relative?'

'I suppose that's one part of it. I'm a single mother and I can't help but worry about what will become of Lilly if I'm not here.'

Alice opened her mouth to say something and then decided against it. She wasn't sure Becky would thank her for sticking her nose in.

'What is it, Alice?'

'I was just thinking … well, I know it's none of my business, but it's not strictly true that you don't have any other family. I don't know what went on, but do you think that maybe it's time to sort things out with them?'

'Absolutely not!' Becky's face turned dark.

'But if it's just family you want to give Lilly, wouldn't that be an easier way?'

'Believe me, Alice. There's nothing easy about my family and I have no intention of ever introducing them to Lilly.'

'Family feuds can be difficult I know but—'

'Alice, you don't know anything about it! The past few years have been the happiest of my life and that's mainly because my parents and my sister didn't figure in them. Now can we just forget about them? They're nothing to me.'

Alice was stunned by the ferocity with which Becky spat out the words. She'd never seen her like that before. 'I … I'm sorry, Becky. I honestly didn't mean to upset you.'

'Don't worry.' She stood up and began to clean away the cups. 'And I shouldn't have shouted but it's such a sore subject, and I *really* don't want to talk about it.'

'Okay. I won't say another word. I'd better be going. Frank is coming over later and we have some things to discuss.'

'Sounds interesting.' Becky smiled, but Alice noticed that the smile didn't reach her eyes.

'It could be. I'm thinking of asking him to move in.'

'Oh, wow! That's brilliant. It's about time you put that man out of his misery. How long now has he been hinting at moving in?'

Alice laughed. 'Ah, poor Frank. I've really kept him hanging, haven't I? Well, hopefully I can fix that later.'

'Well, good for you.' Becky walked out to the hall with her.

'See you Monday, sweetie,' said Alice, blowing a kiss in to Lilly, who was engrossed in *SpongeBob SquarePants*. 'And I'm really sorry again, Becky. You know I didn't mean to hurt you.'

'I know. Don't worry about it. I overreacted. It's just everything that's happening has me on edge.'

'It's understandable. Now, make sure you get some sleep over the weekend. You have a big day on Monday and you want to be fresh and alert for it.'

Alice sat into her little car and headed off down the road. She was still a little rattled from Becky's outburst. She'd thought it had just been a family feud that had kept Becky away, but it must be way more than that. And then there was her response to the black eyes. Alice hoped that whatever had happened within Becky's family wasn't as bad as she was beginning to think it was. There were more and more stories coming out in the news these days about child abuse. God, she hoped it wasn't that. She shuddered at the thought.

She turned down her own road and parked outside her house. She was going to put Becky and her problems firmly out of her head for one night. Tonight was going to be all about her. Her and Frank. She was going to finally put the past to rest and ask him to come and live with her. Becky wasn't the only one looking to make changes. This was going to be a new beginning for Alice and she couldn't wait to start her new life.

# Chapter 16

That morning, Becky had rung in to work to say she was sick. She'd barely had a wink of sleep for worrying about meeting Dennis and had just fallen asleep when the alarm had gone off. It was the first time in her life she'd ever done anything like that. Usually she'd drag herself to work no matter how sick she felt. But between the exhaustion and the worry, she knew she wouldn't be able to face anyone.

Martha's Kitchen was a quaint old coffee shop with blue-and-white checked tablecloths and real home baking displayed in the glass case at the counter. The tea was served in china mugs with flower patterns and Becky felt like she'd stepped back in time as soon as she'd walked through the door. She wished she could embrace places like this. She wished she could enjoy a big slice of the home-made apple pie or a scone and butter. But the truth was places like this made her imagine dirty kitchens with cats roaming around and old women barely rinsing cups under the tap before sending them out to be used again. She knew she was being unreasonable and Martha probably had the most pristine kitchen you could imagine, but she just preferred modern, clean-cut places where she knew there were dishwashers and stainless steel counters.

She checked her watch for about the tenth time in as many minutes. Still only five to one. She'd been worried that Dennis wouldn't wait if she was late, now she was worried that he might not come at all. The old lady behind the counter stared over at her so she took a pretend sip from her unwanted cup of tea so as not to look conspicuous.

'Hi, Alice. Sorry I'm late.'

Becky looked up and her heart gave a leap. 'No, *I* am. Early, I mean. I'm early. You're not late.'

'Right, now that we've established that, can I sit down?'

His face was dark and Becky felt a little intimidated. 'Of course. Can I get you a tea or coffee? Or anything to eat?'

'A cup of tea would be nice. And I'd murder a bacon sandwich.'

Becky didn't wait for service but went to the counter to order instead. She needed to get herself together. She felt her chest tightening and prayed she wasn't going to have another panic attack. *Breathe, Becky, breathe.* This was just an informal chat. She was completely in control. She didn't have to tell him anything she didn't want to. Not until she was ready.

'Here you go,' she said, placing the tea in front of Dennis. 'The sandwich will be ready in a minute.'

'Thanks, Alice.'

It was strange to hear him call her by her friend's name. She watched as he stirred spoonful after spoonful of sugar into his tea before taking a big gulp.

'So this article – is it for a newspaper or something?' His deep brown eyes bore into hers and she felt uneasy.

'Yes. It's, em, for one of the nationals.'

'Which one?'

Oh, God. 'I'm not sure yet. I'm freelance so I'm putting a few things together for pitches.'

'I see.' Still those eyes.

'So anyway, Dennis. Do you mind if I ask you a few questions?' She was anxious to just get on with it.

'That's what we're here for, isn't it?' The woman arrived with his sandwich and placed it down in front of him. 'As long as you don't mind me eating at the same time.'

'Of course.' Becky winced as he launched on the sandwich with gusto, taking almost half of it in his mouth at once. 'So you were a very successful businessman, I believe. When did that start to change?'

His face seemed to crumble and Becky felt sorry for him. He looked down at the table and for a moment, she panicked that she was pushing him too soon. 'Look, Dennis. If you're not comfortable with me asking—'

'No, it's fine. It was probably around the start of 2012. I'd struggled for a year or so before that, but 2012 was a bad year. I couldn't meet any of my repayments to the bank and I was getting letters almost every day, threatening repossession. It got to a stage where I just stopped opening the post. There was nothing but bills and bad news.'

'That sounds tough. And how did it feel to go from being top of the world to losing everything?'

He frowned. 'You did say you'd write this piece in such a way that it might help others, didn't you? I mean, the only reason I'm talking to you at all is the thought that I can warn people against letting themselves fall into this shitty life.'

Becky balked at the vehemence in his voice. 'Of course. It will be a very empathetic piece. I want people to be able to relate to what you've been through.'

'It's just not easy thinking back to that time in my life. At first, I thought I'd be able to get back on my feet easily enough. I thought I was savvy enough to be able to start again and work my way up, but sometimes shit happens.'

'Is your life really that bad now, Dennis? I know things have changed, but sometimes change can be good.'

He looked at her then as though she was a mad woman. '*Good?* Are you serious? You should try living in my head for a while and feel the stress, the loss, the pain, the guilt …'

'I don't understand. There are so many people out there just like you. What have you to feel guilty about?'

His voice became quiet. 'I wouldn't even know where to start.'

Things weren't going exactly to plan and Becky wasn't sure she wanted to continue with the conversation. The man sitting in front of her was broken. He wasn't the man she remembered. The man who'd sparkled with wit and confidence. The man who'd dazzled her with his charm and had put her under his spell.

'Do you want another one of those?' she asked finally, pointing to his empty plate. 'You look like you enjoyed it.'

'Go on, then. Sure, I might as well.'

Becky felt slightly miffed. Who ate more than one sandwich in one sitting? Was he just making a point that everything came at a price? The woman who'd served her was clearing a table beside them so Becky asked her for the same again.

'So these articles – I suppose you'll be getting a decent amount of dosh for them. I hear the nationals pay pretty well.'

And there it was. The old Dennis Prendergast – money always at the forefront of his mind. 'Well, they haven't accepted them yet. I'll just have to wait and see. So tell me about your personal life – your family.'

'What family?'

'Well, my source said you were single when you ran the business. Has that changed?' Oh, shit. She hadn't planned on being so blunt and she didn't want to risk alienating him.

'Nothing has changed. No family. It's just me.' His face was sad but suddenly there was a flicker of a smile. 'Are these questions really necessary, Alice? Or are you just fishing for information for yourself?'

Becky felt her cheeks burning and she tried to keep her voice from shaking. 'I can assure you, Dennis, anything I ask you is purely for the purpose of the article.'

'Relax. I'm just teasing you.' But the smile was gone and he looked broody again.

Becky wanted to keep things going. 'And the place down the road where I met you yesterday – it's a sort of social club for the homeless?'

'Yeah. It's run by a homeless charity and it's a real lifeline to people on the streets.'

'I can imagine. I didn't even know places like that existed.'

'Oh, they exist all right. The Simon Community and other charities like it provide wonderful services for the homeless. Did you know volunteers go out every night on a soup run, providing food for people on the streets?'

'No, I didn't.'

'And did you know they have a team who go out every night, checking the rough sleepers, providing them with sleeping bags and blankets and anything else they might need?'

He was certainly very passionate about the charity. A noble trait. She didn't need to know any more. 'Dennis, you know I said I was writing these articles? Well, I wasn't exactly—'

'Oh, yes, and can you mention the fact that the government is cutting funding to these homeless charities? It's a travesty. As it is, they're hugely stretched and the government wants to make it more difficult for them.'

'That's awful, but I just—'

'To be brutally honest, I could well be dead now if it wasn't for the Simon Community. I can't tell you the number of times I've contemplated ending it all.'

'Wh – what do you mean?'

'Well, since I became homeless I—'

'You're *homeless*?' Becky couldn't contain her shock.

'Of course,' said Dennis, looking at her quizzically. 'Isn't that what all this is about?'

'I was just about to ask you what you did at that homeless place. I thought you *worked* there.'

'Nope. I aspire to bigger things but, right now, I'm homeless, jobless and pretty much desperate to get my life back on track.'

Becky didn't know what to say. She suddenly just wanted to get out of there. It was all going wrong. And to think she'd been just about to tell him about Lilly. Thank God she hadn't said anything.

'Does it make a difference?'

'What?' Becky tried to focus.

'Does it make a difference to what you're writing about – the fact that I'm homeless?'

'B – but you don't look like a homeless person.' She was trying to get her head around it.

'And what exactly does a homeless person look like? Is there a dress code?'

'I didn't mean … what I meant was that you seem like a decent sort – very respectable.' Shit. It was all coming out wrong.

'There are a lot of respectable homeless people. Homelessness doesn't necessarily mean unclean.' He had an edge to his voice now and Becky could tell he was getting agitated.

'I wasn't suggesting that. It's just hard to take in.'

Dennis stood up suddenly. 'Well, I'm sorry that my homelessness has unsettled you. And *you* came to *me*, remember?'

'Sit down, Dennis. Please. It's all just come out wrong. Maybe we could talk about it a little more.'

'I have to be somewhere. Even homeless people have lives, you know. I hope you get over the shock of coming into contact with one of *my* sort.'

'Dennis, please—'

'Goodbye, Alice.'

'Hold on.' Becky grabbed his arm as he was about to walk away. Part of her wanted him to disappear and the other part was scared she might never see him again. She rooted in her bag and pulled out a fifty euro note. 'Please take this for your time. As you said, I'll get paid well for the articles.'

He glared at her. 'And as *you* said, they haven't been accepted yet. I just wanted to make sure you could cover the cost of the food. I don't want your money.' He turned with a flourish and headed outside.

She suddenly felt conscious that the woman behind the counter and a few people at other tables were watching the show. She quickly pulled out a twenty euro note and threw it on the table before rushing out after him.

'Dennis, Dennis, wait a sec.' He was already halfway down the street when she caught up with him. 'I'm sorry about how I came across in there. I honestly didn't mean to offend you.'

He dropped his rucksack on the ground beside him and looked at her with loathing. 'Alice, you represent everything I hate about my old life. Everything I don't want to be.'

'What do you mean by that?' It was her turn to be offended.

'Look, when I was a high flyer, I was selfish. I judged people by how rich they were, how successful they were and what they could do for me. I'm not that man any more.'

'And you think *I'm* that person?'

'Well, aren't you?'

'No, that's not who I am. You know nothing about me.'

'And let's just leave it that way.' He nodded, hauled his rucksack up on his back and continued down the street.

Becky stared after him and felt a mixture of relief and rage. How dare he! How dare he try to make her feel bad. Surely she was entitled to be shocked by his revelation. She turned in the direction of her bus stop. She'd never been so glad about not going to work. There was no way she could concentrate on anything else after what she'd just heard.

Suddenly she felt all her hopes and dreams crash through the floor. Dennis Prendergast – Lilly's father – was an unemployed, homeless bum. Whatever way he tried to dress it up, that's what he was. She wasn't upset for herself, of course. But she did feel bad for Lilly. Deep down she had hoped she could bring a father into her little girl's life. A good, solid man who'd welcome the fact that he had a daughter he hadn't known about. A man who'd embrace his new role and be a real daddy, just like the one Lilly had drawn in the picture. Whether he was a decent sort or not, it didn't matter. She couldn't expose her daughter to the homeless world that had scared Becky so much when she was a child herself. She'd only wanted to make her little girl's dreams come true but there was no chance of that happening now.

# Chapter 17

Kate sat on the loo in work, praying nobody would come in. She knew the laxatives she'd taken would clear her out, but she really hadn't imagined there was so much to get rid of. After searching the internet for weight-loss solutions, she'd found a company who supplied laxatives online that they said were proven to work. They seemed harmless enough and she knew she'd only use them for a short period of time. If she could just drop a dress size or two quickly, she'd have no further need for them.

God, stuff was still coming out of her and she felt like she was getting lighter by the second. Maybe even a few days of this and she'd have achieved her goal. But her stomach was starting to cramp and she was beginning to wonder if she'd ever be able to get off the toilet. And what about going home? She really hadn't thought of that. How was she going to get on a bus if there was a chance this might happen again? She'd got up early to take them. The packet had said they should work within forty-five minutes. But nothing had happened – she hadn't even felt a twinge, and had headed off to work thinking they just hadn't worked. And now she was stuck in this bloody loo.

Five minutes later, things seemed to have dried up, so she fixed herself and went to wash her hands. She looked at her face in the mirror and couldn't believe how grey she looked. She really wasn't feeling the best. She was glad Becky wasn't in because she'd only be questioning her. Although Becky was so preoccupied with Dennis Prendergast at the moment that Kate thought Becky probably wouldn't even notice anything amiss.

She washed her hands and walked back out into the main office.

She suddenly had to steady herself at a desk because the room started to sway in front of her.

'Kate, are you okay? What's wrong?' It was Lynda, one of the cashiers, looking at her with concern.

'I … I'm just not feeling very well. In fact, I think I should just go home.'

'Oh, you poor thing. Will I call you a taxi?'

'That would be good, thanks.' She gratefully sat down on a chair that Lynda brought over to her and felt like death.

Lynda was still fussing. 'I'll just go and tell Andrew you're going home and I'll grab you a glass of water.'

Kate felt too weak to argue and was glad someone was taking charge. She hoped this would all be worth it. It had probably been a mistake to come to work. If she'd taken a few days off and dealt with things at home, it would have been fine. She'd go home now and go to bed for a few hours so she'd be okay when Garreth came home. Now that she knew how those laxatives worked, she'd just have to time them better. She wouldn't slip up like that again. She was in control now and the results would be worth the pain in the end.

❀

Dennis had planned to go and see his mother after lunch with the journalist but had changed his mind. He'd felt too angry after their exchange and he didn't wanted to upset her. Instead he'd found himself on a bus to Swords and was now sitting at the bus stop across the road from Isabella's house.

He didn't usually come at this time of day. It was always early morning when he knew he'd see her frazzled and exhausted, loading the car with kids and bags, getting ready for the day ahead. There was no car there now, but he suspected school was probably finished and they'd be home soon. It would be strange to see them at the other end of the day. He wondered if Isabella would look any less stressed.

Right on cue, the silver Zafira appeared from around the corner and turned into the driveway. The street was quiet and suddenly Dennis felt exposed. In the mornings, there was the hustle and bustle of people waiting for a bus or rushing past. He was able to feel invisible. But sitting there without a soul around, he felt very conspicuous. He pulled up the hood of his jacket and kept his eyes firmly fixed on the car as the doors opened.

Isabella was first out, followed by one of the boys, who'd obviously commandeered the front seat. She lifted the little girl out of her car seat and the other boy hopped out. Dennis noticed they all seemed calmer than they did in the mornings. He was thankful for that at least.

He watched carefully as she expertly juggled the child onto her left hip while she opened the front door with her right hand. Letting the three children inside, she paused for a moment. That's when Dennis' heart almost stopped. She swung around and looked at him. She stared right at him and didn't move for what seemed like an eternity. He didn't breathe. And then she was gone, closing the door firmly behind her.

He hadn't been able to tell whether it had been a menacing look or one of recognition. She'd been expressionless. Or had he imagined the whole thing? But whatever it was, it had unsettled him. He slung his rucksack over his back and headed down the road as fast as his feet would take him. He probably shouldn't be watching her. It wasn't a clever thing to do. Maybe he should just stop. But he knew he couldn't.

'Are you okay, chicken?' Garreth said, watching Kate from the kitchen door. 'You look really pale.'

'I'm grand.' Kate tried to muster up a bit of enthusiasm. 'I just have a bit of an upset stomach. Must have been something I ate.'

'Well, what are you doing in here making dinner? I can look after myself. You take yourself off to bed.'

'Honestly, I'm fine. I left work early and had a bit of a sleep when

I got in, so I just thought I'd throw something together for when you got home.'

Garreth came over and wrapped his arms around her waist as she stirred some sauce into a pot of pasta. 'You're too good to me. Now, I insist. At least take yourself off into the sitting room and I'll be in to you in a minute.'

She didn't object. She still wasn't feeling the better of the diarrhoea that had plagued her for most of the day and although she'd slept for the last few hours, she still felt weak and exhausted. She gladly flopped onto the sofa and flicked on the telly. Urgh! *Come Dine with Me*. Much as she loved that programme, she couldn't face watching food at the moment.

She could hear Garreth clattering around in the kitchen and smiled to herself. He was a really good guy. She'd want to be careful, though – she didn't want him finding out what she was up to. Usually they were really up front with each other and told each other everything but this was something she needed to keep to herself. She felt bad about it but she knew that he'd put a stop to it immediately if he knew.

Her reaction to the laxatives seemed quite severe but she was sure it was just until her body adjusted. And anyway, it was only a quick fix. She'd ditch them as soon as she was down a couple of dress sizes.

'This is great, love,' said Garreth, coming in and sitting down on the chair beside her with his bowl of pasta. 'I'm assuming you didn't want any yourself.'

'Not at the moment. Maybe I'll have a bit later.'

She was afraid to look at him. They were usually so in tune with each other that she was sure he'd notice there was something more to it than a stomach upset.

'Kate?'

Oh, God. 'I'm fine, Garreth. Stop worrying.'

'Listen, love, you'd tell me if there was something else going on, wouldn't you? I mean, you really don't seem yourself lately.'

'Of course I would. And there's nothing wrong – except for this bloody stomach upset. I'll be as right as rain in the morning. Actually, maybe I *will* head to bed after all.' She couldn't wait to get away from his questions.

He reached out his hand and pulled her towards him as she got up from the sofa. 'You won't like me saying it but I hope you're not on one of these weird diets. I know you were disappointed about missing out on that modelling job, but you don't need to change yourself. You're absolutely gorgeous and if they don't want you as you are, then they're the ones missing out.'

She was stunned at his perceptiveness and had to swallow a lump in her throat. She bent down and placed a soft kiss on his lips. 'You're lovely, Garreth. But honestly, there's no need to worry. And when have you ever known me to diet? I love my food too much.'

'Well, I suppose that's true.' He smiled and seemed to relax a little. 'Maybe you just need a good tonic or something. Get yourself off to bed and call me if you need anything. I'm going to watch the football and I'll be up then.'

She felt rotten lying to him but she didn't have a choice. She didn't want to worry him. And there was really nothing to worry about. She was in control. She'd never become a victim of a food disorder. She was too strong for that. In fact, she could never understand those people who wrecked their bodies with anorexia or bulimia.

Her stomach growled as she curled up in bed. She was actually feeling hungry now. Maybe she'd just have a nap and then slip down for some tea and toast. And surely being hungry must be a sign that things were settling down. She was right not to be worried. Nobody need ever know.

# Chapter 18

'It's just so strange, Kate. It's been over a week now and she won't even *hear* of his name being mentioned.' Alice was whispering into the phone in the kitchen for fear Lilly would hear the conversation.

Kate sighed. 'I know. She's the same in here. It's just business as usual, as if the whole Dennis Prendergast thing never happened.'

'I sort of wish it hadn't. She was happy before she got this whole notion into her head and now it's as though she has the weight of the world on her shoulders.'

'It's obvious she's still thinking about him so why won't she talk to us? We're supposed to be her best friends. I thought she told us everything.'

Alice could almost hear Kate's pout, reminding her of how young the girl was. 'It doesn't always work like that, Kate. I think she's just trying to forget. Didn't she say that she felt she'd let Lilly down? We both know that's not the case, but try telling *her* that.'

'But she hasn't even mentioned him since she told us about the meeting. Any time I've tried to bring up the subject, she holds her hand up and stops me.'

'Well, she's much the same with me,' Alice said, peeping into the sitting room to make sure Lilly was still happily watching telly. 'And she makes sure Lilly is in the room with us most of the time so that I can't talk to her about it.'

'We're just going to have to corner her and get her talking.' Kate sounded decisive. 'Dennis is obviously still on her mind so she needs to stop ignoring the matter.'

'I agree. So what do you suggest?'

'Maybe if you hang around some evening and I can come round after work? We can both talk to her then.'

Alice thought it was a good idea. She hadn't always got on with Kate, but she knew that Becky listened to her. 'That sounds like a plan. You know, it's times like this that I wish Becky was in touch with her family. I know she always says *we're* her family but it's not the same.'

'I know,' said Kate. I often think about that too. Doesn't she have family over in the UK, though? Maybe we should give her a gentle nudge. Maybe it's time for her to build bridges.'

'I wouldn't bother. I mentioned her family to her a couple of weeks ago and she almost bit my head off. She said that they're nothing to her.'

'I wonder what went on there. It all sounds very strange.'

'It does,' Alice conceded. 'But all I know is that something huge must have happened to make her fall out so much with her parents *and* her sister. I suppose it's not our place to judge, though.'

'I'm sure she'll tell us one day. But, in the meantime, I'll come over tomorrow evening if it suits you to stay on and we can both confront her then.'

'Alice! The telly's not working. It's gone all fuzzy and noisy.'

'Sorry, Kate. Lilly's calling so I'd better go. I'll see you tomorrow evening and we'll see if we can get her talking.'

By the time Alice had gone into the sitting room, the telly was working again and she wasn't needed. She headed back into the kitchen and poured herself a glass of cold water. She certainly had no problem drinking her recommended eight glasses of water a day at the moment because she was always thirsty. She seemed to remember some connection between thirst and diabetes and made a mental note to check it out.

She felt really sad for Becky and what she was going through, but that couldn't stop her being happy about her own life. She was happier than she'd been in a long time. Frank had jumped at the chance of moving in. It had only taken them two days to move his stuff and he was already a welcome fixture in her house. Alice was bursting to talk to Becky about this new phase in her life, but she didn't feel comfortable saying anything at the moment. In fact, she didn't even feel comfortable about being happy. It sounded ridiculous but that's the way it was.

Alice checked the big clock on the kitchen wall and saw it was almost five. She wouldn't be hanging around this evening when Becky came home, especially since she was going to stay around tomorrow night. She'd never been in a hurry to leave in the past and had often stayed to have dinner with Becky and Lilly, but things were different now. She had a couple of steaks in the fridge and a nice bottle of Chilean red on the wine rack. If she managed to get home before Frank, she could have a nice romantic dinner ready for the two of them. He'd only been living with her for a week, but it had been one of the best of her life. She wondered what on earth had taken her so long.

Life was strange. There was Becky, with no man but a beautiful daughter, and there *she* was happy with her man but still grieving for the children she never had. But she had a feeling that Frank was going to fill some of that void. He was a good man and she was very lucky to have him. Now if only she could get Becky sorted. She hadn't said it, but she'd secretly hoped that Dennis would turn out to be her knight in shining armour. She'd warned Becky against hoping for a fairy tale but, in truth, that's what Alice had secretly wished for. Things seemed pretty grim at the moment, but Alice trusted they'd get better. Becky deserved a bit of happiness and Alice was going to do all she could to make sure she got it.

❁

'Look at the state of your desk, Geraldine.' Becky stood with her hands on her hips, shaking her head. 'It's like a bomb's hit it. How are you supposed to find anything in that mess?'

'It's organised chaos,' grinned Geraldine, one of the older bank officials. 'If I cleaned it up, I wouldn't be able to find anything.'

Becky grunted a disapproving noise and breezed off to the toilets. She just couldn't help herself. Her head was bursting with so much emotion that she felt she was on the brink of some sort of breakdown. Finding Dennis Prendergast had become the most important thing in her life and now that it had ended badly, she felt cheated.

There was nobody else in the toilets so she leaned on the counter and looked at her reflection in the mirror. Maybe she should be trying out some of Alice's remedies. Her skin looked dry and her eyes were dull and bloodshot. Even her usually bouncy hair seemed tired and devoid of life. Damn that man for getting into her head like this.

The sound of footsteps outside the door prompted her to go into a cubicle. She locked the door and put the seat down so she could sit on it.

'Becky, are you in there?'

It was Kate. Becky was sick of her constantly sticking her nose in and wanting her to talk about things – especially lately. She was trying to forget and didn't need constant reminders of how she'd failed.

'Becky, I know it's you. I just want to see if you're okay.'

Becky sighed and flushed the toilet before coming out. 'Of course I'm okay. Why wouldn't I be?'

Kate's face was riddled with concern. 'It's just I saw you having words with Geraldine. She's in her sixties, Becks. She didn't deserve that.'

'Oh, for God's sake! I only mentioned about her desk being a mess. How is she supposed to—?'

'But it's not about the desk really, is it?' Kate's voice softened. 'You've been like a bulldog since the day you met Dennis.'

Becky turned and glared at Kate. 'Don't even say his name, Kate! That subject is well and truly closed.'

'But is it really?'

'Well, it would be if people weren't so nosy and wanted me to talk about it all the time.'

'I'm sorry you feel like that, Becks, but I'm just concerned about you. You can't go on being angry. I think you need to confront—'

'Kate! Shut up, will you! I'm a grown woman – and seven years older than you, might I add. I don't need a little girl telling me how to run my life. Now can you just leave me alone?'

Kate's face crumbled. Becky had never spoken to her like that before. 'Okay, you win. I'm sorry.'

'Kate, wait …' Becky grabbed the younger girl's arm as she headed out the door. 'I shouldn't have spoken to you like that. I'm just going through some stuff at the moment.'

'It's okay,' said Kate, looking at her sadly. 'Don't worry about it.'

Becky felt like an absolute shit as she watched her friend walk out the door. What was happening to her? Why was she letting all this Dennis stuff turn her into some sort of demon? She'd always been determined that she didn't need a father for Lilly so why was it bothering her now? It didn't make sense.

Her mind wandered back to when she'd discovered she was pregnant. It had been a scary time for her – especially when she'd made the decision to do it alone. But she'd believed in herself and knew she could be everything her baby needed. Why had that changed? What had she wanted from Dennis? Had she wanted the fairy-tale ending? Whatever her reasons, having found him, she now knew that she had to stay away from Dennis. But even though her head was telling her she didn't need the complication, her heart just wouldn't agree.

❀

'Ah for fuck's sake, Deano. Are you in this game at all?' They were in the social club and John had just hit a table-tennis ball to him, which he'd missed for about the tenth time.

'Sorry, John. My mind's not on it. I think I'll call it a day.'

'So what's up with you?'

Dennis sighed. 'I'm just on a bit of a downer. You know how it is.'

'I certainly do.' John clapped him on the back. 'Hang in there, mate.'

'Thanks. Think I'll head off for a bit. Catch up with you again.' He grabbed his belongings and went outside into the cool air. At least it wasn't raining. Rain was the enemy of the homeless. You could layer up to fend off the cold but the rain was a different story.

He headed down towards the quays but just as he came to the end of the road, Martha's Kitchen caught his eye. His mood darkened even further. Every time he thought of that ignorant journalist and the way she'd looked down her nose at him, he wanted to scream. She was no better than him, with her posh clothes and designer handbag. How dare she. How bloody dare she!

Before he realised what he was doing, he'd walked across the road and stepped inside the little coffee shop. He was met with the beaming smile of the old lady who'd served them the last time.

'Nice crisp day out there, isn't it?' She was out like a shot from behind the counter, indicating a table for him to sit down. There wasn't another soul in the shop and she was obviously delighted to see a customer. 'Just yourself, is it?'

'Yes, just me.' Now that he was here, he might as well indulge in a cup of tea.

'Not with that lady of yours today, then?'

'Excuse me?'

'That lady of yours. The one you were with the last time you were in. I couldn't help but notice you two having a bit of a ding dong.'

Dennis sat down at a table at the window. 'Well, she's no lady of mine. It was purely a business thing.'

'Sure it was, love. Now what can I get you?'

'Just a tea, please,' said Dennis, annoyed that the woman didn't seem to believe him.

'Coming up. And just shout if you want anything else. Martha's the name. As in Martha's Kitchen. My own little slice of the pie, so to speak.' She headed back behind the counter chuckling at her little joke and Dennis was left with his own thoughts.

He'd encountered plenty of ignorant people this last year. People who made assumptions. Some would walk past indifferently and others would stare. Some gave him a look of pity and some disgust. They were all as bad as each other. There were a few genuine ones who'd stop to chat and find out more. Those were the good ones, but they were few and far between.

So if he was so used to a certain reaction, why then had this Alice girl got under his skin? She'd seemed nice at first. A bit ditsy, but beautiful with it. She'd been genuinely interested in him and his story and even though he'd been wary at first, he'd enjoyed sitting chatting to her. But as soon as she'd found out he was homeless, she'd clammed up. It was like she suddenly saw him through different eyes. He'd gone from being a guy down on his luck to someone who was the bane of society. Bloody princess!

'There you go, love,' said Martha, putting a steaming cup of tea down in front of him. 'And there's a slice of my home-made apple pie too.'

'Oh, I didn't order any—'

'On the house. You look like you could do with feeding up.'

Dennis watched as she disappeared through a door behind the counter. People like Martha gave him hope. She was one of the good ones. He launched at the warm cake and took a huge spoonful. Why should he give that silly Alice woman another thought? She was just one of the ignorant ones.

As he let the buttery pastry melt in his mouth, it dawned on him why she'd got to him so much – she reminded him of who he used to be. He wanted a piece of his old life back again. He wanted to be working and self-sufficient. But one thing he didn't want to be was the stuck-up, money-grabbing, selfish person he'd been. This past year had changed him. He was a different person. It was easy to change the sort of person you were if you really wanted to. If only it was as easy to change the things you'd done.

# Chapter 19

'Poor Becky,' said Frank, pouring gravy over his steak and chips. 'Sounds like she's having a really hard time at the moment.'

Alice nodded, her own mouth full of the succulent meat. 'She really is. You know, it's funny. I've always envied her. I always felt she had the perfect life. But it just goes to show, we all have our crosses to bear.'

'That's true. But right now, I feel like the luckiest man in the world.' He reached over and put his hand over hers.

'Ah, Frank. I'm the lucky one. I never thought I'd be this happy again. You're very special, you know.'

'You're not too bad yourself. Especially with these haute-cuisine cooking skills.' He stabbed a chip with his fork and dipped it into the dollop of tomato ketchup on the side of his plate.

Alice laughed. 'Well, I may not be Nigella, but you won't go hungry here. Oh, and speaking of which, you might want to pick up a takeaway on the way home tomorrow. I'm staying on for a while at Becky's. Kate is coming over and we're going to try and get her talking about Dennis.'

'Do you really think she's going to shut him out now completely? Surely it can't be as cut and dried as that for her.'

'I honestly don't know, Frank. I know that it's not an ideal situation but he's still Lilly's father. I can't imagine it would be that easy to just forget about him.'

'And do you think she should? Forget about him, I mean?'

'If I'm really honest, I wish she'd never looked for him in the first place.'

Frank looked taken aback. 'Do you really mean that? So you think she should just walk away?'

'No, I don't. Not now that she's found him. I think she needs to stop pretending nothing's happened and start thinking about what to do next. Although I do understand that she's trying to protect Lilly.'

'But don't you think this Dennis guy deserves to know he has a child? Just because he's homeless doesn't mean he couldn't be a good father. Maybe if she had told him from the beginning, things would have been different.'

'In what way?' Alice put her knife and fork down and pushed her plate away.

'Well, for starters, he may not have ended up in the situation he's in now. If he'd had a child to support, he may have been more careful about his choices.'

'But we don't really know his situation – other than he's homeless. And surely homelessness is not a lifestyle choice.'

'I'm not saying that, Alice. But having children makes you think twice before making decisions. When you know that you have a little person relying on you, you want to make sure you do right by them.'

Alice felt tears well up in her eyes and willed them not to fall.

'Oh, God, Alice, I'm sorry. I didn't think.' He pulled her hand up to his lips and kissed it gently. 'I was thinking of my own situation and just forgot about yours.'

'It's okay, Frank. You don't have to tip-toe around the subject of children. I can't go to pieces every time a child is mentioned.'

'Still, I should be more considerate.'

'Stop it, would you, Frank? I'm a big girl now. But what was it you were saying about your own situation? Are you talking about Louise?'

'Yes. I suppose I can't help sticking up for dads. I'd hate to have been deprived of even a small piece of Louise's life. I was lucky to have been there from the beginning and I couldn't imagine my life without her.'

'Of course you couldn't, Frank.' Alice loved seeing Frank's fatherly side. His whole face became soft and gentle when he mentioned his daughter's name.

Frank continued. 'And when I see that gorgeous little girl, I think of the fact that some guy is missing out on one of the most wonderful things in life. There's just nothing like the feeling of— Oh, Jesus, Alice. There I go again. I'm so sorry.'

'It's okay, Frank. Really it is. And I completely see where you're coming from. Dennis has already missed out on so much. It would seem cruel to not give him a chance to be a part of Lilly's life now.'

'Exactly! Now, I know Becky will have to tread carefully. She'll need to know more about him before she jumps in, but it would be a travesty if she never gave him a chance.'

Alice was fuelled with a renewed enthusiasm. 'You're dead right. That's exactly what I'm going to tell her tomorrow night. Or maybe you should come over too. You know she loves you and would listen to what you had to say.'

'Ah now, I think I'll leave the talking to you ladies. God knows you're experts at it.'

'I'll let you off with that one – only because you're right!' Alice stood up to clear the plates. 'But let's not spend the night talking about Becky. I'll be doing enough of that tomorrow night.'

'Here, leave that and come into the sitting room,' said Frank, taking her hand and leading her away from the dishwasher. 'I'm sure we can find much better ways to spend the night.'

'Oooh, Mr Doyle! What might you be suggesting?'

'Come here and I'll show you.'

He lowered himself onto the smooth velvet sofa, pulling her gently on top of him. She didn't hesitate. Her mouth was on his; her tongue urgently probing, tasting, wanting more. As Frank slowly and sensually removed each piece of her clothing, a swell of desire rose up inside her and she just wanted to stay in that moment forever.

Never in her wildest dreams had she imagined that she'd want to be with someone this way again – wanting them to make love to her, desperate to have them inside her. At forty-seven, she was experiencing things with Frank that she'd never experienced before and she loved every minute of it.

'A penny for them.' Frank's voice broke into her thoughts as they lay sated on the sofa. 'What are you thinking about?'

'Nothing really,' said Alice, pulling her top on and snuggling back into him. 'Just how happy I am – how happy you make me feel.'

'Well, the feeling is mutual. And I can't wait to spend the rest of my life with you.'

Alice sat up and looked at him. 'Do you mean that, Frank? Is that honestly what you want?'

'Of course it is.' He looked confused.

'It's just … it's just that …' Alice felt stupidly needy but she had to say it. 'I'm almost afraid to breathe because I'm so happy. I keep expecting you to say it's not working or you need your own space. I know it's stupid but I just couldn't bear to be hurt like that again.'

'Ah, poor Alice.' Frank pulled her into his arms. 'I'm here to stay, if you'll have me. I've even spoken to an estate agent about the apartment.'

'Have you? Already?' Alice was stunned.

'Well, there's no point in leaving it sitting there. I'm meeting him over there later in the week and he's going to do a valuation. The market is picking up in Dublin so I might even get a decent price for it.'

'Gosh, you're not wasting any time, are you? I thought you'd just rent it first until you see how things went.'

Frank shook his head. 'I couldn't be bothered with all that messing about. No, selling is the way to go. I don't have much of a mortgage, so it should make us a tidy sum.'

'Us?'

'Yes, of course, us. And the way I see it, we might need a bob or two if we're going to look into fostering. Kids don't come cheap, you know.'

Alice could have burst with happiness. 'Oh, Frank, what did I ever do to deserve you? You're one in a million.'

'I've actually made some enquiries. It might take some time and there's a lot of red tape to go through first, but I don't see why we shouldn't get the wheels in motion soon. What do you say?'

'I say let's do it. I can't believe you'd do this for me.'

'It's not just for you, Alice. You're not the only one who'd love to have some little ones around the house. I never had that chance with Louise. She lived with her mam so other than the odd night here and there, I was just a weekend dad.'

'But I'd say you were the best dad ever. Louise is very lucky to have you. What do you think she'll make of all this fostering business?'

'She'll be thrilled. Just as she was about me moving in here. She thinks you're a great catch.'

'Even though I'm way older than you?'

'Three years is nothing. And, besides, you look way younger than me. You'll have to get me using some of those anti-ageing remedies of yours.'

'You know, it's funny. I haven't needed my potions and lotions these past couple of weeks. Maybe I'm finally going to allow myself to grow old gracefully.'

'You mean you're letting yourself go because you've snared your man? Alice O'Malley, I'm shocked and appalled.'

'Ha! You make me feel liberated. I may even have put on a few pounds since you moved in.'

'Well, you still look pretty gorgeous to me. Now let me see, where were we?' He reached up under her top and Alice closed her eyes to enjoy the sensation of his hand cupping her breast. So what if she was heading for fifty. It was just a number. It was how you felt inside that counted and right now, she felt like a teenager in the flush of first love.

❀

'Are you happy, sweetie?' It was late in the evening and close to Lilly's bed time but Becky had decided to bring her to McDonald's for a treat. The little girl was lining her fries out on a serviette.

'Yes, Mummy. McDonald's is soooo nice. 'Cept for the green thing in the burger. That's yuck.'

Becky smiled at her daughter. 'Well, I'm glad you like it. But what about other things? Like playschool, for example. Are you happy there?'

Lilly thought for a moment. 'Well, maybe not *every* day.'

'And why is that? What things make you sad?'

'Well, some days Jamie Donnelly wants to be the cook in the kitchen in playschool. It's not really fair because he knows *I'm* the cook and I give out all the dinners.'

'But you know what Glenda says.' Becky laughed at her daughter's determined face. 'Sharing is caring.'

'I suppose,' Lilly pouted. 'But you wanted to know what makes me sad and Jamie Donnelly is the only thing that makes me sad.'

Becky stirred her tea, choosing her words carefully. 'And do you still feel sad that you don't have a daddy?'

'Not really. I have you and Alice. It's kind of like having two mummies – like Samantha in playschool. Are you sad?'

'What do you mean?' Becky was taken aback. 'Why would I be sad?'

'You seem sad sometimes. Is it because I don't have a daddy?'

Jesus. Lilly was only four years old and already had amazing powers of perception. 'I'm not sad at all, sweetheart. I've just been tired lately, that's all.'

'Oh, good,' Lilly said, stuffing the last piece of her burger into her mouth. 'Because boys are silly and daddies just make you play football and stuff, and I *hate* football.'

Becky laughed. 'Well, that's settled then. We don't need a silly, football-playing daddy in our lives. We can manage just fine by ourselves.'

'Can I get a strawberry milkshake, Mummy? Pleeeease?' Lilly's big eyes pleaded with Becky, the daddy conversation already forgotten.

'I suppose so. But just a small one and we'll get it on the way out.'

'Yay! Thank you, Mummy.' Becky smiled at Lilly's enthusiasm. If only all life's problems could be solved with a strawberry milkshake. But she felt better about her decision not to see Dennis Prendergast again. Lilly no longer seemed to feel that a dad would make her life better, and Dennis Prendergast was a complication they didn't need.

She thought back to the day in the coffee shop, how his big brown eyes had filled with hatred when she'd balked at the fact he was homeless. He'd looked at her with such disdain. She hadn't meant to be nasty or insulting – she just hadn't known what to say. But he'd completely overreacted and had made her feel so small. Well, she and Lilly had been fine for the past four years on their own and would continue to be fine. Good riddance to Dennis Prendergast and if she never heard his name again, it would be too soon.

# Chapter 20

'You can head off now, Alice. I'd have thought you'd be rushing out the door to get home to Frank.'

'Well, I just thought I'd stay for a little while so we could have a chat.'

Becky watched as Alice busied herself cleaning the already clean kitchen table. 'A chat! About what? Why are you acting so suspiciously?'

'I'm not,' Alice said, still rubbing at an imaginary stain on the table. 'I'm just, em, I just want us to sit down and talk. We haven't had a proper chat in ages.'

'Alice, we chat every day. Is there something wrong? Is it you and Frank? Don't tell me you're having problems already.'

'There's nothing wrong, Becky. I just want to—'

The doorbell rang, startling Becky, who stood up to go and answer it. 'Bloody salesmen, I bet. They're always calling at this time of the evening. I hate being rude to them but sometimes they just won't take no for an answer.'

As she opened the door, Kate pushed her way in through the hall door, shrugging off her leather jacket and popping it on the banister. 'Hello, Becks. Stick the kettle on, will you? I'm parched.'

'What brings you over here?' Becky followed her into the kitchen. 'Have I forgotten about something? Did we have something planned?'

'I just wanted to come over for a chat. Hi, Alice. Fancy seeing you here.'

Alice rolled her eyes and Becky looked from one to the other. 'I

135

suddenly feel hoodwinked. I take it it's not a coincidence you both want a chat?'

'Come on and sit down, Becky,' said Alice gently. 'We're just concerned, that's all. I was talking to Kate and we agreed we'd get together to talk to you.'

Becky wasn't happy. 'I can't sit down. I need to give Lilly a bath and get her to bed and I really don't appreciate you two plotting behind my back.'

Kate filled the kettle with water herself. 'Don't be like that, Becks. If you hadn't been shutting us both out over the past couple of weeks, we wouldn't be doing this now.'

'What are you talking about? I haven't been shutting anyone out. I've just been busy, that's all.'

'Becky, we're your friends.' Alice reached out and took her hand. 'We know you had a shock with Dennis but you can't keep it all to yourself. You need to talk about it – about how you're feeling and what you're thinking of doing next.'

Becky sat down heavily on a chair. 'I know you two mean well, but I'm not planning on doing anything next. I did what I set out to do – I found out more about Dennis Prendergast. And now that I know more about him, I've chosen not to take things any further.'

'But that's just it, Becks,' said Kate, placing three mugs and a pot of tea on the table. 'What *do* you know? You know he said he's homeless but nothing more. Aren't you a tiny bit interested in what happened to him? How he ended up homeless and what his life is like now?'

'No more curious than I'd be about anyone else.' Becky was defiant. 'He's nothing to me – just a guy who may or may not have an interesting story to tell.'

'Well, don't you want to know that story?' Kate wasn't letting it go. 'Don't you want to find out more from him – what sort of person he is?'

'I think Kate has a point. You should go and talk to him again and see where it leads.'

Becky was baffled. 'Since when did you two agree on anything? And Alice, I thought you'd be the one warning me off. Why are you so keen on me talking to Dennis now?'

'Because I think it's the right thing to do. Because I think you'll regret it if you don't. And—'

'And what? Becky was getting impatient.

'And because I think that Dennis is entitled to know he has a daughter.'

Silence filled the room and even Kate looked a little shocked at Alice's words. Becky could feel the rage rising up inside her and was almost afraid to speak.

Alice continued. 'And what about Lilly? Don't you think she's entitled to know who her father is? I know you're doing a great job with her, but it seems sort of cruel to keep Dennis from her. I think they both need to be told.'

'I've had enough of this,' Becky said, jumping up and slamming her hands down on the table. 'How dare you both come into my house and try and send me on some sort of guilt trip. I'm more than a mother and father to that little girl, and I won't have you saying otherwise. Now I'll expect you both to be gone when I get down from bathing Lilly.'

She stormed out of the kitchen, slamming the door behind her and rushed upstairs. She ran into her room and threw herself on the bed. 'Interfering bitches!' She slammed her fist on the bed again and again until the tears started to flow. How dare they do this to her. Just when she was beginning to pick herself up from the disastrous meeting with Dennis, they had to go and ruin everything. Well, she wasn't going to be bullied into meeting him again. No way.

The sound of Lilly's voice singing from her bedroom prompted her to wipe her eyes and get herself together. She'd go and bathe her daughter. It always relaxed her to see her daughter splash around in the bubbles. And she'd give her plenty of time in there tonight. There was no way she was going back downstairs while either of that pair was there. She wouldn't be responsible for what she'd say. This was the very reason she'd kept her distance from people in the past. Everyone was a problem solver. Everyone thought they knew what was best. When you lived in Ireland, it was as though people felt it was their right to know your personal details. It was crazy.

Sometimes she wished she hadn't allowed Alice and Kate to get so close to her. She was Becky Greene – a strong, independent woman who didn't need anyone. She'd always handled everything life had thrown at her and it had certainly thrown some hard punches. Well, she was still standing and that was a true sign of her strength.

But she'd also grown in the past few years, and a lot of that was as a result of what she'd learned from her friends. Strength came in a lot of different forms and it had taken strength to allow her barriers to be broken down and to let people in.

'Am I having a bath, Mummy?' Lilly's eyes were wide as she watched her mother pour half a bottle of bubble bath into the water.

'You certainly are, sweetie. And it's going to be the biggest, bubbliest bath you've ever had.'

'Yay!' She began to strip off her clothes and Becky smiled. No matter what else was going on in her life, nothing was as important as Lilly. She was everything to her and if she was happy, then so was Becky.

❀

'Jesus, Alice. And you say I'm the impetuous one. What was that all about?'

Alice bit her lip and tried to rub the stress from her temples. 'I honestly don't know what came over me. I knew what point I was going to make to Becky, but I didn't mean to blurt it out like that.'

'Well, you certainly took her, and me, by surprise. Is that really how you feel? That Dennis is *entitled* to know about Lilly?'

'Yes. No. Well, sort of.'

'Make your mind up, will you? What's got into you?'

'Oh, God, I should really go up there after her, shouldn't I? She must think I'm a right cow.'

Kate spoke softly. 'No, she doesn't. She adores you. And I think we should leave her with Lilly for a bit. She'll calm down soon enough and when she does, she'll realise we're only thinking of her best interests.'

'But what I said was so insensitive. I should have thought about what I was going to say a bit more.'

The sound of little footsteps meant that Lilly was out of the bath already so it wouldn't be long before Becky was back downstairs. Alice really needed to make her understand she hadn't meant to hurt her.

'Look, we all say things on the spur of the moment,' said Kate, 'but what brought it on?'

'It was something Frank said last night that got me thinking.' She launched into the whole story of Frank's past. How he got his girlfriend pregnant at eighteen and how they hadn't stayed together but he'd stayed involved in his daughter's life.'

'I had no idea,' said Kate, shaking her head. 'So you have a sort of step-daughter, then?'

'Well, not exactly, but Louise is a great kid and I'm very lucky we get on brilliantly.'

Kate was counting on her fingers. 'Oh, my God! So your step-daughter would be older than me. That's gas.'

'Stop, will you? You're making me feel ancient.'

'But at least you didn't have to go through all that pregnancy and baby stuff. And she even had those horrible teenage years behind her by the time she came into your life.'

'Kate!' Becky was back in the room, and this time it was Kate who was subject to her glare. 'I can't believe you said that.'

'Jesus, Becks. You gave me the fright of my life. What have I done now?'

'It's okay, Becky.' Alice didn't want a scene.

'It's not okay, Alice! Kate, you really need to think before you speak. You know Alice wasn't able to have children so why would you say something cruel like that?'

Alice recoiled at Becky's words. Just hearing them spoken out loud was very confronting. 'Don't worry about—'

'Oh, God. I'm so sorry, Alice. Me and my big mouth. Again.'

'Well, I can hardly admonish you when I've just put my foot in it myself.' Alice turned to Becky. 'I'm really sorry for saying what I did, Becky. I didn't mean it to come out quite like that.'

'I know,' sighed Becky, sitting back down at the table. 'And I'm sorry I reacted that way but you'll both have to understand that although I asked for your help, the final decision lies with me. This is not something that's going to affect *your* lives – it's mine and Lilly's that would be turned upside down and I can't let that happen without good reason.'

Kate nodded. 'But you were so excited about finding him a few weeks ago. What's changed so much? I mean, I know the whole homeless thing was a shock, but it seems like there's more to it.'

Suddenly Becky put her hands up to her face and a muffled sob escaped her lips. Alice was quick to run to her side.

'Becky, what is it? What's upsetting you so much? I hate seeing you like this.'

'I … I can't …'

'Come on, let's get you into the sitting room where it's more comfortable and we can talk about this properly. Kate, grab that bottle of red that's opened over there and a large glass for Becky.'

'I really don't want to talk about—'

'I'm not taking no for an answer.' Alice spoke with authority but inside she was shaking. She was worried what she was going to find out.

They sat on the brown leather sofa in uncomfortable silence for a few minutes while Becky cried quietly. When she eventually stopped, Alice, who was still holding her hand, was first to speak. 'What is it, Becky? I suspect this is about more than just Dennis Prendergast.'

'It *is* about him,' insisted Becky. 'Nobody seems to understand that I don't want to have anything to do with him. He's a homeless, no good, alcoholic, druggie—'

'Jesus, Becks.' Kate looked shocked. 'How do you know that? Have I missed something?'

'He's homeless, Kate. Aren't all homeless people the same? Why else would they be in that situation?'

Alice shook her head. 'Ah, come on, Becky. You can't be serious. You can't tar them all with the same brush.'

'You know *nothing*, Alice,' said Becky, pulling her hand away and dabbing at her eyes with her sleeve. 'Neither of you do. You don't know *anything* about my life.'

'Well then, tell us.' Kate's voice was barely audible. She was visibly shaken by Becky's outburst.

Becky hesitated, then looked at the two girls. 'I promised myself I wouldn't talk about it but if it will get you two off my back …'

'What is it, love?' Alice was almost afraid to breathe.

'Well, I reckon I know a thing or two about homelessness. When he wasn't hanging around making our lives hell, my father lived on the streets.'

Alice couldn't help her sharp intake of breath and Kate's jaw almost dropped to the floor. Nobody spoke for a few seconds and Alice willed Becky to continue.

'And don't feel sorry for him, whatever you do. He was a no-good, violent drunk who took every opportunity to knock seven bells out of my mother.'

'Oh, God, Becky,' Alice said, tears welling up in her eyes. 'I'm so sorry. I didn't know.'

'Of course you didn't. When I left London, I left that part of my life behind and I never, ever want to go back to it.'

'That's awful, Becks.' Kate shook her head. 'I can't imagine how that must have been for your family. Did he hit you and your sister too?'

'Kate!' Alice couldn't believe she'd be so blunt.

'It's a fair question,' said Becky, curling her feet up beneath her on the sofa. 'He didn't, actually. It was always just her. But Joanna and I got to witness it often enough. And that's something you *never* forget.'

'The black eyes!' blurted Alice. 'I knew something wasn't right.'

'What black eyes?' Kate looked puzzled.

'I had a procedure a few weeks ago and ended up with two shiners. Becky immediately assumed Frank was knocking me about.'

Becky nodded. 'Sorry about that, Alice. But you can see why I'd think it. I lost count of the number of black eyes I watched my father give my mother over the years.'

Kate wanted to know more. 'But you said your dad was homeless sometimes. Did he not live with you?'

'He did mostly. Then he'd go on a mad drunken binge and spend months on end on the streets. My mum would often go and find him and try to persuade him to come home, but me and Joanna used to pray that he wouldn't.'

'God, what a horrible way to live your lives,' said Alice, tears welling up in her eyes. 'And why did your mother want him home if he was treating her so badly?'

'She loved him. It seems ridiculous and unbelievable, but she really loved him.'

'So she'd bring him back home, the beatings would start again and he'd eventually go away on another binge?' Kate looked ashen at the thought.

'Yep. That's about it. It was a vicious circle. We begged her to leave him. We tried to show her how much better our lives were when he wasn't there, but she just wouldn't listen. She said she'd rather have him with all his flaws than not have him at all.'

'The poor woman. It must have been—'

'Save your sympathy, Alice. She made her decision. She had plenty of chances to get away but she chose the way she wanted to live. That's why I couldn't wait to get away.'

'I honestly don't know what to say,' Alice said, upset to think of the horrors Becky had gone through. 'I'm glad you told us, though. Have you not had any contact with your mum since you came to Ireland?'

'I've never been back. Things had got really bad before I left. Mum's depression had consumed her and she'd turned to alcohol herself. I think Dad was happy to see her drinking and somehow the beatings weren't as frequent when they were getting drunk together.'

Silence hung in the room again until Kate piped up. 'It must have been horrific for you, Becks. I'm really sorry you had to go through that, but, at the risk of sounding stupid, how does this relate to Dennis? Are you comparing him to your father?'

Becky thought for a moment. 'I was often dragged along with Mum when she went out looking for Dad. My memories of the streets are of drunks or druggies looking for a piece of Mum in exchange for information about Dad's whereabouts.'

'But that doesn't sound like the Dennis you described to us,' said Alice, watching Becky carefully. 'From what you said, he seemed like a respectable guy who's just fallen on hard times.'

Becky stood up suddenly. 'Listen, I don't want to be rude but I told you my story so you'd understand. I want … no, I *need* you to back off. I really don't care what sort of person Dennis Prendergast is because I'm having nothing more to do with him.'

'Becky, I think that you're—'

'Shut up, Kate. Just shut up. I really don't want to argue with you again. My mind is made up and considering what I've just told you, I think you should back off.'

Alice stood up and grabbed Becky into a hug. 'Of course we will, Becky. Won't we, Kate?'

Kate nodded her head reluctantly.

Alice continued. 'We won't say another word about him but you know where we are if you want to talk. Now we'll head off and leave you in peace, unless you want us to stay for another while?'

'No!' Becky was quick to answer. 'I don't mean to sound rude but I really could do with just getting some sleep now. I'm exhausted.'

'Of course you are. Come on, Kate. Let's leave her in peace.'

They said their goodbyes and Alice dropped Kate to the bus stop. What a night that had turned out to be, Alice thought as she drove off. She couldn't wait to get home to Frank and tell him all about it. It felt good to be going home to someone. She'd spent far too many lonely nights with just her own thoughts for company. Poor Becky was missing out by not having someone special in her life. It wasn't as if she didn't get offers – a stunner like her wouldn't be single for long if she didn't want to be. Maybe she should give her a gentle nudge towards a man to help her forget all this Dennis Prendergast stuff. Yes, that's what she'd do. She'd help her find a man of her own so she could begin to build a future – just like she and Frank were doing. Letting go of the past was the best thing Alice had done in years and it would be the same for Becky – as soon as Becky was willing to let it go.

# Chapter 21

'Take a seat there, Len. I'll be with you in just a minute.' Becky was completing a large transfer from a client's account and needed to give it her full attention before dealing with Len Sherwood.

'No problem, Becky. I'm early anyway.'

She tapped away on her computer, aware of Len's eyes watching her every move. Len owned Sherwood's Wholesale and was a very good customer. He regularly transferred money overseas to suppliers and always insisted that Becky looked after him. He asked her out almost every time he saw her, but she'd always politely refused, telling him that she couldn't date a customer. She knew from his file that he was thirty-five, single and loaded – on paper, he was the perfect catch.

'Now, Len. Sorry about that. I just needed to get those off before three. So what can I do for you today?'

'I have a couple of transfers here but I need them to go as soon as possible. Any chance you could stick them in today?' He ran his hands through the tight curls in his hair and his blue eyes twinkled.

Becky glanced at her watch. 'It's cutting it a bit tight, but give them here and I'll see what I can do.'

'Ah, you're an angel. I should have got them in to you yesterday but I was just so busy it slipped my mind.'

'Well, all I can do is try. I'll input them now and see if the system accepts them. Hang on there just a moment.' She typed furiously, determined to get the transfers through if she could. She hated to let anything beat her and, besides, Len was on the list of customers the bank wanted to keep sweet.

'There you go,' she said, beaming. 'All gone through. And just in the nick of time too.'

'Thanks, Becky. I owe you one. Why don't you let me take you out to dinner tonight to say thanks?'

'Len, you know I can't date you. And, besides, I have Lilly. I can't just go swanning out whenever it suits me.' Len had commented once on the picture of Lilly on Becky's desk and she'd told him all about her little girl.

'Of course, I totally forgot about your daughter. Well, why don't we make it lunch? Just name the day.'

Becky laughed. 'Len, you're impossible. You know I'm going to say no, don't you?'

'I know,' Len sighed. 'But you can't blame a guy for trying.'

'You need to give up on me and go and find yourself a nice girl.'

Len stood up and pushed his chair under the desk. 'I'll never give up on you, Becky. What fun would that be?'

'Go on, Mr Sherwood, before I have you thrown out for harassment.' But Becky was smiling as she watched him walk away. She liked Len. She liked the banter they had together. She liked a lot of things about him – but she didn't fancy him. She wanted someone who made her heart beat fast and filled her with feelings of passion. Suddenly a picture of Dennis Prendergast popped into her head and she had to shake herself. What was she thinking? She could never, ever fancy a man like that. God, she needed to get a grip.

'So what's the story with lover boy, then?'

Becky almost jumped out of her skin as Kate appeared beside her desk. 'Wh – what? Who do you mean?'

'Luscious Len, of course. Who did you think I meant?'

'Oh! Len was just doing some transfers. Nothing out of the ordinary.' Becky could feel the heat rise in her cheeks.

'Becky Greene! Are you blushing? Did he ask you out again? He did, didn't he?'

'Well, if you must know, yes, he did. And I refused, as usual.'

'Ah, come on, Becks. You'll have to put the guy out of his misery at some stage. You can't keep on telling him no.'

'I can and I will. How many times do I have to tell you I'm not interested in Len Sherwood?'

Kate raised her eyebrows. 'But you did say you were open to finding a man now. You said you were ready.'

'I know, Kate. And that still goes. But it has to be the right man.'

'Like Dennis Prendergast, you mean.'

'Oh, for God's sake, Kate. Didn't you hear a word I said the other night? Not only am I not interested in Dennis Prendergast, but the man repulses me.'

'Okay, okay. I'm sorry. You know how I speak without thinking. I suppose I'm still living in a fairy-tale world where you and Lilly's father live happily ever after.'

'Well, that's *never* going to happen so you can get it out of your head right now.'

Kate sighed. 'I know. Let's have lunch tomorrow and we can have a chat. I promise I won't mention the name Dennis Prendergast even once.'

'That's a deal. Now I'd better get on with this lot or I'll never get home this evening.'

Becky felt unsettled by both Kate's mention of Dennis and by the fact that he'd popped into her own head so easily. She wanted him out of her life and out of her mind. Maybe she should consider going out with Len after all. It might get Kate and Alice off her back and would also give her someone else to think about. And, besides, maybe she wasn't giving him a proper chance. Who knew, she might even grow to fancy him in time. She could feel a plan forming and felt a bubble of excitement rise up inside her. Len Sherwood was very soon going to get the surprise of his life.

Dennis took his time walking down Grafton Street. It was just after midnight, but he couldn't face settling down for the night just yet. The street was buzzing with people coming out of pubs and pouring into fast-food restaurants for a post-booze burger. He remembered those nights well.

Sometimes he allowed himself to think that things could get better. But then he'd think of Isabella and it would bring him right back down again. He wanted to get off the streets but sometimes he wondered if he deserved to. The cold truth of it was that the transition from homelessness was never an easy one, but the recession meant that jobs were even harder to come by for people like him. It was a vicious circle and sometimes he wondered if he'd ever get out of it.

He'd slept in the same spot in the city for months now. You could never say the streets were safe, but his little recessed doorway provided a bit of shelter, and he found that people bothered him less there – apart from the odd asshole coming out of the pub and thinking they were funny for mocking the homeless guy. In other spots, he'd been kicked, spat on and even robbed of the measly few euro in his tapping box.

He was glad things were quietening down when he arrived to set up his sleeping bag for the night. He hated having an audience while he was getting himself settled. It was humiliating. He usually got himself into the sleeping bag as quickly as he could, pulling his hat half way down his face. This made him feel invisible. And to most, he probably was. Just another one of the rapidly growing homeless community. Just another nuisance on the streets.

He closed his eyes and thought of Martha, his new friend in the coffee shop. She reminded him of his mother – all clucky and full of chat. At least that's how his mother *used* to be. God love her. If only she knew what had become of her son. But Martha had proven to be the one bright light in his day. He'd taken to popping in to her shop almost every day now and she'd always have a slice of cake at the ready for him. He always offered to pay, of course, but she'd never hear of it.

'Let's just call you a taster,' she smiled one day as she presented an enormous piece of strawberry cheesecake to him. 'You taste the cakes and tell me whether I should keep them on the menu or not.'

He'd always be grateful to her – not just for the cake but for the kind words. No matter how busy she was, she always took the time to chat to him and see how he was doing. She didn't pry but had told him that if he ever wanted to chat, she was there. She didn't judge. Not like so many others.

He pulled his sleeping bag tighter up to his neck and reached into his trouser pocket for his old Cartier watch. It was one of the things he'd held on to from his previous life. Only the battered face remained. It was hard to believe that it had once cost over two thousand euro and had been attached to the most exquisite leather strap. It was almost two o'clock. In another few hours, it would be getting bright and the city would come alive again. These were the worse few hours. They were the hours when all the loss, shame and uncertainty would fill his head and thoughts of how he could end it all flashed through his mind.

He'd planned it more than once. Suicide often seemed like a blessed escape from the misery, and in his darkest moments, he even craved death. He'd walk alongside the River Liffey and imagine jumping in. Drowning was supposed to be the best way to go – painless and even peaceful. He'd imagine that feeling of freedom – no more pain and misery and hopelessness. But every time he reached rock bottom, he managed to pull himself back. The fighter in him would tell himself that he'd find a way out. Suicide wasn't the answer. Determination and hope were. Although with every passing day, his guilt was swallowing up every last bit of hope he had.

Just as he was dropping off to sleep, he felt a jab in his side and his eyes shot open. It took him a moment to focus and just as he did, another sharp pain hit his arm.

'Oh, look, it actually moves!'

Shit! That was all he needed – drunken assholes. He rubbed his side that had started throbbing from the kick but kept his mouth closed.

'Well, old man, don't you have a tongue in your head? Or are you mute as well as stupid?'

The guy couldn't have been more than eighteen or nineteen, clearly drunk, as were his friends, who were finding the whole thing hilarious.

'What do you think, lads? Maybe if I pissed on him, he'd have something to say.'

'Ah, leave him alone, Shay,' slurred one of the girls. 'Sure he's not doing any harm.'

Dennis didn't dare move an inch, willing them all to do as the girl said. To his great relief, they all started to walk on, too drunk to really know what was happening. Except for the Shay guy. Dennis could read him like a book. He wasn't going to be told what to do by some girl.

'Well, maybe I'll let you off today since I'm in such a good mood. But I'll just take this as a memento of when we met.' He reached down and whipped the rucksack from under Dennis' head.

'No!' roared Dennis, jumping up and grabbing at his bag. Everything he owned in the world was in there and he'd already lost way too much.

'Here, lads,' laughed Shay, shouting after his friends. 'The mute *does* talk after all.' To Dennis' horror, two of the lads came back and the three of them proceeded to toss the bag from one to the other.

'Look, boys, I don't want any trouble. Just give me back the bag and we'll leave it at that.'

'Haha! The old man thinks he can call the shots.' It was another of the guys talking and Dennis was beginning to realise he wasn't going to win this one.

But he wasn't letting his bag go that easily so he made a swipe at it and in doing so, elbowed one of the guys in the face. And that was it. The three of them launched at him, punching and kicking until he had no other choice but to just curl up in the foetal position and let them at it.

Seconds later they were gone, their drunken cackles ringing in his ears. He was at least glad to see they'd left his bag, so he managed to drag it and himself back over to where his sleeping bag was. He noticed a few people across the street had stopped to watch the show but when he made eye contact with them, they walked on with their heads down. Their indifference hurt as much as his wounds.

Suddenly, he felt exhausted. He reckoned he'd be bruised when he woke up in the morning but the damage didn't seem to be too bad. He was probably lucky they were so drunk and hadn't been at their full strength. He zipped his sleeping back up around him again and settled down for the second time. It was funny that he didn't even feel afraid anymore. In theory, he should be living in fear of those guys coming back but so what if they did? They couldn't break him any more than he was broken already. All he wanted to do now was sleep. As he drifted off, he was aware of people passing by. People with a life. He wondered if he'd ever have a life again.

# Chapter 22

'Come on, Alice. Don't you want to be young any more?'

'Ah, Lilly, love, of course I do. But I'm not sure anything is working. Maybe I should just grow old gracefully.'

'What does "grace-illy" mean?'

Alice laughed at how Lilly's big brown eyes opened wide in her inquisitive face, as she stood there with a tub of kiwi face mask in her hands.

'It means that maybe I should accept that I'm forty-seven and stop trying to make myself look thirty-seven!'

'Oh, but it's sooooo much fun. Can we just have one mask before Mummy comes home? Pleeeeease?'

How could she resist. 'Okay, Lillypops. Just a quick one though because I don't want your mummy coming home to a mess.'

'Yay!' The little girl squealed with delight as Alice slapped the gritty green cream over her face.

'Why is Mummy so grumpy?' Lilly asked, as they lay back on the sofa to let their masks dry.

Oh, God, she was off again. 'She's not grumpy, darling. She's just tired.'

'But why is she tired? She told me she sits down all day.'

'Yes, but that doesn't mean she's not busy. She has to work all day and then come home and look after you.'

'But she was never grumpy before. Do you think it's my fault?'

'Of course it's not your fault. Why would you think that?'

'Dunno. Maybe because I drew that picture of a daddy. That's when she started to get grumpy so I think she's just cross with me.'

'Sweetheart, I promise you, she's not cross with you. I think she's probably just busy with stuff in work.'

'Like Dennis?'

Alice froze. 'What do you mean?'

'Dennis, 'member? The man in work who was always being late and she had to talk to him.'

'Oh, yes, that's probably what it is. I bet your mummy will come through that door in a few minutes with a big smile on her face. You just wait and see.'

'I think I don't want this mask on any more, Alice. It smells like the taste of kiwi.'

'You're absolutely right,' Alice smiled. 'And I love kiwis so if you're not careful, I might just lick it off your face.'

'Eeewww! That's 'gusting.' The little girl recoiled as Alice made a lunge for her. Her giggles filled the room as Alice tickled her and they both fell off the sofa, laughing.

'What's going on in here, then?'

'Mummy, Mummy. We putted on horrible masks so Alice could be young but she wanted to lick mine off and I wouldn't let her.'

Becky smiled and lifted Lilly up into her arms. 'Well, I agree with Alice, sweetie. I think you're good enough to eat!'

'Noooooo!' Lilly wriggled out of her mother's arms and went running out into the hall. 'You can't catch me!'

'Come back in here, Lillypops,' laughed Alice. If I don't take that stuff off your face, your mummy will be picking bits of kiwi sludge up off the floor for weeks.'

Five minutes later, Lilly was cleaned up and sitting watching *The Simpsons* on telly. Becky walked Alice out to the door.

'I have to admit, Alice. I've always been sceptical about all this anti-ageing stuff but your skin is positively glowing. It really seems to be working.'

Alice took her coat from the banisters. 'Do you think so? To be honest, since Frank moved in, I haven't had as much time for my skincare regime.'

'Ha! That's typical, isn't it? Maybe you've been using all that stuff for too long and now you've allowed your skin to take a break, it's finally able to breathe.'

'Maybe. Or maybe it's the hot flushes giving me the glow from within!'

'Oh, God. You and your menopause. I'll be an expert on it when my time comes.'

'That won't be for a long time yet, Becky. Sure you're only a young one.'

Becky opened the front door and closed it over again when a blast of cold air hit them. 'Sometimes I feel way older than my years. If I'm not careful, I'll be an old woman way before you.'

'Well, that will never happen. But ...' Alice wasn't sure whether to say anything about her conversation with Lilly.

'But what?'

'Nothing. I was just thinking, I mean, Lilly was saying—'

'Well, spit it out, Alice.'

'It's just that I was chatting to Lilly earlier and she was saying how you were grumpy lately. I told her you were just busy in work but she said that she thought it was her fault.'

Becky looked shocked. 'God, the poor thing. Where did she get that idea from? Have I really been grumpy? I may have been a bit distracted by the whole Dennis thing, but that's over now.'

'If I'm honest, you *have* been a bit grumpy,' Alice said. 'And I know it's none of my business and with the risk of getting my head bitten off again, are you sure the whole Dennis Prendergast thing isn't still playing on your mind?'

Becky looked angry for a moment and then her face softened. 'Honestly, that's all in the past. I've moved on.'

'Really?'

'Honestly, Alice. I know it consumed me for a while, but not anymore. In fact, the only man I'll be thinking about for the next while is the one I'm going on a date with.'

Alice's jaw dropped. 'A date? You? Really?'

'Yes, me. Why is that so surprising?'

'Don't get me wrong – I'm delighted. Thrilled, in fact. But I just didn't think you'd ever … well, you know. Tell me all. Who is he and where did you meet him?'

Becky laughed. 'His name is Len Sherwood and he's a customer in work.'

'Ah, he's the one who's always asking you out.'

'Yep, that's him. I've decided to give in to his charms. I honestly don't know why I've refused him for so long. He's a really nice guy and very handsome too.'

'That's fantastic, Becky. I'm really happy for you. So when is this big date, then?'

'We haven't firmed up on arrangements yet, but I'll be talking to him tomorrow. And I know I might be pushing things, considering how I've spoken to you lately, but could I ask you to mind Lilly again if we arrange a date?'

'Of course. That goes without saying. And speaking of Lilly, maybe you should talk to her. Let her know she's not to blame for you being in bad form.'

Becky shook her head. 'I feel awful that she didn't say something to me about it. What does it say about me that she'd prefer to talk to the nanny?'

Alice felt a sudden rage. 'Well, this *nanny* spends an awful lot of time with Lilly so maybe she just feels close to me.'

'God, Alice. I didn't mean that the way it sounded. Of course she's close to you. She loves you. I just feel like a failure sometimes. I go to work every day just so I can give Lilly everything she needs but I worry that I'm not there enough for her emotionally.'

'Don't worry.' Alice softened when she saw the look of distress on Becky's face. 'You're a great mum and Lilly knows that too. I just think this whole Dennis thing has stressed you out and Lilly has been picking up on it. Take her out for a pizza tomorrow and all will be fine again.'

To Alice's surprise, Becky threw her arms around her and hugged her tight. 'Thanks, Alice. And I'm sorry again for what I said. You're way more than a nanny to us. You're my best friend and a second mother to Lilly. She wouldn't be turning out to be such a wonderful girl if it wasn't for your input.'

Alice blushed. 'Thanks for saying that, Becky. You know how much she means to me. If I'd ever been lucky enough to have a girl of my own, I'd have wanted her to be exactly like Lilly.'

There was nothing to be said after that. Becky hugged her again as she headed out the door, pulling up the collar of her winter coat to fend off the cold wind as she ran to her car. She was exhausted. Her skin may be glowing but the rest of her body was letting her down. She was too tired lately to do any exercise and she'd noticed the extra pounds piling on. Bloody menopause. She'd willingly accept her womanly workings shutting down if they'd ever worked properly in the first place. It seemed so unfair. But, funnily enough, it didn't make her cry as often as it used to. Frank had come into her life at just the right time and saved her from herself. He was a spiritual man and some of it was rubbing off on her. He believed that everyone was dealt particular cards in life for a reason. The way things were was the way they were meant to be. Alice had to believe that now.

❀

Kate heard Garreth's key in the door and rushed into the kitchen. She filled the kettle with water and pottered around, trying to look normal. He'd been out at a gig all evening and, despite how she felt, she was dying to see him.

'Jesus, Kate. You look like death. What's up with you?'

'Oh, thanks for that.'

'Don't be like that. It's just you look so pale.' He walked over to her and planted a kiss on her lips. 'You're not sick again, are you?'

'Garreth, I'm fine. Stop fussing, will you?'

'I can't help worrying, Kate. You almost fainted yesterday and you don't look too steady on your feet now either. Maybe that bug you got a couple of weeks ago hasn't gone. You should go and see the doctor.'

'Maybe,' Kate conceded. She just wanted to get him off her back. 'But I'm actually feeling better tonight than I have in the past couple of weeks so hopefully I'm on the mend.'

'But I still think you should—'

'Garreth, honestly, I'm fine. Go and have a shower and I'll make us a pot of tea and some sandwiches. We can have them in front of the telly. I recorded *Homeland* earlier on.'

He seemed reluctant but nodded. 'Okay, sounds good to me. Just give me five minutes.'

Kate breathed a sigh of relief when he disappeared up the stairs. She was now using the laxatives regularly and they were really beginning to take their toll. She felt sick most of the time – and she was terrified when she left the house in case she had an accident – but she was also starting to see results. Her jeans were loose around her waist and her hip bone was beginning to protrude. She was going to a casting the following week for an ad campaign for a well-known clothing label and if she kept going like this, she'd be skinny enough by then to compete with any size zero teenager.

Poor Garreth. He was so patient and kind. She'd rebuffed his advances for the last few nights, claiming she felt exhausted, and he'd backed away to give her space. Much as she loved sex, she didn't think her nether regions would be up to much fun at the moment. She bloody well hoped all this would be worth it in the end.

She poured boiling water into the teapot to heat it up and began to root in the fridge for something to put on their sandwiches. Even the thought of eating was making her stomach do somersaults. But she'd persevere. She needed this. Nothing in this life came without a price and this was a small price to pay to finally be who she wanted to be.

# Chapter 23

'So, Len, how come a catch like you is still single? Is there something I should know?'

'I just haven't found the right girl yet. God, that sounds so clichéd, doesn't it? But unfortunately it's true.'

'So you're telling me that in all your thirty-five years on this earth, nobody suitable has come along?' The wine was loosening Becky's tongue and she was enjoying flirting.

Len raised his eyebrows. 'Thirty-five! Hmmmm, I think somebody has been snooping in my personal file.'

'Ooops,' giggled Becky. 'I may have come across the information at some stage. Of course it would be completely inappropriate if I'd looked it up for my own personal reasons.'

'Well, I won't tell if you don't. To be honest, I think it's very flattering. It's not every day that a gorgeous lady seeks out my credentials.'

Becky took another sip of her wine. 'No need to flatter yourself. I just wanted to make sure you weren't an axe murderer or anything.'

'And would it be likely to say that in my bank details if I was?'

'Ha! You got me there.'

Becky was really enjoying herself. It was her second date with Len in as many days. She'd shocked the life out of him by ringing him and telling him she'd go out with him. He'd insisted on bringing her to lunch the very next day and she'd surprised herself at how much fun she'd had. Tonight, they were in a small, intimate pub just off O'Connell Street in the city centre and things were going well.

'Ready for another?' Len pointed to her almost empty glass but she placed her hand over it.

'Not for me, thanks. I should really be heading off soon. I promised Alice I'd only be a couple of hours.'

'Not even one for the road?'

'Nope. Sorry. I've really had a lovely time, Len, but—'

'I know, I know. You've had a lovely time but you're not ready for a relationship. I know the score.'

Becky glared at him, her good mood fading. 'Actually, I was simply going to say I've had a lovely time but you know how it is. Lilly comes first and I need to get home.'

'Oh! Sorry, I just assumed. Ignore me. I'm an asshole.'

'Yes, you are. But a nice asshole.'

Len beamed. 'So I haven't ruined my chances, then?'

'Well, let's just say if I'm home before eleven, you've passed the first test.'

'Come on, then – what are you waiting for?' He jumped up from his stool and grabbed his jacket. 'I can never resist a challenge.'

They walked outside and headed towards the taxi rank. There was no hand-holding but that suited Becky perfectly. She'd never been a touchy-feely sort of girl and hated public displays of affection. But she had to admit she liked the feeling of being out with a man again. Len was good company and a perfect gentleman. He looked hot too, in his jeans and casual shirt, strands of his dark curly hair falling haphazardly over his blue eyes.

They walked more or less in silence and when they reached the line of taxis, he offered to drop her first before going home himself.

'Don't be silly,' Becky said, surprised but pleased by his generous offer. 'We live in completely different directions. But thanks anyway.'

'Well, if you're sure. I had a great night. I hope we can do it again soon?'

Becky looked at his earnest face and knew she wanted that too. 'Give me a ring next week and we'll arrange something.'

His six foot frame towered over her and he hesitated before bending down to place a short, soft kiss on her lips. It took her by surprise but not in an unpleasant way. She hopped into the waiting taxi and waved as they sped off. It had been a long time since she'd been kissed and it felt good. If that was a taster of what was to come, she couldn't wait to see what would happen next.

She closed her eyes to relive the moment in her mind. Those soft lips. The taste of his maleness. She pictured her hand stroking Dennis' beard as their lips met in a long, passionate kiss— Oh, for God's sake! How could she picture Dennis Prendergast at a time like this? She'd gone there once but never again. She could never be with a man like that. She needed somebody like Len and when she gave herself to him, Dennis Prendergast would be out of her mind for good.

❋

Dennis pushed the door of Martha's Kitchen and stepped inside. It was a few days since his altercation on the street and he'd been keeping a low profile. The bruises were mostly on his stomach and side but he'd copped a nasty shoe to the face and his left eye had blown up like a balloon. The swelling had gone down but a nasty yellowish-purple bruise was still visible.

'Jesus, Dennis. What happened? Come on and sit down.' Martha spotted him as soon as he walked in and fussed around him, showing him to his usual table.

'I'm grand. Nothing to worry about. You'd want to see the other guy.'

'Don't make a joke of it, love. Who did this to you? I hope you told the police.'

'What good would it do? Do you actually think they'd have gone off looking for some random drunks who kicked a homeless guy?'

Martha's eyes filled with tears and he had to fight back his own. He wasn't used to such compassion and Martha was slowly becoming his lifeline in a world that was feeling more unbearable.

'Well, let me get you something to eat, then. I reckon that eye could do with more than a slice of cake. I'll get you a bacon sandwich and a nice mug of tea.'

'Thanks, Martha. That's very kind of you, but you'll have to let me pay today. The tapping has been quite lucrative these past few days. The bashed up face is quite a money spinner.'

'Listen, I've a couple of things need shifting in the kitchen if you're up to it after, so it's not as if you're not earning it. And, anyway, it's quiet in here today and I'll only end up throwing out stuff if it's not used.' She shuffled off and as Dennis watched after her, he was reminded once again of his own mother. She used to love baking too. When his dad had died of a stroke when Dennis was just fourteen, his mother had been amazingly strong. She'd put her own grief aside and had given all her time and energy to him. It wasn't an easy thing to lose your dad at such a young age and Dennis had been traumatised. The smell of baking always brought him back to those days because each day when he'd come home from school, the waft of something delicious in the oven would always hit him even before he'd walk through the door. It was only years later that his mother told him that baking had saved her.

'Here we go.' Martha was back with a whopping triple-decker sandwich and a mug of tea. 'And there's a slice of whatever cake you fancy behind the counter for when you're finished that.'

Dennis nodded his thanks, grateful for what Martha was doing. She'd asked him to do a couple of odd jobs over the past number of weeks and it had made him feel worth something again. It didn't matter that it was only lifting something heavy or fixing a broken drawer – it gave him hope. He didn't need to be wheeler-dealing in the business world. He didn't need to be dripping in money. In fact, those sorts of values didn't impress him any more. He just needed an honest day's work to afford him a little place of his own and a sense of purpose in the world.

'So what can I tempt you with now, then?' He hadn't even noticed

Martha hovering over him with a fresh mug of tea. 'The apple pie is all gone but I have a lovely strawberry cheesecake or a rhubarb crumble.'

'Rhubarb crumble sounds delicious, thanks.'

'Custard?'

'Of course.'

'Be back in a jiffy.'

Dennis watched as she deftly served a couple of customers at the same time, juggling hot drinks and slicing cakes. He reckoned she was about seventy but it was hard to tell. She seemed to manage in the shop mostly on her own and she did all her own baking. She often had work-experience students come in for a few hours here and there and there was a girl who helped with the early-morning baking but, other than that, she was a one-woman show.

'Here you go. An extra large slice since I'm never going to sell the rest of it before closing. May I?' She pointed to the seat opposite him.

'Of course.' Dennis could feel her eyes on him as he ate spoonfuls of the cake. He could feel a lecture coming on and he really wasn't in the mood.

'I don't want to intrude,' she began. 'But I'm just a little curious.'

'About what?'

'It just seems that … you just seem an unlikely person to be on the streets. Come upon hard times, did you?'

Dennis sighed and nodded. 'You could say that. Would you believe that a couple of years ago, I ran a business, owned my own apartment and had a decent lifestyle?'

'I'd well believe it, love. These are hard times we live in. I often think to myself: There but for the grace of God, go I. None of us are much different really – a piece of bad luck or a bit of good fortune is all that separates us.'

'You're very wise, Martha. And I really appreciate your kindness.'

'Ah, it's nothing. But why don't you go back to the beginning and tell me your story. That is, if you want to.'

Suddenly he *did* want to. It was the first time anyone had ever really shown an interest in his life. Except of course for that journalist who, as it turned out, just couldn't handle it. The words spilled out. He told her everything – well, almost everything. He still couldn't bring himself to talk about Alan McCabe. He didn't want Martha to know. Some things were better left in his head.

# Chapter 24

Dennis did a final check in the mirror. Much better. He'd trimmed his beard right back and had even tidied up his hair with a little scissors. He was still a bit rough around the edges and there were still traces of his bruising, but there was a spark of something in his eyes that had been missing for a long time.

Ever since he'd started going to Martha's and chatting to the old lady, something had changed for him. She'd made him see that there was a thin line between everyone's lives and the only way of stepping over that line onto the other side was to put in the effort and do something about it. Luck didn't just happen – you had to make it happen. At least that's what she said. Martha was a very wise woman.

His brown corduroy trousers had seen better days but they were clean, and the mustard jumper he'd picked up in a charity shop was as good as new. He'd had a good wash at the sink and was actually smelling soapy clean for once. He slung his rucksack over his back and headed out into the cold October air. Today, he was a man with a purpose. He was just like thousands of others – nervous, excited, filled with anticipation. Today he was going for a job interview.

*No experience necessary*, the card had said. *Must be fit and strong, as heavy lifting is involved. Must be available for shift work.* It was perfect for him. He'd taken the card from the notice board in Eurospar in the hope that nobody else would have seen it. He knew it was underhand, but he wanted to give himself the best chance possible of getting the job. Doing odd jobs for Martha had given him the taste of what it was like to be working again, and although she only paid him in food, it felt good.

It didn't take him long to walk down the quays towards Smithfield Square. Dennis had always liked it there. A marketplace since the seventeenth century, it had been rejuvenated during the Celtic Tiger and had become a hive of activity for businesses and tourists. Although no longer open to the public, the observation tower of the old Jameson Whiskey Distillery dominated the landscape and Dennis suddenly felt excited at the thought of working in the area.

He checked the address of the warehouse on the card and headed down the street. They were doing open interviews between twelve and two so there hadn't been any need to ring in advance. The little bubbles of excitement he felt in his stomach were alien to him but it was a good feeling. He had this job in the bag – he was sure of it.

He rounded the corner and his heart almost stopped. Surely this couldn't be it. Surely there must be something else going on. There was a queue of mostly men and a few women, spanning the whole length of the little laneway. Some wore suits and some were more casually dressed but most held folders in their hands – probably CVs and references, something Dennis hadn't figured he'd need for such a casual job.

'Excuse me,' he said to a man at the back of the queue. 'Is this for the warehouse job?'

'Yep. Can you believe it? I was told about it on the qt by a guy who works in there. I told the wife I should get it no problem. I didn't bank on so much competition.'

Dennis' heart sank, but he still joined the queue. He had to remain positive. Martha had taught him that. He'd made so many attempts to pull himself out of the rut he'd fallen into, and each time had given up when the going had got tough. Martha's words rang in his head. *You have to make it happen*. Well, now that he was here, he may as well present himself and see what they had to say.

It took an hour and a half but he was at last sitting in front of a burly-looking man with a double chin and glasses that were way too small for his rounded face. He shifted uncomfortably in his chair while the interviewer looked through some files on his desk. Dennis knew what his game was. He'd done the same himself back in the day when the roles were reversed and he was the interviewer. Keep them waiting so they know who's boss. There was nothing surer to make a potential employee sweat.

'Right, then. Richard Cooney.' The guy held out a large, workman's hand for Dennis to shake. 'And you are?'

'Dennis Prendergast.'

'So Dennis, do you have anything to show us? CV, references?'

Dennis shrank under Richard's stare. 'I didn't bring anything, actually. I thought it was a casual job. It said no experience necessary. But I can tell you about previous jobs, if it helps.'

'That won't be necessary. Can you lift heavy loads?'

'Well, yes, I'm pretty strong. I—'

'Are you flexible with your hours?'

'Definitely. I've nothing going on at—'

'Right, just fill in that form with your name, address and telephone number and we'll be back to you as soon as possible.'

And there was the stumbling block. He stared at the form.

'Is there a problem?' Richard looked over the rim of his glasses.

'No problem, no. It's just that I'm between addresses at the moment. Can I leave that out and just give you my phone number?'

It seemed like ages before he responded. 'Homeless, are you?'

'I … well, I'm just …'

'Listen, son, it doesn't matter a damn to me. I've hired plenty of lads with no home. They're often the ones who'll put in the hard work. Stick in your phone number there and we'll let you know. But there are a lot of people here for just two jobs so don't lose heart if it's a no this time.'

'Thanks very much,' Dennis said, standing up and shaking Richard's hand. He felt a little choked up and couldn't say any more.

Even if he didn't get the job, a little piece of him felt fixed by Richard's words. Maybe there was hope for him yet.

He stepped outside and blinked as the October sun hit his face. He checked his phone and was glad to see the battery was still half charged. He doubted he'd get a call so quickly about the job but he would hate to miss one because his phone was dead. He might even treat himself to a fiver credit and a nice cup of tea.

But as he walked up the quays towards O'Connell Bridge, his mood began to dip again. If only there were some words that could help him forget the guilt he felt. Even if he got himself straightened out with a home and a job, he'd never be free from the torment that occupied his mind.

He stopped and leaned on the wall, looking into the River Liffey. For fuck's sake. Why did he always do this to himself? Why could he not enjoy the little victories instead of always allowing the guilt to win? He raised his fist and punched himself hard on the side of the head. Jesus! He did it again, and again, and again. He knew he must look like a crazy man, but sometimes he honestly thought he was losing his mind. Why did everything have to be so complicated?

He had a sudden urge to see Isabella. He always knew that one day he'd speak to her and maybe now was as good a time as any. He didn't know how he'd do it or what he'd say, but he knew that she was the only one who could set him free. It could go the other way, of course, and he might end up feeling worse, but it was something he had to do.

Ten minutes later, he was on the bus to Swords, his head a myriad of emotions. Saturday shoppers chatted happily to each other as he looked out the window at the world passing by. Would he ever feel normal like these people again?

He'd been so lost in thought that he almost missed the stop, but he managed to hop off just in time. He looked across the road and was disappointed to see there was no car at the house. Damn! He'd psyched himself up so much to talk to her and now he felt like he was back to square one. Typical of his luck.

He walked on down the road towards the Pavilions Shopping Centre. He needed to just sit and think. Everything was becoming muddled in his head, and that usually signalled the start of a downward spiral. But he wasn't going to let it happen again. Today had been an okay day, and okay was a hell of a lot better than awful.

He was glad to sit down in McDonald's with a cup of tea and an apple pie. He was still living off the money he'd made from tapping when he had a bruised face. He wouldn't recommend it, but a battered-up look was definitely the way to get noticed. He took a slug of the tea and sat back and closed his eyes. He wished he could just have a sleep in the warmth of the restaurant but he'd probably be thrown out. And besides, the place seemed to be full of kids screaming and shouting so he wouldn't get much rest anyway.

'Mummmmyyyy! Ryan took the green thing out of my burger and ate it.'

'But he hates the green thing. He *never* eats it.'

'Yes I do. He's just saying that. I'm not eating it now. Buy me another one.'

'That's enough, Gino,' came a woman's shrill, accented voice. 'Ryan is right – you never eat it.'

Dennis had been aware of the kids fighting behind him but when he heard the name Gino, coupled with the woman's voice, he swung around. And there they were. Isabella and her three children right behind him. His heart began to beat faster and he suddenly felt conspicuous. He was sure she didn't even know he existed but it was still very confronting to see her at such close quarters. He slipped seamlessly into the seat to his side so that he could have a better view. She looked older close-up. More stressed. But it was no wonder. The kids were a handful and there was nobody there to help her look after them.

'Right, come on, I've had enough of this.' Isabella threw all the leftovers onto the tray and ushered the children out of their seats. 'Gino, put that rubbish in the bin and I don't want to hear another word about that burger.'

'But, Mum—'

'Gino is the rubbish man, Gino is the rubbish man …' sang the other twin, causing Gino to hit out at him, barely missing his face.

Dennis' heart went out to Isabella as she practically dragged the two boys away from each other, lifted her daughter onto her hip and rushed off. Dennis stared after her and felt numb. To think he'd planned to talk to her today. What had he been thinking? Did he expect that she'd free him from his guilt? Did he actually think she'd even want to look at him when she realised who he was? He must have been deluded.

A beep came from his phone that was charging beside him. It wasn't often he got messages so he grabbed it up to check.

Sorry, you haven't been successful today. Best of luck with the job hunt. Richard Cooney.

He wasn't surprised. But he wasn't going to let himself be defeated. He didn't get the job but at least the guy had been decent enough to let him know. He felt exhausted and all he wanted to do at that moment was bury his head and sleep. But he wouldn't let Martha down – he'd take the glimmer of hope he'd felt today and do his best to build on it in the weeks ahead.

# Chapter 25

'Lunch is better for me, Len. I can hardly ask Alice to babysit again. It hasn't even been a week since she did it last.'

'Lunch it is so. How about tomorrow?'

'Yep, tomorrow is good. Let's say I'll meet you at Bewley's in Grafton Street. I fancy getting well away from this place for an hour – it'll be a good way to start the weekend.'

'Becky.' A voice shouted across the office. 'Joe Feeley is on line two. He wants to talk to you about some transfers you did yesterday.'

Becky placed the palm of her hand over the phone. 'Tell him I'll call him back. I'm busy.'

'But he said it's important.'

'Len, sorry about this. I just need to put you on hold for a minute.' She switched to line two and had Joe sorted in no time. Some of her customers drove her mad. They always wanted *her* to deal with things when sometimes it was just a simple matter that anyone could handle.

'I'm back, Len. Sorry about that. You know what it's like.'

'It's no problem. It's part of what makes you so attractive. I love a powerful woman.'

'Ha! You wouldn't say that about me if you saw me on the floor, playing Twister with Lilly.'

'Don't put yourself down, Becky. You're gorgeous and strong and I'm mad about you.'

Becky blushed. Len was easy to be with. They hadn't got past a peck on the lips yet but the way things were going, she felt sure they'd be at the next level very soon. It excited and scared her in equal measure.

'Are you still there, Becky?'

'Yes, yes, sorry. What were we saying?'

'I was just saying how strong and beautiful you are. And I was thinking, if babysitters are a problem, why don't I come over to your place some night. We can watch a movie and I'll bring the wine. What do you say?'

'I'm not sure. I have to think about Lilly. Maybe you can call to the house next time we go out and you can say hello to her – get to know her a bit first.'

'Okay. If that's what you want.'

Becky noticed the slight edge to his voice. 'Well, having a child means that it's *never* about what *I* want. Lilly always has to come first.'

'Of course she does. I didn't mean to be flippant about it. I bet you're a wonderful mother.'

He sounded sincere. 'Thanks. I try my—'

'Becky, Becky, there's someone out at the front of the office to see you.'

'Kate, can't you see I'm on the phone? Just get somebody else to deal with them. Sorry about that again, Len. Where were we?'

'But she wants to see *you*. I really think you should go out there.' Kate was hopping from foot to foot and Becky was getting annoyed with her.

'No, Kate. I'm just finishing up on a call here and I have someone coming in to me in five minutes. She'll just have to deal with—'

'It's your sister.'

Becky almost dropped the phone. 'Wh – what did you say? Len, I'll have to call you back.'

Kate rushed over to her side. 'I couldn't believe it. She said her name is Joanna and she's your sister.'

'Joanna.'

'Yes, Joanna. Are you okay? What should I tell her?'

'I – I don't know. Maybe you got it wrong. I haven't seen Joanna in years.'

'Well, she's your double, Becks. She may be older and a lot rougher around the edges, but I don't think there's any denying you're related.'

Becky couldn't take it in and put her head into her hands. 'Oh, God, I don't know what to do. She's part of a life I don't even know any more.'

'But aren't you curious to see her? To talk to her and see what's happening in her life?'

'Yes. No. I don't know.'

Kate's voice was gentle and she placed a hand on Becky's. 'Just go and talk to her.'

Becky straightened her navy pencil skirt and ran her hands through her hair. She wished she could have taken the time to check her make-up and smarten herself up but what was the point anyway? She didn't need to impress Joanna. She may be her sister, but she was nothing to her any more. She'd left home when Becky was just eight, left her to deal with their violent alcoholic of a father and unstable mother. Who'd do that to their own sister? No, she'd go out there and say hello and see what she wanted, but she wasn't going to let Joanna Greene back into her life and turn it upside down. She took a deep breath and walked out to the front of the office.

She spotted her immediately, her blonde bobbed hair covering her face as she pored over something on her phone. Becky approached her tentatively. She was wary of her, scared of the memories that would be unfolded just by seeing her. She paused in front of her, willing herself to speak but no words came out. Suddenly Joanna looked up. She had bright eyes – not a trace of the trauma of the past. She looked healthy. She looked beautiful. A million miles from the troubled teen who'd run away from home in search of a better life. It was clear she'd found it.

'Hello, Becky. Long time no see.'

They grabbed an empty table at the back of the coffee shop. Becky had finished work for the day and had agreed to hear what her sister had to say. They'd walked down the road in relative silence, both lost in thought, Becky remembering those tough years of their youth.

'You're looking well, Becky. The Irish air is obviously agreeing with you.'

'Thanks. You're looking good yourself.' And she was. Joanna was almost forty now but looked years younger. She looked as though she worked out too because her short-sleeved dress showed off her toned arms.

'So you're probably wondering why I'm here after all these years.'

'Well, it's a bit of a shock, to tell you the truth.'

Joanna looked down and said nothing.

This was excruciating. Becky continued. 'I mean, it's not as if I've never thought about you, but you seemed to just wash your hands of us all when you left.'

'I know and I'm sorry for that. But you know how it was.'

She did. Only too well. 'But I was only eight, Joanna. Eight years old and you left me to deal with those two on my own.'

Tears sprang to Joanna's eyes. 'I know, and I don't even know where to begin to make it up to you. It wasn't as if I just didn't care. I couldn't take any more of what was going on. I know I should have considered you but the truth of it is I was young and selfish and just needed to get out of there.'

Silence fell again and Becky didn't know whether to feel anger or relief.

'Well, say something, Becky. Shout at me. Scream at me. But please don't shut me out. We have a lifetime of news to catch up on and whether we like it or not, we're still sisters.'

'It's just a lot to come to terms with. It's been twenty-two years since you walked out. I know you came back once or twice but they were just fleeting visits and you left as soon as you realised Dad was home or Mum was drunk.'

Joanna looked sheepish. 'Don't remind me. God, I couldn't stick it in that house. I was lucky enough to get a job in retail and was able to pay my way in a shared flat for a while. I came back initially because I thought I could persuade Mum to leave him. I told her I was earning money and could help her get out of the trap she was in. The trap both of you were in.'

Becky hadn't known that. She thought Joanna had just come back once or twice out of duty but hadn't bothered when she'd found a new life. 'I didn't realise. I did the same thing when I left school. I was working and earning money and I begged her to leave with me. But she stuck her heels in. She said she'd never leave him, no matter what he did to her.'

Joanna shook her head. 'Hard to imagine, isn't it? But look at both of us. We didn't do too badly in the end, did we?'

'I suppose not,' said Becky, noticing the Prada handbag by her sister's side.

'And that brings me to why I came over. I made some enquiries and heard you were over here working in the bank. It didn't take me long to—'

'So go on, what is it you want from me?'

'What?' Joanna looked confused.

'Just get to the point, Joanna. I'm sure you're not here to rekindle our sisterly bond after all these years.'

Joanna's face crumbled and her eyes filled with tears. 'I understand you're bitter, Becky. But I didn't come here because I wanted something. You're my sister and I love you, despite what—'

'Well, now I *know* you're talking bullshit. How can you say you love me when you abandoned me? How can you have the nerve?' It was Becky's turn to get upset.

'You have every right to think that way,' Joanna said, reaching across the table to take her sister's hand. 'And I'll get to all that in a minute. But right now, there's something I came to tell you. I thought it would be better to do it in person.'

'What is it?' Becky began to feel her heart beat up into her throat. Please not here. Please not another panic attack.

'Are you okay?' Joanna placed a well-manicured hand on hers and she felt strangely calmer.

'Please just tell me, Joanna. What's brought you here after all these years?'

'I don't know how else to say this except to come right out with it. I just wanted to let you know that' – the words caught in her throat and Becky's panic rose further – 'she's dead, Becky. Mum is dead.'

# Chapter 26

Becky stared at her sister. She'd heard the words but was finding it difficult to process them. She didn't know how she felt. She should feel devastated. She should feel a huge sense of loss. She'd just heard her mother had died, but all she felt was numb.

'Say something, Becky. I know it's a shock. It was for me too.'

'I – I don't know what to say. When? How?'

'You've gone as white as a ghost. Let me grab us another couple of teas and I can tell you what I know.'

Becky watched as Joanna went to the counter to order the teas. It was bizarre. It was years since she'd felt part of a family and now it was as though she was a little girl again with her big sister looking after her. She'd allowed bad thoughts of Joanna to fill her head over the years – blaming her for leaving and writing her off as a bad person. But now she was here, Becky's mind flooded with scenes that had been buried in the back of her mind.

*She crept out of her room when she heard the raised voices. Sitting at the top of the stairs, peering through the banisters, she saw her father pinning her mother up against the wall. Her little six-year-old body stiffened when she saw the first blow being delivered. Her mother's muffled screams rang in her head. She wanted to look away but something wouldn't let her. She felt compelled to watch as blood trickled down her mother's lip from the cutting blow of her father's hand.*

*'Becky, come away from there,' Joanna said, pulling at her arm so she was forced to stand up. 'Quickly, into my room.'*

Becky reluctantly followed her sister into her room as she tried to fight back the tears.

'Come on, pet. Don't cry.' Joanna put her arm around her and led her to the bed. 'You hop in there and we'll have a bit of a midnight feast.'

'But why does Daddy hurt Mummy? Was she bad?'

Joanna produced a big bag of crisps from her wardrobe and brought them over, snuggling in beside her in the bed. 'No, Mummy isn't bad at all. Daddy just isn't well and when he drinks beer, it makes him do things he shouldn't.'

Becky nodded and snuggled in further beside Joanna. Sometimes things were all mixed up and she just couldn't understand anything. She was glad she had her big sister to explain things to her and make her feel better.

Joanna placed the two cups of tea on the table and sat back down. 'Right, I'd better start from the beginning.'

'You were good to me, Joanna. You looked after me.'

'Sorry?'

'I've always blamed you for leaving me when I was so young but I just remembered some of the times when you protected me when ... you know ...'

'It wasn't nice for either of us, Becky. I had to get out of there but I'll always regret leaving you like I did.'

Becky nodded. Her feelings of anger were being replaced by an excitement to have Joanna here now. She was her sister. A part of her family. The only piece of her past that held any decent memories. Because they'd had a bond at one time. 'So tell me about Mum. I can't believe she's gone. And I can't believe I'm so calm about it. What happened?'

'I only just found out myself. I bumped into old Mrs Tubbery on Oxford Street last week. Honestly, if we thought she was old back then, you'd want to see her now. She must be heading for a hundred.'

'So go on, what did she say?'

'At first she sympathised with me about Mum. I was struck dumb because I hadn't heard a thing. Then she got all accusing, saying how the whole thing was a sad state of affairs and how awful it was that she hadn't even had a proper funeral.'

'So this happened a while ago? She's buried and everything already?' Becky was struggling to take it all in.

'It happened six weeks ago, apparently. I went to the house to check things out for myself because I found it all hard to believe.'

'And was *he* there?'

'Yes, out of his head, as usual. It was hard to get any sense out of him but I found Mum's old address book and got the number for her GP.'

'Did you ring? What did he say?'

'He was very nice, actually. Apparently Mum suffered from a heart defect called arrhythmia. When it's diagnosed, it can usually be treated but it seems Mum was missing appointments and not taking her meds.'

'God, I never knew she had any heart problems. So did she have a heart attack?'

'From what I can gather, it was similar to a heart attack but more of a sudden death. The doctor said she'd had a turn last year and that's when the arrhythmia was detected. He'd lectured her on what she needed to do but he said that unfortunately, she was too drunk most of the time to know what was happening.'

Becky blinked away the tears. 'I want to feel sorry for her – really I do. She had an awful life. But then I think back to all the times I was scared. All the times I tried to get her to leave. All the times when I had to go to school hungry because they'd either spent all the money on booze or were in too much of a drunken stupor to buy any food.'

'Don't beat yourself up over how you feel, Becky.' Joanna reached across the table and took her hand. 'I feel the same. We both have our own lives now and although it's sad to think we never had parents we could rely on, at least we managed to get out before it was too late for us.'

Becky nodded and looked at her sister. 'And what about you? What are you up to these days? Are you still working in that shop in London?'

'Still in retail but I'm a buyer now for a big chain. In fact, I'm over here on business. When I heard about Mum last week, I was going to give you a call but as I was coming over anyway, I thought I'd see you in person.'

'Well, I'm glad you did.' And she meant it. 'But how did you find me? I didn't think anyone knew where I was working. I kept in touch with Mum for a while after I came to Ireland but she only ever seemed to want me to send money so I just cut myself off completely after a while.'

Joanna nodded. 'That's exactly how it was with me. When I left, I didn't plan to stay away completely but I soon realised that the money was being used for drink and probably drugs and I just distanced myself.'

'I do remember. And I lived for your visits. So go on. Tell me how you found me.'

'When I got my hands on Mum's address book last week, I kept hold of it. I looked you up and found the details of the last bank you worked in. I went to them first this morning and they sent me here. Said you'd been transferred a few years ago.'

'Yes, I wanted to start afresh after my maternity lea—' Becky barely had the words out before she realised that Joanna wouldn't know a thing about Lilly. She watched as her sister's mouth opened wide.

'Maternity leave! You have a child. Oh, Becky, that's wonderful. A girl or boy?'

Becky smiled. 'A girl – Lilly. She's just gone four and she's the most wonderful child you could imagine.'

Tears poured down Joanna's face as she tried hard to gulp them in. But it was useless. When she'd started, it was like opening the floodgates. She sniffled and snotted through both the serviettes on the table before rummaging in her bag for tissues. Becky was finding it hard to fight back her own tears.

'I'm sorry,' said Joanna, when she'd finally managed to get herself together. 'Lilly. What a gorgeous name. I can't believe I'm an aunty. I can't wait for her to meet her cousins.'

'Cousins? You have children too?'

'Yes, two. Sarah is five and a half and Adam is just gone two. I don't know why it never occurred to me you'd have children. Maybe it's because you're still a child in my eyes. My little sister.' She was off crying again and this time Becky joined in.

'It's overwhelming, isn't it?' Becky said, when she managed to compose herself. 'I can't believe my little family has just increased by over a hundred per cent in the past hour. Up until now, it's just been Lilly and me.'

'I know. Crazy, isn't it? And you said it's just the two of you – are you not with Lilly's dad any more?'

'No, I never was really. Well, except for the obvious …'

'And what happened there? Did he not want to be involved?'

'He never knew. I didn't tell him.'

'What? He doesn't know about Lilly even now?'

Becky sighed. 'It's a long story.'

'Well, I have time. Come on – I want to know everything.'

It took half an hour and another round of tea before Becky had filled Joanna in on everything. She told her all the details – from that night with Dennis right up to her recent meeting with him.

When she was finished, Joanna sat back on her chair and exhaled a long breath. 'That's some story, Becky. And are you really not going to pursue Dennis any further?'

'No. He's not the sort of father I want for Lilly and I'm not going to expose her to that sort of stuff.'

'What sort of stuff? Homelessness?'

'No, not exactly. Well, yes, I suppose so. But not *just* that – it's the things associated with it. The drugs, the alcohol, the abuse … I don't ever want my daughter exposed to the sort of things I was exposed to as a child.'

'I understand, Becky. But how do you know this guy is involved in all that? Homelessness can happen for any number of reasons.'

Becky suddenly felt annoyed. 'Who do you think you are coming over here and preaching to me about my life? You know nothing about me or my daughter so you can save your sanctimonious advice for someone else.'

'Don't be like that. I'm not preaching to you – far from it. I just know what it's like to not trust men. I've been there too and probably for the same reasons. We saw stuff that children should never see, and it's made us cagey. It was only when I decided to let my guard down that I met George, and he's the most wonderful, gorgeous man on the planet and a brilliant dad to Sarah and Adam.'

'You see? You've got the perfect little family and you think we should all be the same. But life isn't like that, Joanna. You can't always have everything packaged up nicely and tied with a bow.'

'God, don't you think I know that, Becky? I've had some shit relationships through the years and I had some really hard times. I'm just trying to tell you that you don't have to let the past rule you. You can set yourself free.'

'I *am* free. I have a boyfriend who I'm crazy about. He's a decent, hard-working man who'd do anything for me. So maybe I just don't need someone like Dennis Prendergast coming into our lives and upsetting things.'

'But, Becky, you wouldn't be bringing Dennis into your life as your boyfriend. If this guy of yours is so special, he shouldn't have a problem with Lilly seeing her real dad. Do you still have feelings for Dennis?'

Becky slammed her fist down on the table, causing other customers to look around. 'As I said, there was *never* anything between us except for that one night. Lilly is my only concern in all this and I won't have her upset for anything.'

'Okay, okay.' Joanna put her hand up, conceding the argument. 'I'm sorry if I upset you. I suppose I just feel I've been through a lot of stuff and I want to pass on my experiences to my little sister.'

Becky rubbed her temples. 'I'm sorry too. It's just that there's been so much happening lately and now you come along to add to it all.'

'Oh, thanks for that.' But she was smiling.

'Sorry, that came out wrong, but you know what I mean.' Becky was glad the mood was lightened again. It was all so intense. 'So getting back to Mum – was she buried or cremated? I can't even believe I'm asking that question. It sounds so weird.'

'She's buried in with Granny and Granddad. Apparently it was all done quickly enough and nobody was invited to the funeral. It's mad to think you could spend so many years on this earth and leave without anybody really caring.'

Becky nodded, feeling somewhat sad for her mother but even sadder for herself and the childhood she never really had.

Joanna continued. 'And before I forget, the doctor said we should get our hearts checked too, just as a precaution. Sometimes the condition can run in families but it's probably more likely Mum's was brought on by her alcohol abuse.'

Becky suddenly remembered all her 'fake heart attacks', as she called them. Her panic attacks where she felt her heart beat up into her throat. Oh, God. Maybe they were more than just panic attacks. Maybe, after giving her nothing for most of her life, her mother had left her with a parting gift of a heart defect. She felt almost faint at the thought.

'Have you been checked yet yourself?' she asked her sister, her palms sweating at the mere thought of it.

'Not yet. I have an appointment with my GP for next week and I'll take it from there. I'm sure we're both fine but there's no point in taking any chances.'

'So when do you go back? Are you staying around for a while?'

'Unfortunately not. I'm on a late flight tonight. I came yesterday for the meetings and just booked in for one night so that I could come and look for you today.'

'Oh.' Becky felt gutted.

'But you can be damn sure I'll be back again soon – and I'll be bringing the children too so they can meet their aunty and cousin. That's if you'll have us.'

'Of course. I can't wait to meet them and for you to meet Lilly. Speaking of which, I'd better get home. Alice, my nanny, will be wondering where I am.'

'Okay.' Joanna rooted in her bag and produced a card. 'All my details are on that so give me a ring soon and we'll arrange something.'

Becky looked at the card: Joanna Greene, Chief Buyer. 'Wow, haven't you come up in the world?'

'I worked my way up. Like you, I was determined to make something of myself. You're not doing too badly yourself from what I can see.'

'I suppose I'm not. Listen to us two – we're living proof that people can get over all sorts of things.' Becky stood up and embraced her sister. 'It's been really good to see you, Joanna. And let's not lose touch again.'

'Never. You'll be sick of the sight of me soon.'

They said their goodbyes and Becky walked towards her bus stop in a daze. God, that had been a heavy afternoon. Heavy and emotional but good. Part of her felt guilty for not feeling devastated about her mother's passing. She felt sad, but only a little. Her main feeling was one of elation for having found her sister again. Her sister. It felt good to say it.

As she made her way through the busy streets, she was aware of her heart beating. It was a strong beat and seemed to be keeping in time with her footsteps. An uneasy feeling came over her and she suddenly felt that her life was about to change. It was a scary feeling but maybe change didn't always have to be bad. Maybe it was time to stop being afraid and embrace some positive changes in her life.

# Chapter 27

It was already six and Becky was just leaving the office. Damn that customer and his urgent query. Len was taking her out to dinner and she badly needed to shower and wash her hair. It was too late now to start queuing for a bus so she'd just head over O'Connell Bridge and hop into a taxi on Westmoreland Street.

She stopped at the traffic lights before crossing the bridge, and that's when she saw him. He was walking right towards her and her heart began to beat like crazy. Dennis Prendergast. It had been over a month since she'd met him but he'd clearly noticed her too, so she was going to have to talk to him.

'Hi, Dennis. How have you been?'

'Let me see. Do you want to hear the prettied-up version or the truth?' His eyes looked just as angry as when she'd last seen him.

'I suppose I deserved that,' she said, moving aside to let the crowds cross the road. 'Listen, I'm really sorry about how things went when we last met. I really didn't mean to be offensive or to upset you.'

'You didn't upset me, Alice. I've got thicker skin than that. You did annoy me, though. Your reaction was just typical of the ignorant people I come across every day.'

Becky shrank at that but decided to let it go. 'I've been planning to get in touch with you again, actually.'

'Sure you have.'

'No, honestly. I've just been so busy with other stuff that I haven't had a chance yet.' It wasn't entirely a lie. She'd been toying with the idea since talking to Joanna.

'So I take it you haven't got everything you need for your article yet, then?'

'Not entirely, no. I know it's a bit of a cheek to be asking you, considering how things went last time, but would you be willing to chat to me again? I promise to behave myself.'

There was a flicker of a smile on his lips. 'I suppose it wouldn't hurt. How about Martha's again some day next week?'

'Perfect. But can we say Friday at one? I'm on a course earlier in the week so won't be free.'

'Suits me.' His eyes bore into hers and she felt something stir inside her. Dennis was different to the man he used to be but his eyes were exactly the same.

'Em, right, I'd better get going. See you next week.'

She was relieved to walk away but was determined to try and see beyond the crumpled corduroy trousers and well-worn shirt. She needed to look past the matted beard and defeated face. She was going to look into those Spanish eyes and see right into his soul. Lilly was the most important thing in all this and she needed to do what was best for her.

Suddenly there was only one person she wanted to talk to. She whipped her phone out of her bag as she headed towards the taxi rank and tapped into her phonebook. It was funny to think she'd only been given the number just over a week ago and it was already stored under 'most used'.

'Hi, Joanna. It's me.'

'Becky, how are you doing, love? This is early for you.'

'I know,' said Becky, clutching the phone close to her ear to drown out the noise of the busy city centre. 'But I just couldn't wait to tell you. You'd never guess who I just bumped into.'

'Go on – don't keep me in suspense.'

She began the story of her chance meeting with Dennis as Joanna listened intently. It was weird how well the two sisters had connected. Weird but wonderful. It was as though they hadn't missed out on the past twenty years of each other's lives. They'd spoken on the phone almost every day since they'd met, and Becky was excited about Joanna and her family coming over for Christmas.

'I'm glad you're going to meet him again,' said Joanna, after she'd listened to the whole story. 'What harm can it do? And you'd never know – maybe if you get to know him a bit better, you might find the time is right to introduce him to Lilly.'

Becky hopped into a taxi and gave the driver her address. 'Maybe. We'll just have to wait and see.'

'Remember what Mum used to say? "What doesn't kill you makes you stronger." And no matter what happens with Dennis, you'll come out of this a stronger person for having the balls to confront it.'

Becky smiled as she listened to her sister's words of wisdom. Her sister. She loved how it sounded. Joanna had spoken about becoming a stronger person but Becky already felt stronger for having her sister by her side.

❁

'It's fate, Becky. I'm telling you,' said Alice, her eyes twinkling. 'I can't believe you just bumped into him like that.'

'I couldn't believe it either. I've been trying to decide whether or not to contact him again and up he pops. Just like that.'

'Well, I'm delighted. Are you going to tell Len about him?'

'I don't think I'll say anything yet. It's still early days for us so there's no need to complicate things.'

'Probably wise. And speak of the devil, this must be him now.'

The sound of the doorbell echoed in the house and Becky suddenly felt nervous. He was going to be meeting Lilly before they went out and Becky really hoped the two of them would hit it off.

'Well, go on then,' said Alice, as the bell rang for the second time. 'I'll join Lilly in the sitting room to watch telly and you just bring him in when you're ready.'

'Thanks, Alice.' She rushed out to the door, smoothing down the pink and black Julien Macdonald dress that she'd picked up that lunchtime. Len was taking her to a posh restaurant in Howth and she wanted to look the part.

'Well, hello, gorgeous,' Len said, as Becky swung the door open. 'Wow! You're a sight for sore eyes.'

Becky stood back to let him in. 'Thanks. Come on into the kitchen. Lilly is in the sitting room with Alice so you can meet her in a minute. Coffee?'

'Not for me, thanks. Nice little place you've got here.'

'Little being the operative word. But it's perfect for just the two of us.' Becky was conscious of Len's eyes scanning the place. He was obviously used to much grander accommodation.

'Of course it is. You wouldn't want to be rattling around in a big place when there are only two of you. And speaking of which, maybe I could pop my head in and say hi to Lilly now? The table is booked for eight and it will take us at least forty minutes to get there.'

'Oh, I thought we weren't eating until nine?' Becky was disappointed. She'd wanted Len to take a bit of time with her daughter and she'd hoped he'd want that too.

'Yes, that was the plan but they only had an eight o'clock sitting left. I'll spend more time with Lilly next time. And, anyway, we don't want to overwhelm her with too much of me at once.' His eyes twinkled and Becky relaxed. It wasn't his fault that the restaurant didn't have a table for a later time.

'Right, we'd better make a move so.' She took her silver cardigan from the back of the kitchen chair and grabbed her matching bag. 'We'll pop our heads in on the way out.'

'After you.' He made a sweeping gesture with his hand and Becky headed out towards the sitting room.

'Lilly, Alice, this is Len. We're in a bit of a hurry but he just wanted to say hello before we left.'

'Nice to meet you, Len.' Alice jumped up from the sofa, extending a hand to shake his. 'Lilly and I were just settling down to watch *Alvin and the Chipmunks*.'

'Nice to meet you too, Alice. And hello there, little lady.' He held out his hand to shake Lilly's. 'I've heard a lot about you.'

Lilly stared at him and snuggled further into the sofa.

'Lilly, sweetheart, say hello to Len.'

The little girl looked at her mother and pouted.

'Lilly! Don't be rude. Len has come in to see you. Now, say hello.' Becky was mortified. She'd told Len how bubbly and friendly her little girl was and here she was being the complete opposite.

'It's okay, Becky,' said Len, smiling at Lilly. 'I'm sure she's just shy.'

'Wait a minute. Lilly, what's wrong, sweetheart. I told you Len would be coming to say hello. It's not like you to be like this.'

'I have a pain in my tummy.'

'You never said anything to me,' Alice piped up, looking at the little girl suspiciously. 'And you were just asking for popcorn for the movie.'

'Well, I have a pain now and it's sooooo bad.' She doubled over to show everyone just how bad the pain was.

'Oh, sweetheart, I didn't realise. Come here.'

Lilly ran to her mother and Becky swept her up in her arms. 'Show me where the pain is. Maybe I should just stay home.'

'Yes, Mummy. I need you to mind me.'

Becky felt torn and looked up at Len. 'I'm sorry. We may have to postpone until another night.'

'Ah,' said Len, tapping the side of his nose. 'But Lilly doesn't know about the magic beans I brought with me.'

Lilly was suddenly interested and pulled away from her mother to look at Len. 'What beans?' she asked shyly.

'These ones.' Len produced a bag of jelly beans from his jacket pocket and dangled them in front of Lilly's nose. 'I've been told the orange ones make you see in the dark, the red ones make your brain work better, the pink ones make you pretty and the green ones make sore tummies go away.'

'Wow!' said Alice, smiling. 'Isn't that amazing, Lilly?'

The little girl's eyes lit up and she gingerly took the bag from Len's hands. Becky was impressed. She didn't know Len was so good with children.

'Can I have some of these now, Mummy?'

Becky nodded. 'Maybe just a few. You can save the rest until tomorrow.'

'Yay!' Lilly hopped down from her mother's arms and ran to sit beside Alice on the sofa. 'I'm going to eat all the green ones to make my tummy better. Alice, you can have some pink ones to make you pretty.'

'Oh, thanks for that.' But Alice looked impressed by Len, and Becky felt relieved.

'Right,' said Len, looking at his watch. 'We'd better make a move if we're to get to the restaurant on time.'

Becky looked over at Lilly. 'Is that okay with you, sweetheart? I won't be late and I'll come up and give you a kiss when I get in.'

Lilly looked unsure again but Len was quick to cut in. 'How about we bring you back some nice dessert from the restaurant and you can have it tomorrow? You'd like that, wouldn't you?'

'What a good idea,' said Alice. 'Maybe you can even ring us to tell us what's on the menu. How about that, Lilly?'

'I s'ppose.'

'And by the time we've finished watching the movie, your mummy will be on her way home.'

That seemed to appease Lilly and Becky left her tucking in to her precious jelly beans.

'You were so good with her,' said Becky, as they sped off down the road in Len's brand new Audi. 'I didn't think you had any experience with kids.'

'Nieces and nephews. I have them in abundance so I've learned what works over the years. And besides, I was really scared there for a minute that you'd cancel our date. I've been really looking forward to it – and when I saw you in that dress …' He gave a low whistle and Becky laughed.

'But you do know Lilly always comes first, don't you? If she'd really been sick, I'd have had to cancel.'

'I know, but thankfully it didn't come to that. Now let's just enjoy our dinner and maybe we'll even have a little walk along the pier in Howth after. It's such a gorgeous, romantic place at night.'

'Let's just see how it goes. I don't want to be out too long in case Lilly is fretting.'

Len nodded. 'Well, there'll be plenty of other nights. I plan to wine and dine you and treat you like a princess for as long as you'll let me. You deserve to be looked after.'

Becky put her hand on his knee but didn't say anything. She couldn't help feeling a little uneasy. Len seemed to be looking way into the future when she really wasn't sure what she wanted yet. He was definitely a good catch. Everything about him seemed perfect but she was still waiting for that spark. She settled back into her seat for the drive and noticed how handsome Len looked. His suit was impeccable and his aftershave was sexy and alluring. She just needed to learn how to be with a man again. She deserved to have some adult time and she couldn't think of a better way than to spend time with a gorgeous man like Len.

❦

'Alice, can we have the popcorn now?'

'But you've already had a load of jelly beans. And what about that pain in your tummy?'

'I think that man was right. The green ones made it better.'

'Hmmmm. Are you sure you really had a pain or were you just pretending?'

'I really, really did, Alice. It was right here.' Lilly lifted up the top of her pyjamas and pointed to her stomach.

Alice laughed. 'That looks like a very sore place to have a pain all right. Well, how about I make us a small bowl. I wouldn't want that pain to come back.'

'Okay. And some orange. You promised, 'member?'

Alice headed into the kitchen and filled a bowl with popcorn and two glasses with Fanta. It had been an interesting scene earlier. She was sure Lilly hadn't had a pain and was playing up because her mother was going out with a man. Alice had also been sure that Becky would cancel but Len had come to the rescue. He seemed like a really decent guy – charming and polite and very easy on the eye. Becky deserved a bit of happiness and if Len was going to give that to her, Alice hoped nothing was going to get in the way.

'Here we go.' Alice placed the tray of goodies on the coffee table. 'And remember, eat slowly in case your pain comes back.'

'I think it's gone for good now,' said Lilly, launching into the popcorn. 'Can we have hot chocolate after?'

Alice smiled at her earnest face and decided to question her a little about earlier. 'So what did you think of Len? I thought he seemed like a nice man.'

Lilly's face darkened a little as she stuffed her mouth with popcorn.

'Lilly? Did you hear what I said?'

'He's okay, I s'ppose.'

'Just okay? But didn't he give you those lovely sweeties and he's going to bring you home some dessert too.'

Lilly looked up with big teary eyes. 'I know. But I don't want him to take my mummy away.'

Ah, there it was. Alice put her arm around Lilly, and pulled her in close.

'Nobody is ever going to take your mummy away, do you hear me? Your mummy loves you more than anyone in the world. She's just having a bit of fun, that's all.'

'But she can have fun here with me. She always says she loves playing games with me before I go to bed.'

'I know, sweetie. And she does. But sometimes mummies just like to do something different. They like having other adults to talk to.'

'You mean like you and Frank?'

'Well, yes, sort of.'

'I like Frank. He's funny.'

'And I'm sure you'll like Len too once you get to know him.' Alice hoped she was right. Lilly had been appeased with the sweets but it was going to take more than that to make her understand the situation. She needed to know she was top of her mother's list and that nothing would ever change that.

# Chapter 28

Dennis sat at his usual table in Martha's, his heart beating like crazy and his palms sweating. It was out of character for him to feel so anxious, but he couldn't help it. Ever since he'd bumped into Alice last week, he hadn't been able to get her out of his head. Despite the fact that he thought she was a judgemental, stuck-up snob who didn't understand what went on in the real world, she still intrigued him. Something about her reminded him of the past. He'd been a bit of a womaniser in his day and he always would have gone for women like her – tall, leggy blondes with pretty faces and great figures. He didn't want to be that man any more but it didn't stop him from being turned on by a beautiful woman.

'Here you go, pet.' Martha placed another mug of tea in front of him, taking the cold one away. 'And are you sure I can't get you anything to eat?'

'I'm fine, Martha, thanks. I'm meeting someone and she should be here any minute.'

'Ah, a woman. Sure it's no wonder you're all spruced up.'

Dennis blushed. 'Don't be silly. Don't I always make an effort when I'm coming in to you? And she's not *that* sort of a woman.'

'Oh, I was unaware there were different sorts,' Martha chuckled. 'And what sort would this one be?'

'She's a journalist, if you must know. The woman you saw me in here with a few weeks ago. She's doing some articles about the recession and how it's affected people and she thought I'd be a good one to talk to.'

'Of course you would. Your story is a very touching one, and very inspiring too.'

'It's hardly inspiring, Martha. But thanks.'

'Don't put yourself down, pet. You've lived for almost a year on the streets and look at you. You're a decent, kind man who's refused to get caught up in the sordid world of drugs or alcohol. You have a good head on your shoulders and it's going to be your saviour. You mark my words – you'll get out of this rut you're in and it might be sooner than you think.'

'I hope so. I sometimes wonder if I'll ever get a break or if this is it for the rest of my life.'

'You've got to stay positive, pet. Now it looks like your lady friend has arrived.' Martha nodded towards the door where Becky had just come in. 'I'll leave you to it, good luck.'

'Dennis! Thank you so much for coming. I wasn't sure if you would.' Becky shook her umbrella and put it under the table before sitting down opposite him.

'I didn't know if I would either, to be honest.' He was such a liar. 'I mean, how is this going to benefit me?'

She shifted awkwardly in her chair. 'Well, you'll be reaching out to a lot of people. You can inspire them with your story.'

That was the second time he'd been referred to as inspiring. He felt anything but. If only they knew the truth.

'So,' Becky continued, indicating to Martha that she'd like a coffee. 'Can we put the last disastrous meeting behind us and start again?'

'Fine by me. So what can I tell you?' She was wearing that same perfume and it was making his head fuzzy.

'Well, first of all, tell me what it means to be homeless. You don't look like you live on the streets – and I don't mean that to be disrespectful to people who do, it's just that you look as though you look after yourself. I don't imagine most people on the streets take such care.'

'Well, actually I *do* live mostly on the streets. I've stayed on sofas in friends' houses and I've done the hostel and shelter thing, but none of it has really worked out for me.'

'I can't imagine how awful that must be. How do you keep warm? And what about food?'

'The winter is tough and sometimes it's impossible to fend off the cold. But the charities do their best to help us out. It's hardly a pleasurable existence, but we get by.'

'But surely it's dangerous out there. Are you not afraid? This city isn't exactly the safest place to be at night, even if you're just passing through. But to have to sleep on the streets night after night ...'

Dennis sipped his tea and looked at her. She seemed horrified at the thoughts of him sleeping rough. Maybe he'd have a bit of fun with her. She needed a good dose of reality.

'Dennis?'

'You'd think the streets would be the scariest place to be but they're nothing compared to some of the shelters.'

'You mean it's actually *safer* on the streets?'

'It depends. I'm not into the whole drug scene. In fact, I don't even drink any more because I want to keep my wits about me. Most of those shelters are littered with druggies. Some of them would sell their granny for their next fix. You just never feel safe when you're in their company.'

Dennis noticed how she visibly shrank and he couldn't help taking delight in it. 'And the alcoholics aren't much better. When they're out of their heads, there's just no telling what they might do. I could tell you some stories.'

'Go on,' said Becky, reluctantly.

'One day, my friend John was just minding his own business, sitting on his bed in the hostel and two guys jumped on him, punched him in the face and took the shoes off his feet.'

'Oh, that's awful—'

'Shoes are a big deal in this world, Alice. They're one of the most robbed things in the hostels. Especially in the winter. Can you imagine how hard it is to get through a night of below zero temperatures while wearing shoes with holes in them?'

She shook her head and looked close to tears. 'I can't even begin to imagine. I don't know what to say.'

'Just make sure you say it all in your article. Tell it as it is and don't pretty it up.'

'Okay. I probably have all I need for the moment. I won't take up any more of your time.' She rooted in her bag and threw a five euro note on the table.

'You're heading off so soon?' Dennis was disappointed. He'd been enjoying watching her discomfort. He knew it was cruel, but she needed to see what it was like. If she was going to report on it, she may as well do it properly.

'Sorry, yes.' She was already on her feet, her coat and umbrella in her hands. 'But can we meet again? Do you have a phone?'

'I do, as it happens. I don't usually have any credit though so I won't be able to ring you back.'

'Call me out the number,' she said, tapping into her own phone. 'Can I ring you about meeting again in a few days?'

'I suppose so. And maybe next time I'll take you on a little trip.'

'T – trip? What do you mean? Where?'

'Well, I was thinking; if you really want a taste of what it's like to be homeless, you should walk in my footsteps for a bit – the places I go and the people I meet along the way. Maybe that would give your articles the authenticity they need.'

'Em, yes, that would be good. Let's do that. I'll give you a ring tomorrow.'

She was gone out of the place like a light and Dennis didn't know whether to laugh or cry. He'd enjoyed his little taunt but he actually felt quite sorry for her. She'd gone pale as he was talking. And he hadn't expected she'd agree to the 'walking in his shoes' thing. He'd only really said it to horrify her but fair play to her, she seemed willing to give it a go.

He took a gulp of his almost cold tea and realised his mood had lifted a little. Just like it had when he'd gone for that job two weeks ago. His life was such drudgery that anything that lifted his spirits, even for a short while, had to be a good thing. And it felt good to be doing something positive for a change. If even one person learned from his mistakes, it would be worth it. He also wanted to make sure Alice knew how important the homeless charities were to people like him, and he wanted to make sure she stressed that in her article. They kept so many people alive with the services they provided and yet the government was planning to cut their budget. It was insane. In his previous life, he used to complain about taxes on cigarettes and booze and when they'd put the price of diesel up – and they were probably the things that still concerned Alice and people like her – but now he saw things differently. If talking to Alice and educating her on homelessness could bring some much-needed publicity to the cause, well that's what he was going to do.

'Here you go, pet. You look like you need this.' Martha placed a huge slice of lemon meringue pie in front of him and he looked at her gratefully.

'Thanks, Martha. I won't say no.' As he spooned the gooey, lemon sauce into his mouth, he wanted to think about Alice but a picture of Isabella came into his head. It seemed that every time a bit of positivity came into his life, his conscience reminded him that he didn't deserve it. Why should things improve for him when Isabella was locked into a life of sadness? His head told him it was time to move on and stop dwelling on the past, but his heart refused to let the past go. But he was going to have to find a way. It was almost a year now since he'd landed on the streets and one way or the other, there was no way he was going to be there for another one.

❁

'Becky, what happened?' Kate had spotted Becky rushing in the door and heading straight for the toilets so had followed her in. 'Talk to me.'

'Just let me do this first,' said Becky, squirting out handfuls of soap from the dispenser and working up a lather. 'I need to get clean.'

'Why? What's happened? Did he turn up?'

Becky rubbed the suds right up to her elbows before letting the water from the tap wash them away. 'Yes, he turned up all right.'

'And what's with the cleaning?'

'I – I don't know. I just feel dirty. How could I have done it, Kate? How could I have slept with a random guy who sleeps on the street? How could I have done it to Lilly? Imagine if she found out her father is a man like that.'

'But you're not making any sense. Dennis wasn't homeless when you first met him. What's happened?'

Becky pulled down some paper towel from the dispenser and stared at Kate. 'Nothing's happened. But how do you think Lilly would feel if she knew her father was a man like that? I've really let her down.'

'Kate, cop on to yourself, would you? Haven't we been here before? Now let's get you into the kitchen for a cuppa. There's still ten minutes of lunch left.'

Kate sighed to herself as she led Becky over to a table in the corner of the little kitchen. She was beginning to get annoyed with all the drama. Becky wasn't the only one with stuff going on in her life but sometimes it seemed like she wanted everyone to run around her, pandering to her every whim. Kate wanted to be supportive. She wanted to hold Becky's hand through it all and tell her it would be okay. But she couldn't guarantee that it would be okay and, besides, she had her own problems to deal with too.

'Right, start from the beginning.' Kate leaned on the table and mustered up as much enthusiasm as she could. 'Did you find out something bad about Dennis today?'

Becky sighed. 'Not exactly. He just painted a picture of what it's like to be homeless. Oh, Kate, it's awful. Just hearing about the shelters and the streets made me wish I'd never looked for him in the first place. The alcohol, the drugs ... it's just such an awful way to live.'

'God. Are you saying he's into drugs?'

'Well, no. He says he steers well away from them.'

'Alcohol, then?'

'Doesn't drink at all. He says he needs to keep his wits about him at all times.'

Kate was exasperated. 'Well, what's the problem then, Becky? It sounds to me like he's a decent sort of guy.'

Becky nodded. 'I know, I know. I suppose he is. I just got rattled when he started talking about the homeless scene. I had flashbacks to my mother dragging me around the streets looking for my father when he'd go AWOL.'

'Oh, of course. I'm sure you could do without having those memories dredged up. And it must be a difficult time for you, hearing about your mother and everything.'

Becky's eyes glistened with tears. 'It's been a strange couple of weeks. I felt mostly numb when Joanna told me the news but as it's sinking in, I'm remembering some of the good times. There weren't many but they were definitely there. I remember when I was really small, maybe about three or four, and my mother took me to a cake shop. She let me pick anything I wanted and we went home and snuggled under a blanket on the sofa, watching telly and stuffing our faces. It was funny, I didn't even question where my father was then – he was probably off on one of his drunken binges.'

'I'm glad you have some good memories. It's good to hold on to those.'

'Well, there's no point in "what ifs" any more. Things were what they were. And although I didn't do anything about it, there was probably always a tiny piece of me that felt a connection with London because of Mum, but no more. She's gone now and my father can rot in hell as far as I'm concerned.'

Kate winced at that. Her own parents were so loving and kind that she couldn't imagine having a mother and father who didn't care. No matter how much Becky pretended, it must be like a knife through her heart.

Becky was still talking. 'And really, I suppose I shouldn't let the past rule me any more. I shouldn't be making assumptions about Dennis because of my father. My life is Lilly now and that's what's important. And Dennis is *her* father, whether I like it or not. I need to give him a chance – see what he's like and maybe then think about bringing Lilly into the equation.'

Kate grinned and clapped her hands together.

'What?' Becky looked at her blankly.

'Well, it looks as though you don't need me here at all,' said Kate, amused by Becky's summing up of things. 'You seem to have it all sorted now.'

Becky grinned too. 'I guess I just needed to say it all out loud. My head has been so mixed up lately but I'm beginning to see things more clearly.'

'Well, I'm happy for you. And how are things going with Len?'

'Surprisingly well, actually. He's a good guy and he's brilliant with Lilly. She's been a bit reluctant with him but she's coming around.'

'Ah, that's understandable, I suppose. She's not used to seeing you with a man.'

I know. And he knows exactly how to win her around. You'd want to see the amount of stuff he's bought her just this past week. I think she's actually beginning to look forward to seeing him.'

'You see? What did I tell you? I always knew he'd be a great catch. But never mind Lilly – how do *you* feel about him?'

'It's early days but I'm enjoying having the company of a man again.'

'I bet you are.' Kate leaned forward. 'And have you taken that enjoyment into the bedroom yet? I'm dying to know what he's like.'

'Kate!'

'Ah, come on, Becky. If the saying about feet and willies is true, he must be a sex god. Have you seen the size of his feet?'

'No, I have not – nor anything else, for that matter.'

'And are you not dying to … you know …'

Becky blushed and Kate grinned.

'You see, you *are* hanging for it, aren't you? How could you not be? Well, hurry up, will you? I want a full report back.'

'Well, I'm not saying we won't go there, but we're just taking our time. And if and when we do, there'll certainly be no report!'

'Spoilsport!'

'Anyway, how are things with you? You're looking a bit pale these days – are you still feeling sick?'

'I'm fine,' said Kate, not wanting the conversation to turn to her. 'Just a bit run down.'

'But you look as though you're losing weight too – and you can't afford to get any thinner than you already are. Are you eating properly?'

'Of course I am. Have you ever seen me off my food? And to be honest, I could do with losing a few inches and pounds if I'm to compete with other girls for modelling places. They're all so beautiful and thin.'

'Don't be ridiculous, Kate. You're gorgeous and a perfect size. I'd kill to be so thin. Don't go changing yourself for anyone.'

'Okay, Mammy. But we'd better get back. Have you seen the time?'

Becky groaned. 'I was forgetting where we were for a minute. And thanks for the chat. I feel so much better now.'

Kate watched as Becky rushed out of the kitchen. She hadn't told a lie really. She was eating plenty – the problem was that with those laxatives, it was all just running right through her. She seemed permanently hungry while she was taking them but the more she ate, the more she emptied from her bowels. It was like a vicious circle. Sometimes, she wished she'd never started with them but the fact she was seeing results made her want to continue. But maybe there was an easier way. She knew she could never deprive herself of food but maybe laxatives weren't the best way of getting rid of it.

She stood up and felt herself wobble. Another side effect of the drugs seemed to be dizziness and she'd sometimes find herself swaying from side to side as if she was on a boat. She wasn't sure she could put up with this much longer. But giving up wasn't an option. She'd just have to find another way.

# Chapter 29

Becky stepped down from the bus and headed towards the quays. She felt strange wearing a tracksuit out in public. She'd resisted the urge to buy a new one but instead had chosen the old grey one she used when cleaning the house. Under normal circumstances, she'd never be seen dead wearing it in public, but these circumstances were far from normal. Today she was meeting Dennis to be given the grand tour of his life – and she was absolutely dreading it.

She checked her watch as she approached the social club and breathed a sigh of relief to see she was early by about ten minutes. She wasn't ready yet. She needed time to get herself together and stave off the panic attack she could feel rising inside her. She really didn't want to do this, but if it gave her an insight into the life of Dennis Prendergast, it would be worth it.

The previous night, she'd had a long phone chat with Len and had told him all about Dennis. She hadn't planned to, but she found herself wanting to share more and more of her life with him. He'd listened attentively and had then given his opinion. To him, it was black and white. If the guy had no money or prospects, he wasn't worth pursuing. But Becky didn't see it that way. He may be homeless, but he was intelligent and articulate and she just couldn't help feeling drawn to him. Who was she to say he wouldn't make a good father for Lilly, despite his lack of wealth?

'Hello, Alice.' Becky almost jumped out of her skin as she swung around to see Dennis looking at her. 'I see you're dressed to fit in with us unclean folk.'

'Yes, I mean no, I mean—'

'Relax. I'm just having you on. You look fine.'

Becky blushed. 'I didn't know what to wear and since we'll be doing some walking, I thought this would be more appropriate than a dress and heels.'

'It's perfect. Now, are you ready to come inside and meet some of the lads?'

'Of course.' That was a lie. She'd never be ready.

'Right, after you.'

He held open the door and she stepped inside, every part of her shaking at the thought of what she was going to see.

The air was like dirty, grey socks. It was a drab space, badly in need of a lick of paint and a bit of loving care. There was a group of men sitting at a table playing cards and a couple more playing pool. A few were chatting, their hands cupped around hot drinks, and others sitting alone, lost in their own world.

'John, come over here and meet Alice. Remember the girl I was telling you about?'

A man rose immediately from the card game and headed in their direction. 'I was doing shite anyway. Red Ron has been winning everything all afternoon. Hi there. Nice to meet you. Alice, is it?'

'Yes. Lovely to meet you too.'

'John here is an inspiration,' said Dennis. 'How about we have a cup of tea and he can tell you his story. Is that okay with you, John?'

'Of course. I'm never happier than when I'm blowing my own trumpet.' He cackled and Becky noticed his brown, broken teeth. Her stomach did a flip and she cursed the cheese sandwich she'd had before leaving home.

They sat on some uncomfortable grey plastic chairs that reminded Becky of sitting through endless concerts in the school hall when she was a kid, and John began his story. Dennis went to get the teas, leaving her alone with the old man. She watched how his eyes glistened when he spoke about his wife and his two gorgeous little girls. His pain was unimaginable. How life can change in the blink of an eye. Here was a man who'd had it all and a cruel twist of fate had catapulted him into this horrendous life.

'Here you go.' Dennis placed the mugs of tea on the table and sat back down. 'Has John been filling you in?'

'Yes, he has. And what a sad, sad story. I don't know what to say to you, John.'

'No need to say anything, love. I'm climbing back into life now, bit by bit. I have my own place, a little job in the bookies and a load of friends I wouldn't have met if life had taken a different turn.'

'But how can you stay so positive?' Becky was on the verge of tears, especially at the thought of him losing those two little girls.

'Well, if you want a piece of this life, you've got to be. You may as well be dead as miserable.'

'Too much milk?' Dennis indicated the mug he'd put in front of Becky, which remained untouched.

'No, it's fine, thanks.' She couldn't bear the thought of having to put her lips to the mug but as she didn't want to offend either of them, she forced herself to do it. 'So did you get your place through the homeless charity, John? Dennis was telling me how valuable they are.'

'I did, yes. And they *are* amazing. I wouldn't be here now if it wasn't for them. They give us all hope.'

'And what about you?' She turned to look at Dennis. 'Is there any chance they'll help you out in the same way?'

'Eventually. I'm one of the newer homeless, so with the cuts in funding and a list of people before me, I could be waiting some time.'

'Oh.' Becky was disappointed. She would have loved to hear that there was something in the pipeline – something to cling on to – for her as well as him.

'But I have other plans,' continued Dennis. 'I've been looking for a job – anything at all just to get my foot on the ladder. When I can get a few bob coming in, I can get my own place. I won't have to be relying on the charity and, in fact, when I get myself sorted, I'd like to do some volunteer work with them.'

Becky was shocked. 'I'd have thought you'd want to get away from this life and never look back.'

'Alice, no matter what happens, I'll never turn my back on these people.' Dennis was looking at her earnestly. 'I hope that when I get myself sorted, I'll never be homeless again, but I'll definitely want to help those who are.'

'Sure, look at me,' said John, slugging back the last of his tea. 'I'm well set up now but they can't keep me away. It's just a part of my life now.'

'I see.' Becky didn't really. She was beginning to feel really nauseous and just wanted to get out of there. 'Dennis, didn't you say you were going to take me to some other spots too? Maybe we should move on before it gets too late.'

'And how about you, Alice?' John leaned his elbows on the old wooden table. 'Do you have someone to go home to of an evening?'

'I don't have a husband, if that's what you mean. It's just me and my dau—' Oh, Jesus! She hadn't wanted to mention Lilly. It was too soon. She didn't need Dennis to be asking questions. It was all far too awkward.

'A daughter!' John clapped his hands together. 'You have a daughter. How old is she? I bet she's a cracker.'

Becky was aware of Dennis watching her, waiting for an answer. 'Y – yes. I have a little girl. She's four years old.'

'So no dad on the scene, then?' Oh, God! John wasn't shy about asking questions. She knew this had been a bad idea.

'Ah, leave her alone, John,' said Dennis, playfully punching the other man. 'I'm sure she doesn't want to be interrogated by you. Her job is to ask the questions, not to answer them.'

Thank God for Dennis. 'As I said, we should probably make a move. I need to get home in the next hour or so.'

'Right, let's go.' He hauled his rucksack onto his back. 'I'll talk to you tomorrow, John.'

They headed towards the door and Becky was aware of a number of eyes on her. The place had begun to creep her out and she was glad to be leaving. A few men standing at the wall whistled as she passed and one even had the nerve to try to cop a feel of her boob.

'Fuck off and leave the woman alone, Lazzer.' Dennis put a protective arm around her. 'Sorry about that. Some of them are just idiots.'

'It's okay.' Becky was glad to breathe the fresh air again. 'But I really do have to go soon so where else did you want to take me?'

'Well, it's up to you but I thought you might like to see where I put my head down at night. It will give you a real sense of what it's like to be homeless.'

'Well, if you didn't mind, that would be great.' Becky hated the thought of it, but she could hardly say no.

'Right, let's head over there straight away. Now the cleaners haven't been in today and I haven't had a chance to tidy or anything, so you'll have to close your eyes to any mess.'

Becky didn't know whether to laugh or cry. They walked in silence most of the way and she wondered what he was thinking. Was he embarrassed to bring her to where he sleeps? No, he wouldn't have suggested it if he was. Or was he thinking about the injustice of life that he was going to be settling down in a sleeping bag on the streets tonight while she was going home to luxury.

They passed through Grafton Street, where the Christmas lights had been switched on only days before, and even though it was still daylight, Becky loved the Christmassy atmosphere. She idly wondered if homeless people enjoyed the build-up to the festive season or if it just brought misery with it. Dennis stopped suddenly and broke into her thoughts.

'So here it is – my humble abode.'

'You sleep *here*?' She felt choked up. Although she knew he slept on the streets, it was very confronting to see the space where he spent his nights.'

'Most nights, yes. You learn things when you've been on the streets for a while. You learn where the best spots are and where you're most likely to be left alone.'

'So does nobody bother you here?'

'Not usually. I've had a few incidents – even as recently as a few weeks ago.' He told her the story of the drunken teens who'd kicked him black and blue.

Becky was appalled and felt physically sick. 'I don't know what to say. How could they treat you like that?'

'It's not nice but it's one of the hazards of living on the streets.'

'And does anyone ever talk to you or try to help you?'

'Sometimes people will stop and ask if I'm okay. They might throw a bit of change in my box. It makes them feel better, I suppose.'

Becky hung her head. She'd often thrown a few euro into a homeless person's begging box. Dennis was right. It was just to make herself feel better. She'd throw in her loose change and then go about her business feeling like she deserved her own good fortune.

'So have I shocked you enough yet?'

'I just think it's such a sad life, Dennis. You deserve better. Surely you can get yourself out of this rut. Is there nobody that could help you? I know you said you had no family, but what about friends?'

Dennis shook his head. 'As I told you before, they didn't stick around when I hit rock bottom.'

'That's awful.' Becky thought of her own two best friends and thanked God for them both.

'Look, it is what it is. Just make sure you mention the homeless charities and all the cuts the government are making to the homeless budget.'

'I'll do my best.' How was she ever going to tell him there wouldn't be any article?

'So if you have everything you need, I'll say goodbye, then.'

Becky felt a sudden panic rise up inside her. 'But we didn't even discuss how you got here in the first place – how you lost your business and how things went so wrong for you.'

'Well, we could always meet in the social club again for a chat. We could have a cup of tea and you could meet some more of the lads.'

Becky's face fell. She didn't know what to say.

'Ha! Relax, Alice. I wouldn't put you through that again. Let's meet in Martha's. You name the day and time – it's not as though my calendar is filling up quickly.'

Thank God for that. 'Okay. But I'll have to give you a ring. I'm not sure when I'm free yet.'

'No problem. Get yourself home to that little girl of yours and give her a big kiss. Tell her how lucky she is and to appreciate every moment.'

Tears sprang to Becky's eyes and she thought she'd never get away. She shook his hand before rushing off down the street. Hearing him mention Lilly had been weird. He was her father, for God's sake. The whole thing was ridiculous and if Becky didn't rein it in, it could well spin out of control. She couldn't drift along like this, pretending she was a journalist and not facing the real issues. She had to make a decision soon. But right now, she still didn't know whether that decision would bring Dennis Prendergast into their lives or not.

# Chapter 30

Becky checked on the salmon in the oven before putting the finishing touches to the table. She'd toyed with the idea of buying a nice tablecloth for the occasion and some fancy napkins, but in the end had decided to keep it simple. The little cream wooden table was usually strewn with plastic table mats so she'd cleared it and added a few red candles across the centre to create a bit of colour and atmosphere.

Tonight she was entertaining Len, and she'd never been so nervous. She'd told him to come at eight, giving him just enough time for a bonding chat with Lilly before she went to bed. The little girl had already eaten and was in her pyjamas watching telly and Becky was looking forward to having a child-free meal with Len later. She wasn't exactly Nigella when it came to cooking, but had managed to make a pesto crumb and stick it on top of a couple of salmon fillets. She had baby potatoes simmering in a pot and some carrots and broccoli ready to go. It would have to do. And besides, the food probably wouldn't be top of his agenda.

That was another thing that was worrying her. They still hadn't managed to get past first base and it was like an unspoken thing between them that tonight would be the night. But it had been a long time for Becky and she really didn't know if she was ready. She'd changed her clothes about five times before settling on a pair of tapered black trousers and a green silk top.

'Mummy, is the man here yet?' Lilly's voice echoed into the kitchen, jolting Becky out of her reverie. Switching the oven to low, she headed into the sitting room to wait with her daughter.

'Push up there,' said Becky, half-sitting on Lilly on the sofa. 'You're taking up all the space.'

'Mummmmyyy! You're squishing me.'

'Well, you'll have to move, then, won't you?' Becky laughed as Lilly struggled to free herself and wriggled over to the other end of the sofa. 'And Lilly, remember I told you not to call him "the man". His name is Len. It's rude not to use someone's name.'

A pout began to form on her lips and then her eyes lit up. 'Is he going to bring me something? I hope he brings a DVD.'

'I don't know, sweetheart. But you shouldn't always expect something.'

'But I don't 'spect it. He just brings it and I don't even ask him. I think he likes me.'

'Of course he does. You're perfect.' Becky placed a kiss on the top of her head. 'And do you like him?'

'He's nice, but I don't really want him to be your friend.'

Becky's heart dropped. She'd thought Lilly was coming around to the idea of a man in their lives. 'But why not, love?'

'Because you've got me and Alice and all your other friends. You don't need another one.'

'Sweetheart, there's always room for more friends. Look at you and all the new friends you've made in playschool. Len is *my* new friend and I want the two of you to get on because you're the most important thing in the world to me.'

This seemed to appease her and Becky headed back into the kitchen to check on dinner. This was all new to Lilly – to them both. She couldn't expect her daughter to embrace change when she was still getting used to it herself.

The potatoes and salmon were done so she put them on a low heat and switched on the cooker under the vegetables. It was almost eight and from what she'd seen of Len so far, he was a meticulous timekeeper. Everything about him was meticulous really; his hair, his clothes, even how he spoke. On paper, he was her perfect man. So why didn't she feel those tingles of anticipation when he held her close or kissed her? Why did she not feel flutters in her stomach when his hand brushed 'accidentally' against her breasts? Maybe it was because she was older. Maybe those feelings were exclusive to young people in the first flush of love. That was probably what it was. She'd just have to learn to adjust and realise that things were different to what they were five or ten years ago. *She* was different.

The doorbell rang. Eight o'clock on the button. Becky smiled as she smoothed down her silk top, stepped into her black heels that she'd left at the kitchen door and headed out to greet Len.

'Is that the man, Mummy?' Lilly shouted as Becky passed the door of the sitting room.

Becky rolled her eyes. So much for Lilly doing as she was told. As she opened the door, the scent of Len's aftershave wafted in and with it brought memories of the past. They were good memories. Things suddenly felt right.

'Hiya, gorgeous,' he said, a bottle of wine in one hand, a bunch of roses in the other. 'Hope I'm not too early.'

Becky smiled. 'Bang on time – but I suspect you knew that. Come on in.'

He kissed her lightly on the cheek before following her into the kitchen. 'Something smells delicious. I hope you haven't gone to too much trouble.'

'I *never* go to too much trouble in the kitchen, I'm afraid. I hope you like salmon.'

'Love it.' He began to pull out a chair before Becky stopped him.

'I thought we'd sit in with Lilly for a bit. Give you two a chance to chat before dinner.'

'Oh! I thought it would be just the two of us for dinner.'

'You thought I'd lock her up in a dungeon while we had dinner?' Becky laughed. 'She isn't Cinderella, you know.'

Len smiled. 'I didn't mean that and you know it. I just thought maybe she'd be going to bed.'

'I'm only having you on, Len. She's eaten and ready for bed. She'll be fast asleep before we sit down to eat.'

'Right, then, let's go in and chat to the little lady.'

Becky led the way into the sitting room and hoped Lilly would be on her best behaviour. 'Lilly, Len's here. I thought we'd sit in here with you while we're waiting for dinner.'

'Hi again, Lilly.' Len held out his hand but Lilly kept hers under her chin as she lay on her front, her eyes firmly glued to the telly.

'Lilly! Say hello to Len.'

'Hello.' Her glance flicked to him and then back to the telly.

He sat on the armchair under the window and tried again. 'So how's playschool going? Your mummy tells me you're very clever. Do you like it?'

'Yes. Did you bring me something?'

'Lilly, watch your manners.' Becky was mortified.

'Well, actually,' said Len, reaching into his pocket, 'I have a little something I thought would look lovely on a princess. Are there any princesses here?' He pretended to look around the room and Lilly jumped up, squealing.

'Me, me! I'm a princess. Give it to me.'

'Of course you are. Silly me for forgetting.' He pulled out a little box and handed it to Lilly, whose eyes almost popped out of her head.

'Len, you shouldn't have,' said Becky, staring in amazement as her daughter grabbed the box from his hands. 'You don't have to keep buying her presents.'

'But I want to. I can't think of a better way to spend my money.'

'Look, Mummy, look.' It was a little silver Pandora charm bracelet and Becky's eyes filled with tears at his thoughtfulness.

'It's beautiful, darling. Say thank you to Len.'

'Thank you, Len. Can I put it on now, Mummy, pleeeeease?'

'Maybe Len will put it on for you while I go and check on the dinner.' She smiled to herself as she heard Len ask Lilly loads of questions. 'So what do you like watching on telly? Do you have a best friend in school? What's your teddy's name?' He was really doing everything he could to get her to like him. But another half-hour and Lilly would be asleep, leaving them to enjoy the rest of the evening themselves.

The salmon was well done so she lifted the two pieces out of the oven and put them on the plates she had warming. She strained the water from the potatoes and vegetables and added those to the plates. She'd leave the plates in the oven while she got Lilly to bed.

'Right, Lilly love,' she said, holding out her arms. 'Let's get you up to bed so Mummy and Len can have dinner.'

'But I don't want to go. Why can't I just stay here?'

'Because you have school in the morning and because I said so.'

'You should do as your mummy says.'

Lilly glared at Len. 'You can't tell me what to do. You're not the boss of me.'

Becky had to stifle a giggle. She found it hilarious but she couldn't let Lilly away with talking to Len like that. 'That's very rude, Lilly. Say you're sorry right now.'

'But Mummy, it's true. Only *you* are the boss of me.'

It was hard to argue with that. 'Come on, Missy. We'll talk about this later.'

'But, Mummyyyyyy, I don't want to go.'

'I'm not arguing with you.' She scooped the little girl up in her arms and turned to Len. 'Sorry about that. And after you bought her that gorgeous bracelet and everything.'

'Don't worry, Becky. I'm sure she's just tired. Why don't you get her to bed and we can relax over dinner.'

Big fat tears streamed down Lilly's face as Becky carried her upstairs and tucked her into bed. 'I'm very disappointed in you, Miss. I can't believe you spoke to Len like that after he was so good to you.'

'I'm sorry, Mummy. Please don't be cross.'

Becky's heart melted. 'It's okay, love. You're tired. Just go to sleep now and we'll talk about it in the morning.' She kissed her on the forehead and turned off the light. Leaving the door a little open so the light from the landing would seep in just as Lilly liked it, she headed back downstairs. She took the plates out of the oven and put them on two leather placemats on the table. Perfect.

'You can come in now,' she said, peeping into the sitting room where Len was still waiting. 'It's a Lilly-free zone in the kitchen.'

'Phew! Thank God for that.' But he was smiling.

Becky indicated for him to sit down and she poured some white wine into his glass. 'I'm sorry about Lilly. She really does like you but I think she's just afraid you'll take me away from her.'

'No need to be sorry. She's just a kid. I'm sure it's not easy to see someone else taking her mum's attention. And I'm sure bringing up a child on your own can't be easy either.'

'It can be hard at times, but at least I have great support in Alice. She's like another mother to Lilly.'

'And how are you feeling now about the father?'

'You mean Dennis? I'm still torn. Part of me wants to follow through and tell him and the other part of me wants to run a mile.'

'Well, I think you're mad even contemplating telling him. What good could come of it?'

'As I said to you before, it's for Lilly I'd be doing it. So that she can get to know her father.'

'But biology is a bit overrated, don't you think? What good would he be? He was really only a glorified sperm donor and has had nothing to do with the child since she was born.'

Becky placed her knife and fork down on the plate and stared at Len. 'A glorified sperm donor? What a crude thing to say.'

'I don't mean for it to be crude, Becky. But it's a fact. Does he really deserve to be part of your lives now?'

'I honestly don't know. I keep changing my mind about what I want to do.'

Len pushed his own plate away and Becky was happy to see he'd eaten everything. 'Look, Becky. The fact is he's homeless. What could he offer Lilly? He has no home, no money and no prospects.'

Becky nodded. What Len was saying was true up to a point, but she didn't agree entirely. There was just something about Dennis Prendergast. He seemed strong and focused, despite his situation. It was true that he had no money and no home but she saw something in his eyes that told her he was going to make something of himself again. He had a grim determination that was very appealing and the more she thought about it, the more she felt that Lilly should get to know him.

'Are you still with me, Becky?'

'Sorry, I was miles away. I hear what you're saying about Dennis, but I'm just not sure. Now are you ready for dessert or should we wait a while?'

'How about we take our glasses into the sitting room and not worry about dessert just yet.'

'Good idea,' said Becky, relieved that she didn't have to produce her shop-bought pecan pie. 'You go on in. I just have to nip to the loo.'

With the toilet door firmly closed behind her, she rooted in her bag for her lipstick. After she'd applied the pink gloss, she brushed her hair until it was silky and adjusted her top so that just the right amount of cleavage showed. She tried to muster up a bit of excitement, but all she felt was trepidation.

'This is nice, isn't it?' said Len, as she kicked off her shoes and joined him on the sofa. 'I'm glad we didn't go out, are you?'

'Definitely.'

He pulled her a little closer and moved in for a kiss.

'I have a headache, Mummy. And I'm sooo hot. I think I need medicine.'

'Lilly!' Becky jumped back to the other side of the sofa. 'I didn't hear you coming down the stairs.'

'I don't want to stay in bed. My headache is too bad.'

'Come here then and let me feel your forehead.'

'She's only having you on,' whispered Len, who didn't look a bit pleased at having their intimate moment interrupted. Becky was inclined to agree, but she couldn't just dismiss her daughter.

'How about I get you some medicine and then you'll be able to sleep.'

'Okay, Mummy.'

Becky flew into the kitchen and pulled the first aid box from a cupboard. She pulled out a bottle of Calpol and took a 5ml measuring spoon from the drawer. A spoonful of this should settle her down and they could get back to what they were doing – not that they'd even really got started.

'Here you go, sweetie. You like this one. It's strawberry.'

'I think I'll just go up to bed now, Mummy. I'm feeling better.'

'Are you? But I thought you said your headache was really bad?' Becky noticed a look between Lilly and Len and she wondered what had transpired when she was out of the room.

'It's gone now. Night night.'

'Well, if you're sure?' She watched as Lilly left the room and made her way up the stairs. 'You obviously have the magic touch, Len. What did you say to her?'

'I didn't say a thing. Now come on over here and let's finish what we started.'

'But—'

His lips were on hers and she gave in to his passion. He was a brilliant kisser. She wrapped her arms around him and they fell back on the sofa. His kissing became more urgent and he began to unbutton her blouse. She allowed him to undo the first few before pulling away suddenly.

'What's wrong?'

'I … I'm sorry. It's just with Lilly and everything. It doesn't feel right.'

'Come on. She's probably fast asleep by now.' He tried to pull her back to him but she didn't let him.

'I'll go and check. I don't feel comfortable knowing she could be lying awake listening to us.' She rushed upstairs before he could say another word. She got to Lilly's room and peeped in. She was, just as Len had said, fast asleep, her blonde hair fanned out on the pillow. Becky quietly stepped inside and closed the door. She sat down on the end of the bed and tried to get herself together. She needed to think. Len was gorgeous and great company. She enjoyed his kisses and the feel of his arms around her. He was all man and his musky scent had been driving her mad tonight. But she wasn't sure she wanted more. Much as she wanted him to be the man of her dreams, there was just no spark. She didn't get that knot of excitement in her stomach when she saw him the way she did when she looked into Dennis Prendergast's eyes.

# Chapter 31

'Are you sure you're okay to go to work, Alice? Why don't I ring Becky for you and tell her you're not feeling well?'

Alice shook her head and hauled herself out of the bed. 'You can't do that, Frank. I'll be fine. It's nothing I can't handle.'

Frank looked at her with concern. 'But you've barely slept and I hate to say it, but you really don't look too good.'

'Thanks, cheer me up, why don't you!'

'Don't be like that. I'm just concerned, that's all. You've been exhausted for weeks now, you're off your food and you're snapping the head off me for every little thing.'

'Don't be such a pig, Frank. I don't snap the—'

'Ha! You see?'

Alice couldn't help laughing. 'God, I hate that you're always right. I suppose I have been a bit off lately, but it's nothing a good tonic and a bit more sleep won't cure.'

Frank grinned. 'Well, you'd get a lot more sleep if you didn't keep pestering me for sex in the middle of the night.'

'Bloody cheek,' laughed Alice, picking up a pillow and slapping him over the head with it. 'When do I ever do that?'

'You can't blame a man for dreaming. Seriously, though, I think you should go to the doctor. Just get some blood tests done to reassure us there's nothing else going on.'

Alice wrapped her robe around her and slipped her feet into her slippers. 'Frank, I don't need to go to the doctor. Do the maths. I'm a forty-seven-year-old woman.'

He pulled her back down onto the bed. 'I know you said you're menopausal but shouldn't you just get checked anyway? I'm sure there are things you can take to help you through it. It's the twenty-first century, for God's sake. Women don't have to suffer like this.'

'Leave it, will you.' She pulled away from him and headed for the door. 'You have no idea what it's like. I'm not exactly dying. I have a few minor symptoms and if it's okay with you, I'd prefer not to have to deal with the inevitable yet. At least let me get into my fifties before I have to admit I'm a failure as a woman.'

'Ah, Alice. Don't say that. You'll never be a failure. You're a wonderful woman and no matter what happens to your body, your heart will never change. And it's a big, big heart.'

'What would I do without you, Frank?' Big tears welled up in her eyes and began to slide down her nose. 'I love you so much.'

Frank was out of the bed like a light and over with his arms around her. 'I love you too, pet. Now are you going to get back into that bed and let me ring Becky? I'm sure she can make other arrangements for Lilly today. You really should rest.'

'I really *shouldn't*, actually. It gives me too much time to think. I'd prefer to keep busy and Lilly is the perfect company.'

'Well, if there's nothing I can say to make you change your mind, I'll make dinner this evening. I should be finished that job in Finglas by lunchtime so I'll pick up a few bits in Tesco and rustle us up something.'

Alice touched his face gently and kissed him on the lips. 'You're an angel. And sorry for being such a grump lately. This weather isn't helping either. Maybe I have that SAD thing. I'm always so much happier when the sun is shining.'

'That's it!'

'What is?' Alice was confused.

'The sun. Maybe we should take off somewhere nice and warm for a week. It would do us both good.'

'Do you really mean it? I'd love that. Where would we go? And can you get time off? I wonder if Becky would be able to make alternative arrangements for Lilly.'

Frank laughed.

'What?' said Alice, staring at him.

'Just you. You're adorable when you get all excited. I'll make some enquiries when I'm home this afternoon and we can chat about it over dinner.'

'Lovely. Now I'd better get my ass into gear or I'll be late. Bags first in the shower.'

She shot into the bathroom before he could answer but she was laughing. Frank certainly knew how to cheer her up. She'd been feeling really hormonal lately – grumpy for no reason and getting annoyed by the least little thing. Another man wouldn't stand for it but not her Frank. He understood. He was one of the good ones.

She stepped into the shower and let the warm water sluice over her body. She was alarmed to feel the pockets of fat around her middle that hadn't been there before. She'd become a bit complacent since Frank had moved in. But she was determined not to let herself go. She'd start exercising again as soon as she felt a bit better. It shouldn't take her long to get back into shape. Her skin was feeling a bit lacklustre too, so maybe she'd get Lilly to help her make a nice olive oil face mask later.

She smiled to herself when she thought of the little girl. She was such a joy. Suddenly realisation dawned on her and it was like she was seeing things clearly for the first time in ages. She, Alice O'Malley, was one of the luckiest people in the world. She spent too much time mourning the child she never had instead of embracing the wonderful people she *did* have in her life. Well, she was giving herself a mental kick and things were going to be different from now on. Frank, Becky, Lilly – they were the people that mattered and she was going to make sure they knew how much they meant to her.

❀

'Hi, Alice,' said Becky, opening the door for Alice to step in out of the rain. 'Miserable day out there. I can't say I'm looking forward to the bus journey to work.'

'It's horrible.' Alice followed her into the kitchen. 'But Frank and I are thinking of escaping it soon.'

'What?' Becky swung around to look at her. All she needed now was Alice deserting her.'

'Don't worry. We're just talking about it at the moment. We thought it would be nice to have a week away somewhere nice and warm. But it would be depending on how you're fixed.'

'Well, I suppose I still have some days due to me.'

'Brilliant. Why don't you and Len take Lilly away somewhere for a few days? It would be a good way to get her to bond with him.'

'Hmmmm.'

'Uh, oh. I take it last night didn't go well so? Right, I'm sticking the kettle on and you can tell me all about it. Is Lilly still asleep?'

Becky sighed. 'Yes. The poor little thing is exhausted – she had a bit of a late night. I thought I'd just leave her there for a bit.'

'Late night? I thought you were going to get her to bed early so you and Len could have some time alone.' Alice stuck teabags in two mugs and stood waiting for the kettle to boil.

'Yes, but Lilly had other ideas. She came downstairs complaining of a headache just as we were about to … well, you know.'

'Oh, God. She didn't see anything, did she?'

'There was nothing to see, thankfully.'

Alice giggled. 'I'm sorry but I can just picture the scene. Were you mortified? How was he about it?'

'He was great, actually. He knows she needs time to adjust and he's being very good to her.'

'Fair play to him. You should really think about a few days away. It might help Lilly see that she's not being left out and that having Len in your lives is a good thing.'

'The idea of a holiday sounds great, but I can't see it happening any time soon.'

'Why? Is it because of Lilly?'

'That's only part of it. We still haven't … you know …'

'Oh! But it wouldn't be that sort of holiday anyway with Lilly there. And are you planning to … you know … any time soon?'

Becky laughed. 'I'm really not sure, Alice. He's a nice guy. He's gorgeous, kind and considerate. But the passion isn't quite there. Not on my part, anyway.'

'But that might come with time, Becky. You're older than you were when you last dated and your life is different. Maybe you shouldn't expect the fanfares and fireworks.'

'So is it that way with you and Frank? Is it less passionate than what you had with your husband?'

Alice thought for a few seconds. 'It's different, Becky. I really can't compare the two. I had a good marriage for a while, but Frank and I have a special relationship. We do have great sex, but it's not all we're about. Just think about it.'

'You're right. I'm probably clinging on to my youth too much – thinking about those days when you'd see a guy you fancy and your whole insides would do somersaults. I need to give Len a chance.'

'That's all I'm saying,' Alice said, placing two mugs of steaming tea on the table. 'And give Lilly a chance too. Maybe Len will use his charms to win her over the way he did with you.'

'Is he gone, Mummy?'

'Lilly, you're awake.' Becky looked over at the door where Lilly was standing and her heart melted. She was wearing a pair of pink princess pyjamas and holding her teddy by one of his ears. Her blonde hair fell in loose messy pigtails over her shoulders and her eyes were only half open. 'Come on over here and sit on my knee. Alice and I were just having a cup of tea before I have to go to work.'

'Is the man gone?'

'If you mean Len, then yes, he is. He went home last night soon after you went back to bed.'

Lilly nodded and didn't say anything.

'I'm sure when you get to know Len, you'll really like him,' said Alice, watching the little girl carefully. 'Your mummy likes him and you like *everything* your mummy likes.'

''Cept pineapple.'

Becky laughed. 'Let's just forget about Len for now. Be a good girl for Alice, sweetie, and I'll see you later.'

'Bye, Mummy.'

Becky slipped on her shoes out in the hall and wrapped up in her new grey winter coat. She hadn't been able to face another conversation with Lilly about Len. Maybe Alice was right. Maybe she should think of all three of them taking a few days away. She'd put it to Len later and see what he thought. It was only early days for them, but she wanted to make Lilly comfortable about her seeing someone. She always wanted to make her little girl happy, and maybe that would be going on holiday with Len – or maybe it would be allowing her to finally get to know her father.

# Chapter 32

Kate steadied herself by leaning against the toilet door. She really wasn't feeling very well, but she couldn't stop taking the laxatives now or she'd balloon back up to her larger size.

She'd gone to an audition for a television ad yesterday and for the first time ever, she felt like somebody. She felt the judges were really sitting up taking notice when she sashayed out onto the runway. Her green silk, flowing dress from River Island had fallen loosely to her thighs, giving her legs a sense of length, and her red hair had beautifully framed her much thinner face. She'd been called back with five other girls and was due to go for another audition next week.

She looked at her face in the mirror and noticed the grey tinge to her skin, but that was a small price to pay – besides, she could easily cover it up with make-up. The pain struck again and she rushed back into the toilet just in time. She hoped to God nobody else would come in this early. She reckoned there couldn't be much else left in her so she should be fine for the rest of the day.

When she'd realised how hard it was to deal with the effects of the laxatives, she'd thought about other quick measures to lose the pounds. She wasn't stupid but reckoned that she could handle anything just until she got to the size she wanted to be. She didn't have an addictive nature, so she felt it should be easy to stop. She'd contemplated starving herself but she loved her food too much and hated feeling hungry. Then she'd contemplated binging and purging. That hadn't enticed her either because she hated vomiting. She had never understood how people could stick their fingers down their throats to make themselves vomit. No, the laxatives, although uncomfortable, were the best option for the moment. She'd reduce them gradually as soon as she was happy with how she looked.

She pulled the chain and came out of the cubicle just as the door opened and Becky walked in.

'Morning, Kate. You're early this morning. God, what's that smell?'

'Awful, isn't it? Edith O'Connor was in here when I came in. I think she must have had a dodgy curry or something.' It was the best she could think of. She didn't want Becky on her back, asking questions about things.

'I saw her out there at her desk. She did look a bit pale. Poor Edith.'

'So how are things with you?' Kate asked, wanting to change the subject. 'How is it going juggling two men in your life?'

'Excuse me?'

'Len and Dennis. It must be exhausting having them both on the go.'

Becky looked furious. 'If I had the energy, I'd slap you.'

'Ah, don't be like that. I was only having a laugh.'

'I know,' sighed Becky. 'It's just things are never straightforward, are they? I honestly don't know what to do with either of them.'

'Well, let's have lunch and you can tell me all about it.' Kate's stomach was rumbling again and she really didn't feel like getting into a long chat at that moment.

'Suits me.' Becky quickly applied some lip gloss and headed for the door. 'I can't bear the smell in here for a minute longer anyway. I'll chat to you later.'

Kate pretended to root in her bag for something until Becky disappeared, then rushed straight back into the toilet. She'd better bloody well get that job now after all this. Just one big break – that's all she needed. One chance to prove that she was worthy of being picked over and above everyone else. She needed it for all those times she'd been the last girl standing when the other girls would pick teams for netball at school or when the bullies would beg the teacher not to put her in their group for projects. She needed to prove something to them. She needed to prove to herself she was worth something.

❖

Becky headed back to her desk but something was bothering her. Kate was never in work this early. She'd usually rush in at the last minute, just about making it to her desk on time. And she'd been acting a bit shifty too. It was as though she was hiding something. Becky hoped she wasn't having problems with Garreth. He was such a lovely guy and they were perfect for each other. They were both still young, but Becky would hate to see them splitting up.

But she had enough of her own problems and didn't need to be worrying about anyone else. She was really warming to the idea of a few days with Len, so maybe she'd give him a ring and talk to him about it. She looked around to make sure nobody was listening and quickly dialled the number.

'Hi, Len, it's Becky.'

'Hi there, you. I was just thinking about you.'

'All good, I hope?'

'Of course. I was thinking about last night and how it was a pity things didn't go to plan. We'll have to reschedule soon. You can't expect to look as hot as you do and not drive me mad with desire.'

Becky laughed. 'Well, if it's more time with me you want, I might have the perfect plan.'

'Well, don't keep me in suspense.'

'I was thinking … it's just a thought and I know we've only been seeing each other a short time and I don't want you to think I'm being too forward but—'

'Come on, stop being all coy and just tell me!'

'I was hoping maybe we could get away for a few days. Nothing fancy and not too far away. Maybe two or three nights somewhere like Galway or something? What do you say?'

'I say it's a brilliant idea. When were you thinking?'

'I was hoping maybe this side of Christmas. We could even do a bit of Christmas shopping too.'

'That sounds great. Let me know dates that suit and I'll see if I can work around them. It will be nice to spend some quality time together.'

Thank God he was so enthusiastic. 'I'll have to wait until Alice gets back to me with dates. She's off on holidays for a week so I'll have to take that time off to mind Lilly. But I'm easy about whether you'd prefer early or later in the week.'

There was a silence on the other end of the phone.

'Len, are you there?'

'Em, yes, sorry. I'm not sure I understand. How can you go away if Alice isn't there? Or do you have someone else to mind Lilly?'

'What are you talking about? I don't need anyone else. Lilly will be with me.'

'Oh! I thought you meant for just you and me to have a few days away together.'

Becky laughed. 'Well, that would never happen. Lilly and I come as a package. I could never go away and leave her.'

'Well, yes, of course. I just thought ... you know.'

'You just thought what?'

'I just thought it would have been nice to be on our own for a change.'

Becky sighed. 'Len, how many times do I have to tell you, I can't just ignore Lilly. She's a part of me, and where I go, she goes.'

'Ah, don't be cross, Becky.' His voice was soft. 'You can't blame me for wanting some alone time with you. I'm a hot-blooded male and I might just spontaneously combust if you put me off any longer.'

She laughed at that. 'Our time will come. But as far as a holiday goes, if it happens, it will be all three of us.'

'Well, if you let me know the dates you're thinking of, I'll see if I can manage the time off. The only thing is it's hectic here coming up to Christmas. It might be difficult to organise but I'll try.'

'Okay so. I'll chat to you later.' Hmmm! Difficult to organise. He hadn't said that when he thought it was just the two of them, Becky thought to herself. Still, it was hard to be cross with him. As he said himself, he was a hot-blooded male and they'd hardly got past first base.

She flicked on her computer and began to sort out the post in her in-tray. Her job was beginning to feel more and more like a chore to her lately. She used to love coming in and dealing with customers. She loved the cut and thrust of the business world and would get huge satisfaction out of getting things done. Not any more. Her mind was rarely on the job these days. She was either thinking about her relationship with Len and all the possibilities that brought with it or she was thinking about the situation with Dennis.

Dennis Prendergast. What was it about that man that kept her wanting more? It seemed ridiculous that she'd enjoy the company of someone like that. Maybe she was getting soft in her old age – or maybe she was just realising that life could sometimes be cruel and one wrong turn and any of us could be in his situation.

Her mind wandered back to her childhood and she shuddered. She was so lucky to have escaped. She could so easily have gone down the same route as her parents. And now her mother was dead and her father may as well be. But at least she had Joanna. She couldn't believe how close she felt to her, even after their years apart. And she'd been so encouraging and supportive about Dennis. It was wonderful to have a sister again.

A beep from her mobile in her bag caused her to jump and she grabbed it out quickly. It was from Alice to say she and Lilly were going for a burger and chips after playschool. She was about to put the phone back in her bag when she had a sudden thought.

She tapped in Dennis' name and let her fingers hover over the number. She wanted to ring him but a little voice in her head was telling her not to be so keen. And was it really fair to continue with this charade if she wasn't going to tell him the truth?

But she chose to ignore the little voice and pressed the number.

'Hello,' came a wary voice.

Her heart gave a little leap. 'Hi, Dennis. It's Be ... It's Alice. I just wondered if you'd like to meet again. For the articles. I mean to chat. Again.'

'Don't you have those articles finished yet? Surely you have enough information by now.'

'There was just one or two more things, but if you're busy ...'

'Is that meant to be a joke?' He sounded annoyed.

'Of course not. I didn't mean anything by it. I just meant that if you'd rather not ...'

'It's fine. How about lunchtime today? I was going to pop in to Martha's anyway.'

She'd promised Kate. She couldn't just cancel her like that. 'That's perfect. I'll see you shortly after one?'

'Right you are. I'll see you then.' And he was gone.

She suddenly noticed a few sets of eyes looking in her direction. She was always on at the staff for making personal calls during work time, so it wasn't surprising they'd be happy to catch her doing the same. She slipped the phone back into her bag and began to tap away at her computer. She felt guilty about Kate. But she knew the other girl would understand when she found out why she had to cancel. She'd make sure to spend some time with her over the coming days because it was clear there was something going on with her. If there was one thing she'd learned from Dennis Prendergast, it was compassion. He made her want to be a better person. And there was no better place to start than with her friends.

# Chapter 33

Becky sat in Martha's feeling nervous and wondering why Dennis Prendergast had such an effect on her. She was sure about one thing, though, she was tired of all the lies. Today, she was going to make a decision whether to walk away from Dennis for good or to come clean and include him in their lives. That's assuming he'd want to be included.

Glancing at her watch, she realised they wouldn't have much time. She'd already been slacking off work this morning, so she'd really need to be back by two to catch up.

'Can I get you something to eat with that tea?' It was the old lady who ran the shop.

'I'm actually waiting for someone, but thanks.'

'Everything is freshly made, you know. And we use the best of ingredients.'

She had her notebook poised and Becky realised she wasn't going away. 'Okay, I'll have a cheese salad sandwich on brown please. No butter.'

'Coming right up.' And then to Becky's surprise, the old lady bent in close to her. 'And if it's Dennis you're waiting for, go easy on him, okay? He's a good lad and needs to be treated with respect.'

Becky's mouth gaped open as she watched her disappear behind the counter. Well, that was weird. How did the woman know she was meeting Dennis? There must be hundreds of people who come and go in the busy shop every day. And why was it that she'd almost sounded threatening? She wondered how she knew Dennis and why she was being so protective of him.

'Hi, Alice. Sorry I'm late.'

Becky jumped as Dennis rushed in. 'Don't worry about it. Good to see you.'

He sat opposite her, keeping his jacket on and blowing on his hands. 'Bloody freezing out there, isn't it?'

'It's cold all right. They say we're in for a cold snap over the next few weeks.' Becky could have kicked herself. It wasn't exactly a great thing to say to a man who lived on the streets.

'You should try sleeping in it. I woke up like an ice block and haven't got the heat into me ever since.'

'God, that must be awful. You should get something warm into you.' As if by magic, the old lady appeared again, pen poised over her notebook.'

'Hi, Martha,' Dennis said, smiling at her. 'I'll have a club sandwich please and a nice mug of tea.'

'Right you are. It'll just be a few minutes.'

Becky noticed the look between the two. 'Do you know each other?'

'Yep. Martha's great. She gets me to do some odd jobs and feeds me up in return. This place has become a bit of a sanctuary for me, to be honest.'

'I'm really curious about something, Dennis. Do you not actually have any family or have they just turned their backs on you?' She'd been thinking about her own situation and had begun to feel some empathy for Dennis.

'No family, except for my mother. And let's just say we don't talk much.'

'It must have been so hard not to have any support when you went from being a high flyer to a … a …'

'… a bum?'

Becky could feel the colour creep up her neck. 'I wasn't going to say that. I was going to say a homeless person. And what about children?' Becky held her breath.

Martha chose that moment to arrive over with the tea and sandwiches. 'There you go. Enjoy.'

They both nodded their thanks but Becky was anxious to get an answer to her question. 'So, I was asking you whether you have any children.'

He shook his head. 'Probably just as well.'

Becky couldn't help her sigh of relief.

'But don't feel sorry for me. Maybe if I'd found myself a wife and settled down back in the good days instead of being a player, I wouldn't have ended up in this mess.'

'You never did tell me what exactly happened. I still can't get my head around how someone like you could end up on the streets.'

Dennis took a large bite of his sandwich and chewed slowly. 'It's just one of those things. It's like when you hear about a horrible car crash or someone being shot, you always think it could never happen to you. But it could – and for me, it did. The homelessness, I mean.'

'But didn't you have people around you? Even work colleagues? Surely there was someone you could have turned to when things got really bad.'

'I was an idiot, Alice. When things were going well, I was loaded. I threw my money around, playing the big-shot estate agent. I'd go out every night partying and I just completely lost sight of the important things in life.'

'Which are?'

'Well, friendship, I suppose. And the simple things like common decency and kindness. If I'd been a better person, then there'd have been people who'd have been there for me. But when I didn't have any money left, most of the so-called friends I had disappeared. I'd have been better off holding on to a couple of good friends instead of collecting a load of fair-weather ones, who were only hanging around to feed off my good fortune.'

Becky shook her head. 'So you literally had nobody. You lost everything and had nobody to help you through it.'

'That's about it. There were a few who helped initially, but pride is one sure way to self-destruct. I was too proud to admit how bad things were. And then with the guilt weighing me down ...'

'What guilt? You mentioned guilt before but how can you feel guilty about things that were out of your control. A lot of businesses failed during the recession. You're not alone.'

'Believe me, Alice. When you feel consumed by failure, loss and guilt, you live in your own head and it's the loneliest place you could ever imagine.' His head dropped and he began to tear pieces off his serviette.

Becky nibbled at her sandwich, unsure what to say. She could feel tears threaten to surface and she tried her best to hold them back. He was a decent guy who'd just fallen on hard times. Life could be so cruel.

'I see you're still not taking notes.'

'Sorry?'

'No notebook and pen,' said Dennis, nodding at her empty hands. I thought you journalists always had a little spiral notebook where you wrote everything down and a recording device so as not to miss a single word.'

'Well, as I said before, I just like to take it all in.' It sounded lame but it was the best she had. 'It's a fascinating story. You said you were hoping to change things – maybe get a job and a place of your own. Anything happening with that?'

'Nothing at all.' Becky noticed how his face fell as he said it. 'I sometimes get bursts of energy and positivity and think that things are going to happen for me. But the reality is quite different. Even non-homeless people are finding it hard enough to get a job these days, never mind me.'

'But you can't lose hope. You've got to stay positive and believe it will happen for you.'

Dennis stared at her, his eyes cold, and she could feel herself shrink. 'And you know that, do you? God, I hate how people like you patronise people like me.'

'I'm sorry, I wasn't—'

'No, Alice. Honestly, you should hear yourself. You have a family, a job, a life. How can you tell me it's going to be all right? I'm not a six-year-old who's afraid of the dark. This is real life and things don't happen just because you believe!'

'Dennis, I really *am* sorry. I was just trying to look on the bright side.'

'Bright side? There *is* no bright side.' His voice was getting louder and his eyes were glistening. 'You've no idea how shit my life is.'

'So let me help you.' Before she realised what she was doing, she reached across and touched his hand. 'Just tell me what I can do to help you get out of this awful situation.'

Dennis looked at her as if she was mad. 'But why would you want to help me? You're just a reporter, doing a job. You'll write the article, the paper will print it and the next day you'll have moved on to the next article. I'll be just another one of those nameless faces who bring down the tone of the city.'

'That's not true, Dennis. I – I like you. You're a decent man and you've made me look at myself and my own life too. I really would like to help, if I can. I could write you a reference for a job, give you a little bit of money to get some decent clothes for interviews – whatever might help.'

He stood up all of a sudden. 'Look, I'm sorry if I seemed a bit aggressive. It just all gets to me sometimes. Thanks for the nice thoughts but I'll be fine. I hope you have all you need for your article.'

'Wait. I don't want you to be angry with me.'

'I'm not, Alice.' His eyes were softer now. 'I'm just tired and fed up. Maybe I'll see you around sometime.'

She felt a panic rise up inside her. 'I'll ring you. We can meet again soon. That's if you want to?'

'Whatever.' He was already walking away.

She felt numb as she sat there alone, her barely eaten sandwich making her stomach lurch. That had been intense. And it had started off so lovely. It was such a shame it had ended like that. She felt guilty somehow. All she'd been trying to do was help. She noticed the time and realised she was already late for work but she didn't care. At this very minute, she didn't care if she never worked in that place again. She had bigger things to worry about.

'Finished with that?' Martha was there beside her, pointing to her sandwich. 'Didn't you like it?'

'Yes, it was lovely, thanks. I guess I just wasn't that hungry.'

'He's gone, then?' The old woman raised her eyebrows.

'Yes, he had to leave.'

'He told me you're a reporter. I hope you treat him with the respect he deserves in that story.'

Becky felt rattled that Dennis had spoken about her to this woman. 'Well, yes, of course. How much do you know about him?'

'I know it all,' said Martha, checking for customers before sitting down in the seat Dennis had just left. 'He comes in here most days and he tells me what's going on. He's a good lad.'

'He seems like a decent guy all right. It must be hard for him. His life has changed so drastically from what it was before.'

Martha nodded. 'Aye. As I said to Dennis himself, there but for the grace of God, go I. None of us can know what's in store and any one of us could be in his situation if things took a turn for the worse.'

'I'm sorry, Martha, I have to run. I'm already late for work.' Becky stood up quickly, her breathing beginning to quicken. She put a twenty euro note on the table. 'That should cover it. Thanks for the chat.'

She could feel Martha's eyes on her as she almost ran for the door. Outside, she gulped in the cold air, trying to slow down her breathing. It took a couple of minutes but eventually her breath began to even out and she felt less panicked. It was Martha's words that had done it. *There but for the grace of God, go I.* The words kept going around and around in her head, like a song on a loop. They were words that were so true for her own life. If she hadn't been so determined, her life could be very different. With parents like hers, she could easily have turned into a drug addict or an alcoholic. She could have ended up on the streets, just like Dennis. She suddenly felt a huge affinity with the father of her child. How could she have reacted so badly to his situation?

She was going to be at least a half an hour late so she began to walk quickly back towards the bank. As she came close to O'Connell Bridge, she could hear the soft sounds of 'Silent Night' in the air. She'd always loved that hymn. She remembered feeling soothed by it during one particular Christmas Eve when her mother had brought her to midnight mass. It had been a particularly bad few days, with her father drinking heavily to celebrate the festive season, and when she'd heard 'Silent Night' being sung in the church, she'd closed her eyes and allowed herself to be transported to a better place.

As she turned onto O'Connell Street, she saw the carollers outside Easons, all wearing Santa hats and looking happy as they swayed from side to side. She paused as she rooted for change in her purse. A young girl held out a bucket and smiled as Becky put the money in. It was then that a banner caught her eye. 'Help the Homeless'. What were the chances that a homeless charity would be collecting right at that moment? It was definitely a sign.

A surge of happiness washed over her and for the first time in ages, she felt really decisive. Tonight she'd go home and cuddle up with Lilly on the sofa. She'd chat to her like she always did and smother her with hugs and kisses. Then tomorrow, she'd finally do it. She'd go and talk to Dennis Prendergast and tell him that he *does* have family after all. She knew it would be a shock, but when he'd had a chance to take it in, Becky would introduce him to his beautiful daughter.

❖

Dennis had walked around the city for ages after his meeting with Alice. He'd needed to clear his head. Her offer of help had unsettled him and all the thoughts he'd tried to suppress about the past kept flooding his brain. His head said he'd need help if he was to get out of the situation he was in, but his heart said he didn't deserve it. Who'd been there to help Alan McCabe? Had anyone offered to help him out of the terrible situation he'd been in?

The weather was unusually warm and Dennis could feel himself sweating under the heap of clothes he was wearing. He'd definitely need to find somewhere to shower later. But right now, he needed to rest. He was happy to see his favourite bench in St Stephen's Green was free so he settled himself down for a nap.

He thought about the first time he'd spoken to Alan McCabe, six years earlier.

Alan had rung the office, saying he'd seen the 'For Sale' sign going up on a house and wanted to find out more. Dennis had been delighted to get a call so soon after the house had gone on the market, and he'd immediately gone into salesman mode. And that's what he was good at.

He'd recited the blurb from the brochure as if his life depended on it. He'd told Alan that he'd be mad to let such an opportunity pass. The house was well constructed and lovingly crafted to the highest standards. It was far superior to any house he'd find in a housing estate and certainly better value for money. It had the best of both worlds – it was on its own grounds but just a stone's throw from a very busy shopping centre.

It had ticked all the boxes for Alan. He'd said he wanted to move his family away from what his wife called 'rural hell'. She was a city girl and although they'd built their own house in a lovely quiet area just outside Skerries a few years earlier, she'd never really settled. She was originally from Italy and had grown up in a busy town with all her family around her. She wasn't used to the silence of rural life and felt isolated. Alan said he just wanted her to be happy and the house in Swords seemed just the thing.

The deal had been sealed in a matter of weeks. But Dennis hadn't stopped at that. He'd sensed the other man's weakness and had taken advantage. Much like himself, Alan was a bit of a wheeler-dealer and always on the lookout for an investment opportunity. And Dennis had known just the thing. Paudie Lenihan, a local developer, had approached Dennis about sending potential investors his way. He'd been planning a big project and needed funding. Alan had suited the bill and had been a willing investor in Paudie's project. But within a few years, Paudie had been declared bankrupt and had disappeared out of the country, leaving his investors with no hope of ever seeing their money again.

At that point, Dennis had been trying to keep his own business going and had blocked all calls from Alan and the other investors he'd sent to Paudie. He'd felt guilty when he'd heard about them losing all their money – of course he had – but what was he to do? He hadn't thought much more about it until the day his mate Simon said, 'Did you hear about Alan McCabe?' And that's when he'd known his life would never be the same again.

# Chapter 34

'This smoked salmon is delicious,' said Becky, tucking into her lunch. 'I can't believe I've never been here before.'

Len nodded. 'There are some great restaurants on Dawson Street. This one is my favourite. They do a lovely dinner in the evening too. We must come back some night.'

'That would be lovely.' But Becky's mind was on other things. She kept thinking about her chat with Dennis the previous day and how she was going to tell him about Lilly. She felt a mixture of excitement and dread. It was the right thing to do. She knew that now. But she needed to make sure nobody got hurt in the process – especially Lilly.

'So, I decided to buy an elephant and use it as my mode of transport.'

'What?'

'Ha! Gotcha. You're miles away, Becky. What's up?'

'Sorry, I just have a few things on my mind.'

'Like our little trip away?'

'Well, yes.' In fact, she'd completely forgotten about that. 'But I thought you were too busy at the moment?'

'I'm busy all right ... and I was thinking, maybe it would work out better if we left it until after Christmas. I'd be less busy and you'd have time to plan to get Lilly looked after.'

Becky fought the urge to scream. 'I told you, Len. I can't just go off and leave her. Where I go, she goes.'

He reached across and took her hand. 'Becky, I'm just thinking of you. You never really get a break from her. You need to take more time for yourself.'

'That's just it, Len. I'm probably away from her far more than I'd like to be. Sometimes I think Alice is more of a mother to her than I am.'

'You know that's not the case,' he said, squeezing her hand. 'You're a great mother. And look at what they tell you on a plane. There's a reason they say you must put your own lifejacket on before that of your child. You need to look after yourself before you can look after a little one.'

'I know what you're saying, Len, and in an ideal world, that would work. I try to get the balance right.'

'But just imagine the two of us on our own for a few days with no cares in the world. We could get up to whatever we wanted to.' He reached across and took her hand. 'I'm crazy about you, Becky Greene, and my one wish in life is to make you happy.'

Becky wasn't sure what to say. She was overwhelmed by how much he cared about her. It was very flattering and, if she was honest, it felt good having someone who wanted to look after her.

'So what do you say?' Len looked at her with puppy-dog eyes.

'I say we get Christmas over with first and if we still feel like getting away at that stage, we'll talk about it then.'

'And you'll think about getting Lilly looked after so we can get away by ourselves?' He obviously caught her look because he quickly added, 'It's not that I don't want Lilly to come with us. I just think we just need to kick start our relationship on our own.'

Maybe he was right. 'I'm not promising anything, but I'll think about it.'

'That's all I'm asking. And we have loads of time where we can bring Lilly on holidays. I have some brilliant places in mind for next year.'

God, he was so intense. 'Let's just deal with one thing at a time. Right now, I need to put all my energy into the situation with Dennis.

If he reacts well when I tell him about Lilly, I'll need to speak to her about him. It will be a big deal for her and I'll need to give her plenty of attention while she adjusts to the situation.'

'Well, you know how I feel about *that*.' The waiter came to take the empty plates and Len asked him to bring two coffees. 'I think you're bringing a lot of unnecessary grief into your life.'

'I don't want to go through everything again, Len. Seeing Dennis yesterday made my mind up for me. He's a good man and deserves to know about Lilly. Who knows – she could be the incentive he needs to get himself out of the situation he's in.'

'But I thought you said his situation wasn't a choice. Now you're suggesting that he just needs a push to get himself out of it?'

'Stop trying to twist my words.' The waiter arrived with the coffees and Becky couldn't help feeling agitated. She didn't even like coffee much and if Len had bothered to ask, she'd have ordered a tea.

'I'm not twisting anything, Becky. You're saying Lilly might give him the incentive to get off the streets. It's totally contrary to what you said before. You said he'd been trying but it wasn't that easy.'

Becky had heard enough. 'I'm not having this conversation with you, Len. I've been thinking about this since before I even started going out with you so you can't try and make me think differently now.'

'And would there be another reason you want to bring this Dennis guy into your lives?'

'What exactly do you mean by that?'

'Well, is there any other attraction?'

'Len!'

'What? I just can't get my head around why you keep pursuing him. I think it has to be about more than just telling him about Lilly.'

'That's *exactly* what it's about. I'm not sure I like where you're going with this.'

'Come on, Becky. If it was just about Lilly, you'd have told him by now. Instead you're making dates with him and drawing the whole thing out. I'd prefer if you just said if you like him.'

'For God's sake, Len. Of course I don't. Why does it have to come down to that? My only interest in Dennis Prendergast is the fact he's Lilly's father.'

'But you were obviously attracted to him once. Or was it just a sex thing?'

Becky was furious. 'That's it, I'm out of here. I can't believe you'd talk to me like that.'

'Come on, Becky. Sit down.' He pulled at her arm and she sat back down so as not to make a scene. 'I'm really sorry. I didn't mean that to come out like it did.'

'Well, how did you mean it to come out? You were obviously just saying what you were thinking.' Tears stung Becky's eyes and she fought hard to keep them from spilling out.

'And I'm sorry for thinking it. I was just jealous, if you must know.' He took her hand again but she stiffened. 'Becky, I'm really falling for you. If I'm honest, I've been in love with you for years and now that I have you, the thought of you being attracted to someone else just kills me.'

'But I've told you, Len. I'm not attracted to Dennis. This is purely about him and Lilly.'

'Okay, okay. I believe you. It's just that when you mention him, you seem so excited and enthusiastic about involving him in your life. I suppose I'm just feeling a bit neglected.'

'But we've only been going out two minutes, Len. And, as I said earlier, this whole thing with Dennis had started even before we got together.'

'That's just it, Becky. We haven't "got together" yet. Well, not properly anyway.'

'So is that what all this is about? The fact we haven't had sex yet?'

Becky was surprised to see him blush. 'Of course not. But you can't blame me for wondering if there's any connection between our lack of intimacy and the fact you're thinking about Lilly's dad all the time.'

'I am *not* thinking about him all the time!'

'Becky, I'm not condemning you for it. I've told you now that I'm crazy about you. Try and see it from my point of view. If you were crazy about me and I was thinking about another woman, you might wonder about it too.'

'I suppose.'

'Ahem! This is where you say you *are* crazy about me!'

Becky couldn't help laughing. 'I thought it was the fact that I'm so vague and mysterious that attracted you to me in the first place.'

'You're right. I love a mysterious woman. So can we forget about Dennis Prendergast and all the other stuff that's getting between us and just enjoy each other's company?'

'That's fine by me.' She noticed the clock on the wall and realised she only had ten minutes to get back to work. 'I have to fly, though. I'll give you a call later.'

'I'll walk back with you.'

'No!' She hadn't meant it to sound so sharp. 'What I mean is, I have to call into the chemist for a few bits and pieces so I'd rather just head off myself, if you don't mind.'

'Okay, I'll give you a ring later.' He stood up to kiss her on the lips before she flew out the door of the little restaurant.

Although she was in a rush, she decided it would be nicer to walk down Grafton Street, with its pretty Christmas lights and shops belting out Christmas songs. She hadn't always loved Christmas – it had never been a happy time when she was little – but with Lilly's arrival, Becky had a newfound joy for all things festive. She loved how the little girl's eyes would light up at the mention of Santa and how she'd squeal at the sight of the Christmas trees and lights around the city. She smiled to herself as she passed the Brown Thomas window and vowed to bring Lilly in there for a look.

It had been a strange lunch with Len. He said he'd been in love with her for years. That had shocked her. She'd always known he fancied her, but saying he'd been 'in love' with her was a whole different ball game. But it also gave her a feeling of warmth and security. It was nice to be loved. And considering how he felt about her, it couldn't be easy listening to her going on about another man. And she had been pretty obsessed with Dennis Prendergast even if her interest in him was purely because of Lilly.

She pulled up the hood of her navy parka to warm up her ears as she crossed O'Connell Bridge. She'd bought the coat in Debenhams last week and with the weather having turned icy these last few days, it was already proving a great investment. The festiveness around Grafton Street had lifted her spirits but she was glad when she pushed open the door of the bank and was met with a blast of warm air.

She noticed Kate heading into the toilets. She'd been feeling ill yesterday and didn't look too good today either so Becky decided to have a quick chat with her before starting back to work.

'Hi, Kate. Are you taking a late lunch?' The other girl had her coat on and was rooting for something in her large handbag.

'I'm off home, actually. I've cleared it with Andrew.'

'What's wrong? Are you still not feeling well?'

Kate was already at the door. 'I think I must have picked up a bug or something. I might just take a few days off in case I end up spreading it around to everyone else.'

'You poor thing. Will Garreth be at home to look after you?'

'He's doing an early evening gig but, to be honest, I just want to get to bed.'

'Well, look after yourself and I'll give you a buzz tomorrow.'

She waved and disappeared out the door. Kate was never sick and Becky hated to see her looking so pale and exhausted. Then a sudden thought struck Becky – maybe Kate was pregnant. That would explain her symptoms. God, that would be exciting. Still, it could be early days so she wouldn't say anything to her yet. Hopefully, if she really *was* pregnant, she'd share her news soon enough.

She was just heading back out the door when something caught her eye on the floor. Kate's wallet! Becky picked it up and rushed out, hoping to catch Kate but there was no sign of her. Ah, well, if Kate was going straight home and to bed, she wouldn't need it tonight. She'd let her know she had it and maybe drop it over tomorrow.

As she passed the post desk, two of the girls were looking at pictures on an iPhone and cooing over them. When they saw Becky, they stiffened.

'We're just heading back to our desks now, Becky. We didn't realise the—'

'It's fine. Is that your daughter, Frances? Let's have a look.'

Frances looked at her in shock. 'Well, yes, it is, actually. It's a picture of her dressed up as a bee for Halloween.'

'She's gorgeous. They're so cute at that age.' Becky handed back the phone and continued to her desk. She could hear the whispers and feel the stares. They definitely hadn't been expecting that. She smiled to herself as she settled into her chair and fired up the computer. Kate would be proud.

# Chapter 35

'But *why* can't we put up our decorations now? All the shops have them up and it's soooo close to Christmas.'

'I've told you, Lilly. The shops put them up early so that the customers can enjoy them while they're out shopping. Nobody puts decorations up in their houses before December.' Becky was blue in the face trying to reason with Lilly but the little girl was determined to win the argument.

'They do so. There are two houses around the corner all decorated. They have huge big Santas on the roof and everything. Can we get Santas on the roof?'

Oh, God. Becky wasn't a fan of the big tacky decorations, preferring the more subtle, classy ones. She had let Lilly pick out a few Santas and snowmen the previous year but she was definitely going to draw the line at putting them up on the roof.

'She's been at it all afternoon,' Alice laughed, putting on her coat. 'Ever since she saw those houses on the way home from playschool, she's been talking about her plan for *your* house decorations.'

'Ha. She has no chance.' Becky walked Alice out to the door. 'So, any plans for this evening?'

'Not a thing. I'm feeling tired so I'll probably just have an early night.'

'There must be something in the air. Kate went home sick this afternoon. Said she felt exhausted and was going to bed.'

'Oh. Maybe a dose of lazyitus!'

'Ah, Alice, don't be like that. She really didn't look well.'

'Sorry. So what do you think is wrong with her?'

'Well, it's only a hunch but' – Becky almost said what she was thinking about Kate being pregnant but caught herself in time – 'but I think she must be low in iron. She's very pale these days.'

'It'll just be something like that. Don't be worrying about her. Will she be back to work tomorrow?'

'I don't think so. Actually, she left her wallet behind today so I'll have to try and get it back to her. I'll give her a ring later to see how she is and see if maybe Garreth can come and collect it.'

'I can drop it over to her, if you like. I've nothing else planned this evening and Frank is out with a few friends so there's no hurry on me getting home.'

Becky was delighted. 'If you're sure you don't mind, that would be great.'

'No problem. I'd hate to be without my wallet. And it should only take me ten minutes to get over there.'

Becky rooted in her bag which she'd left in the hall when she came home. 'Here you go. Tell her I said hello and I'll give her a buzz tomorrow.'

She waved Alice off, delighted to mark another thing off her list. She wanted to ring Dennis when Lilly had gone to bed and so hadn't wanted to get into a long chat with Kate on the phone. She was going to tell Lilly that Santa would be watching so she'd need to start going to bed a little earlier from now on.

'Mummy, are we going to decide what decorations to get?'

Becky walked back into the kitchen, where Lilly had the Argos catalogue open on the table. She'd managed to find the Christmas decorations pages and was eagerly awaiting her mother's decision. Becky looked at her daughter's wide eyes and smiled. Well, maybe one large Santa wouldn't hurt, especially since Joanna and the family were coming over.

She was excited about their visit but a little nervous. She and Joanna had spent such a long time apart that it seemed almost too good to be true that they'd become so close so quickly. She was anxious about meeting the rest of the family too, but she knew Joanna shared that same anxiety about meeting Lilly. It certainly wouldn't be the sort of Christmas she and Lilly were used to. But one thing was for sure, she was going to make sure it was the happiest Christmas they'd ever had.

✤

Alice stepped out of the car outside number twenty-three. The traffic had been surprisingly light for this time of the evening and she'd flown up the Navan Road in minutes. She'd been to Kate's house in Blanchardstown a couple of times before, but only to drop her home when they'd been having a night in Becky's. In truth, Alice didn't like the girl much at all, but she always tried to get along with her for Becky's sake. And if it wasn't for the fact that she wanted to save Becky a job, Alice wouldn't be here at all.

She stepped up to the door and rang the bell. There wasn't a sound from inside. She rang again but thought maybe she shouldn't wait in case Kate was in bed. But just as she was about to walk away, she saw a shadow through the stained glass of the front door. Someone was definitely in. Well, she hadn't come all this way to be ignored so if Kate was there, she'd better bloody well answer the door. She rang again, this time keeping her finger on the bell for longer. It obviously worked because only seconds later, the door was swung open and Kate stood there looking at her.

'Alice! What brings you here?'

'Well, that's a nice welcome. I've just come to drop this off.' She held out the wallet and waited while Kate stared at it.

'That's my wallet!'

'Well, of course it is. Why else would I be here to give it to you?'

'But how did you get it?' She rubbed her head, looking confused.

'You dropped it in work today. Becky picked it up and was planning to try and get it to you but I offered to bring it. It's not as easy for her to do deliveries when she has Lilly.' Alice knew she sounded sarcastic but she couldn't help it. Kate hadn't even said thanks.

'Oh … I didn't realise.'

'Well, now that you and your wallet are reunited, I'll be off.' She couldn't get over the rudeness of the girl. It cost nothing to be polite.

'Alice, I …'

To Alice's shock, Kate leaned on the door and began to slide downwards. 'Kate, Kate, what's wrong? Oh, Jesus!'

She just about got her shoulder under the other girl's arm to support her and they both leaned against the door. Kate seemed to come around within seconds, just as Alice was beginning to panic about what to do.

'S – sorry about that, Alice. I just had a dizzy spell. I'll be okay now.'

'You look shocking, Kate. Come on, let's get you inside. Is Garreth here?'

'No, but he'll be back soon. I don't need help, honestly.'

'I'm not taking no for an answer.' Alice pushed her way inside, still supporting Kate, and walked straight through the door in front of them.

'Sorry about the state of the kitchen,' said Kate, flopping down on a chair. 'I was just in the middle of a clean up.'

Alice quickly surveyed the scene in front of her and she knew something wasn't right. The table was full of food. There were freshly made sandwiches, bowls of crisps, bars of chocolate and a melting Vienetta ice-cream amongst other things. She sat down in the chair beside Kate.

'Were you planning a party or something, Kate? I wouldn't have thought you were in any state to have guests over.'

'I wasn't … I'm not …' Kate rubbed her head and Alice noticed her colour. She looked pale and drawn. She definitely wasn't well. And judging by how skinny she looked, she hadn't been eating properly either. Slowly, realisation began to dawn and Alice's heart sank.

'Kate, all this food – is it what I think it is?'

'I – I don't know what you're talking about. And honestly, I feel much better now. I'd ask you to stay for a cuppa except I think I'll just take myself back to bed.'

She was avoiding the question. 'I've seen it before, Kate. A long time ago, I had a friend who went through this. Please don't hide it any more. The first step is admitting you have a problem.'

Kate bowed her head and Alice knew she'd got through to her so she kept going. 'You have nothing to be ashamed of. Bulimia is a horrible disease and I can help you with it, if you'll let me.'

'I have *not* got bulimia.' Kate had tears running down her cheeks.

'You've got to admit to—'

'No, listen,' said Kate, wiping her eyes. 'I don't have bulimia, I swear. But you're right. That's what the food was here for.'

'And I came before you went through with it?'

'Yes. Well, no. It was a sort of experiment. I'd already decided before you came that I couldn't do it.'

Alice was doubtful. 'But why were you even thinking about it? Have you done it before?'

Kate shook her head. 'I've never done this. *Ever*. I swear. I've just been trying to lose weight and I thought this might be the answer.'

'Oh, God, Kate. You're absolutely gorgeous with a figure to die for. Why would you want to lose weight?'

'It's a long story.'

'Right.' Alice stood up and took off her coat. 'I'll stick the kettle on and you can tell me all about it.'

Kate didn't refuse. Alice knew how important it was to talk. She suddenly felt an urge to wrap Kate up and look after her. She was just a child really. A young impressionable kid who was obviously going through something that made her think that this was the best solution to her problems. It felt good to be looking after someone. Alice was old enough to be Kate's mother and she was happy to take on the role. She put the two steaming mugs on the table and sat back down opposite Kate.

'Right, now start from the beginning.'

❊

'I'm home.'

Alice and Kate almost jumped out of their skins when Garreth's voice came booming into the kitchen.'

'Oh, hello, Alice. Good to see you. I haven't seen … Jesus, what's wrong, Kate?'

Kate's hand automatically flew to her eyes that were red and swollen from crying. 'I'm sorry, Garreth. I'm really sorry.'

He ran to her and bent to wrap her in his arms. 'You're scaring me now. What is it? What's wrong?'

'It's just … I should have told you before but I didn't want you to worry. Then Alice came over and …' She started sobbing again.

Garreth looked from Kate to Alice.

'Go on, Kate,' said Alice gently. 'He needs to know.'

Kate nodded and wiped her eyes. 'I've been having problems with my eating. I – I've been using laxatives to try and lose weight and it's all getting out of hand.'

'Jesus, Kate. You should have told me. Actually, no, I should have known. I knew things weren't right with you and I could see you were losing weight.'

Seeing his distress upset Kate even more and she leaned on the table with her head in her hands. 'I'm such a fool for doing this to myself and for upsetting everyone. I'm so, so sorry.'

'I think that's my cue to leave,' said Alice, standing up. 'And remember, Kate. You don't need to be sorry. We just want you to be well again, isn't that right, Garreth?'

'Of course. How bad is it? I mean, should we be getting you to hospital?'

'No!' Kate was adamant. 'I'm going to deal with it. Alice has been brilliant tonight and I'm going to see my GP first thing in the morning. We can take things from there.'

'Just make sure you make that appointment,' said Alice, walking towards the door. 'It's really important to make that first step.'

'I will.' Kate stood up. 'I'll walk you out.'

'Bye, Garreth. And remember I'm here for both of you if you need me. Kate has my number.'

'Thanks, Alice. It looks like you've already done plenty for Kate. We're both really grateful.'

Kate hugged Alice tight before she headed out to her car. 'Honestly, Alice. You've been brilliant today. I really can't thank you enough.'

'I just want you to get yourself well – physically and mentally. I know how eating disorders can affect your life but the hardest part is admitting you have a problem.'

'But I *don't* have an eating disorder, Alice. It's just … it's just …'

'Whatever way you want to present it, love, you still have a problem. Just please make sure you follow through with seeing the doctor.'

Kate nodded. 'You're right. Actually, you're right about everything. I think that's why we never really got on. I hated the fact you always seemed so perfect while I was suffering from foot-in-mouth disease!'

'I'm far from perfect, Kate, believe me. Now you'd better go back in to Garreth and talk to him. Tell him everything you told me and let him help.'

Kate threw her arms around Alice again before waving her off. Alice O'Malley – her new best friend. Who'd have thought it? Wait until Becky heard. Alice had been amazing to talk to. She'd managed to get to the root of the problem straight away. It all came back to Kate's low self-esteem at school. She'd become fixated on being successful and, in her head, modelling had become that gateway to success. Alice had pointed out that she was already successful because she had a great career, a lovely house, a wonderful boyfriend and a load of great friends. And now she could call Alice a friend. Sometimes, life worked in mysterious ways.

She closed the front door and headed back towards the kitchen. She paused in the hall and took a few deep breaths. This wasn't going to be easy. She knew how much Garreth loved her and how he'd hate to think of her shutting him out. She just hoped he'd understand. She had a long, hard road ahead of her but she was determined to get well again. And with so many people who loved her, she was definitely going to succeed.

❀

Dennis arrived at his usual spot and threw his rucksack on the ground. The sprinkling of rain that had fallen earlier was already beginning to crystallise and the icy air was biting at his ears, despite his woolly hat. He was lucky he had plenty of warm clothes because he was going to need them. He sat down in the recessed doorway and began to take the heavier clothing out of his bag.

He thought about Alice and his chat with her the previous day. He'd been very aggressive towards her and he felt bad for it. She was only doing her job and had even gone above and beyond it by offering him help. But of course, he'd refused. You'd think he'd have got over his stupid pride by now. It wasn't that he was averse to accepting help in general, but there was just something about Alice. While he was with her, he tried to imagine he had a normal life and was out with a girl under normal circumstances. By offering to help him, she had burst that bubble. But the harsh reality was that pride wouldn't keep him warm at night or put a roof over his head. He'd need to cop on to himself and think about what he hoped to achieve.

'Hey, scum. Stop dirtying our streets and go and find yourself a hole to crawl into.'

Dennis had been lost in thought and looked up when he heard the voice. There were two young guys looking down at him. They wore expensive-looking clothes and spoke in a refined Dublin accent. One of them, obviously the ringleader, was speaking.

'Did you hear me, old man? Get out of here.'

'Look, I don't want any trouble.'

'Oh, it knows how to speak.' They both laughed hysterically. Dennis guessed immediately they were high on something – he knew the signs. Their eyes were manic and they looked like they meant business. In his experience, you just didn't mess with people like that. He stood up and tried not to meet their eyes. He knew he needed to get out of there.

'What? You're going without saying goodbye?' It was the second guy. 'That's a bit rude now.'

'Yes,' said the ringleader, putting out his arm to stop Dennis from going anywhere. 'Where's your manners?'

'As I said, I don't want any trouble, lads.'

'Trouble? We're just trying to make Dublin a cleaner place.'

Dennis pushed through them roughly and began to walk down the street. He was suddenly aware of how quiet it was. There wasn't a single person around except for himself and the two lads he'd left behind.

'Nobody pushes me like that.'

It felt like a punch in the back and then the sound of something falling to the ground.

'Oh, shit,' he heard one of them say, and then the sound of footsteps running away.

He turned around and looked down. That's when he saw the blood-stained penknife on the ground. The two lads had disappeared, leaving him alone on the street. It didn't make sense. While he was trying to figure out what had just happened, he felt a cold, wet sensation on his back. It didn't take him long to realise that blood was seeping through his clothes. He'd been stabbed. He suddenly felt short of breath and the world started spinning. The last thing he remembered was the sound of his head smashing off the pavement.

# Chapter 36

'Sorry, but nobody has seen him in the last few days.'

'Well, thanks for your help anyway,' said Becky, smiling at Martina, the woman who looked after the social club. Dennis had referred to her on a couple of occasions as the 'Mammy' because she made it her business to know each of the homeless people who spent time there and was very protective of them all. 'If he comes back, would you mind telling him I'm trying to get in touch with him?'

'No problem. Alice, isn't it? I never forget a name.'

'That's right.' Becky reddened. 'Just tell him Alice was looking for him and I'll call back at lunchtime tomorrow and see if there's any news of him.'

Becky was walking away when Martina shouted after her. 'Actually, tonight is art night and I've never known Deano to miss it. I'll pass on your message if he's here and tell him you'll be back in tomorrow.'

'Brilliant. Thanks for that.'

The air was cool and crisp, perfect for a nice, long walk, so Becky decided to take a stroll up Grafton Street before heading back to work. She didn't feel like eating, so she still had half an hour to kill. In fact, she'd barely eaten since Tuesday night, when she'd phoned Dennis.

She'd been excited to get Lilly to bed that night so that she could ring him and arrange to meet again. She'd been planning on telling him everything. She'd been nervous at the prospect but she'd made up her mind and it had just felt right. But Dennis hadn't answered. She'd waited a half-hour and rung again, but still nothing. By the time she'd gone to bed, she'd rung him several times with no success. She knew he wouldn't have credit to ring back or even listen to his voicemail messages so she'd sent a couple of texts too just to say she wanted to meet him again.

She reached the top of Grafton Street and stood for a moment to enjoy the magnificent Christmas tree that crowned the street just outside the gates of St Stephen's Green. It reminded her of how close it was getting to Christmas and she had nothing organised. Christmas dinner was usually just her and Lilly, with Alice calling in at some stage during the day. But this year she'd be cooking for Joanna, her husband and two children as well. Joanna had rung her excitedly the previous evening to confirm that she'd booked the flights and they'd be arriving over early on Christmas Eve. Lilly was so excited at the prospect of having cousins and Becky wanted to make sure it would be the best Christmas ever.

Why wasn't Dennis answering her calls? Had he just had enough of her? She knew things had ended quite badly the last time they'd met, but she'd hoped he wouldn't hold a grudge. She'd meant well by offering him help – surely he could see that. And how was he ever supposed to get out of the terrible situation he was in without accepting help. She didn't get it.

She arrived back to work just at two on the dot, and smiled to herself when she thought of the many times she'd either just work through lunch or get in early to get on top of the workload. Now, she just did the bare minimum. She still worked hard, but her job wasn't the most important thing in her life any more. It was a means to an end and she'd realised that she'd much rather spend those extra minutes or hours with her family and friends than catching up on the endless paperwork that seemed to amass on her desk each day.

She threw her handbag under her chair and flicked on her computer. Three more hours and she'd be out of there. Maybe she'd have a chat with Alice when she got home and see if she had any thoughts on Dennis and what she should do next. Alice was great for giving sensible advice, but it was Kate who came up with the great ideas. It was strange not to have her in work. She wasn't going to be back until next week and even though it was only a few days, Becky missed her.

'Becky, can I have a word, please?' Andrew, the branch manager, stood over her desk, shifting from foot to foot and looking uncomfortable.

'What's up, Andrew?'

'Well, it's just that I noticed you put yourself down for holidays the week after Christmas. I can give you a week off later in January but we'll definitely need you in on the thirtieth and thirty-first of December.'

Becky shook her head. 'Sorry, I can't do that.'

'What?'

'Those two days. I won't be able to come in. I have other things planned for that week so I'm going to need the whole week off.'

'But I can't give it to you, Becky. You know what it's like just after Christmas. I don't have anyone to cover for you.'

'Well, you'll have to find someone.' She wasn't going to give in.

'But you *always* work those days. I just assumed—'

'That's just it, Andrew. I *always* work those days. Isn't it about time somebody else did it? I have family plans this year and I'm not cancelling them.'

'Well, I don't know about this. I'll have to check with head office to see if they have anyone. It's highly inconvenient.'

He walked off mumbling to himself and Becky couldn't help laughing. It was good to take control of her life instead of her job controlling her. Dennis had given her some good advice on that score. He'd said that it was important to get perspective and not to lose sight of what really mattered. He'd learned the hard way.

She became sombre again as she thought about him. He couldn't have just vanished into thin air. Although maybe it would be easy for a homeless person to disappear if they wanted to. She glanced around and everyone seemed to be busy with their own work so she pulled her mobile out of her bag. She wasn't going to give up until she found him again. She scrolled down and found his number.

❀

'Mummy, Mummy, come and see what me and Alice are doing. It's so much fun.'

'Come here and give me a hug first,' Becky said, closing the front door behind her. 'I've missed you so much today.'

Lilly hugged her tightly then pulled her hand. 'Come in and watch Alice. She's sooooo funny.'

Becky walked into the kitchen, where Alice was sitting with a mirror in front of her. 'Hi, Alice. So come on. Show me what's making Lilly so excited.'

Alice blushed. 'We were just messing around. It's nothing really.'

'Alice, show Mummy. You're so good at it.'

'Yes, come on, I have to see it now.' Becky pulled up a chair and waited.

'It's silly really,' said Alice, standing up and filling the kettle with water. 'Just something I was reading about and thought I'd give it a try.'

'It's like this, Mummy. But I only 'member two things.' She sucked her cheeks in and opened her eyes wide and both Alice and Becky laughed.

'Very pretty, darling. So this is how you've been amusing yourselves?'

'That's called the fish face and look, I can do the lion too.' The little girl stuck her tongue out as far as she could and rolled her eyes upwards.'

'Well, I'm glad to see Alice is teaching you the important things in life.'

Alice laughed and sat back down. 'It's called facial yoga. Apparently a lot of celebrities are ditching the Botox in favour of the natural approach.'

'You're hilarious, Alice. I thought you were giving up all this anti-ageing stuff.'

'I've given up on the expensive stuff but I'm willing to try anything that doesn't cost and might knock a few years off. So how was work?'

Becky glanced at Lilly, who was holding the mirror in front of her face and practising various poses. 'Lilly, why don't you go up to your room and play with your dollies for a bit. Mummy and Alice are just going to have a chat.'

'Okay. I'm gonna teach them face yoga.'

When she was out of earshot, Becky sighed. 'Work was the same as ever but I can't get Dennis out of my head.'

'Still no reply?'

'Nothing. I've rung him about twenty times now and left a few text messages.'

'Maybe he's lost his phone or something.' Alice was back on her feet again, sticking teabags into two mugs and pouring water in. 'There's bound to be a reasonable explanation.'

'I'm not sure about that, Alice. I went to the social club this afternoon and they haven't seen him either. I can't help thinking he just got fed up with me pestering him so he's moved on.'

'That's hardly the case. It's not as if you made him meet you. From what you said, he's been quite willing to chat.'

'I don't know, I can't help thinking he doesn't want to see me again.' Tears sprang to Becky's eyes as she said the words. 'God, what's wrong with me? I've managed this long without Dennis Prendergast, so why does it matter so much now?'

'If you want my advice, Becky, I'd leave it for a bit. If you have scared him off with all your questions, ringing him twenty times is hardly going to entice him back. Send him another text and let him know you'll be at a certain place at a certain time if he's willing to meet you again, but make it next week. Give him a bit of space and time.'

Becky sighed. 'I suppose you're right. I just really want to move things on now. I'm ready to tell him about Lilly and I want everything to be perfect.'

'But life doesn't work that way, Becky. You should know that.'

'I know. But I'm going to do my best to make it as perfect as possible for Lilly. I'll do as you suggest and we'll see what happens. And on another note, have you and Frank made any decisions on a holiday?'

Alice shook her head. 'Not yet. It's probably a bit close to Christmas so we might go in January, if you can arrange the time off work.'

'That shouldn't be a problem.' Becky thought of Andrew and how he'd offered her a week off later in January. Well, she'd take that as well as her Christmas week. It was about time that job started paying her back for all the work she put in. 'So I take it you're happy about him moving in?'

'I couldn't be happier. Honestly, what was I thinking all those times I put him off. I should have had him living with me ages ago. We get on so well and it's brilliant having somebody there every night.'

Becky thought of Len and wondered if they'd ever get to that stage.

'And how are things with you and Len?' It was as though Alice was reading her thoughts.

'Things are really good. I wasn't sure about him at first but I think it was just me being nervous about being with a man again. I think I may really be falling for him.'

'That's brilliant news, Becky. He's a lovely guy and you deserve a bit of happiness. Now, I'll have to love you and leave you. Frank and I are heading out for a bite to eat and then going to see that movie, *Prisoners*. It's getting great reviews.'

'Lucky you,' said Becky, walking Alice to the door. 'The only thing I have a hope of seeing in the cinema is *Frozen*. Lilly is dying to see it.'

'Well, why don't you and Len get off to the cinema one night next week and I'll babysit. Just name the day.'

'Thanks, Alice. I might just do that. Enjoy your night and tell Frank I said hello.'

She closed the door and listened at the bottom of the stairs. Lilly was chatting away to her dolls so she'd leave her there for a while.

She headed into the sitting room and flopped down on the sofa. Her mind wandered to Len and she wished he was there with her. She'd been putting up barriers since they met, but maybe now was the time to let them down. She needed to stop pushing him away and allow him to share her life properly. He'd declared his love for her and she'd shied away from it. But not any more – maybe Len would turn out to be *the one.*

She'd invite him over tomorrow night and they could watch a movie and have pizza or something. Nothing formal – just a nice, relaxed night. She wouldn't have any preconceived ideas about where the night would go but instead, just relax and see what would happen. Besides, if she was going to put Dennis out of her mind for a few days, she'd need lots of distractions.

She went to the hall where she'd left her bag and pulled out her phone. Heading back into the sitting room, she scrolled down through the numbers until she found the one she was looking for. Dennis. She'd just try him one last time before ringing Len. Then she'd definitely put him out of her mind until next week.

# Chapter 37

Kate looked at herself in the mirror and saw how pale and thin she'd become. How had she not noticed that before? It was her first day back in work after a week off and although she was feeling marginally better, she knew it would be months, if not longer, before she felt like herself again. But she was on the right road. Alice had been a great support, ringing her every night and checking how she was feeling. Now *there* was one friendship she hadn't seen coming!

She carefully applied her blue-black mascara and added some colour to her pale cheeks. It was only 8.30, but she'd come in early to have a chat with Becky. They'd had a couple of quick phone calls since last week but Kate hadn't felt like chatting much or explaining what was going on. She wanted to tell her everything now – not for sympathy but simply as a way of facing up to her problems. She was putting the final touches to her make-up when the door opened and Becky walked in.

'Hiya, Kate. Welcome back. How are you feeling?'

'Thanks, Becky. I'm not too bad.' She threw her make-up bag into her handbag and turned to look at her friend. 'But I have so much to tell you.'

Becky looked intrigued. 'Really? I'd have thought you'd have no news, having been laid up this last week.'

'Well, it's about that, really. I wanted to tell you what's going on. I know I told you I had a bug, but that wasn't the case.'

'I knew it!' Becky dropped her handbag on the floor and hugged Kate tightly. 'I just had a feeling and I was hoping I was right.'

Kate stared at her. 'What feeling?'

'I had a feeling you were pregnant. I didn't want to say anything because I was hoping you'd—'

'Hang on, hang on, Becky. I'm not pregnant. What on earth made you think that? Me of all people.'

'Oh.' Becky looked disappointed. 'I'm sorry. I just suspected it and when you said you wanted to tell me the *real* reason you were sick, I just assumed.'

Kate hooshed herself up onto the counter beside the sink and indicated for Becky to do the same. 'Park your bum here for a few minutes and I'll fill you in on everything.'

Ten minutes later, Becky was shaking her head, having heard the full story. 'I'm so sorry you've been going through that, Kate. And I'm raging with myself for not noticing. I should have seen you were losing weight and that something wasn't right.'

'Don't blame yourself,' said Kate, patting Becky's hand. 'How could you have known? I'm living with Garreth and he didn't even know.'

'And what did he say when he found out? Was he devastated?'

'Yep. You can imagine. But he's been so supportive. And so has Alice.'

Becky nodded. 'I still can't believe you told Alice everything. She never said a word to me. When I asked her if she'd dropped in the wallet, she just said she gave it to you at the door.'

Kate was delighted that Alice had kept her secret. 'I asked her not to say anything until I was able to tell you about it myself. She's great, isn't she? I never realised.'

'Yep. She's one of the best. Does that mean that you two might even be friends now?'

'Of course. We've been on the phone every night since.'

Becky gasped. 'I don't believe it. Well, I never thought I'd hear that. But I really am happy she was able to help you. It sounds like the universe was doing its job, bringing her to you at the right time.'

'Definitely. She's a friend for life now.'

Becky started to say something and then stopped.

'What is it?' asked Kate, searching her face.

'It's just … I was just wondering about the binge eating. Do you think you would have gone through with it if Alice hadn't arrived?'

'No, I don't. I know I have problems but things hadn't got that bad. I know it sounds stupid but I'd really let this whole modelling thing get into my head and losing weight seemed like the most important thing in the world to me.'

'And it's not now?'

'I'd be lying if I said it wasn't important, Becky. It's going to take me a while. I still hate the thought of getting fat, but I just need to learn to relax about it.'

'And the modelling?'

'I'm not going to bother any more. And it's funny, as soon as I made that decision, it was as though a weight had been lifted off my shoulders. I'm going to concentrate on just getting better now.'

The door opened suddenly and a couple of girls walked in, chatting and laughing, but stopped when they saw Becky and Kate sitting on the counter.

'Don't mind us,' said Becky, hopping down and looking a little embarrassed. 'We were just going.'

They headed out to the main office and Kate turned to Becky before she headed to her desk. 'Thanks for not judging, Becky. I'm lucky to have you as a friend.'

'Don't be silly. You've spent the past few months advising me on the Dennis situation. *I'm* the one who's lucky to have *you*.'

'And speaking about Dennis, what's the story there? Any developments? And is Luscious Len still trying to get his leg over?'

Becky laughed. 'No to developments and yes to the leg over. But I'd need at least an hour to fill you in.'

'Great. Well, let's go for lunch today and you can tell me everything.'

Becky suddenly looked awkward. 'Em, not today. Sorry. I have to be somewhere. Maybe tomorrow?'

'Yep, tomorrow is fine. Where are you off to today?'

'Oh, it's just a thing. I'll tell you about it over lunch tomorrow. Now I'd better get some work done.'

Kate watched Becky busying herself at her desk and wondered why she was being so mysterious. Still, she'd find out soon enough.

'Morning, Kate.' It was Andrew. 'Good to have you back. And just to let you know, I've made a few changes in the safe in relation to the sacks of coins.'

'Oh?'

'Yes, I've changed the height of the coin shelf to the same height as the trolley so you'll just have to slip the coin bags off the shelf onto the trolley. It'll reduce the amount of lifting so it should save your back.'

'That's brilliant, thanks.' Kate went off to take out the cash and smiled to herself. Becky must have spoken to him about it. It was good to know she was looking out for her. Just as Alice and Garreth were. She was one lucky girl.

❦

Becky felt nervous as she sat in Martha's at lunchtime. Kate had seen her rushing out the door and had raised her eyebrows but Becky hadn't waited to give her an explanation. She felt bad for not telling her where she was going but she didn't want to say anything just yet. It was ten past one and Becky was hoping that Dennis Prendergast was going to walk in the door any minute.

It was over a week since she'd met him and she still hadn't managed to get in touch with him. So she'd taken Alice's advice and hadn't called for a few days but had sent a message yesterday to say she'd be at Martha's at lunchtime today. She'd popped in a couple of times over the past week to ask if Martha had seen him, but she hadn't. Becky hadn't been able to read the old lady and wasn't sure if she'd been telling the truth.

Of course, Len was happy with the situation. He'd been delighted when Dennis had disappeared because he wanted all Becky's attention. He'd advised Becky that she should just leave things and not pursue him any more. Needless to say, Becky had kept quiet about today, but time was pushing on and there was still no sign of Dennis.

'You wouldn't be waiting for our mutual friend, would you?' Martha placed another mug of tea down in front of Becky. 'It's just that I'm beginning to worry. I still haven't seen him since last week and he rarely misses even a day of coming in.'

Becky knew then she was telling the truth. 'Yes, I *am* waiting for him. But I don't know if he's going to turn up. I haven't managed to find him yet either so I sent him a text to ask him to meet me here.'

'Well, let's hope he does turn up. I've been imagining all sorts of things. It's not safe on the streets, you know. I know he acts all tough and streetwise, but he's as vulnerable as any one of us would be in that situation.'

'I know,' said Becky. 'And I probably haven't been as understanding as I should have been. But that's why I want to meet him again. I need to explain.'

Martha patted her on the hand. 'Well, I'll be watching that door like a hawk. I hope to God he turns up.'

It was already 1.40 and Becky knew she only had ten minutes before she had to leave. She felt like she was in the last-chance saloon. She'd decided that if he didn't turn up today, she was going to put him out of her head. She didn't know how she'd do it, but she needed to stop letting Dennis Prendergast take up so much of her head space. She needed to give more of herself to Lilly, and even to Len.

She glanced over at Martha, who was dealing with three customers at the one time. She really was a remarkable woman for her age and ran a surprisingly good business. It suddenly dawned on Becky that Dennis wasn't the sort of person who'd desert an old lady. They'd become friends and whatever about him growing tired of Becky and her questions, she was sure he wouldn't have turned his back on

Martha. Her time was almost up, and she began to feel worried. She had assumed that Dennis was avoiding her, but now she was thinking that maybe something awful had happened. What if he'd been in an accident? Or worse still, what if he was dead? The thought filled her with dread and she could feel panic rising. Oh. God, please don't let her have a panic attack in here. She closed her eyes and. cupping her hands over her mouth, she began to breathe slowly and deeply. She'd read that it worked just as well as the paper bag technique and she felt her breathing levelling out straight away. Thank God for that.

'Hello, Alice.'

She jumped when she heard the voice and was suddenly filled with relief. She looked up to see Dennis standing over her but her delight quickly turned to shock. 'Jesus, what the hell happened to you?'

# Chapter 38

'It's not as bad as it looks,' Dennis said, sitting down opposite Becky.
'But you can see why I was otherwise occupied when you were trying
to get in touch.'

Becky's eyes tried to take it all in – the bruises, the stitches – he
was in a right state. 'God, Dennis. Who did this to you? Tell me what
happened.'

Before he could say another word, Martha was over to the table,
her face crinkled with worry. 'Dennis, love, what happened?'

'Listen, it's nice that you're both concerned, but I'm fine really. I
got attacked – it happens. I spent a few days in hospital but I'm out
now and on the mend.'

'Well, I'm glad you're okay,' said Martha, rubbing his arm gently.
'You'll have to fill me in on the whole story later. I'd better go and
serve these customers.'

Becky wasn't sure what to say. She had a whole speech ready in
her head but now didn't seem like the right time to tell Dennis he
had a daughter. She watched as he carefully took off his coat, wincing
with the pain as he did so. Besides his obvious injuries, she noticed
how he looked different – broken. His clothes were crinkled and he
smelled bad but his eyes were the worst. They looked sad and lifeless.
Something told Becky that Dennis had given up.

'Am I putting you off your food?' he said, nodding towards the
half-eaten apple pie in front of her.

'Don't be silly. I'd finished long before you came. So do you want
to tell me what happened?'

'Would this be for your article or for your own interest?'

She wasn't sure how to respond but decided that the truth would be best. 'No, Dennis. It's not for any article. I'm genuinely concerned about you. I was worried when I couldn't reach you.'

'I was in hospital and just didn't bother charging up my phone. There didn't seem any point. Nobody really contacts me on it anyway.'

'So this attack – when did it happen?'

'God, don't ask me the day – I barely know what day it is now. But it was about a week ago. They stabbed me in—'

'You got stabbed?' Becky was horrified.

'Yes, but the stab wound wasn't the worst of it. I fell to the ground and smashed my head. They had to put fifteen stitches across my forehead and, as you can see, there's a lot of bruising.'

'Here you go,' said Martha, putting a large sandwich and a mug of tea in front of Dennis. 'You look like you need that.'

'Thanks, Martha.' Dennis smiled at the old lady but Becky noticed how the smile didn't reach his eyes.

'There's something different about you, Dennis. You're not the same as you were when we last spoke.'

'Different how?'

'I'm not sure. It's as though you've lost your spark or something.'

'Alice, I'm just out of hospital after an attack, excuse me if I'm not dancing on the tables.'

She felt stupid. 'I'm sorry. Of course you're not going to be in great form. But I just feel you've lost your spirit, which I suppose is completely understandable under the circumstances.'

Dennis sighed and took a half-hearted bite of his sandwich. He chewed for what seemed like ages before he spoke again. 'You're right, actually. I've been up and down all year but this incident has knocked me right back.'

'It's not surprising. Do you want to tell me exactly what happened?'

It took about a half-hour, with Dennis alternating between talking and eating. He told her everything from the attack to when he was released from hospital the previous day. Becky was aware that she was dead late for work, but she didn't care. This was far more important than a load of foreign transfers. This was real life.

'So where did you sleep last night if you came out of hospital yesterday?'

'I found another spot not too far away from my usual place. I didn't feel like going back to the scene of the crime.'

'I'm not surprised. But would you not have gone into a shelter or something, at least until you recover. It's freezing cold at night.'

'Who are you telling? I could hardly feel my fingers this morning.'

'And tonight?'

'It's not as though I have choices, Alice. It doesn't work like that when you're homeless. I'll go back to the same place.' He looked defeated and Becky felt a sudden urge to look after him.

'Right, you're coming with me.'

'What?'

'I'm going to take you back to my house so you can have a nice warm shower, change your clothes and have a bite to eat. We can throw stuff from your rucksack into the wash if you like. I'm afraid I can't offer you a bed or anything but at least it will give you a few hours of normality.'

'Okay.'

Becky was shocked. She'd expected at the very least for him to be indignant about it and refuse to go. It seemed he'd lost every bit of fight he'd had in him. 'Right, that's settled then. Just let me make a couple of calls before we go.'

'Take your time. I'm not going anywhere.'

She grabbed her bag from under the table and rushed into the toilets. First she called the bank to let them know she wouldn't be coming in for the afternoon and then dialled Alice's number.

'Hi, Alice. It's me. I need a favour, please.'

'Hiya, Becky. What's up?'

'I need you to head out with Lilly for a few hours. Just take her to a movie and McDonald's or something.'

'Well, we were just about to bake. Can we do it tomorrow instead?'

'No! I mean, I just need for both of you to get out of the house for a bit. I can't say why now, but I'll explain everything later.' She didn't want to tell Alice about her plan in case she'd tell her not to do it.

'Okay, so. We'll leave the baking for today and we'll go and check out what's on in the cinema in Blanchardstown.'

'Thanks, Alice. You're a star. We'll chat later.'

Becky rushed back out, half-expecting to see an empty chair where Dennis had been, but thankfully, he was still there. 'Right, let's go. We can get a taxi from the quays and we'll be home in twenty minutes.'

'Thanks for this,' he said, standing up with difficulty. 'You're a decent sort. I'm sorry if I've been narky with you in the past.'

'Don't worry about that now.' Becky just wanted to get him in a taxi before he changed his mind. 'And I wouldn't blame you for it. You've got the best reason out of everyone I know to be narky, the way life's treated you.'

'I only have myself to blame. I was a first-class prick.'

Becky led him outside after paying for lunch and they headed towards the quays. 'I'm sure you weren't that bad. And nobody deserves to go through what you've been through, no matter what.'

He didn't respond and they walked in silence side by side until they got to the quays. Becky flagged a taxi down and, within seconds, they were heading towards Cabra. She glanced sideways at Dennis and, seeing his battered face, she got a sudden rush of nerves. Was she crazy, inviting him into her house? Yes, he was Lilly's father, but did she really know him? Well, she'd already given the taxi man her address so only time would tell if she was doing the right thing or making the biggest mistake of her life.

❋

Becky rustled around in the cupboards, trying to find the makings of a dinner. She'd showed Dennis up to the shower and handed him some soft, fresh towels. She'd felt choked up when she saw him put his face on them and close his eyes. It was probably a comfort he hadn't experienced in a long, long time. She could still hear the shower going so she had some time to get organised.

She found some leftover chicken in the fridge and opened a tin of condensed chicken soup. She'd mix it all together with a tin of corn and cook a pot of pasta too. That was her quick-fix dinner – and one Lilly loved. She heard the shower stop and knew he'd be down soon. She suddenly felt scared. What the hell was she doing? What had she been thinking?

'Thanks for that, Alice.' Dennis appeared at the kitchen door, crumpled jeans and a jumper on him, a pile of clothes in his hands. 'Did you say I could throw these into the washing machine?'

Becky ran to help him with the load. 'Of course. Give them here and I'll stick them in. Sit down there and make yourself comfortable. Dinner will be another few minutes.'

He handed over the clothes willingly and sat down at the table. Becky bent to fill the machine, keeping one eye on Dennis. She could smell her coconut shower gel off him. He must have used half a bottle. She could hardly blame him. His dark hair fell in wet curls over his forehead and little beads of water dropped down his cheeks. He rubbed his beard with his right hand and Becky noted that it could do with a trim.

❄

'Here we go,' Becky said, ten minutes later, as she placed two bowls of the creamy pasta on the table. 'I hope you enjoy.'

'Are you kidding me? Of course I'll enjoy it. Do you know how long it's been since I've sat in someone's kitchen and eaten a meal?'

Becky nodded. Sometimes there just weren't words.

'So what about these articles?' Dennis continued. 'Have you found a home for them yet?'

She had to say something. He was clearly getting suspicious and she couldn't keep up the pretence any longer. 'Dennis, I have a story of my own to tell you. And to start it off, my name isn't really Alice.'

'But … Why would you give me a false name? I don't get it.'

'It just sort of happened. And I may as well tell you, I'm not a reporter either. I work for a bank.'

Dennis was in the process of putting a forkful of pasta in his mouth

but paused with it midair. 'What? But the articles? All the interviews
– what were they all about?'

Becky sighed. 'Well, first of all, my name is Becky – Becky Greene.'

Dennis narrowed his eyes. 'That name sounds familiar. And come
to think of it, I thought I recognised you when we first met.'

'Really?' Becky's stomach gave a little leap. Could it be possible
that he remembered her from their night together?

'Go on, then. Tell me why you've been lying to me.'

Just as Becky was going to tell her story, they were both startled by
the sound of keys in the door.

'Sorry, Becky,' said Alice, appearing in front of them and looking
quizzically from Becky to Dennis. 'We've just come back to collect
Lilly's teddy. She didn't want to go to the cinema without him. I'll fly
up and get it and we'll be out of your way in one minute.'

'Hiya, Mummy.' Lilly came running over to hug her mother,
eyeing Dennis suspiciously. 'Who's that?'

Becky froze. She looked from Lilly to Dennis. It felt strange to see
them together – two pairs of the same eyes sizing up each other.

'Mummy, who's that man?' Lilly repeated.

'I'm Dennis. And you must be Lilly.' He held out his hand to
shake hers and Becky felt her world spinning around.

Lilly watched him suspiciously. 'How do you know my name?'

'Because your mummy talks about you *all* the time. And because
Lilly sounds like a princess name and you look like a princess.'

'I *am* a princess. Len said so. He even gave me this.' She held out
her arm to show off her Pandora bracelet.'

'That's very pretty. Len has great taste.' He raised an eyebrow to
Becky and she blushed deep red. She couldn't think of a single word
to say.

'Come on, Lilly,' said Alice, appearing at the kitchen door. 'We
need to rush if we're going to be on time for that movie.'

'Okay, Alice.' She turned back to Dennis and stared at him for a
moment. Why does your face look funny?'

'Lilly!' Becky was mortified. Why hadn't Alice just bloody stayed away like she'd asked?

'It's okay, Al … I mean, Becky.' He turned to Lilly. 'Well, Lilly, I was very silly and tripped coming down the stairs. Look, I have an injury for every stair I fell down.' He began pointing to his wounds and counting, much to Lilly's fascination.

'Lilly, we really have to go now.' Alice was getting agitated and mouthed 'sorry' to Becky.

'Okay, see you later, Mummy. Bye, Dennis.'

'Bye, Lilly. It was nice to meet you.' He turned to Becky. 'She's a lovely kid. You're very lucky.'

There would never be a better time. She shoved her barely eaten pasta aside and leaned on the table. 'Dennis, I have something to tell you and it's going to come as quite a surprise.'

'God, you're full of surprises today.' His eyes narrowed and he looked suspicious.

'It's about Lilly.'

'Go on.'

'You were asking me why I changed my name and pretended to be a reporter. Well, it was just a way to get to know you. I'd been looking for you for a while.'

Dennis stared at her. 'I don't understand.'

Becky sighed. 'I was going to start from the beginning, but I think I'll just come right out with it and we can work backwards.'

'What are you talking about?'

'It's Lilly.'

'So you said. But what about her?' Dennis managed to shovel the last of his pasta into his mouth before pushing the bowl away. 'Becky, tell me.'

She could barely get the words out but there was no going back now. She looked into his eyes and said the words. 'Lilly is your daughter.'

# Chapter 39

'Is this some sort of a joke?' Dennis stared at Becky as if she was mad.

'It's no joke, Dennis. It's the truth.'

'Don't be ridiculous. Why are you saying this?'

'I swear. Why would I lie to you?'

He stood up suddenly. 'I don't know what's going on here, but I'm not going to play a game with you so you can write a story for the paper. What sort of sick mind do you have?'

'Dennis, please. Sit down. I'm telling you the truth. And I already told you, I'm not a journalist. I work in the bank.'

He seemed unsure of what to do next so Becky continued. 'Come on, sit down please and listen to what I have to say. I know it's a shock but let me explain.'

'Go on, then. But I'm telling you, I'm no fool.' He sat back down on the edge of the chair, as if ready for a quick escape.

'I worked and lived close to where you had your business. We didn't know each other but I knew who you were. We met in Gillick's one night and went back to your apartment. I know you won't remember, because I was just one of many women, but you can imagine what happened next.'

She watched as he began to take in the information. She could almost see his mind ticking over, trying to make sense of it all.

'Do you understand what I'm saying, Dennis? We had a one-night stand almost five years ago and Lilly was the result of that night.'

'I knew I recognised you.' He looked pale. Stunned.

'What?'

'That perfume, that face. It all felt really familiar but I couldn't think why. I remember you now. I remember that night.'

Becky was thrown by that. 'You don't have to say that. I'm under no illusion – I know there were a lot of women.'

'It's true. I can see it now. You had a purple silk dress on that came to just above your knees. I remember the feel of that dress and how it slipped so easily over your head.'

Becky blushed a deep red. 'I can't believe you actually remember. I honestly thought all your conquests would be jumbled up in your brain.'

He winced. 'I suppose I deserved that. I can't believe I didn't remember who you were straight away. You stuck in my mind for ages after that night. And your hair was different – shorter and straighter I think.'

'Yes, I've been letting it grow. But none of that's important now. Lilly is what matters.'

Dennis looked at her. 'Are you sure?'

'What do you mean?'

'I mean, how can you know she's mine?'

'Because I wasn't like you. I didn't sleep with somebody different every night. In fact, you were the first man I'd been with in a while and then after … well, it was difficult.' She stood up and took a framed picture of Lilly from a shelf and handed it to him. 'Look at her eyes, Dennis. There's no denying it.'

'I – I don't know what to say. And why now?'

'It's really a combination of things – Lilly's been asking questions and it just felt like the time was right.'

'I take it you haven't said anything to her yet?' Dennis was shifting uncomfortably in the chair. 'Because if you haven't said anything, maybe you shouldn't.'

'No, I haven't said anything yet. I wanted to discuss it with you first. I was hoping you'd agree to meet her and we could take it from there.'

He stood up again suddenly and moved away from the table. 'What can I offer her, Becky? I have nothing. I'm a nobody. Why would you want Lilly to have a father like me?'

Becky was alarmed. 'Don't be silly. You're a good man, Dennis.'

'That might be the case. But that's not enough. Just make up a lie and tell Lilly that her father was some wonderful hero who died saving someone's life. Give her something good to cling on to.'

'No, Dennis. I want her to know *you*. I've got to know you over the past couple of months and I think you're a genuine, decent guy who's just had some really bad luck.'

He already had his coat on and his rucksack slung over his shoulder. He turned and looked at her with angry eyes. 'Well, I don't want her in my life. You can't just decide to turn someone's life upside down like that. Hers or mine. No, I'm sorry. This just isn't for me.'

'But, Dennis, she's your daughter. I know it's been a shock but at least give the information a chance to sink in before you decide you want nothing to do with her.' She followed him out to the door, panic rising inside.

'You can't keep something like this from me for years and then decide the time is right when *you're* ready.' He was really angry now and Becky felt close to tears. 'If you know what's good for you, you'll forget you ever found me and just get on with your lives.'

'I can't do that. Like it or not, you're Lilly's father and nothing's going to change that.'

'Bye, Becky. Have a good life and I hope Lilly will have a successful, happy life too.' He began walking down towards the gate.

'What about your clothes? They're not ready yet.' Becky was desperate to get him to come back.

'Drop them into the social club for me. But please don't come looking for me. I don't want anything to do with you or your family.'

Becky opened her mouth to say something else, but the words wouldn't come out. She had a sob stuck in her throat as she watched Dennis disappear around the corner. What a disaster. In all the scenarios she'd imagined in her head, she'd never thought it would end up like this. Dennis had been really angry and Becky felt sure he wouldn't change his mind. It felt like the end.

She closed the door and leaned against it while she tried to get her breathing under control. What a mess. At least she hadn't mentioned any of this to Lilly. The little girl could continue with her life, completely oblivious to the drama her mother had created. But it wouldn't be so easy for her. Dennis Prendergast was ingrained on her brain and it would be a long time until she'd be able to forget him.

❦

'Oh, God, Becky. I'm so sorry.' Alice had come back from her outing with a happy but tired Lilly. The little girl had been happy to sprawl out on the sofa in front of the telly while Alice and Becky had a chat.

'It's my own stupid fault,' said Becky, cupping her hands around the hot mug of sweet tea Alice had made for her. 'Why did I expect things to work out? This isn't a fairy tale!'

'Stop being so hard on yourself. You had to try. If you hadn't gone after Dennis, you would have thought about it for the rest of your life. It's his loss if he doesn't want to be involved.'

'But it must have been such a shock for him. Maybe if I give him a few days and then—'

'No, Becky.'

'What?'

'I think you should leave it now.' Alice knew she needed to be firm. 'You've given it your best shot and you can't do any more.'

'But if you'd seen him, Alice. He just feels he's not worthy. He actually said he's a nobody.'

'I feel sorry for the guy, I really do. But I don't see what going after him again can achieve. He knows about Lilly now so if he wants to be involved in any way, he'll come back to you.'

'But what if he doesn't?'

Alice could see the panic in Becky's eyes and felt sorry for her. 'It's unfortunate but you can't make someone *want* to be a dad.'

'I know, but he's had so many knocks – so much bad luck. If I can prove to him that we really want him to be involved, that it's not just a sympathy thing.'

'Listen to yourself, Becky. Did it occur to you that maybe Dennis really doesn't want to be involved? Maybe the thought of having a child fills him with dread.' Alice saw Becky recoil and felt bad. But she needed to hear it. 'We can't imagine the pain he's been through. It just might be too much for him.'

'I know you're right. I should leave him now and let the information sink in. He knows where I am.'

'But?'

'But it's just so bloody hard to forget about him after everything that's happened these past couple of months.'

Alice looked at her friend and felt a surge of love for her. Becky acted tough sometimes but that was just a front. Alice wanted to protect her but she also knew that some tough love was required.

'Becky, when exactly did all this become about *you*?'

'Wh – what do you mean?'

'I mean this whole Dennis Prendergast situation. It seems to me that you've forgotten the reason you started this thing in the first place.'

Becky stood up and put her mug in the sink. When she turned around, she looked angry. 'How dare you suggest that I've forgotten about Lilly. She's the *only* reason I did this.'

'Is she?'

'Yes! You know she is. Why are you being like this?'

'Maybe she was the reason you started, but I think somewhere along the line, things got muddled up.'

Becky leaned against the counter and stared at Alice. 'You're wrong.'

'Am I?'

'Yes! All I care about is Lilly.'

'Is she happy?'

'Yes.'

'Has she been upset about not having a father in her life?'

'Well, no, but—'

'So it didn't work out with Dennis. Lilly isn't any the wiser. Leave it now, Becky. Don't make this a mission for your own gratification.'

Becky looked as though she was about to give Alice a piece of her mind and then thought better of it. She sighed and nodded. 'You're right. I hate to admit it but Dennis has become like a project for me. The more elusive he seemed, the more I wanted to chase him.'

Alice stood up and put her arms around her friend. 'I can understand that, pet, but it's time to let it go. And who knows? When he's had time to think about things or if things improve for him, he might come back. You've given him the information now and it's up to him what he does with it.'

'You're such a rock of sense. What would I do without you?'

'Why are you hugging each other?' Lilly appeared at the kitchen door, startling them both. 'And why are you crying, Mummy?'

Becky quickly wiped a few stray tears with her sleeve before going to pick Lilly up. 'Because I'm happy.'

'You don't cry when you're happy, silly. Look, I'm happy and I'm not crying.' Her smile almost cut her face in two and Becky laughed.

'Well, I'm glad you're happy because that's the most important thing in the world to me.'

Alice slipped out the door quietly, tears in her own eyes, as Becky hugged Lilly tightly. There was nothing so powerful as the bond between a mother and child.

❀

Dennis walked alongside the River Liffey, his head awash with emotions and his heart heavy. The warmth of Becky's house made the outside temperatures almost unbearable and, at that moment, he hated his life more than ever. He'd learned over the last couple of years to expect the unexpected, but he really hadn't been ready for what he'd heard today.

He had a daughter. He couldn't believe it. Lilly. 'Lilly.' He said the name out loud to see how it sounded. It sounded beautiful, but it filled him with fear. He couldn't be a father. He couldn't look after himself, let alone a child. What the bloody hell had Becky been thinking? What did she want from him?

His time in hospital had brought him to a crossroads in his life where he was either going to find a way to make things better or just end it all. Ending it all often seemed like the easier option, but since he'd befriended Martha, he'd allowed himself a glimmer of hope. He'd accepted Becky's help earlier and it had made him feel good. For that short hour or so, he'd thought that maybe things were looking up. But then she'd hit him with her news.

He stopped to look into the river and wondered what it would feel like to sink below the murky water. They say drowning is a peaceful way to go and, right now, it was looking very enticing. Who'd miss him if he was gone? Would anyone really care? His mother came into his mind and he immediately felt guilty. He thought about Lilly. What did he have to give that little girl? How could he enhance her life? He had nothing – he *was* nothing. Yet how could he live with himself, knowing he had a child and not doing anything about it?

He didn't have a choice. You lose the luxury of choice when you become a nobody. Choice was for people who had a life. He looked around him at the busy street and felt invisible. He idly wondered if anyone would even notice if he were to jump. Would he have noticed back in the day when he was dashing around, being a successful businessman? Probably not. He dropped his rucksack beside him at the dirty wall and leaned over. It was now or never.

# Chapter 40

'Come on, Lilly. Let's get you ready for bed.'

'I don't want to. It's too early.'

Becky resisted the urge to scream. 'Remember our deal? If you're a good girl tonight, we'll put up our Christmas decorations tomorrow.'

'But *why* does Len have to come over *all* the time. It's just not fair.'

'Sweetie, Len doesn't come over all the time, and doesn't he always bring you something nice? I think you're a very lucky girl.'

Lilly made a face. 'But why can't I just stay down here and watch telly? I'll be as quiet as a mouse. I promise.'

'Lilly, you need your sleep. You're exhausted. And besides, sometimes Mummy just wants some adult time.'

'Why?'

'Because … because I just do.'

'To do adult stuff?'

'Well, yes … I mean, to talk about adult things and stuff.'

'What stuff?'

Colour rose in Becky's cheeks. 'Lilly, stop trying to delay things. You're going to bed now and that's that.'

'You're mean and so is Len. You're two meanies.'

'Right, I've had enough of your cheek. Upstairs to your room now and have a think about what you've just said. Len has been nothing but kind to you. I'll be up in a minute and if you're sorry, you can come down and watch a bit of telly for a while.'

'But, Mummy.'

'No buts, young lady. Now *go!*'

Lilly looked at her before bursting into tears and flying out of the room. Becky heard her stomp up the stairs and slam her bedroom door – if this was the way she acted at four, what would her teenage years be like? But she couldn't help feeling bad about being so hard on her. Lilly was a good kid and was trying to deal with a tricky situation. Sometimes, she seemed to really like Len and other times she was wary of him. But that was to be expected. And Len was great with her so Becky had no doubt that the two of them would become friends eventually.

She headed into the kitchen where she stuck some cans of beer in the fridge and opened a bottle of red wine. She'd cooked for Len a couple of times lately but was relieved earlier when he'd suggested they order a takeaway. She wasn't sure if that was a reflection on her cooking, but she didn't really care. Things had been going well between them lately and she was beginning to see a future.

She could now see how much Dennis had complicated things. She'd become so immersed in the situation, she hadn't given Len the time he deserved. But in the past week alone, he'd been over to the house three times and Becky was really falling for him. She wasn't sure it was love yet, but it was definitely getting there.

It was nine days since she'd told Dennis about Lilly and there'd been no contact from him. She'd taken Alice's advice and decided to leave things well enough alone. Dennis knew about his daughter and if he ever wanted to pursue things, he knew where they were. But no matter how hard she'd tried to forget, there were reminders everywhere. There'd been horrific news of a homeless man found dead in the Phoenix Park; she'd panicked when she'd heard the news, convincing herself it was Dennis, until they'd said the man was thought to be in his fifties. But that had been little comfort to her. It had made her think more about the plight of the homeless and what a horrible world Dennis had found himself in.

'I'm sorry, Mummy.' Lilly stood at the kitchen door, hugging her teddy, her face blotchy from tears.

'Come here,' said Becky, holding out her arms. 'I'm sorry for being cross too, but you can't say things like that about people – especially about Len, who's generous and kind and treats you like a princess.'

'But, Mummy, I have enough things now. I don't want any more stuff from him.'

Becky looked at her quizzically. 'Since when did you ever refuse a present? Is this because he got you that *Cinderella* DVD?'

'I told you, I hate Cinderella,' pouted Lilly. 'He doesn't even know what I like.'

'Don't be so ungrateful, Lilly. Len doesn't have any children so it's hard for him to pick presents. He's doing his best.'

'Is he going to be my daddy?'

Becky almost fell off the chair. 'Of course not! What gave you that idea?'

'Dunno. I just thought.'

'Well, you can get that thought right out of your head, sweetie. Len is just my friend – he's not your daddy.' Thoughts of Dennis came flooding into her mind and she hugged her daughter tightly. 'Go on, off with you into the sitting room and see what's on telly. I'll bring you in some popcorn, then it's bed in twenty minutes.'

The doorbell rang just as she was taking popcorn out of the microwave. Perfect timing. She smoothed down her grey knitted dress and adjusted her stockings. She felt really sexy in the sheer knit dress and loved how it just sat below the top of her stockings. She knew Len would appreciate it and she looked forward to letting him check her out later. She slipped her feet into her black stilettos, after dropping the bowl of popcorn in to Lilly, and went to answer the door.

'Hi, darling.' He looked very handsome in his loose-fit jeans and fur-trimmed parka and she breathed in his heady scent as he leaned in to kiss her.

'Come on in,' she said, opening the door wide. 'Lilly will be heading to bed shortly and we can order the food.'

'Great. I brought her a little something so should I give it to her now or wait?'

'Let's have a drink first while she's happy watching telly. You can give it to her when she's going to bed. But you really don't have to keep buying her things, Len.'

'I know, but I want to. You're very special to me, Becky. And she's special to you, so I want to make my two girls happy.'

Becky glowed with happiness as she led the way into the kitchen. 'Now, what can I get you? Beer or wine?'

'I wouldn't mind a beer, please.' Just as she turned to get it, he pulled her back into his arms and ran his hands up her thighs. 'Ah, thought so. What are you trying to do to me, woman?'

'What do you mean?' she asked innocently, as he fingered the top of her stockings. 'I'm not doing anything.'

'You're driving me crazy. Why do you have to be so damn sexy?'

Becky laughed and pulled away. 'Settle down. There'll be plenty of time for that later when Lilly is asleep.'

'I like the sound of that. It had better be soon, though, or I won't be responsible for my actions.' He found the top of her stockings again and Becky was delighted her outfit was having the desired effect.

'Right,' she said, shoving some menus in front of him. 'Have a look through those and see what you fancy. I'm going to put Lilly to bed and then I'm all yours.'

'See what I fancy? Are you kidding me?' He pinched her bum as she left the room and she smiled to herself. A minute later she was back in the kitchen, Lilly in her arms. 'Say goodnight to Len, sweetie.'

'Night,' she said, eyeing up the package on the counter. 'Is that for me?'

'It certainly is.' Len handed her the present and she had the paper torn off in seconds.'

'Look, Mummy. It's a Peppa Pig bag. Can I bring it to playschool next week? Can I?'

Becky laughed at her enthusiasm and shot Len a grateful look. 'Of course you can, sweetie. Now say thank you to Len.'

Lilly murmured her thanks without looking at him. Becky decided to let it go because Lilly was obviously exhausted. Thank God. She carried her upstairs and supervised as she brushed her teeth. Becky had been pleasantly surprised at how her body had responded earlier to Len's advances. Oh, God, when he'd touched the top of her thighs, she'd felt things stir inside her that she'd long forgotten about. Everything was falling into place. She felt ready now to take things to the next level.

'Right, Missy. Hop into bed and I'll come up and check on you when I've had my dinner, okay?'

'When is he going home?'

Becky sighed. 'Not until later, sweetie. And when he's gone, I'll come up and give you another cuddle. But you have to promise to be good and go to sleep. Deal?'

'Okay. And we can put up the Christmas decorations tomorrow?'

'Yes. I promised, didn't I?'

'Night, Mummy.'

Becky headed back down to where Len was poring over the menus. 'Right, have you decided what we're having yet?'

'Well, I've marked a few things on here,' he said, pointing to the Chinese menu. 'And I was hoping for a double portion of you for dessert.'

Becky laughed. 'I'm sure that can be arranged. Now let's order. I'm starving.'

An hour later, their food eaten, they headed into the sitting room where they made themselves comfortable on the sofa. The heady combination of wine and Len's musky scent was beginning to drive Becky wild and she was more than happy when he began to kiss her. She groaned with pleasure when his mouth began to explore her neck and made its way down to her cleavage. She could feel her nipples harden as he fondled them through her dress and it was all she could do not to rip her clothes off. It was a long time since she'd felt like this and she was glad that Len was finally able to stir up those long-lost feelings.

'What are you doing, Mummy?' Becky almost died of shock when she heard Lilly's voice and sat upright on the sofa.

'Len was just tickling me, sweetie. Why are you up?'

'Why was he tickling you?'

'We were just playing. Now come on, let's get you back up to bed.' Becky felt awful that Lilly had seen them, but at least they were both still fully clothed. Lilly allowed her mother to pick her up. 'I was trying to go asleep but I have a pain in my tooth.'

Becky looked at her suspiciously. 'You didn't have a sore tooth before you went to bed.'

'But I really, really do, Mummy. I can't go asleep because it's sooooo sore.'

Becky sighed. 'Right, sit down there beside Len and I'll go and get you some hot milk. That should make you sleepy, and you'll forget all about the pain.'

'But, Mummy, I don't want to go back to bed.'

'Lilly, you'll do as you're told.' Becky was getting fed up with Lilly always interrupting and especially tonight when things had really been hotting up.

She rushed into the kitchen and poured some milk into a cup. She stuck it in the microwave for thirty seconds and gave it a little stir. She was still feeling really turned on and wanted to get Lilly back to bed while she and Len were in the zone. Just as she was about to go back into the sitting room, she heard Len chatting to Lilly. She smiled to herself and paused to listen to what he was saying. For somebody with no children himself, he really knew the right things to say.

'Remember what I said last time, Lilly?'

Lilly pouted but didn't say anything.

'Surely you haven't forgotten already.' Len was leaning in close to her.

'No,' said Lilly, her voice barely a whisper.

'Well, it looks like you need to be reminded.'

Chills suddenly shot through Becky. Len's voice sounded a bit menacing and yet he was smiling. Maybe she was imagining it. She stood completely still, barely breathing, wanting to hear more.

'You know that evil step-mother in the *Cinderella* DVD I gave you?' continued Len. 'Well, I could be just like her – except I'd be the evil step-father. And if you keep disturbing me and your mummy like this, I might have to lock you away and you'll never see your mummy again.'

'Len!' Becky burst in the door and scooped Lilly up in her arms. 'What the hell do you think you're doing?'

'Oh, I was just … I mean, me and Lilly were talking about her favourite fairy tales.'

'Get out! How dare you. I heard it all. I heard what you were saying to her.' Lilly snuggled into her and Becky held on to her tightly. 'I can't believe you'd say something like that.'

Len stood up. 'Calm down, Becky. We were just messing about – weren't we, Lilly?'

Lilly buried her face into her mother's chest and didn't say anything.

'Come on, Lilly. Tell your mother that we were just playing. Don't be naughty now.'

It was all Becky could do not to slap him. 'Get OUT! I swear, if you're not out of here in ten seconds, I'm calling the police.'

'Well, there's no need for—'

'OUT!'

He grabbed his coat off the banister on his way to the door and turned around to plead with Becky again. 'Come on, Becky. You know what Lilly's like. Even you were getting fed up with her antics. I was just doing it for us.'

'Never, ever speak my daughter's name again. I can't believe you've behaved like that. She's four years old, Len. Four years old!' Becky was in tears.

'Okay, okay, I'm going. But when you've had time to calm down, we can talk about this.'

'I don't think so. I never want to see you again.'

'But it's just because I love you so much, Becks. Come on, I was just frustrated. You can't say you weren't feeling the same yourself.'

'Even looking at you is making me sick. Now GET LOST!' She gave him a shove out the door and slammed it behind him.

Lilly looked up. 'Is he gone, Mummy?'

'Yes, he is, sweetie. And I'm so sorry I brought him here in the first place.'

'I was trying not to be bold but he was kind of scary.'

Becky's head was awash with emotions. She couldn't believe what had just happened. 'Well, he certainly won't be coming back here again.'

'Yay!' She jumped down from her mother's arms. 'Can we have some hot chocolate, then? With marshmallows and flake?'

Becky smiled through her tears. 'Of course we can. Why don't you and me snuggle under a blanket in the sitting room with our hot chocolates and watch a movie. It's very late but we're celebrating.'

'What are we celebrating?'

'We're celebrating the fact that I love you more than anything in the world and that it's just the two of us again.' Becky settled Lilly on the sofa and headed into the kitchen.

Her own words were ringing in her ears. It was just her and Lilly again. Is that the way it would always be? Was she destined to not have a man in her life? Tears poured down her cheeks as she spooned the chocolate powder into the milk. She wasn't crying for Len. Not really. But she *was* crying for what he represented – an end to her loneliness.

Not for the first time, she thought about Dennis and what might have happened if she'd told him about her pregnancy from the beginning. Would they have got together? Maybe she could have saved him from a life on the streets. Maybe he could have saved her from a life of loneliness.

She gave herself a mental shake and forced herself to concentrate on the here and now. Hindsight was all very good but it wouldn't change anything. Dennis had his chance and he'd thrown it back in her face. Maybe he'd have done the same five years ago. She'd never know. She took the two cups and headed into the sitting room. Lilly had her head rested on the arm of the sofa and was almost asleep. Becky realised at that moment that she could never love anyone like she loved Lilly. She was the centre of her life and she was going to make sure that no man – not Len Sherwood and not Dennis Prendergast – was ever going to come between the two of them.

# Chapter 41

'So I was thinking,' Alice whispered, cupping her hand over the phone and peeping into the sitting room to make sure Lilly wasn't listening. 'Since she wouldn't go to the Christmas party on Monday, why don't I make a night of it here on Friday night for the three of us?'

'Brilliant idea.' Kate sounded delighted. 'What were you thinking exactly?'

'I was thinking I could cook a nice, Christmassy meal and you could come over later. I know it's close to Christmas and everyone's busy, but I think it would do us all good.'

'That's perfect. And will we make it a surprise?'

Alice thought about all the surprises Becky had been through over the past few months and knew instinctively it would be the wrong thing to do. 'No surprises, Kate. I think she's had enough of those to last her a lifetime. I just wanted to run it by you first and if you're on board, I'll tell her this evening.'

'Well, you can count me in. Garreth has a gig on Friday night anyway so I would have been home alone.'

'Right, that settles it. Let's say eight o'clock. I was thinking of doing a roast beef with all the trimmings – we'll have turkey and ham coming out of our ears in another couple of weeks.'

'Sounds great. There's nothing like a good old-fashioned roast to fatten a person up.'

'God, Kate. I wasn't trying to … I didn't mean to … Maybe we could have something simpler, like a nice salad or a—'

'Relax, Alice. I'm just having you on. You know I really do love my food. Even when I had my *problems*, I could never resist a big chunk of meat.'

'And speaking of problems, how's the counselling going? Is it any help at all?'

'It's good actually. I hated the thought of it at first but Dr Gulati is brilliant. I sometimes forget it's a counselling session and we just chat.'

'That's great, Kate.'

'Well, you were the one who kick-started it. I won't forget that, you know.'

Alice blushed. 'Stop it, will you? You'll have me in tears. Now I'd better go and get Lilly something to eat. I have a doctor's appointment this afternoon, so I'm expecting Becky home early.'

'Ah, so that's why she skulked off half an hour ago. I thought it was strange to see her leave so early.'

Alice glanced at the clock. Only half three, so she'd have plenty of time.

'So why have you to go to the doctor?' continued Kate. 'I hope it's nothing serious.'

'Ah, no, just a check-up really. I've decided to give in and get something for this menopause. There's no point in fighting nature.'

'Oh, poor you. I'd hate to be at an age where everything starts going haywire in my body.'

'Thanks for that, Kate.' But Alice was smiling.

'Oh, Jesus, sorry. That came out wrong. I didn't mean, I mean—'

'Ha! Don't worry. I know you suffer from foot in mouth.'

'I don't know what's wrong with me. I can't seem to help saying the wrong thing. But honestly, I hope you get it sorted. I'm sure it's not a pleasant thing to be going through.'

'Thanks. Listen, I have to fly. I'll see you on Friday at eight, if I don't talk to you before that.'

Alice sat back on the kitchen chair and closed her eyes. She was exhausted. Each day she seemed to be getting more and more tired, despite her daily iron tablet. She was glad she was going for the blood tests today. It was about time really. But she also felt trepidation. What if it wasn't just the menopause? What if it was something else? Her mother had died young of pancreatic cancer and she was terrified it would happen to her too. She hadn't shared her fears with anyone, even Frank. She liked to be the one solving other people's problems, not the other way around.

She thought briefly about sticking on some beans for Lilly but she couldn't resist letting herself drift off to sleep for a few minutes. She didn't usually do it while she was in charge of Lilly, but she literally couldn't keep her eyes open.

'Alice!'

She jumped up with fright, knocking the phone onto the tiled floor, where it smashed to smithereens. 'Oh, no. Look what you did now, Lilly.'

The little girl immediately began to cry. 'I'm sorry.'

'Oh, God, no, *I'm* sorry.' Alice rushed to her and picked her up, hugging her tightly. 'I didn't mean to shout. I fell asleep and still wasn't awake properly when you called me. Please don't cry.'

''Kay,' said Lilly, big tears in the corners of her eyes, ready to plop out. 'But the phone is all broken.'

'Don't worry about that. I can clean it up and we can go and buy a new one tomorrow. Now, are you hungry?'

Lilly shook her head. 'Not really. Can we do face masks instead?'

'Not today, Lilly. Your mummy is going to be home soon, I have somewhere to go.'

'Where?'

'I'm just going to the doctor so he can give me tablets so I won't be so tired any more.'

'Yay! Then we can do more stuff like we used to.'

Alice immediately felt bad. Her tiredness had meant that she and Lilly had spent a lot of time lately watching telly. 'Yes, we'll be able to do more stuff. Maybe we'll do some baking tomorrow.'

'Oooh, can we make the chocolate chunk muffins? They're my favourites.'

'Of course. As soon as you come home from playschool we'll make them.'

'But pleeeeease can we do a face mask now before Mummy comes home? Just a little teeny weeny one?'

Alice looked at the clock. 'I really don't think I have time today.'

'But Alice. You're starting to look old. I thought you didn't want to be fifty.'

'Oh, Lilly,' Alice laughed. 'Your honesty is brilliant. Right, let's make a quick olive oil one. I still don't want to be fifty, so let's see if we can stop time before it's too late.'

Her own words rang in her ears as she mixed the oatmeal and brown sugar in with the olive oil: 'before it's too late'. She suddenly felt really nervous about going to the doctor. She even contemplated ringing to cancel. But no, it needed to be done and whatever the outcome, she'd deal with it.

❁

'Mummy, look at Santa climbing down from the ceiling and the polar bears singing and the snow and everything.'

'I know. Isn't it wonderful?' Lilly's face was a picture and Becky was delighted she'd brought her to see the lights. She'd arrived home early to let Alice go to her appointment and decided at the last minute to hop in the car with Lilly and drive back into town. She'd been doing her best to spend more quality time with Lilly since the whole Len Sherwood episode. He'd been trying to worm his way in to her affections again, but she was having none of it. There was no taking him back after the way he'd treated Lilly. Becky had cried a lot afterwards but they were mostly tears of anger. She'd thought she was falling for him but it turned out she was just falling in love with the idea of a romance. Len Sherwood meant nothing to her.

'It's nearly my turn, Mummy. Will you come in with me?'

'Of course I will. Have you decided what you're going to say to Santa?'

'Can't I just have a present? I don't want to talk to him.'

'But don't you want to tell him what you want for Christmas?'

'I wrote him a letter. He'll know.'

Becky had to stifle a giggle. 'That's true, but there's no harm in reminding him.'

'Okay. Will he give it to me today?'

'Of course not. You know you have to wait until Christmas morning. But he'll give you something little now and, if you like, we can get a picture and put it in one of those pretty snow-globes.'

'Yay,' said Lilly, picking up one from the counter and shaking it. 'These are so much fun.'

'If you want to just step inside now, Santa will be with you in a moment.' A girl dressed as an elf smiled at them and Lilly's eyes lit up.

They stepped into Santa's grotto where the booming laugh of Santa echoed from his room. Lilly stiffened but Becky held on to her hand tightly. 'Don't be scared, sweetie. Santa is really lovely.'

'So who have we got here, then?' said Santa, holding out his white-gloved hand for Lilly to take. 'You're a beautiful little girl. Are you an angel?'

Lilly giggled and took a few steps forward. 'No, I'm Lilly.'

'Lilly! What a lovely name. Are you going to come over here and stand beside Santa for a picture?'

'Okay.' She inched her way forward until she was just within comfortable distance of him but not too close. 'Can I have my present now?'

'Well, how about you tell Santa what you want for Christmas. I've been so busy, I haven't had a chance to go through all my letters yet.'

Becky smiled as she watched. He was a brilliant Santa, very authentic looking, and she could see Lilly was getting more and more comfortable as he spoke to her.

Lilly moved a bit closer and smiled for the elf who was pointing the camera at them. 'I'd like a Flutterbye Flying Fairy Doll, a Furby Boom and a surprise.'

Santa glanced quickly at Becky, who nodded. 'Well, I'm sure we'll be able to organise that for you, because I heard that you've been a very good girl.'

'Thank you, Santa.' Lilly beamed at him but Becky could see she was eager to leave. Just as she got to the door, she turned back. 'And for the surprise, could I have a baby sister or brother? That would be really cool.'

Becky almost died of shock and she suspected Santa's 'ho-ho-ho' response was genuine laughter. She didn't want to say anything until Lilly had collected her present and they got the receipt to come back for the snow-globe later. They sat down on a bench so that Lilly could open her present.

'Why did you say that to Santa, sweetie?'

'Say what?'

'About getting a baby sister or brother.'

'Because I want one.'

'But you know we can't just *get* a baby like that. We've talked about this before.'

'I know,' said Lilly, looking at the princess dress-up set she got from Santa. 'But it's not fair. Erin has a baby brother *and* her mummy is getting another one. She said it might even be a girl. She's soooo lucky.'

Becky felt sorry for the little girl. If things were different, she'd love to be able to give her a brother or sister. Maybe some day, but she wasn't holding her breath.

Lilly was still talking. 'And if we can't get a baby, can we have a puppy?'

Oh, God, things were going from bad to worse. 'Puppies are a lot of hard work, sweetie. They're lovely to cuddle but not when you have to pick up their poo from all over the house.'

'Eeewww! I'm not doing that.'

Thank God for that. 'Me neither. Now let's go and get a burger. We might even stretch to a McFlurry, if you're good.'

'Yay. Thank you, Mummy. This is the best day.'

Becky smiled as they headed to McDonald's. How easily kids can be distracted. They'd gone from babies to puppies to ice-cream in minutes. If only it was so easy for adults. In movies the women always turned to a tub of Ben & Jerry's double chocolate to cheer them up. She somehow doubted whether any amount of ice-cream would make her forget about Dennis Prendergast and what could have been.

❉

Alice came out of the doctor's surgery in Phibsboro and began to walk aimlessly. She was in a daze. She'd thought she'd been prepared, but obviously she wasn't. The rain had begun to fall but she didn't care. What did it matter if she got wet? Her head was in a spin – there'd be tests, then more tests, check-ups, treatments, but the doctor had been in no doubt.

She found herself at the entrance to the Botanic Gardens and thought it would be a good place to think. The beautiful manicured lawns and winter blooms began to calm her and she soon felt more at peace. There were a surprising number of people around, considering the icy temperatures, and she found an empty bench where she could sit and watch the world go by.

There was a woman wheeling an empty double buggy, both children obviously preferring to walk. Alice stared at her for a moment and felt a strange feeling in the pit of her stomach. The woman looked frazzled as she tried to manage the tots, who couldn't be much more than two. An old man passed and tipped his cap, offering her a toothy smile. She smiled back, an automatic response. Her mother would have been proud. And then there were the three girls. Fourteen or fifteen perhaps. That horrible age where they were neither child nor adult. They defied the cold weather with their short skirts and their faces were made up well beyond their years. But their giggles portrayed their youth and Alice couldn't help thinking they were lucky. Their lives were still blank canvases. They could choose to do or to be whatever they wanted. She hoped they'd choose well.

She stood up suddenly. She needed to get home. She wasn't alone any more. She'd become very used to dealing with things on her own, but she didn't have to do that now. She had Frank and he needed to know. Her steps quickened at the thought of her wonderful Frank. He was her rock. She just wanted to be home now for him to put his arms around her and tell her everything would be okay. Because it would. Things happened for a reason and no matter how surprising or shocking they were, she was strong – *they* were strong – and they'd deal with whatever came their way.

# Chapter 42

'This looks gorgeous, Alice,' Becky said, coming into the kitchen to check out the table. 'You've really surpassed yourself.'

'It's nothing, really. I just wanted to make it festive so we could get into the spirit.'

'Well, you've certainly done that. You've a real eye for colour. I'd never have thought of putting purple and silver together.'

Alice beamed. 'To be honest, I nicked the idea from a magazine. These are bits I bought for our own Christmas table so I'm trialling them here tonight.'

'Good idea. So what can I help with?'

'Not a thing. The meat is cooked and resting and everything else is almost ready. Let's sit down and I'll pour us a mulled wine.'

'Ooh, so that's what the cinnamon smell is. Yum! You've really thought of everything.' Becky sat down and gratefully took a glass of the warmed wine from Alice.

'Well?' Alice watched as Becky took a large sip.

'It's absolutely delicious. Thanks so much for doing this. It's exactly what I needed.'

'No problem,' Alice said, wiping down the counter. 'And with only twelve days left to Christmas Day, it's nice to start the countdown.'

'Speaking of which, I assume you and Frank will have Christmas dinner at home.'

'Yep. Our first time to spend Christmas Day together. That's why I'm making a special effort to make the table look nice. And Louise, his daughter, will be coming over in the evening for tea.'

'Ah, that's brilliant. You'll have a great time.'

'And what about you? Looks like you'll be having a different sort of Christmas yourself this year. Are Joanna and the gang still coming?'

Becky couldn't contain her excitement. 'Oh, Alice, it's going to be great. Joanna, her husband and the two children are coming for a week and spending the whole of Christmas Day here with us. I can't believe this house will be so full of people and Lilly is beside herself with excitement.'

'It'll be brilliant all right. I hope the kids get on well.'

'I'm sure they will. You know how Lilly has been going on about having a brother or a sister? Well, I've told her that a couple of cousins will have to do for now.'

'She'll be in her element. And I can't wait to meet them all.'

Becky suddenly had a brainwave. 'Come over on Christmas morning. I'll make some nibbles and I can introduce everyone.'

Alice looked hesitant. 'I'm not sure, Becky. You'll have enough with your family there and I wouldn't like to leave Frank on our first—'

'Ah, you big eejit. Bring Frank of course. And you *are* family, Alice. I'd really love you to meet everyone.'

'Okay, then. I'll just check with Frank, but thanks. It sounds like a lovely idea.'

The doorbell rang at that moment and Becky jumped up to answer it. 'That'll be Kate. You'd better pour another glass of that mulled wine. She'll have smelled it from down the street.'

'Hi, Becky,' Kate said, stepping in and bringing with her a waft of cold air. 'Is that mulled wine I can smell?'

Becky laughed as she took Kate's coat. 'It certainly is. Alice has a big pot on the go.'

'Hi, Kate. Lovely to see you.' Alice handed her a glass as she came into the kitchen. 'Get that down you and you won't be long warming up.'

'Thanks, Alice. The table looks fabulous. Ooh, I can't believe Christmas is so close. It's my favourite day of the whole year.'

'I only ever really liked it for Lilly's sake.' Becky held out her glass for Alice to top up. 'But this year feels different.'

'And what about you, Alice?' said Kate. 'Are you a lover of all things Christmas?'

'I suppose, like Becky, I haven't been in the past. But this year I'm going to make it really special. I think we should all appreciate what we have more. None of us ever know what's going to hit us in our lives so we should live for the moment.'

Becky looked at her in alarm. 'What do you mean? Has something happened?'

'Oh, God, I never asked you about your tests,' said Kate, her hand flying to her mouth. 'What did the doctor say?'

Alice shook her head adamantly. 'Everything is fine and no, nothing has happened. I was actually thinking of Dennis when I said that. I was thinking about how his life must have been a few years ago and now he'll be spending Christmas on the streets.'

Silence filled the room. Becky wished things could be different, but she'd done all she could. Maybe sometime in the future they'd get in touch again and he might be more receptive to the idea of meeting Lilly if things have improved for him.

'Sorry, I didn't mean to bring the mood down.' Alice was the first to break the silence. 'It was just a fleeting thought. I shouldn't have opened my mouth.'

'It's fine,' Becky said, trying to lift her mood again. 'I suppose we should always think of the less fortunate while we enjoy a great Christmas.'

'Right, you two, out of here.' Alice changed the subject by standing up and shooing the two of them towards the door. 'I just have the finishing touches to put on this meal and I'll be serving up in ten minutes.'

'Are you sure you don't need any help?'

'Thanks, Becky, but I'm fine. I just need the kitchen to myself and I'll have everything done in a flash.'

Kate plonked down on the leather sofa in the sitting room and curled her legs up beneath her. 'Where's Lilly? Is she not eating with us?'

'God, no. She's been up in bed for the past hour. She was exhausted, poor thing. Ever since she started playschool, she gets really tired by the end of the week. All that playing is hard work, you know.'

'Oh, I'm sure it is,' giggled Kate. 'But what do you think about Alice?'

Becky raised her eyebrows. 'What about Alice?'

'Do you think there's something wrong?'

'What do you mean?'

'I don't know. I just got the impression she wasn't herself. When I mentioned about the tests, she sort of fobbed me off, but I thought she was being a bit melancholic.'

Becky nodded. 'Now that you mention it, she's been in a funny sort of mood the past couple of days. It's like her mind is somewhere else entirely. But what can we do if she says there's nothing wrong?'

'I think maybe we should just keep an eye on her. I can't believe I used to dislike her. She's brilliant and has been very good to me.'

'She's been like a mother to me, although she'd prefer the title of sister. She's just one of those people who likes to look after others and people like that often forget about looking after themselves.'

'Right, dinner's ready,' Alice said, appearing at the door of the sitting room. 'Let's get it while it's hot.'

Kate jumped up. 'You don't have to ask me twice – I'm starving.'

Becky's eyes almost popped out of her head when she saw the plates on the table. There was enough food on them to feed an army. The beef was well done, just as they all liked it, the roasted vegetables were shining with a glaze of some sort and the roast potatoes were crisp and looked delicious. There were orange-glazed carrots, sprouts with almonds and bacon, and minted mushy peas.

'Well, come on then, don't just stare at it, tuck in.' Alice beamed as they complimented her, and Becky wondered if they'd been reading too much into her mood. She seemed happy enough and was definitely getting into the festive spirit. But as Kate said, they'd just have to keep an eye on her.

The conversation flowed as they ploughed through the huge meal, and the sound of laughter and clinking of glasses made Becky more excited about Christmas Day. Having the house full of people and full of noise was going to be fantastic. Just as she was thinking she couldn't eat another mouthful, the doorbell rang.

'Are you expecting anyone else?' said Alice. 'We could definitely use another guest to finish off this food.'

Becky stood up and threw her serviette on the table. 'I'm not expecting anyone. Maybe someone has reported us for being too noisy.'

She was still giggling when she swung open the door, but stopped as soon as she saw who was there.

'Hello, Becky.' Len stood there like a fashion model, his navy parka zipped up to his chin and his Vans shoes looking as though they hadn't even left the shop. His aftershave filled her nostrils and she felt sick.

'What do you want?'

'Ah, don't be like that, Becky. You wouldn't take any of my calls so I had to come.'

'You're an intelligent man. Surely me not taking your calls is an indication that I didn't want to talk to you.'

'But it was all just a misunderstanding. Look, I even bought this for Lilly to say sorry.' He held out a box and Becky's eyes widened when she saw it was a Kindle.

'Len, you don't get it. We don't want you here and we don't want your presents. Now I have guests, can you please just go?'

'Becky, please. Don't let a four-year-old dictate your life. You're a grown woman, and you'll never be happy if you let her rule you.'

'How dare you! You have no right to say things like that. Now just go.'

'But Becky, we can work this out. Just give me a chance.'

Becky just needed him to be gone. 'Goodbye. And, for the record, Lilly is a four-year-old child, who's just beginning to learn her ABCs. A Kindle? You're not as smart as I thought you were!'

She slammed the door before he could say another word and leaned her back against it. Prat! How could she ever have liked him? He'd really had her fooled. Tears stung her eyes. God, what a bad judge of character she'd been. She gathered herself together and peeped back into the kitchen, where the girls were chatting animatedly.

'I'm just going up to check on Lilly. I'll be back in a minute.'

She flew into the bathroom and closed the door and waited for the tears to come. But there were none. She looked at her reflection in the mirror and suddenly a sense of calm came over her. What was there to cry about? She was well rid of Len Sherwood. She actually didn't feel sad at all. She hadn't loved him and now she didn't even like him. He'd been nothing more than someone to spend some time with – a man to snuggle up to on otherwise lonely evenings. She felt lucky that she'd seen his true colours before she'd let things go any further.

She heard the sound of laughter from downstairs and suddenly couldn't wait to get back down to the girls. They were all that mattered. Them and Lilly. She'd just go and check on Lilly and then enjoy the rest of the evening. The next week would be filled with Christmas shopping and planning for the big day so she wouldn't have time to wallow in any regrets. She smiled at herself in the mirror and for the first time in a long time, she noticed that her eyes smiled too.

✸

Alice crept quietly into the room. She could tell from Frank's snores that he was sleeping soundly and she didn't want to wake him. They'd spent the past two nights talking into the early hours and both were exhausted as a result. There was a lot to take in and a lot to discuss.

She gently pulled back her side of the cream-covered duvet and slipped in over the soft Egyptian cotton sheets. She'd bought new bedding when Frank had moved in and, instead of her usual Penneys bargains, she'd gone to Arnotts and indulged in some more expensive stuff. It had definitely been worth it because she'd been sleeping like a baby since he'd moved in.

She shivered and moved her body in close to Frank's to warm herself up. Still not a stir from him. She'd had a really good night but it had been hard to put everything out of her mind. Over the past couple of days, she'd been so tempted to talk to Becky about everything, but she wasn't ready yet. She wanted to have a full picture of things before she shared with anyone else.

Kate had taken her by surprise when she'd asked about the tests but she'd been able to divert their attention away by talking about Dennis. Poor Becky. She'd looked sad at the mention of his name. It was such a pity how things had worked out but she was glad that Becky hadn't pursued him any more. If he did come back at any stage, it would be because *he* wanted to and not because she'd forced him into it. Still, at least Becky would have Joanna and her family to distract her at Christmas.

Frank gave a loud snort before turning towards Alice and pulling her to him. He was still asleep but it was comforting for her to feel his arm around her. She watched as he ground his teeth between every snore. Her ex-husband used to do that too, and she'd hated it. Somehow with Frank, it didn't matter. His bad habits didn't really annoy her like they'd done with her ex. She'd never believed in true love before, but she had no doubt about the depth of her feelings for Frank.

She began to drift off into a lovely sleep as she thought about Christmas Day. She was looking forward to waking up with Frank on Christmas morning. She'd been buying him bits and pieces over the last few weeks and was going to make sure his stocking was full to the brim. They were going to have a wonderful time because God only knew what life would be like next Christmas.

# Chapter 43

He sat staring at his tea. The mug didn't even feel hot and he wasn't sure how long he'd been there. Time meant nothing to him any more. He'd spent the past couple of weeks in a daze and hadn't been sure whether he wanted to live or die. Limbo was a strange place to be and he prayed for the ability to make some decisions.

'Dennis, Dennis! Are you okay?'

He looked up to see Martha hovering over him with a fresh mug of tea in her hands. Her face was full of concern and she kept her eyes fixed on him.

'I – I'm grand. I was just thinking.'

'Well, I've been thinking too and I want to talk to you.'

'About what?'

'Look, I have someone coming in to give me a hand in a few minutes. It's been crazy here, what with it being so close to Christmas and the shoppers out in force. When she arrives, I'll come and sit with you and we can have a chat.'

Dennis watched as she tottered off to serve the next batch of customers. He realised that he'd never seen the shop so busy, with some people standing at the counter that ran around the back of the shop. Another time he'd have given his seat up but not today. He was tired and miserable and, at that moment, this was the only place he wanted to be. He'd poured his heart out to Martha over the past couple of difficult weeks. She hadn't judged. She hadn't advised him or lectured him. She'd just listened.

When Becky had told him about the child that day, the immediate word that had come into his head was failure. He was a failure. Not only had he messed up his own life but he'd messed up Becky's and the little girl's too. He'd been teetering on the edge for a while at that stage and the news of the child, combined with his fragile state, had almost broken him.

He'd stood at the bridge that day thinking that the best thing for everyone would be for him to disappear. But in a strange twist of events, the thing that had almost driven him to it was the thing that saved him in the end. Lilly. He wasn't sure what was going to happen, but all he knew was that he had a child, and therefore there was some hope for the future.

'Right,' Martha said, pulling over a chair to sit down beside him. 'Trish is here for a couple of hours so I can take a break. I've been doing some thinking.'

'So you said.' Dennis wasn't sure he was in the mood for a chat.

'You were an estate agent, right?'

He hadn't expected that. 'Well, yes, I was.'

'Any good, were you?'

'If you'd asked me that while I was working, I'd have said I was the best. I'd have convinced you that there was nobody in the business as good as me.'

'And now?'

He thought for a minute. 'I suppose I was pretty good really. When I worked for an estate agent, I learned quickly and had enough ambition to go on to open my own shop. Although, given where I am now, I'm not sure it was the best idea.'

'Hmmm.'

'Where exactly is this going, Martha?'

'Well, I might know of a job going.'

'Okay, now you've got me interested. Although if it's as an estate agent, I'm not sure I'd want to go back to all that.'

'It's not. Well, not exactly.'

He leaned forward on the table. 'Now I'm intrigued. Tell me more.'

Martha smiled. 'It's quite close to here, actually. The pay might not be brilliant but the perks are pretty good.'

'Go on.'

'Right, let me start from the beginning. Did I ever tell you my Richard was a property developer?'

'I think you may have mentioned it.' She'd also mentioned that Richard had died five years earlier, so he wasn't sure where she was going with this.

'Look, I'll get to the point and you can ask me questions later. Richard was a wealthy man. He lived and worked through the boom but he was also a savvy man and had the good sense to liquidate a lot of his assets while they were worth something. Let's just say he left me very comfortable.'

Dennis was flabbergasted. He'd always imagined Martha was living on the edge with her finances. He'd always thought she probably took in just enough from her little business to keep a roof over her head and pay the bills. He knew she lived in a small apartment just off Baggot Street and seemed to live a very frugal life.

'So anyway,' Martha continued, 'Richard owned a couple of buildings just off Capel Street. He never sold them because he had them converted into bedsits and they were making quite a bit of money over the years. But since he died, I haven't done anything with them and they've been lying empty for the past few years.'

Dennis could feel his heart beating faster. Even though he didn't want to be the tycoon he'd once been, there was just something about property that excited him. 'Go on, I'm listening.'

Martha nodded and took a slow sip of her tea, as if trying to decide what to say next. 'I have no interest in property, Dennis. All I want to do until the end of my days is run my little shop. But you, on the other hand, know the business and could make something of those places again.'

'So what exactly are you suggesting?'

'Well, you'd have to go and check them out because I don't even know what state they're in but I was hoping you might take them over for me and develop them. After that, you could advertise them and rent them out. I know the property business has been dismal these past few years, but I've heard things are picking up. I'm always getting flyers in my door lately from estate agents looking for properties to let.'

Dennis couldn't believe what he was hearing. 'You'd really do that for me, Martha? You'd hand over a huge project like that for me to manage?'

'I wouldn't be doing it for you, Dennis. Those bloody buildings have been on my mind for ages. There's no good in them just sitting there when they could be earning money. Richard would turn in his grave if he thought I'd let them go to wrack and ruin.'

'I – I don't know what to say.'

'Well, yes would be a good start.'

'Yes, yes! Of course I'll do it. I'd love to. I mean, you wouldn't even have to pay me. If you could just feed me here and let me hang out when it's cold so I—'

'Dennis! Be quiet, would you? Of course I'll pay you, and there'll always be a cup of tea and a sandwich for you here too. But I forgot to say that the deal is that one of the bedsits will be yours when they're all done.'

'You're not serious!'

'I'm deadly serious. And I won't take no for an answer. Listen, love, you know I have nobody – no children or grandchildren, no nieces or nephews. And I can't take it with me when I'm gone.'

'But it's such a generous thing to offer.' Dennis couldn't take it in.

'Look, it will be mutually beneficial. I'll know it's what Richard would have done, and you get a job and a place to stay. You could probably spruce up one of the bedsits straight away and move in.'

It was getting better and better. It was almost too much. Dennis could feel tears forming in the corners of his eyes and he bent forward and put his head in his hands. Could his life be actually turning around at last?

'I'm sorry if I've offended you by offering, Dennis. But if you don't take the job, I'll have to go and advertise it and interview people, check CVs, references – it will be an absolute nightmare.'

He looked at the woman who was turning out to be his saviour and reached out for her hand. 'Thank you.' He couldn't get any more words out.

'Maybe we'll go over there this evening and have a look at the place. I'll give you the keys and you can start to make plans.' Her mood suddenly turned serious. 'But there's one more thing.'

'What's that?'

'You go and see your daughter.'

The words hit him like a bolt of lightning and he started to panic. 'I can't. I've told you, Martha. I just can't do it.'

'That's because you were homeless. You didn't want her to see her father in that situation.'

'Yes, but—'

'You're not homeless now. You have a place to stay and a job. It doesn't have to be today or tomorrow but I want you to think about making contact.'

'And if I don't?'

'The job is still yours. It's not my place to tell you what to do, but what I *can* do is offer you the benefit of my wisdom. And I think that meeting your daughter will be the best thing that's ever happened to you, and she'll be damn lucky to have a dad like you.'

'Thanks.' He sipped his tea while he tried to take in all the information that she'd thrown at him. 'I'll definitely think about it.'

'Good. Now one last thing. Go and talk to your mother and tell her everything. Mammies always know what to do in situations like this.'

'But Martha, you know the story there. What good would it do?'

'You'll never know if you don't go. Even being with her might help you find the answer within yourself. Just give it a try. I'm an old woman – indulge me.'

He laughed at that. 'Okay. You're one in a million, do you know that?'

'You're not so bad yourself. Now, I'd better go and help out before the queue is out the door. We'll talk again later.'

Dennis lost himself in thought for a few minutes. But then it came to him. He knew what he had to do. He pulled on his coat and hooshed his rucksack up onto his back. Martha gave him a knowing nod as he headed out the door. He felt stunned but excited. He still had a long road ahead of him but it was definitely the start of something. But before he could ever discuss things with his mother, there was someone else he had to see.

❀

He was going to talk to her today. No putting it off, no excuses – he just had to do it. He'd allowed the guilt to swallow him up over the last year but now it was time to confront it. If he was going to move on with his life, he needed to make amends for the past. He needed to say sorry. He wasn't expecting forgiveness, but at least it would be something.

He sat on the bench at the bus stop and waited. He wasn't really sure what he'd do or what he'd say, but he just knew today was the day. She'd be home soon. Just like she always was. The bus shelter began to fill with people and he started to sweat. He'd never felt so nervous in his life. He wiped his sweaty hands on his old corduroy trousers and it dawned on him that perhaps he should have made an effort. He hadn't changed his clothes in days, nor had he had a shower. But he dismissed the thought quickly. Those things weren't important right now.

Right on cue, the car rumbled up the street and turned into the driveway. Isabella hopped out and she quickly ran to the passenger seat, where she opened the door. An older lady stepped out, followed by the three children. Dennis' heart began to beat faster.

Just then, a bus arrived, obscuring his view of the house. He willed everyone to get on quickly. When it finally moved off and he looked across the road, he was startled to see Isabella standing in the driveway, looking in his direction. He averted his gaze, worried she'd sense he was looking at her. And then something happened. Something that sent his head into a spin and made him wish he'd never come. She began to walk across the road towards him.

His brain was screaming at his legs to walk away but he was glued to the seat. He'd come with the intention of speaking to her but he really didn't think he could do it. He kept his head down, but heard her footsteps come closer and eventually stop as she sat down on the bench beside him. He daren't move a muscle. He barely allowed himself to breathe.

'It took me a while,' she said, in her mixed accent. 'But I eventually figured out who you are.'

'Wh – what?' Dennis looked at her and saw a deep sadness in her dark brown eyes.

'I've seen you here on and off over the past few months. Initially I thought I was imagining it, but I eventually realised you were watching me.'

'I didn't ... I wasn't ...'

'Dennis Prendergast, right?'

He nodded, scared of what she was going to say. He couldn't believe she'd recognised him. They'd only met briefly a couple of times when she'd come in to sign some documents – the rest of his dealings had been with Alan. They both sat in silence for the next few minutes and Dennis couldn't find the words to say what he needed to say.

'It wasn't your fault, you know.'

He looked at her again and saw she had tears in her eyes. She continued.

'Alan was a gambler – always looking for the next big thing. If he hadn't put money into Paudie's investment, it would have been something else. And, to be honest, the money he lost was not much to him. He lost far more in some of his other ventures.'

'But what makes you think—'

'Are you saying I'm wrong? Are you saying you don't feel responsible? Because all I know is that I've been there. I've felt the guilt and it just rips you apart. When I realised it was you, I put two and two together and guessed you were feeling bad about the investment.'

'I – I don't know what to say. I brought him to that investment. I encouraged him to part with his money. The papers said he couldn't cope with losing so much.'

'I never spoke to any of the papers. They came to their own conclusions. Alan was a manic depressive and his illness contributed to his death more than any stupid investments.'

Dennis was stunned.

'Did you hear about Alan McCabe?' his mate Simon had said one day. 'Gassed himself in his car. Left a wife and three kids behind. Awful stuff.'

He'd blamed himself since that day. The weight of guilt had held him down and stopped him from moving forward. Could it really be that it wasn't his fault?

Isabella stood up. 'Right, I'd better go back. My mum is over from Italy to help organise the twins' birthday. They'll be seven on Sunday.'

Dennis stood up too. 'I'm so sorry for your loss, Isabella. If I can ever do anything for you …'

'Just remember what I said and give yourself a break. Life is too short for regrets.'

He watched her dodge the traffic and disappear inside her front door without a backward glance.

And that's what *he* needed to do. He needed to move on without a backward glance. He'd never forget, but he wouldn't let it hold him back any more. His mind flooded with all the possibilities – the things he could do with his life, the person he could be. He stood up and hauled his rucksack up onto his back. He smiled to himself as he headed on down the road.

# Chapter 44

It was Christmas Eve and Becky and Joanna were sitting in a little coffee shop, eating warm scones and chatting as though they'd never been apart. Joanna and her family had arrived early that morning and George, Joanna's husband, had offered to mind the children while the girls got reacquainted. Becky had been determined not to dwell too much on the past, but there were certain things that needed to be said.

'Do you think about her much?'

Joanna stopped stirring her tea and looked at her sister. 'Mum? Yes, I do, as it happens. I try to remember the good things – the early days when she was just like all the other mums. Before Dad's drinking got out of control and she changed.'

Becky nodded. 'Me too. I was just thinking this morning about the nights when Dad was out and Mum and I would snuggle up on the sofa to watch a movie. She'd always have a stash of chocolate and we'd have a feast. They are precious memories.'

'Precious because they were few and far between.'

'You're right,' said Becky. 'But as you said, I don't want to focus on the bad times. She was still our mother, and now she's gone.'

Silence hung between them until Joanna spoke again. 'I wonder what *he's* doing now.'

'I don't know and I really don't care. I know he's my father but I hate him. I'm sorry. I know it sounds awful, but I do.'

Joanna reached across and took her hand. 'You don't have to be sorry. He was never really a father to either of us. Let's hold on tight to Mum's memory – the memories of the good times, no matter how few.'

Becky suddenly had an idea. 'Let's do something for her. We never got to the funeral so let's do something in her memory. We could do it right now.'

'Like what? Go to church or something?'

'No, something Mum would have liked. Flowers. Let's get some red roses and scatter the petals. Or does that sound cheesy?'

Joanna had tears in her eyes. 'Not at all. It's perfect. Mum loved flowers – not that she got them too often. But I remember her commenting on everyone's garden as we walked to school.'

Becky was already putting her coat on. 'Right, that's settled. There's a little flower shop down the road – although they could be sold out with it being so close to Christmas.'

'Well, let's go and check.'

Fifteen minutes later, they were en route to the Phoenix Park, Joanna holding a bunch of mixed flowers – the best of what was left in the florist. In such an enormous park, they didn't have much trouble finding a quiet area. They parked the car and went to sit on a nearby bench. The wind was blustery but thankfully it wasn't raining. They recounted stories from the past – only the good ones – and laughed and cried as they plucked petals from the flowers and let them fly off in the wind. When they were done, they hugged each other tightly.

'Thanks, Becky,' said Joanna, a sob escaping her lips.

'For what?'

'For not judging. For not hating me. For remembering the good times.'

'I'm just happy I have my sister back. I love you, you know.'

'I love you too, Becks. And I'll never, *ever* abandon you again.'

They sat in silence for a while until the cold wind forced them up off the bench. They walked arm in arm back to the car and despite their reason for being there, Becky felt happier than she had in a long time. She had a sister. She had a future to look forward to.

❁

Dennis sat in the corner of the day room and watched as the various residents went about their everyday business. Some were watching the news on a big screen, some were playing cards and others were just drinking tea and chatting. The room was warm and welcoming with a large Christmas tree in the corner and it struck Dennis how happy everyone looked.

'Here you go, Rose. Dennis is here to see you.' Jean, one of the day nurses, helped his mother onto the chair beside him and made sure she was comfortable before turning to Dennis. 'Can I get you anything? Tea or coffee?'

'Nothing, thanks, Jean. I just want to have a chat with Mam.'

'No problem. Give me a shout if you need anything.'

'Hiya, Mam. You're looking well today.' He bent to kiss her on the cheek and handed her a box of chocolates.

His mother nodded and clasped her hands around the box, but her eyes were glazed over, as usual. Her dementia was advanced and had been getting steadily worse for years. Dennis was aware that she never really knew what he was saying but he still liked to talk to her. He hoped that some part of what he said would sink into her brain and she'd feel a connection with him. His made-up stories always sounded so much better and, sometimes, he even thought she had a smile on her lips. She'd say the odd word now and again but it was usually obscure and had no relevance to him or their conversation.

'Mam, I have something I want to talk to you about and I'd really love your advice.'

She nodded again but he thought he noticed a tiny flicker in her eyes. He needed to tell her about the girl he'd met five years ago who'd only now chosen to tell him he had a daughter. The story poured out and Rose nodded the whole way through.

'So there you go, Mam. What do you think? I have a daughter called Lilly but I can't help thinking she'd be better off without me.

Maybe if I'd been involved from the beginning, but she's four years old now and has a life with her mother.'

'Lilly.'

Dennis couldn't believe his ears. 'What did you say, Mam?'

She looked into the distance and he began to think he'd imagined it. She was still nodding, even though he'd stopped speaking. He felt very lonely at that moment and wished he could have his mother back again – back the way she used to be, full of fun and vitality.

'Granddaughter.'

He definitely hadn't imagined it that time. 'Yes, Mam. She's your granddaughter. You have a granddaughter.'

'A blessing. Children. A blessing.'

'Mam, oh Mam, you heard me. You understand more than we think, don't you?' He looked around to see if any of the nurses were there to tell them what had just happened but none were to be seen. 'So you think I should go and see her?'

Rose was back looking into the distance and nodding.

'Mam. Do you think I should see Lilly?'

Still nothing. She was gone again. He reached over and took her hand. 'Thanks, Mam. I knew I could rely on you.'

He knew what he had to do.

# Chapter 45

The dulcet tones of Frank Sinatra singing 'White Christmas' came from the CD player as Becky happily hummed along. She'd just checked the enormous turkey that had been slowly cooking in the oven for the past few hours and was now peeling the potatoes. Who'd have thought she'd have such a full and happy house on Christmas Day? It was something she'd never experienced and she hoped it was a sign of things to come.

The doorbell rang and she wiped her hands on some kitchen towel before answering. She was expecting Kate and Garreth, and Alice and Frank and was dying to introduce them to her new-found family.

'Hi, Becky,' Kate said, blowing on her hands. 'It's absolutely freezing out there. Seems we might get that snow they've been forecasting.'

'Come in quickly, both of you.' Becky hugged her friend and kissed Garreth on the cheek. 'God, you're both like blocks of ice.'

Garreth handed her a bottle of wine and a beautifully wrapped box. 'Here you go, Becky. Just something small from us.'

'And I have something here for Lilly,' said Kate, pulling a present out of her enormous handbag. 'Where is she?'

'Ah, you're both very good. She's in with her cousins. Come on in and I'll introduce you to everyone.'

The sitting room was quite a picture, with Joanna and George on the floor playing with the three children. Lilly was enjoying sharing her toys with her cousin, Sarah, who was just a little older, and her baby cousin, Adam. Becky had bought a real tree this year – a huge one – and she had to admit, it made the room look so much more Christmassy than the scrawny synthetic one she'd used in the past.

'Hi, Kate.' Lilly ran over to her and hugged her. 'Have you got a present for me?'

'Lilly!' Becky was mortified.

'It's okay, Becky. And yes, of course I have. I thought this would be a good present – something you can play with your cousins.'

'Yay,' squealed Lilly, ripping off the paper and revealing a game called Pop the Pig. 'Come on, Sarah, let's play now. Thank you, Kate.'

'You're very welcome, Lilly. And you must be Joanna.' Kate held out her hand to Becky's sister, who had just stood up to greet her. 'I've heard so much about you.'

'Hi, Kate. Likewise. Becky is very lucky to have such good friends. And this is my husband, George.'

George shook hands firmly with Kate and Garreth. He was a quiet man – nothing at all like Becky had expected. Somehow she'd thought her sister would go for a guy with a bit of a wild side and model looks. On the contrary, George was quite a bit older than her and balding, but Becky had instantly warmed to him when they'd met yesterday.

'Right, I'll go and get some wine while you all get acquainted. I'm sure Alice will be' – right on cue, the doorbell rang and Becky smiled – 'here any minute!'

A few minutes later, Alice and Frank had joined the group and everyone was chatting animatedly in the sitting room. Becky was in the kitchen organising some nibbles and found herself wishing they were all staying for dinner. Not so long ago, she'd have hated the thought of cooking for a big crowd, but now she could think of nothing better.

'Do you need a hand there?' Alice stood in the doorway looking gorgeous in a new purple cashmere dress. Becky couldn't help but notice her curves. Alice had always had a boyish figure but today she looked amazing with the woollen dress accentuating her new feminine figure. Those extra few pounds that she'd been giving out about really suited her.

'Not at all, but sit down there and chat to me while I organise these dips.'

'Oh, Becky, I'm bursting to tell you. I've gone over this moment again and again in my head, trying to figure out the best way to tell you. I've imagined so many different scenarios – where we'd be or what we'd be doing. But I can't keep it in any longer and I'm not going to beat about the bush.'

Becky's heart almost stopped as she spun around to look at her friend. She knew Alice had been keeping something from her. Please don't let it be bad news.

'I'm pregnant.'

'Wh – what?'

'Becky, I'm pregnant. Frank and I are going to have a baby.'

'No way!' She almost fell on top of Alice on the chair in her haste to hug her. 'But when, how, are you sure? Oh, my God! I can't believe it.'

'What can you not believe?' Lilly stood at the door watching the two women hug each other, tears streaming down both their faces.

Becky looked at Alice, who nodded her approval. 'Honey, you'll never guess what. Alice is going to get a new baby.'

'Yay, yay, yay! Thank you, Alice.'

Alice lifted the little girl onto her lap. 'So I take it you're happy, then?'

'It's the best present ever. I asked Santa for a surprise but I told him I wanted a brother or sister. I don't think he was able to give that to me, so this is sort of the same thing. Yay!' She wriggled out of Alice's hold and rushed back into the sitting room.

'Uh, oh!' said Becky, laughing at her daughter's excitement. 'I hope you weren't planning on keeping that a secret.'

'Absolutely not. And anyway, look at me – I can't believe I didn't notice how much my stomach was growing. I just found out a couple of weeks ago and I'm already five months gone.'

'So it's true.' Now it was Kate at the kitchen door, a huge smile on her face. 'Oh, Alice, I'm so happy for you. Was it natural or did you and Frank have treatment? And is everything okay, given your age and everything?'

'Kate!' Becky reprimanded her but for once was grateful for her asking the questions that she herself didn't dare ask.

'No, it's okay. I don't mind telling you. It all came as a complete surprise. Well, shock really. It's the one thing I've wanted to hear for most of my adult life but when I actually heard those words "you're pregnant" I fell to pieces.'

'Oh, you poor thing,' said Becky, reaching for Alice's hand. 'But I assume it was just an initial shock? I mean, you're happy now, right?'

'I couldn't be happier. *We* couldn't be happier. There was just so much to take in at first – not only the fact I was actually pregnant, but all the possible risks associated with being pregnant in my late forties. I know it seems crazy that I'd be upset, given how much I want this, but when the doctor told me the news, I just couldn't believe it. I was sure there was a catch.'

'A catch?' Becky looked at her quizzically.

'That there was something wrong with the baby. But when it sank in, I realised I'd been given a gift and I was going to love that child no matter what.'

Kate, who'd been standing since she'd come into the kitchen, sat down to hear more. 'And have you had tests and stuff?'

'Yes, I've had a few and the initial findings are good. We can never know if a baby is completely healthy until she's born, but …'

'She!' Becky almost shouted the word. 'You said "she". Are you having a girl?'

Alice smiled. 'Oops! Me and my big mouth. But yes, we're having a baby girl and she's due on the thirtieth of April.'

'My birthday,' said Becky, almost falling off her chair with excitement. 'I can't believe your baby is due on my birthday.'

'That was the first thing I thought of when I heard the date. I'm looking on it as a good sign. It has to be a lucky day.'

'I'm just so happy for you, Alice. You're going to be the best mummy ever.'

'Sorry to interrupt,' Joanna said, sticking her head around the kitchen door. 'There's a man at the door looking for you, Becky, and he has the biggest teddy I've ever seen in my life.'

They mustn't have heard the doorbell with all the excitement and Becky felt her mood changing. It had to be Len. He'd been in to see her in the bank a number of times and Becky had insisted that a colleague look after his banking needs. He'd phoned her regularly and she'd politely but firmly told him they were finished. Why could he not take no for an answer?

'I'll be back in a sec.' She closed the kitchen door behind her and was glad to see Joanna had discreetly closed the sitting room door too. This wasn't going to be pretty and she didn't want anyone to hear the tongue-lashing she was going to give Len. She stepped just outside the door and was about to give him a piece of her mind when he moved the enormous teddy away from his face.

'Hi, Becky.'

'Dennis!' He was standing there, looking impeccable in a pair of black loose-fit jeans, a yellow sweater and a tailored jacket. His beard was gone and he looked ten years younger.

'It's probably really bad timing, but I just had to come.'

'Well, yes. I mean no.' She was too shocked to know what she meant.

'I'm sorry, Becky. For all of it. For not being there from the start – if I'd been a more decent sort of guy, you probably would have told me. And I'm sorry for running away when you did tell me.'

Becky's mouth had gone dry and she could barely get the words out. 'It's in the past. You're here now and I'm guessing that teddy isn't for me.'

'I know it's Christmas Day and I know I don't have any rights after everything that happened but—'

'Do you really want to do this? Do you want to get to know Lilly?'

He nodded and the smile lit up his face. 'I really do. But let's just go with Uncle Dennis for now. One step at a time.'

Becky felt overwhelmed. It was like it was meant to be. 'That's good for me. Come on in then, Uncle Dennis. There are some people I'd like you to meet.'

# Acknowledgements

So here we are again. I can barely believe another book is finished. Just three years ago, I was still harbouring the dream of being a published writer and now this, my fourth book, is hitting the shelves. Dreams really can come true. But my dreams would have remained firmly in my head if it wasn't for the wonderful people in my life who made them a reality. I can hear you all shout, 'Oh, no, she's off again!' And you'd be right. But I feel grateful to so many people, so bear with me.

If you've read my other books, you'll be sick of me talking about my wonderful husband, but I have to give credit where credit is due. Paddy *is* wonderful. Whether it's taking the kids out to let me write in peace, catching up on the backlog of ironing when I'm holed up in my office or just letting me rattle on about storylines, Paddy is the backbone of everything I do. As I'm writing this, he's off in Rio taking selfies with Christ the Redeemer, but being without him for two weeks has made me realise just how much I love him. Thank you, Paddy, for everything.

As my children are getting older, they're becoming more conscious of what I'm saying about them. They're always telling me not to tell embarrassing stories and to stop giving 'mortifying' pictures to journalists. With every year that goes by and I see them growing, I thank God for such wonderful gifts. Eoin is seventeen now and has become a wonderful young man. He's kind and caring and, being a big reader himself, is always ready to listen to my book ideas and give feedback. Roisin is sixteen and a beautiful young woman. Her support for me comes in the form of cake! She's an amazing baker and when she sees me under pressure or stressed, she'll whip up something delicious and chocolaty and, of course, I have to eat it. It would be rude not to! Enya is twelve and has a wonderful quiet confidence. She's the calming influence in the house. Nothing fazes her and no matter what flaps I get into, I only have to look at her and I feel calm again. Conor is ten and a little firecracker! He's full of fun and mischief and he certainly keeps me on my toes. But when life is stressful, a cuddle and an 'I love you, Mam' from him can send my heart soaring. Overall, what I'm saying is that each of my children has a part to play in my writing. So thank you, my little munchkins (I'm sure I'll pay for that!) and I love you all very much.

A huge thank you to two of the most important people in my life – my parents, Aileen and Paddy Chaney. They've always supported me in everything I've done and continue to be my biggest cheerleaders when my books hit the shelves. Thanks to my mother-in-law, Mary Duffy, and to all my in-laws for their continued support. To my brother, Gerry Chaney, thank you for all your picture-taking and knowing to delete the wrinkles before you show me the photo! Thanks to his lovely wife, Denyse, for reading my books before I send them to my publisher and for listening to me whittle on about storylines.

I feel very lucky to have professional people around me who help me every step of the way. Without them, my books would never see the light of day. A huge thank you to the wonderful team at Hachette Ireland, who look after me so well. My editor, Ciara Doorley, is a magician of words and although I write the books, she really makes them sparkle. Thanks to Joanna for her patience and help and to Ruth for putting up with me for one long day every year and for allowing me to slip away to buy shoes! Thanks to Breda, Jim, Bernard, Siobhan and the rest of the team at Hachette – it's a real pleasure to work with you all. Thank you to Sheila Crowley for all her help and support and also to Becky and the rest of the team at Curtis Brown. Thank you to my lovely new agent, Madeleine Milburn, for her enthusiasm, encouragement and support. I look forward to a great working relationship, Maddy, and maybe the odd glass of wine or two!

I have so many friends who help and encourage me along the way and I'm always terrified I'll leave someone out. I could just say one big thanks to everyone, but then you wouldn't have pages of acknowledgements to moan about! Thank you to my long-suffering friends Lorraine Hamm, Angie Pierce, Sinead Webb, Rachel Murphy, and Bernie and Dermot Winston. It's great to have friends who understand my antisocial behaviour when I bury my head in a storyline and don't come up for air for months. It's nice to know we can just pick up the telephone and continue where we left off. I owe you all bucket-loads of wine! Thank you to my wonderful friend, Niamh O'Connor, who listens, advises, calms and even organises surprise parties! Your friendship means the world to me. Thank you to Michelle Jackson, Niamh Greene and Denise Deegan, all authors I hugely admire and who have become wonderful friends. Our nights away always come at the right time and give me that extra surge of energy I need to keep writing. One of our brainstorming sessions led to the title of this book so a huge thank you to Niamh Greene for coming up with it. Huge thanks to the wonderful Claudia Carroll for all her support. Thank you to Hazel Gaynor, Barbara Scully, Eleanor Fitzsimons, Hazel Larkin and Jane Travers for the coffees and laughs. Thanks to my writing buddy and partner in heels, Mel Sherratt, for all her support and long phone calls. I've met so many lovely people these past few years through Twitter and Facebook but too many to mention individually. Thank you to all of you who chat to me online and make my writing day less lonely.

I feel very lucky to do a job I love and not only that, to have the luxury of doing it from home. I love where I live and that's mainly down to my wonderful neighbours, who I'm happy to call my friends. Whether it's lending me eggs or milk when I've run out or making me a cup of tea when I'm stressed, my neighbours play a huge part in me getting that book written. And, of course, the stories I gather from our weekends away are always a bonus – you'd never know what might turn up in my next book!

I owe a huge debt of gratitude to my lovely friend and mentor, Vanessa O'Loughlin. Vanessa helped me to get my foot on that writing ladder in the first place and continues to advise and encourage me along the way. She's fast becoming the go-to person for Irish writers and is always ready to help authors to achieve their dreams. She has two websites – www.inkwellwriters.ie and www.writing.ie – and I can't recommend her highly enough to any writers who are looking for help.

Bookshops are very important to writers and I'd like to say a special thank you to my local bookseller Aideen, from Abtree Books in Lucan. Aideen has been supporting me since my first seed of an idea and continues to fly my flag in the local area.

If you've already read *One Wish*, you'll know that there's a homeless theme that runs through the book. There are a number of wonderful charities who support people who are homeless but I want to give a special mention to the Dublin Simon Community. Through my research, I got to know a little more about them and I was staggered when I realised just how much they do. Simon is an organisation that homeless people can turn to. They provide services that empower people living on the streets, helping them to rebuild their broken lives. They have various teams working around the clock to provide food and shelter and they work tirelessly to get to the root of the problem. I spent some time last year with two wonderful Simon workers and I got a real eye-opening insight into life on the streets. Dennis Morris and Martina Bergin are part of Simon's Rough Sleeper Team and it was a very special thing to see them at work. The work they do is wonderful but it's more how they do it. They know most of the homeless people around Dublin city by name and as well as offering practical stuff, like sleeping bags and warm clothes, they always have time for some kind words and a hug where it's needed. Dennis and

Martina are two very special people but so too is each and every person who works or volunteers for the cause. A special thank you to the lovely Helen McCormack, communications officer for Simon, who helped with research and pointed me in the right direction. In *One Wish*, I mention the phrase: 'There, but for the grace of God, go I' because I believe it's so true in this case. Homelessness can happen to anybody. You can find out more about Dublin Simon here: www.dubsimon.ie.

So, my lovely readers, all that's left for me to say is a huge thank you to you! I'm filled with joy every time someone tells me they're reading one of my books and I still have to pinch myself when I see my books in the shops. My readers are a huge part of the process because without them, I wouldn't be able to wake up every morning knowing I'm doing what I love. Feedback is really important to me so if you've read this, or any of my other books, I'd love to hear from you. You can contact me on my website at www.mariaduffy.ie, on Twitter at @mduffywriter or on Facebook at facebook.com/maria.duffy.

I hope you continue to enjoy my books and I wish you all the luck life can bring.

Maria x

Reading is so much more than the act of moving from page to page. It's the exploration of new worlds; the pursuit of adventure; the forging of friendships; the breaking of hearts; and the chance to begin to live through a new story each time the first sentence is devoured.

We at Hachette Ireland are very passionate about what we read, and what we publish. And we'd love to hear what you think about our books.

If you'd like to let us know, or to find out more about us and our titles, please visit www.hachette.ie or our Facebook page www.facebook.com/hachetteireland, or follow us on Twitter @ HachetteIre